"Why is all this happening?"

"At first we thought it was an honest mistake, that the nurse put the wrong ID band on our baby because she was new. Then we started thinking about other possibilities. Suellen said something one day that really upset me. She said it might be more than a mistake . . . that maybe somebody switched babies on purpose to make Lucien look bad, or to get even because he campaigned for the black vote. Now this. Why would somebody give them the wrong blood to test instead of mine? Or was Dr. Crisp lying? Politics is a dirty business, but if someone's trying to make Lucien look bad, is Dr. Crisp in on it? None of this makes any sense, Rona, and my innocent baby's the one who's suffering."

D0253411

WITHOUT SIN

Charles Smithdeal

AN ONYX BOOK

ONYX
Published by New American Library, a division of
Penguin Putnam Inc., 375 Hudson Street,
New York, New York 10014, U.S.A.
Penguin Books Ltd, 27 Wrights Lane,
London W8 5TZ, England
Penguin Books Australia Ltd, Ringwood,
Victoria, Australia
Penguin Books Canada Ltd, 10 Alcorn Avenue,
Toronto, Ontario, Canada M4V 3B2
Penguin Books (N.Z.) Ltd, 182–190 Wairau Road,
Auckland 10, New Zealand

Penguin Books Ltd, Registered Offices:
Harmondsworth, Middlesex, England

First published by Onyx, an imprint of New American Library,
a division of Penguin Putnam Inc.

First Printing, September 2001
10 9 8 7 6 5 4 3 2 1

For my son, David, and my wife, Debbie.

ACKNOWLEDGMENTS

That "no man is an island" could not be better illustrated than in the creation and publication of a work of fiction. This novel would never have been completed without the assistance of several extremely talented and very special people.

Thank you to Shelly Lowenkopf, of Santa Barbara, California, for his lifelong dedication to the written word; also for his keen eye and quick red pen for spotting and dealing with inconsistencies and errors.

Thank you to my agent, Phyllis Westberg, of Harold Ober Associates in New York, for believing in me, and for allowing me to humbly carve my initials on walls that recall F. Scott Fitzgerald, Agatha Christie, Pearl S. Buck, and scores of "real writers" the agency has represented.

A special thanks to Hilary Ross, my esteemed editor at New American Library, for her tireless efforts and sage advice. And to John Paine, whose ability to re-arrange and vastly improve the jigsaw-puzzle intricacies of a novel is truly awe inspiring.

Lastly, my heartfelt thank-you to the women (and a few men) of Natchez, Mississippi, for welcoming people from around the world to enter their magnificent homes, stroll their incomparable gardens, and perhaps, for a moment in time, to glimpse a slice of their lives and heritage. As my novel suggests, "Since before *The War*, Natchez has been a genteel society. It remains so today."

May God bless you all.

—*Charles D. Smithdeal*

"He that is without sin among you, let him first cast a stone at her."

—St. John 8:7

CHAPTER ONE

The audience applauded furiously when Page pointed to a sign suspended over City Auditorium stage:

NATCHEZ 2001: WHERE THE OLD SOUTH STILL LIVES.

The thrill she felt reminded her of a night twelve years earlier, when she was crowned homecoming queen at Ole Miss. Still blond and attractive at thirty-two, Page was now happily married and quite maternal. She'd even had her antique-lace antebellum gown refitted to accommodate her nine-month pregnancy.

Governor-elect Lucien Yarbrough quickly joined Page onstage. Four years older and a head taller than she, the governor was fit and trim, with brown hair, an irresistible smile, and a fair, boyish face. Page thought Lucien especially dashing tonight. He wore an 1860s Southern colonel's evening suit with a fitted frock coat, ruffled shirt, and wide silk tie. They raised their entwined hands to the cheering audience.

With her loving husband at her side, their six-year-old daughter backstage preparing to perform, and their long-awaited first son nestled securely in her womb, life for Page Yarbrough was just about perfect. She couldn't imagine how it could possibly get better.

Two hours later Governor Yarbrough anxiously waited outside the nursery of Doctors' Memorial Hospital. Alongside were his personal aide, Billy Larson, and two other close friends. The men laughed and joked in heavy Southern accents, passing a flask among themselves. When a nurse appeared at the observation window, they turned to view the infant she held.

"He looks black," Troy Carter blurted out.

"That's not my son," Lucien said. He rapped on the glass separating them from the newborns, forcing a short laugh. "Damn, lady, can't you tell a white man's son from a little pickaninny?"

Carter nudged Lucien and glanced furtively to either side before saying, "You sure there's not maybe a woodpile we don't know about back there somewhere, Loosh?"

Lucien's aide chimed in, also teasing. He had an unusually large head and long body, with arms so short they resembled an alligator's. Born and raised in southern Mississippi, Billy "Gator" Larson spoke about as fast as he might pour molasses from a cider jug. "Yeah, Loosh, I remember in the showers after high school football practice we always thought you were hung too heavy for a white dude."

They all laughed, including Lucien.

The nurse brought the baby closer, her face crinkling in a smile. Her eyes searched from face to face.

"Dammit," Lucien said exasperatedly. "How dense can some people be?" He shook his head and tried to signal *no* to the nurse. Raising his voice to a stage whisper, he said, "Wrong baby." Lucien rolled up one sleeve and pointed to the skin on his arm. "See? I'm white. Get it?"

His fists clenched tightly and his tiny body shaking violently in his very first blanket, the little black baby screamed out silently on the other side of the heavy glass, while Lucien and his cronies tried to make the nurse understand.

A short time later Page Yarbrough lay propped up in the hospital bed of her private room. Although still groggy from medications, she was thrilled beyond words that their son had finally arrived. Lucien sat beside the bed and took her hands in his. Page's antique-lace gown lay carefully folded across a nearby chair.

Lucien told his wife some of what had happened.

"I don't understand," she said. She tried to focus her eyes. "Isn't he normal?"

Page's primary concern throughout her pregnancy had been that their baby be normal. Lucien insisted that the child was a boy, and proudly informed anybody who'd listen. That it should also be normal sometimes seemed secondary to him.

Lucien said, "It's a temporary mix-up, Page. The hospital administrator's on the way over now. Gator located him at the pageant."

"Where's our baby?"

"They put them in the wrong bassinets or something, sweetheart. That nurse couldn't pour piss out of a boot with directions on the heel."

"Where's Dr. Archer?"

"Tied up in surgery. The nurse said Dr. Benning delivered our baby."

"Who's he?" Page was able to focus her eyes better now. She tried desperately to follow what Lucien was saying.

"He's a new OB doctor, taking backup call because Dr. Archer's performing emergency surgery."

"What did he say?"

"Benning's doing another delivery right now. They've had three or four already tonight. I guess it's a full moon or something."

Page tried to wipe a piece of fuzz off her cheek. "How do you know they mixed them up? Isn't it a boy?"

"Oh, he's a boy, all right. You should see the wanger on him."

"Then I don't understand . . . the nurse said I had a boy." An ominous warning welled up within Page. "Is something the matter, Lucien? Isn't he normal?"

Lucien lowered his voice and gently took his wife's face in both hands. "It isn't that, Page. The kid they're saying is ours is normal . . . but he's black. A Negro baby.''

After a long pause, Lucien stood and paced the room. Seeing that Page had dozed off again, he addressed nobody in particular. Anger seeped into each word as he said, "This place is unreal. Here I am, the governor of the state, and these imbeciles are trying to say my son is colored. How incompetent can one hospital be? Not two hours ago I told an auditorium full of constituents we were about to have our first son, Jackson Adams Yarbrough the second. I even promised he'd be governor of the great state of Mississippi someday . . . probably president of the United States.'' He paused, the muscles in his jaw working. "Now there'll be reporters all over the hospital wanting a picture of my boy, and these morons have put him in the wrong damn baby bed.''

Page opened her eyes again, but her lids seemed to weigh a hundred pounds each. She could hear the concern in her husband's voice, and was eager to help. She wanted desperately to understand what he was saying. Was Lucien talking to her, making another speech, or was she still dreaming? Despite her struggle, her eyelids involuntarily closed, and the sensation was one of blissful relief. She could relax now. She wasn't sure about the rest of it, but Lucien had said their baby was normal. Maybe she'd just take a little nap. She felt her husband's hand, then squeezed it gently.

"I love you," Page whispered. In her heart, she never doubted that everything would be all right now. Her Lucien was right there beside her. He could fix anything.

CHAPTER TWO

Lucien Yarbrough and Billy Larson sat across a table from Dr. Jefferson Archer in the obstetrical lounge. Archer still wore the scrub suit from his emergency surgery. Despite prominent *No smoking* signs on two walls, Steve Griffith, the hospital's administrator, blew clouds of cigarette smoke into the air as he paced the floor behind them.

Lucien fought to remain courteous and in control. Inside, he was consumed with frustration.

Dr. Archer sipped from a Styrofoam cup, made a face, then set the cup on the table. "We'll have this straightened out the minute Dr. Benning finishes up, Governor. He's putting the last stitches in an episiotomy."

"What's that?" asked Billy Larson.

"We cut the mother's vagina open to keep it from tearing during a delivery. Sometimes the head's too big to pass otherwise."

Billy winced visibly, two shades whiter than before he'd asked. He sat back and silently folded his short arms on his chest.

Lucien said, "Why don't you just go into the nursery and find my son, Doc? How difficult can that be?"

"I've already tried. The other babies are accounted for, according to the identibands."

"Who put the bands on in the first place?"

"The delivery-room nurse."

"Well," Lucien said, "she made a mistake. Have her change mine."

Archer turned to the administrator. "Steve?"

"She's on the way back in," Griffith said, smoke enveloping his words. "She swears she double-checked each one before it left the delivery room."

Just then Dr. Robert Benning came into the lounge. About Lucien's height, Benning wore a scrub suit damp with perspiration at the armpits and across his chest. His athletic shoes were spattered with blood. He tossed his paper hat into the trash container. His hair was almost to his shoulders, peroxide blond.

"Damn, what a night," Benning said, collapsing into a chair. He was the only person in the room without a Southern accent. Dr. Archer had said Benning was a board-certified obstetrician. He hardly looked old enough to be out of college.

Archer said, "Bob, this is Governor Lucien Yarbrough."

Benning came out of his chair and they shook. "Nice to meet you, sir."

"And this is my aide, Billy Larson," Lucien said. As Benning returned to his seat, Lucien forced a smile and added, "I understand you filled in for Dr. Archer tonight and delivered our baby. I want to personally thank you for taking such good care of my wife."

"Glad I could help, sir."

"There is, however, a slight problem." Lucien held his artificial smile. "It appears that one of the nurses put the wrong identification bands on two of the babies. The child wearing my name is not our baby . . . so, obviously, my baby has somebody else's name on his wrist. I'm sure you can identify the one you delivered and switch the identification bands back the way they're supposed to be."

"I delivered three babies tonight," Benning said. "But sure, I'll go check."

"I would appreciate that." Lucien leaned back on the sofa and let out a long breath as the two doctors and the administrator left the room. He nodded to his aide. "You must get to the right person to have a job done properly, Gator. To the source."

Lucien closed his eyes and willed his pulse to stop

pounding in his head. This was nothing more than a temporary mix-up. Minutes from now he'd rejoin Page and they'd embrace and agree that they had produced a magnificent son. Then he'd telephone his father. First thing Monday morning, he'd hand-deliver the birth certificate to the trust company. After that, he could breathe easy for the first time in months.

The doctors and administrator returned, looking as though their undershorts had shrunk about three sizes.

"Governor," Dr. Archer began, "we have a problem."

Dr. Benning added, "The identibands seem to be in order, sir."

Lucien and Billy Larson bolted to their feet. Steve Griffith lit a cigarette.

"Excuse me?" Lucien said. "They sure as hell are not in order. If you'll bring that nurse in here who put them on in the first place, I'm sure she can straighten this mess out." He was struggling to contain himself. The solution seemed so obvious. Why wouldn't they understand?

"She is here, Governor," Griffith said.

"Does she remember helping deliver my wife?"

The administrator lowered his eyes momentarily, then squinted at Lucien through his smoke. "No, sir . . . not for sure. Wanda, our regular delivery-room nurse, is on vacation this week. The nurse who filled in tonight is temporary, so things are sorta new to her. We're not accustomed to having so many deliveries in one night. If Wanda had been here, she'd remember for sure . . . she never forgets a face. I mean . . . well, she never forgets a patient. Or a baby."

Lucien stiffened. "Would you mind bringing that temporary nurse in here, Mr. Griffith?" He reconsidered, breathing harder now. "Better yet, why don't I just go into the nursery and straighten this out myself?" He started for the door, on the edge of decompensating.

"I'm sorry, sir," Griffith said, attempting to block

Lucien's path, "only authorized personnel are allowed inside. We have to be careful about—"

Lucien pushed past them all and raced down the hall, with Billy Larson close behind.

The nursing supervisor went almost apoplectic trying to stop Governor Yarbrough's frantic search through the nursery. Ignoring her protests, Lucien inspected wristbands, opened incubators, and woke sleeping infants. Billy Larson positioned himself between Lucien and another nurse, attempting to justify their actions. Dr. Archer, Dr. Benning, and Steve Griffith came inside after donning sterile gowns, caps, and masks. Lucien still wore his Southern colonel's suit, though he'd removed the tie hours earlier. Actively searching for his son helped him regain some measure of control.

Unable to eject them, the administrator finally convinced Lucien and Billy to wear sterile attire over their clothes. Then he organized a more orderly search, bassinet by bassinet.

"This is baby girl Jones," the nursing supervisor said as they all looked on. She read from a clipboard of names and bassinet numbers, confirming the information on the Caucasian infant's wristband.

Lucien halted the nurse as she started toward the next bassinet. "Take off its diaper."

"What on earth for?"

"I want to be sure it's a girl."

"I know this one's a girl, Mr. Yarbrough. She's been here a full day already."

"Dammit," Lucien said, "nobody in this hospital seems to be sure of anything tonight. Now lower that baby's diaper. I need to be absolutely positive this isn't my son."

When the administrator nodded to the nurse, she did as requested, but a red flush blotched her neck and indignant face. The baby was a girl.

There were eight infants in the nursery. Dr. Benning had delivered three that night, all Dr. Archer's patients: the African-American male wearing the Yarbrough wristband, and two Caucasian males. Two others born that night were delivered by different doctors. One was a Caucasian male, the other an African-American female. The other three babies were a full day older: one Caucasian male, one African-American male, one Caucasian female. In all, there were four white male babies: three born that night, one the night before.

"Obviously one of these four little white boys is my son," Lucien declared. He pointed as he spoke.

"I don't think so, sir," Benning said.

"Then you think wrong, Doctor."

Benning said, "Governor Yarbrough, I delivered three white women tonight. I'll admit I was kind of pressured because they all went into labor about the same time. And I didn't know the women personally, since they're not my patients and I'm new in town. But as hectic as it was, I remember that one of the white women had a black baby. All three babies were boys."

"Then one of the other two is mine," Lucien said. "Which ones belong to the other women you delivered?"

Benning indicated the Caucasian infants in two bassinets. The nurse read the ID tags.

"Webb," she said. "Baby boy Webb." Moving to the next, she said, "Dunbar."

"Lower their diapers." When the nurse hesitated, Lucien added, "I'm not taking any chances."

Both infants were male.

Dr. Archer asked, "What about their medical records, Bob? Did you note anything distinctive about either of them?"

With more than a trace of sarcasm, Lucien added, "For instance, which one wasn't white?"

"Well, I . . . with them all coming at the same time, I didn't write anything on the charts till later. I hadn't finished suturing the episiotomy on the first woman before the second started delivering. The third one was the same. So no, I . . . I didn't record anything that would help us. There wasn't time."

"Well, take a good look now, Doctor," Lucien said. "You're obviously an intelligent man. My wife gave birth to one of those two little white boys right there. Tonight. You delivered him. Which one was it?"

Dr. Benning shook his head. "I don't think so, sir. I'm pretty sure that's your baby over there." He indicated the African-American male.

Lucien bristled. He wanted to grab Benning by the shoulders and shake some sense into him. Instead he forced in several deep inhalations and slowly let them out, then led the group into the hall outside.

Lucien addressed Dr. Benning in a level, controlled tone. "What part of the country are you from, Doctor?"

"Philadelphia, sir. I trained at Jefferson Medical College."

"Well, you're not in Philadelphia now; you are in Mississippi. Are you aware of that?"

"Yes, sir."

None of the others uttered a sound.

"You and I have not met before tonight, Doctor, but I've just been elected to the highest office in this state . . . as the honorable governor of the state of Mississippi. Are you aware of that?"

"I am now, sir."

"Good. Now, I want you to take a close look at me. Study my face. Here . . . look at my arms, my hands." Lucien rolled up his sleeves. "Tell me, Doctor . . . what color is my skin?"

"White, sir."

Though Lucien was smiling, his voice held no trace of warmth. "That's right. Tell me, Dr. Benning, what color is that baby's skin in there with my name on its wrist?"

"Black, sir." Benning's forehead was dotted with perspiration.

"That's also correct. Now . . . are you trying to tell me that this brown-haired, blue-eyed, Caucasian governor of the great state of Mississippi and his blue-eyed, blond-haired Caucasian wife have just given birth to a Negro baby? Is that what you're trying to make all of us believe?"

Benning didn't answer. He swallowed hard.

"Doctor, I'm asking you to go into that nursery and correct your mistake. Or your temporary nurse's mistake. When my grandfather was governor, he used to say, 'Don't fix the blame; fix the problem.' I don't care whose mistake it was as long as it gets fixed. And I mean, gets fixed right now. Tonight. I'm gonna go back to my wife's room and tell her everything's all straightened out down here. That she doesn't have to worry herself sick anymore. I expect you to go into that nursery and put the Yarbrough ID wristband on the right baby. My son. He's a boy. And he'd damned well better be white."

The blood drained from the young doctor's face. His eyes searched for help from Dr. Archer and the administrator. When he looked back at Lucien, a muscle was twitching near one eye. After a long silence, Benning said, "I'm sorry, Governor, I can't do that. I believe the Yarbrough band is on the correct child."

Without taking his eyes from Dr. Benning, Lucien spoke to his aide. "Gator, would you please give Buford Tallant a call? Tell him I apologize for disturbing him at this unspeakable hour, but I would greatly appreciate if he would just run on over here right now." There was a tremor in Lucien's voice when he added, "Tell him he's to shut this hospital down. Tonight. Otherwise I may burn the son of a bitch to the ground."

CHAPTER THREE

Page held one hand over her eyes to block the October sunlight streaming through open venetian blinds. It was not yet seven a.m., but somebody was already in her room, talking. She wanted to pull the covers over her head and sleep for about a week. When she tried to sit up, a stabbing pain in her perineum suddenly reminded her of where she was, and why. She opened her eyes, filled with a joy that blotted out all pain. She tried to raise the head of her electric bed, but raised the foot instead. The bedside control refused to do what it should.

The walls of the hospital room were painted a pastel green. As Page pushed herself upright, a uniformed nurse approached, carrying a blue bundle.

Page extended both arms eagerly, making no effort to suppress the grin on her face. "They found my baby?"

"Yes, ma'am, and he needs to nurse now."

Hardly able to contain her excitement, Page couldn't wait to snuggle her son close and watch him suckle her breast. She jerked away, however, shocked, when she saw the face of the child being offered. "What are you doing?"

"Giving you your baby," the nurse replied.

"Is this supposed to be some kind of prank? If so, I am not amused. Bring me my son this instant."

"This is your son . . . baby boy Yarbrough. Says so right here on his wristband."

"It most certainly is not. Let me see that." Page hurriedly read the plastic band on the baby's wrist.

What the nurse had said was correct. The wristband was not. "It's a mistake," Page said. "Somebody put our name on the wrong baby. I mean . . . my God, it's obvious, isn't it?" She tried to recall what Lucien had said the night before, about a wrong bassinet.

"Mrs. Yarbrough, this was the last infant in the nursery. All the others are with their mothers now, being fed. I wouldn't have thought it was the right one either, but the charge nurse said he was when I came on duty this morning. He has to nurse to get the proper resistance for his immune system. You know, from the colostrum in your milk."

"Then take him to his mother. Some Negro woman has my baby, and I want you to find him right now and take this baby to her and bring me mine." Panic pushed Page onto the verge of crying. "Do you hear me? Don't just stand there; go find my baby and bring him to me right now."

The nurse left, taking the infant with her. Page frantically searched for the call button and pressed it. Nobody came. Her fingers trembling, she pressed it again. And again. And again.

After what seemed an eternity, a different nurse entered the room. "Yes, Mrs. Yarbrough?" The nurse was about thirty-five, brunette, with a round face and body.

Page had to clear her throat before she could make a sound. She tried to appear in control. "I'd like to speak with the head nurse."

"I'm Juanita Ford, the nursing supervisor. Perhaps I can help."

"Miss Ford, I would like my son brought in here immediately. Not somebody else's baby . . . mine. Will you do that for me please?"

"Nurse Barlow brought your baby in, Mrs. Yarbrough. You sent them out."

Page thought she'd surely explode. "Miss Ford, that was not my son; that was a little Negro child." Page's throat tightened until it was almost impossible to speak. She ignored the tears now streaming down her face. "Please," she managed. She had always hated when women whined, but couldn't seem to stop the strange sounds squeaking out of her throat. It had to be the medications in her system making her emotions so transparent. "Where is my husband? I need him here right now. This is not funny, and I want it straightened out this instant."

Lucien perched on the edge of the hospital bed and held Page tightly against him. He was unshaven and wore the clothes he'd had on the night before. It was now ten-thirty in the morning, and the tranquilizers Page had refused until Lucien arrived were beginning to take effect.

"What a mess," Lucien said.

"Oh, God, Luce, it's a nightmare." Thank heaven he was here. Page felt so uncharacteristically helpless. Abandoned, somehow. "I don't understand how this could happen."

"I've never seen anything like it, sweetheart . . . these people refuse to listen to reason. Buford and Gator and I were with the administrator and the doctors all night and all morning. We've been through the nursery a dozen times. We must've talked to every nurse and orderly and nurse's aide in Adams County."

"Ouch. That hurts."

"What hurts?"

"My breasts. They're sore."

"Sorry. Anyhow, there's four white boys in the nursery. One of them has to be ours, because there aren't any more, but everybody swears those four match up with the right mothers. White women."

"They're obviously wrong. Or not telling the truth for some crazy reason." Page's mind searched for an explanation. Anything that might make sense.

Lucien continued, "Gator and I followed the nurses this morning when they took the babies around to be fed. Gator would wait until a nurse took a baby into a room. When she left, he'd walk in like he owned the place and get a good look at that mama and the baby. Then he'd say he'd made a mistake, that he was looking for somebody else. Everybody knows my face, so the rooms I went into, I just introduced myself . . . said I wanted to congratulate them for having such a fine baby."

"And?"

"The black women had black babies; the white women had white babies. Dr. Benning said one of the white women last night had a black baby, but we don't know which one." Lucien let out a sharp sigh. "Son of a bitch!"

When Page tried to raise herself up on one arm, Lucien pressed a button on the bed's remote that elevated her back and head.

A ray of hope penetrated Page's gloom. She excitedly offered, "Lucien, maybe ours wasn't a boy. What if . . . what if that amnio test was wrong and maybe our baby is a girl after all? Maybe they're looking for a boy when it's actually a girl."

"Dr. Archer said those tests are pretty much foolproof nowadays. And Dr. Benning said all the babies he delivered were boys . . . but hell, I'm beginning to doubt if we can believe anything Benning says. He's not much more than a kid."

Disappointed but still hopeful, Page said, "It's possible, though, isn't it? Did you check the women with girl babies, too?"

"We checked them all. Five or six times."

Page wiped her eyes on a tissue, then blew her nose. She reflected on what they knew. And what they didn't. She had always considered herself intelligent. She was perfectly capable of sorting this out, but her brain seemed mired in a dense fog. She should never have agreed to take that tranquilizer. After a lengthy silence, she asked, "What are we gonna do?"

"Buford's talking to Judge Winston now. The first thing we need is an injunction to keep these babies from leaving the hospital. A temporary restraining order."

"Can you do that?"

"We have to. The ones who delivered night before last are scheduled to go home today. One of the women from last night insists on leaving, too. I'm not about to let them take any babies outta here till we know which one is ours."

"Wouldn't a blood test prove whose baby is whose?"

"You can't make somebody submit to an involuntary blood test . . . or their baby. People get real persnickety about things like that."

"But if you tell them what's happened, surely they'll understand."

"We'll do whatever we have to. First, let's see what Buford works out with the judge."

Page was immensely grateful that her husband understood legal things. She certainly didn't. "Oh, God, Lucien, I can't believe . . ." She was unable to complete her thought. Only hours earlier she had felt so blessed. She thanked God every night for granting her the husband she adored, the perfect family, and the perfect home. Their family included Cindy, the most wonderful daughter in the world, and, during the past nine months, their son on the way. Everything she had ever wanted. And now this—this nightmare. After a moment, Page asked, "What have you told your parents?"

"That you were real tired and the doctor said you needed to sleep. I said you'd call them later."

Even sedated, Page knew about how long J.L. and Miss Emma would accept that lame excuse. "They don't know anything?"

"I've had a hell of a time keeping them away from the hospital. Especially J.L. He's already called the newspaper in Jackson about doing a photo session with him, me, and the baby. Three generations of Yarbroughs . . . the senator, the governor, and the next president. Thank God he doesn't know. He'd be over here taking the hospital apart with his bare hands, one brick at a time."

"And Miss Emma?"

"I'm sure Mama has called everybody in town and organized a garden party. She's probably got her maids polishing silver and breaking out deviled-egg plates and making cucumber sandwiches right now. She'll be concocting that awful green punch she serves."

Page felt her mental haze lift momentarily. Noticing Lucien's attire, she asked, "Haven't you gone home at all?"

"No, baby, I've been here all night and all morning, trying to straighten this mess out."

She'd automatically assumed that Lucien had seen to their six-year-old daughter. Suddenly filled with concern, she asked, "What about Cindy? Did you talk to Doris?"

"Checked on them last night and about seven this morning. Rona Green drove Cindy home and put her to bed. Said Cindy was too excited to sleep because they already asked her to be in next spring's pageant, and this time she'll get to dance with a boy just like the older girls. Personally, I think she's too young to be doing that."

Page felt herself relax a bit, and retreated into the comfort of her normal world for an instant. Thank God for Doris—one person she could always depend on. "Cindy'll be seven in January. I danced with my first beau in the pageant at that age."

Lucien reluctantly said, "Well, she's an awfully young seven. We'll see when the time comes."

Page bit her lower lip and shook her head. "Oh, God, Luce, why did this happen to us?"

"I don't know, baby . . . I don't know. But I'm damned sure gonna straighten it out."

There was a soft knock on the door; then it opened a crack. "Lucien?"

Billy Larson eased his head and a portion of his body inside. He had a heavy stubble of beard. "Sorry, Page," he said softly. "I don't mean to intrude." To Lucien he said, "Buford just called and he's on the way back over. Said we should meet him in the administrator's office."

Page asked, "Did he get everything worked out?"

Billy replied, "He just said we should meet him. But don't you worry, Page; we'll get what we want. They're bound to know who they're dealing with here."

Outside the administrator's office, Lucien and Billy Larson conferred in hushed tones with Buford E. Tallant. Tallant had finished Ole Miss law school three years before Lucien, and was immediately invited to join the six-member law firm of Lucien's father, J. L. Yarbrough Senior—former United States senator Yarbrough. Since both the senator and Lucien concentrated almost exclusively on their political careers, Buford was an essential partner in the firm—he practiced law. He was neat, trim, fit, and tanned, his shiny dark hair never out of place. Nothing about him was. To say that Buford was good at what he did would be a gross understatement. Having him there was a huge comfort to Lucien. They made a formidable team.

"I have to agree with the judge," Buford said. "If we try to force them, somebody'll get all bent out of shape and call their attorney and then we'll have a public battle. The newspapers would have a field day. Especially that new editor, Hilary Ross."

"What would you expect?" Lucien said. "She's a damned Republican. I'd hoped we could keep people from finding out about this. Maybe we should have somebody just ease in there and take blood samples from those babies."

Billy Larson spoke up. "A friend of mine's a lab tech. She'd do it for me."

"Too risky," Tallant said. "Lucien'd get sued six ways from Sunday if she ever let on what she'd done. Breaking and entering, assault, battery, theft. It'd be worse than Whitewater or Zippergate. Might cost us the governership."

"I been screwing her for three years and she hasn't ever said anything to her husband or anybody else."

Lucien couldn't resist the opportunity. More secure now that he was among his compatriots, he winked at Tallant. "That either means you're not doing a good enough job for her to brag about, Gator, or you're so incredible that she won't risk losing you by talking."

"It's the second reason," Larson said quite seriously.

Buford Tallant brought them back on track. "There'd be no point trying to stop the black women with black babies, so we can just let them go. If Dr. Archer's a hundred percent certain about that amniocentesis result, we needn't be concerned with the girl baby. That only leaves those four little white boys. Let me talk to their mamas, see if they'll go along. If they do, and one of them doesn't turn out to be yours, then we test the girl baby."

Lucien asked, "Do they have to know who's involved?"

"I'll just say I represent a client."

Lucien breathed a sigh of relief. It felt good to have direction again. "Then let's get it done. Nobody's leaving this hospital with my son."

Dr. Archer accompanied the lab technician into Page's room later that morning. They interrupted a nurse instructing Page on the use of a plastic breast pump.

"Sorry," Archer said. "Shall we come back?"

"It's all right," Page said, closing her gown. "My breasts are so engorged, they hurt. We've just finished."

When the nurse left, the lab tech arranged his syringes and glass tubes for taking Page's blood. Page talked with Dr. Archer, trying to take her mind off the needle aimed at her vein. Needles were right up there with snakes and spiders on her list of the most abhorrent things in life.

"Is this for blood-typing?" asked Page, already pulling her arm away before the tourniquet was in place.

"That and DNA fingerprinting," Archer said. "DNA's the best."

"That lawyer for O. J. Simpson said DNA wasn't reliable. On TV. Ouch, ouch, ohhh . . . that stings." Suddenly snakes and spiders didn't seem nearly as dreadful as stainless-steel needles.

Dr. Archer continued. "If Simpson's attorney said that, he's dead wrong. We can identify either parent to an accuracy of at least one in ten million. Some experts say it's as high as one in eighty million."

The technician finished, apologizing for hurting Page, and left. At least he'd been fast. Page held an alcohol sponge to her stinging arm, still trembling inside. Though she was sitting still, her heart was doing a hundred and sixty. "Did you take Lucien's blood yet?"

"He had to change clothes and hurry to his office . . . some emergency about the inauguration. No matter. Whichever baby matches your DNA will be the right one."

"Have all the others been tested?"

"Two of the women agreed straightaway. One wants to discuss it with her mother first. The other one's husband is coming in to talk to Steve Griffith." Archer hesitated, then added, "Says he's bringing his attorney with him."

CHAPTER FOUR

In spite of it being Saturday afternoon, the offices of Yarbrough, Yarbrough, Tallant, and McCann were bustling with activity. Buford Tallant had called in two associate attorneys, three paralegals, and three secretaries. Lucien and Buford were going over strategy when J.L. arrived. Jackson Lucien Yarbrough Senior—Lucien's father.

J.L.'s hair was longer than was fashionable, wavy, and snow white. Though he had celebrated his seventy-fifth birthday in September, he moved with the vigor of a man half his age. His charming facade belied his pugnacity and well-known drive to win. That combination had been responsible for J.L.'s being elected to six consecutive terms as a United States senator. The voters loved him. But as early as when he was an All-American running back at Ole Miss, people had also learned not to get in his way. Wearing a double-breasted suit and an Ole Miss tie, he approached in that unmistakable manner that said his adrenaline was surging. He was on the hunt, all senses heightened, ready for the kill.

"Why didn't you call me?" J.L. made no attempt to hide his irritation.

"I called Mother this morning," Lucien said. "The doctor said Page needed to sleep today."

"About the baby," J.L. growled. "The mix-up."

"It's nothing to worry about. Buford and I have it under control."

"Nothing to worry about? My only grandson. What's this about a Negro being involved?"

"Who told you that?"

"Everybody in town told me. My phone's ringing off the wall. Three reporters have called already . . . two from here and one from Jackson."

Tallant spoke up. "J.L., why don't you have a seat and we'll go over exactly what we've done so far. It's a temporary situation where the hospital interchanged identification bands on two of the babies. Really quite ludicrous. John Winston issued a TRO to prevent any of the four little white boys from leaving the hospital till we straighten things out. Lucien can fill you in while I get us a fresh pot of coffee."

Unable to stay in bed because of pain in her pelvic region and breasts, Page stood outside the newborn nursery, watching through the observation glass. A nurse had collected a second batch of milk from Page's engorged breasts, but Page still couldn't rest.

She had left a message on Rona Green's answering machine about who should docent which house on the Pilgrimage tour. Being president of her garden club, plus chairperson of Fall Pilgrimage and the Confederate Pageant, Page couldn't have picked a worse time to be in the hospital. Rona—also born and raised in Natchez—was Page's lifelong friend and cochairperson. Page had actually been relieved that Rona hadn't been home. Other than to call Doris several times to check on Cindy, Page was too preoccupied to speak with anybody until this mix-up was straightened out. Lucien had promised to bring her laptop computer tomorrow, so she could leave e-mail for Rona and the other girls.

Through the glass, Page watched one nurse and two nurse's aides tend babies. They bathed, powdered, diapered, took temperatures, and counted little pulses. Fascinated, Page knew that one of the infants was hers. But which one? She had suppressed the unacceptable thought that someone might have taken her son from the nursery and left the African-American child in its place. She'd heard of such things happening in big-city hospitals, apparently because of the demand for white babies. An article in *Family Circle* once said that barren couples would pay up to twenty-five thousand dollars for a white child. She could understand that. With Cindy, she and Lucien had tried to get pregnant for four years. It had taken over five years this time.

She'd also read somewhere that you couldn't give a black baby away. Thank heavens this wasn't a big-city hospital. In Natchez, people still sat on their front porches in the evenings, visiting with neighbors. Clerks in banks and drugstores knew your name and who your parents were. The only time things became hectic was during Pilgrimage, when thousands of tourists flooded in to tour spectacular antebellum mansions and gardens.

Mesmerized by the tiny human forms, Page stood watching perfect little faces, hands, toes. Feet no bigger than boiled peanuts. One by one, the babies were carried out to their mothers for their feedings. Page thought of the impersonal breast pump that had drained her milk. She imagined some woman in a nearby room enjoying the indescribable sensation of holding a newborn to her breast, listening to eager smacking sounds as his lips found her nipple and began to pull, watching contentment spread across his precious face. She imagined having to gently nudge him each time he fell asleep, till his little tummy was full. Page's baby. Her son. She pressed a tissue to her mouth and fought back a sob. Oh, God, she missed him so.

Finally there was one child remaining in the nursery. The nurse who'd helped Page pump her breasts brought the African-American baby to the window. Page couldn't help smiling. He was adorable.

Lucien's father often joked that little pickaninnies were so cute, he'd keep half a dozen around if they just didn't grow up. J.L. was from another generation. Sometimes it seemed like another century. His insensitive comments were often embarrassing to Page when he blurted out things like that without thinking. Lucien assured her it had to do with the way the senator had been raised. He didn't mean any harm.

The nurse shook drops of milk onto her wrist from a plastic bottle, then touched the infant's cheek with the nipple. Though no sound penetrated the glass window, the African-American baby was screaming its lungs out and shaking both fists at the nurse, or Page, or maybe the entire world. His lips eagerly searched for, then found, the bottle's plastic nipple.

Page watched him suck furiously for several seconds, then pause and heave an enormous sigh. She felt a sudden urge to cradle the baby in her arms, to feel his warmth against her, the movement of little arms and legs. She wanted to tell him that she understood, that she knew what an agonizing ache he must feel in the pit of his stomach too, and she was sorry.

The nurse took the bottle from the infant and held it toward Page. She pointed a finger at Page's chest, then held the bottle up again. Nursery charades. Page unfolded her arms and pointed to her own breasts, questioning. The nurse nodded, her eyes crinkling in a smile.

"My milk?" whispered Page.

The nurse nodded again, then let the baby discover the plastic nipple once more.

Page's vision blurred. A tear spilled over and slid down one cheek, followed immediately by others. She wiped them away with a sleeve of her robe. After several moments she turned and slowly walked back toward her empty room. The pain in her heart was far greater than any pain she'd felt from her delivery or episiotomy. Analgesic capsules couldn't begin to relieve an ache this deep.

Lucien, Buford Tallant, Billy Larson, and J.L. sat around a conference table with the hospital administrator, Steve Griffith. The hospital's attorney, Mack Malone, stood beside the table.

Malone said, "If we don't release them, we're exposing ourselves to major damages, gentlemen."

"Not nearly as major," Buford interjected, "as if you release Governor Yarbrough's son to the wrong home."

"Governor-elect Yarbrough," Malone said. Another Republican.

Unable to contain himself, J.L. asked, "Exactly who's refusing the tests? Their names."

Griffith read from a sheet of paper. "Gloria Webb hasn't actually refused; she just hasn't decided. Her mother's visiting another daughter up in Memphis, and Gloria wants to wait till Mama gets here . . . she's due in around five. According to our records, Gloria isn't married. She's only nineteen. Caroline Dunbar is the only one who actually said no."

"Which Dunbar is she?" asked J.L.

"Her husband is Jonathan Dunbar," Lucien said.

"Any kin to Richard or Wayne?"

"I don't think so. Her father is Elmer Harrison, from up in Tupelo. She married this Dunbar fellow in Jackson. Both of them worked at a bank there, I think. Is that right, Buford?"

"Correct. Gator had Sheriff Carswell run a background check on them this morning. As far as we can make out, neither one has family here. Jonathan Dunbar's people are from the Atlanta and Macon area over in Georgia. He went to school at Emory."

J.L. asked, "Which bank does he work for?"

Buford answered. "He got out of that. He and his wife leased that little place on Upper Main that used to be Betty Lynn Crowder's bakery and pie shop. They opened a soup-and-salad place about three months ago."

"I've eaten there," Billy Larson said. "They do a decent lunch business."

"Gentlemen," Malone said, "we need to make a decision. Your restraining order will never hold up. But with this being Saturday afternoon, there's no way I can have it overturned before Monday morning, so let me make a suggestion. Two of the mothers have already allowed blood samples to be taken from their babies."

"From somebody's babies," Buford Tallant corrected.

Malone emitted an audible sigh. "When Miss Webb's mother arrives, she will very likely agree to have her . . ." He hesitated, nodding toward Buford. "Correction, *that* little boy tested as well. I'll be happy to join with Mr. Tallant in recommending that she do so. Which leaves only the Dunbars. I don't know them, but I'm well acquainted with their attorney, Wylie Marsh. Unfortunately, Mr. Marsh is away for the weekend and they won't agree to anything until he returns. I believe I can work with Wylie . . . he's a reasonable man."

"As long as he's billing about three hundred dollars an hour," J.L. said under his breath.

To Malone, Lucien said, "What are you getting at?"

"I suggest a compromise. One of the blood samples already drawn may clear up everything. Assuming that Miss Webb's mama agrees, we'll send samples from three of the four white babies to the lab today. If I had to bet, I'd put my money on the Negro baby belonging to the Webb girl . . . her being unmarried and all. If you agree not to enforce the restraining order, I will strongly recommend that Wylie Marsh have his clients bring their baby in to be tested on Monday."

J.L. asked, "How long will it take to get the results back?"

Griffith answered, "Normally a week or more, but the lab says they can do it in three days in an emergency. There's an extra charge for that, of course."

"To hell with the charge," Lucien said. "This is definitely an emergency."

Griffith added, "Being as it's Saturday, they won't start the tests before Monday anyway."

J.L. asked, "Where is this lab?"

"In Jackson," Griffith said. "The state lab."

J.L. turned to Lucien's aide. "Gator, get me the phone number of whoever runs that lab. I want those tests done today."

Billy Larson left the room.

"Well, gentlemen," Malone said, "do we have an agreement? Will you withdraw your restraining order?"

Lucien didn't speak but had no doubt, without the need for discussion, what was coming. Buford Tallant shut and snapped his briefcase, the faintest hint of a smile crossing his face.

J.L. stood and answered, "Not on your life, Mack. Not a single baby leaves this hospital until I see my grandson sucking at his own mama's teat."

CHAPTER FIVE

Lucien brought Page's laptop and a vase of assorted flowers Sunday morning. Page thanked him with a big hug and a kiss, and immediately began redistributing individual buds in the arrangement. She was eager to hear if Lucien had any new information since they spoke on the phone the night before.

"Oh, Luce, they're beautiful," she said. "Where did you find such pretty flowers on Sunday?"

"Dick Tips opened his floral shop for me. His wife's in your garden club."

"Oh, sure, Julie. She's a love."

"Anyway . . . how're you doing, Page?"

"Okay, I guess. I . . ." She couldn't wait a second longer. "When do you think we'll hear?"

"Tuesday at the earliest. Dad got somebody to open the state lab yesterday, but it still takes three days to do a DNA test even in an emergency situation."

"Is it possible to be on pins and needles and go stir-crazy at the same time?"

"How do you mean?"

"I'm so upset I can't sleep or eat or even sit still, and I'm going out of my mind because there's nothing I can do about it. I've worn a path from here to the nursery and back. I feel like a caged panther."

"Watch TV, sweetheart. They have those daytime talk shows."

"I can't be still that long."

"Would you rather be at home? Doc Archer says you're fine to go whenever you want."

"I can't leave without the baby."

"Well, you know I agree. Hey . . . would a couple of visitors help take your mind off . . . you know, the mix-up?"

"Who?"

Lucien started toward the door.

"Sweetie, visiting hours aren't till one p.m. Where are you going?"

He winked. "If they arrest me, I'll pardon myself." He opened the door and called to somebody in the hall.

"Surprise!"

Page's sister, Laura Mason, raced into the room with an armload of flowers. Immediately behind her was Lucien's sister, who was Page's good friend and confidante, Suellen Whitford. They hugged, each putting forth her best efforts to display a cheerful face. Laura tried to say something, but her voice broke. She turned away and busied herself arranging the flowers they had brought.

Being almost five years older, Page had always been able to see through her sister's facades. She pretended not to notice.

"You look marvelous," Suellen said.

Page knew she didn't, but automatically returned the courtesy, then asked, "How's Bryan? Are the girls all right?"

"They're great. Just great. They all send their love. Of course, with both girls being in the pageant this year, that's all we hear about at our house." Suellen and her husband, Bryan Whitford, had two daughters, ages five and nine. "They've both decided to be movie stars now. Ready to move to Hollywood."

Three years younger than her brother, Suellen was thirty-three. She had the same straight Yarbrough nose and high cheekbones as Lucien, but different coloring. Lucien had inherited his mother's brown hair and blue eyes, while Suellen apparently got more genes from J.L. She was a brunette, about five-five, with an olive complexion. Unlike Laura, who was totally unathletic, Suellen prided herself on staying in

great shape, mostly from swimming and riding
horseback.

Laura finally brought her emotions under control
and rejoined them, exaggerating a smile. Blond and
blue eyed, she looked very much like Page, except she
was taller and thinner. "When does the doctor say you
can come home?"

"Probably Tuesday," Page replied.

For the next several minutes, the three women carefully avoided what they were about to burst to talk
about. They discussed Fall Pilgrimage, how much better their production of the pageant was than that of
the two rival garden clubs. Page said her daughter had
recently learned the story of how the rivalry began.
About how the Natchez Garden Club had started Pilgrimage in 1931. Then women whose ideas differed
from the founders had spun off the Pilgrimage Garden
Club, then the Confederate Garden Club. And how
each garden club now put on its own version of the
original Confederate Pageant. While competition was
fierce, it was also quite stimulating, and made the
event more exciting and more successful.

As they knew he would, Lucien said something
about having to find Billy Larson, then excused
himself.

As soon as the door closed behind him, Suellen
pounced on the bed next to Page and said, "Tell us
everything. My God, did they really try to give you a
Negro baby?"

Swearing them both to secrecy, Page shared what
she knew.

Laura asked, "Are all the other mothers staying in
the hospital, too?"

"The white ones," Page said. "A couple of them
are terribly upset about allowing the tests and not
being able to take their babies home. I don't blame
them. I'd be upset too."

Suellen said, "Not half as much as they'd be if they
were in your shoes. At least they have their babies.
Or they think they do."

"How awful," Laura said. "I mean, it's terrible for you, but can you imagine thinking you have your baby for three or four days, then having somebody take it away? The whole situation's like waking up in the Twilight Zone."

An hour later, Laura said she had to be going. "Bobby needs me to come by the restaurant to help with the lunch crowd. I'm working the cash register today."

Laura and her husband, Bobby Mason, owned a small family restaurant on Main Street. Their financial survival had been touch-and-go for the first few years, but now they were on reasonably solid ground—as long as they avoided paying unnecessary salaries. Page was surprised her sister had stayed as long as she did. They hadn't been close in years. But Page was delighted to have seen her, and told her so.

When Laura was gone, Suellen took Page's hands in hers, looked deep into Page's eyes, and said, "You poor dear. What you must be going through. I could just die for you."

They hugged and cried. When they had regained their composure, Suellen said, "What do you think really happened?"

"Gloria Webb obviously had the black baby, and the new nurse mixed them up. Gloria's the only one who isn't married."

"Mary Lou Snodgrass knows Gloria's sister . . . the one up in Memphis. Says she always was wild."

"When did you speak with Mary Lou?"

"She called late last night. She'd heard all about it from Patty Fulton. I don't know how Patty found out."

"Everybody in town must know by now. It's so embarrassing."

"Well, what would you expect? Daddy says us Yarbroughs have been fodder for gossipmongers since before the war, and that's a hundred and forty years. It goes with being socially and politically prominent, but I must say, nothing like this ever happened before.

Not even that scandal when they tried to say Grand-daddy shot that darky. Of course, I know it's the hospital's mistake . . . everybody knows that. And every woman in town is on your side, Page, even from the other garden clubs." Suellen paused, wrinkling her brow. "Have you considered that somebody might've switched babies because of Lucien's being elected? He made a lot of people mad when he campaigned in those black neighborhoods. Some hotheaded white supremacist might think it a great joke to switch a black baby for the governor's son."

Page's heart sank. She hadn't entertained such a possibility. "Oh, God, Suellen, what a horrible thought."

Suellen let the thought go and changed the subject. "All the girls in the garden club have tried to call you. The switchboard won't put them through."

"Lucien knows I can't lie, so he had my phone blocked. He doesn't want me talking to anybody till this mess is straightened out."

"Have you spoken with your father?"

"He came by for a few minutes yesterday."

"Was he . . . ?"

"Sober enough to talk. It was before noon."

"He's such a wonderful man when he's not drinking. I love his sense of humor. They say he was a great doctor in his time."

"He was. But . . . well, you know. I didn't let on there was anything wrong."

"Didn't he insist on seeing his grandson?"

"I told him the baby was downstairs for a routine check by the pediatrician. He accepted it for now."

Suellen adjusted one of her earrings. "Mother and I were trying to figure out when you finally got pregnant. I said it was on that cruise through the Caribbean. Wasn't it?"

"I think it happened the night of Mayrene Carter's wedding shower, but we left for Miami the next morning . . . that's where the cruise started. It might've been later that week."

"I told Bryan we should take a cruise, but he says ten days away from his business would cost him more than the price of two cruises. I'm lucky if I get him for a full weekend anymore." Suellen stood and gathered her things to leave. "Well, Page, we'll get through this just fine. As soon as those tests come back, you'll get your baby and you'll go home." She paused. "People don't normally have babies DNA tested. Maybe there's a blessing in this somewhere. At least when you get your son, you're gonna *know* he's yours. With the money that's involved, those tests could be really important."

Just then the door opened and Page's six-year-old daughter ran inside. Cindy jumped on the bed and threw her arms around her mother's neck. She was a miniature Page, blond, blue-eyed, with the face of an angel.

"I miss you, Mommy."

Page couldn't begin to describe how wonderful it was to hold her daughter close—to touch that silky hair, smell her freshly scrubbed skin. "And I miss you, Cindy. Daddy tells me you were just wonderful in the pageant."

Cindy presented her mother with a tin of freshly baked chocolate-chip cookies. "Doris made these for you. I ate two already." A smudge of chocolate on one cheek substantiated Cindy's admission.

J. L. Yarbrough came into the room, grinning. "I thought you might like a visitor or two."

"It's a wonderful surprise, Senator, but how did you . . . isn't there a rule about children under the age of twelve not being allowed to visit?"

J.L. winked. "Doesn't apply to Yarbroughs." He laughed. "Cindy, tell your mama who were the prettiest girls in the pageant last night."

"I was."

"And who else?" J.L. asked.

"Betsy and Emma Sue." She referred to Suellen's children.

Suellen spoke up. "Daddy, you shouldn't teach the girls to say things like that. They'll repeat it in public."

The senator beamed. "Why not? They're my grand-daughters, aren't they? Besides, it's true . . . they were the best ones there, just as you and Lucien were when you were in the pageant. And you, too, Page, even if you weren't in the family yet. How long is that, now, twenty-five years? Thirty or so for Lucien. Seems like yesterday." He shook his head. "Speaking of yesterday, your Aunt Belle has called every day since you've been here. She's furious that the switchboard won't put her calls through."

"I'll phone her today." Page smiled. "If I don't, she'll be down here with her shotgun to break me out." She thought of the time her mother's older sister, lovingly known as Auntie Bellum by family and friends, filled one burglar's rear end with buckshot and held another at gunpoint until the sheriff arrived at her 1835 plantation home. That incident had occurred four years ago, when Belle was only seventy-one.

Doris Kern quietly eased into the room, smiling broadly. It was just like Doris to wait outside, unselfishly letting J.L. and Cindy come in first. Fifty-two years old, African-American, five-three, and on the heavy side, Doris had a smile for everybody. She hurried to Page's side and they embraced like the long-time friends they were.

"Oh, you look just beautiful, Page." There were tears in Doris's eyes. She spoke with a heavy Mississippi accent, but her voice was warm and kind, full of love. Page had learned early in life that while Doris didn't exactly waste words, she was considerably wiser than she first appeared.

"So do you, Doris. That's a new dress, isn't it?"

"I bought it for church. Do you like it?" She turned around self-consciously, exhibiting the brightly flowered dress. "I'm going a little later on, while Cindy's at her grandmother's house."

"It's lovely." Page hugged both Cindy and Doris again. "Oh, I missed you two." She asked Doris, "Has everything been all right at home? Cindy eating well for you?"

"Same as if you were there, isn't that right, baby?" Doris looked lovingly at Page's daughter.

"Yes, Doris. I even ate my green beans, didn't I?"

"You sure did. You're a wonderful child, just like your mama was."

Page relaxed. For the first time in days, she felt that everything was going to be all right. Surrounded in this unfamiliar environment by family, she was certain of it now. As she and Lucien had agreed earlier, things were going to be just fine.

Tuesday morning Lucien hurried into Page's hospital room. "We got the results," he said. "Wouldn't you know it? It wasn't any of the three babies we tested. It's the other one."

CHAPTER SIX

Page was halfway between the bed and the bathroom, wearing a terry-cloth robe. She held a toothbrush and tube of toothpaste in one hand. Lucien's words had the same effect as if someone had kicked her in the stomach. She had to sit down.

"You could've blown me over with a gnat's breath," Lucien said.

"What do we do now?" Page tried to gather her thoughts. She'd been convinced that the black child belonged to Gloria Webb. And that Gloria had Page's baby.

Lucien said, "It has to be the Dunbars. The ones who insisted on getting their attorney involved."

"What does their lawyer say?"

"Old Wylie? Well, Mr. Wylie Marsh finally moseyed back into town this morning, and he's meeting with his clients this afternoon. He told Buford he's prepared to file suit against the hospital, the hospital administrator, the hospital's board of directors, which just happens to include J.L. and Mother, and against you and me for seeking, obtaining, and enforcing what he considers an illegal and improper restraining order . . . if his clients agree, of course. From what I can gather, they will. Oh, yeah, he mentioned something about kidnapping and holding people hostage, too."

"Can he do that?"

"Honey, you can sue a cyclops for looking at you cross-eyed, but it doesn't mean you'll win. He's just thumping his chest right now. Probably got laid a couple of times over the weekend and thinks he's King Kong. Buford'll put him back in his cage."

"Thank God Buford is on our side."

"You can say that again. I'm a pretty good attorney myself, but I'd sure hate to go up against Buford in a courtroom."

"I know you are, Luce. You're a wonderful attorney, and a wonderful husband and father. You'll be a fantastic governor, too." Page pulled her husband close and held him. They'd straighten out this nightmare soon. She never doubted that working together, they would prevail.

Lucien said, "I hope the newspapers don't blow this thing all out of proportion. So far they've only said that you and Adam are resting at home. Dad pulled a few strings."

"Adam?"

"We had to give them a name. Jackson Adams Yarbrough the second. I said we call him Adam."

"I like that."

Lucien walked to the door. "Well, we're down to that Dunbar woman. No wonder she refused the DNA test . . . she knew all the time. The little tramp."

"You shouldn't say that, Lucien. You don't know her."

"She lay down with a black man, didn't she? I'm as liberal as the next man, but that's way beyond acceptable behavior. It's against nature."

"Good thing you didn't mention that in your campaign speeches. It sounds like something your father would say."

"The majority of my black supporters would totally agree with me. They don't believe in mixing the races either . . . it just wasn't meant to be. Besides, I promised jobs and schools and low-cost housing for Negroes. That isn't the same as a white woman going to bed with a black man."

Page didn't want to argue, but neither of them knew the Dunbar woman. How could they judge what she'd done or why? She directed the conversation back to her major concern. "You can't let the Dunbars leave here with my son, Lucien."

"Oh, they're damned well not going anywhere. Wylie Marsh can threaten anybody he wants, but that baby stays where we can watch him if I have to hold a gun on them all. I'm gonna have Gator station a couple of men outside the nursery twenty-four hours a day. Make sure they don't try to sneak him outta here."

Page suddenly understood how that man in Greek mythology must have felt. What was his name? Tantalus? The one doomed to eternally stand in freshwater that receded each time he stooped to drink. Meanwhile, hanging over his head were branches laden with fruit that forever remained just beyond his reach. At this very moment, Caroline Dunbar was probably holding Page's baby right down the hall, tantalizingly out of reach.

Jonathan Dunbar was a small man, perhaps five-nine, and thin. A severely receding hairline made him appear older than his stated age of twenty-six. He sat beside his attorney, Wylie Marsh, across the conference table from Buford Tallant, Lucien, and J.L. For nearly an hour Dunbar had silently focused on a yellow pencil he held. He softly tapped its point against a legal pad while the attorneys hashed out their points of disagreement.

Wylie Marsh said, "Gentlemen, we seem to have a stalemate here. My clients are incensed that you would ask them to risk any procedure that is medically unnecessary for their baby's health and well-being."

Buford Tallant said, "Wylie, it's only a blood test. A little needle prick."

"Which, according to my sources, carries the risk of hematoma, infection, blood clot, phlebitis, cellulitis, thrombophlebitis, and hepatitis. Needles are lined with silicone today, and we know how dangerous that is. Even the AIDS virus can be transferred by, as you call them, 'little needle pricks.' "

Lucien said, "Wylie, get real. We're not talking about a dirty needle from some drug addict. Mr. Dunbar's own physician can draw the blood, using his best sterile technique and a disposable needle that's never been out of its package from the factory. Dr. Archer explained all that to us."

Marsh shook his head, frowning. "Gentlemen, you don't have a leg to stand on, making such a request. Obviously the decision rests with my clients, the child's mother and father. It is my recommendation that they allow no such invasion of their child's body."

"Just a minute," J.L. said. "Your assumption that the Dunbars are this child's parents is nothing more than speculation. In the excitement of a flood of deliveries Friday night, an inexperienced nurse put the wrong name tag on his wrist. The Dunbars don't have any right to refuse this test."

Marsh said, "Senator, if you want to try the case right here, don't you think we ought to have a judge? Or do you consider that your role, too? If I understand, you're saying to Mr. Dunbar that his Caucasian wife must have had sex with an African-American man; when the babies somehow got switched, she took advantage of this fortuitous occurrence and kept Mrs. Yarbrough's baby. This presumption is totally ridiculous. Mr. Dunbar and his wife have enjoyed a trusting, monogamous marriage for the past four years. While you're speculating, Senator, have you considered that somebody not even connected with the hospital might have taken your grandson and left that Negro child in his place? There are thousands of strangers in town right now for Pilgrimage. You can see how lax hospital security is. I understand white babies fetch a fair price today. How about one of the maids or janitors, or a deliveryman? Some psycho who just happened to be walking down the hall?"

Buford Tallant interceded. "Gentlemen, if I may . . . We're all reasonable men here. We can speculate all day and wind up no closer to a solution than where we began. I feel certain that Mr. and Mrs. Dunbar would like to end this matter as quickly as possible, the same as Governor Yarbrough and his wife. All anybody wants is to go home with their very own baby."

Wylie argued about the baby's blue eyes, his hint of red hair, which Dunbar also had but covered with brown dye.

Ignoring Wylie, J.L. fixed a piercing gaze on Jonathan Dunbar. "Young man, would you actually take a baby home and feed him and clothe him and raise him up and not even know if he's yours? Your own flesh and blood? Don't you want to know?"

Dunbar's Adam's apple bobbed up and down. After a moment, he said, "I do know."

"No, Jonathan," Buford Tallant said softly. "You *think* you know. Big difference."

Wylie Marsh gathered his notepad and pencils, put them into his briefcase, and closed it. "Gentlemen, I'm sure we all have things to do. Governor, when is inauguration day?"

"Third Monday in January," Lucien replied.

"Well, I wish you the best. These are crucial times. Mississippi needs good leadership."

"Before you go," Buford said, "please remind your client that since the restraining order was upheld, the baby in question is to remain in the hospital until we get a blood test, or the court makes a determination as to which baby is whose. Governor Yarbrough has guards posted around the clock to insure that the baby doesn't leave."

"At state expense, Governor-elect?" said Marsh.

"At Mr. Yarbrough's own personal expense," Buford replied.

Jonathan Dunbar asked, "How is Caroline supposed to nurse our son? I won't have guards watching her do that."

Tallant said, "They'll be posted just outside her room. We don't wish to cause your wife any embarrassment."

Dunbar exhaled noisily. "We don't have medical

insurance. Who's responsible for the cost of staying all these extra days?"

Wylie Marsh said, "I would assume the Yarbroughs will take on that responsibility, since they're forcing your wife to stay."

Tallant quickly countered, "We're not forcing Mrs. Dunbar to stay at all . . . she's free to go at any time. Always has been, as far as we're concerned. Whatever costs you incur will be your own."

Dunbar said, "Caroline won't leave without her baby."

Buford Tallant smiled. "And which baby would that be, Mr. Dunbar? Before you fall asleep tonight, I want you to ask yourself . . . 'Do I *really* know?' "

At six a.m. on Thursday, Page took up her position. It had become her ritual. First she pumped her breasts—the nurse hadn't had to help. She no longer felt like such a klutz performing that little procedure. Then she took the milk to the nurse and stationed herself outside the nursery to watch the black baby being fed. Since the others had gone home, the white child with the Dunbar name on its wristband—Page knew in her heart he was her son—and the baby wearing the Yarbrough wristband were the only ones left.

Page thought of the clothes she'd buy for her son. She could see him in one of those fuzzy, zip-front bunting bags. Blue, with a matching knit cap. How she'd enjoy shopping for him, searching through racks of adorable clothes till she'd find the perfect ones. She couldn't wait to buy his first pair of shoes. They'd be so tiny. So perfect. For his perfect little feet with their perfect little toes, like his perfect little fingers that would cling to one of hers while she nursed him.

Her heart felt bruised as she watched her son being taken, under guard, to Caroline Dunbar for his breakfast. She wanted to call out for them to stop, to bring him back to her.

Moments later, a nurse came into the hall. "Would you like to help me?" asked the nurse.

"Help you what?"

"Give him his bottle." The nurse nodded toward the black child.

"I'll just watch."

"I thought maybe . . . well, it is your milk and all. And since you don't have your own baby to hold. . . . Sorry, ma'am, it was just a thought." The nurse turned away.

"What about germs?" asked Page.

"He's big enough now that you don't have to worry so much about germs. Besides, he's immune to any you'd have, from the antibodies in your milk."

Page hesitated. God, how she ached to hold a baby. Maybe if she closed her eyes and imagined this were her son in her arms—*No!* He most assuredly was not her son. No amount of imagining could change that. Page shook her head.

"It's okay," the nurse said. She went back inside the nursery.

Moments later Page tapped on the nursery window. The gnawing ache was more than she could bear. When the nurse opened the door, Page said, "You know that he's not my child . . . everybody knows that. But I was thinking . . . he's not your baby either; still, you feed him every day. Maybe if you brought him to my room, I could hold him while you give him his bottle. He doesn't have anybody, and I wouldn't mind helping until he goes to his real mother. When those awful people give my baby back."

CHAPTER SEVEN

Lucien came by at eleven Friday morning. Page had just washed her hair. She turned off the blow-dryer and hurried to embrace him. He looked particularly handsome today, and smelled of aftershave. It felt wonderful to be surrounded by his strong arms. Safe. She loved him for that. For so many things.

"How much longer?" she asked.

"We've scheduled an emergency hearing on Tuesday about the DNA test. The other things can drag on for months, but they're just smoke and mirrors anyway. The test is what we need."

"Is there any doubt we'll get it?"

Lucien pulled back and walked to the window. He adjusted the blinds to look outside, then turned back to face his wife. "I feel confident Judge Winston will allow it."

"I only want our son, Luce, and to go home." Page tried to keep her tears from starting. She didn't want Lucien to see her break down. She'd never been one to cry easily, and had held it back all week. But she was so miserable, and her emotions were barely beneath the surface. She longed to hold Cindy and listen to her excited stories about what she'd discovered in her world that day. She ached to curl up against Lucien and watch TV at night, or fall asleep in his arms. She wanted to walk through her own home in the middle of the afternoon with nobody around, just looking, touching, appreciating.

She buried her face in Lucien's chest. "I miss Cindy. I miss you. I miss Doris. I miss my home."

"We all miss you, too, baby."

"I'm sorry. I've tried to be strong, but it's so hard without you here. I feel so . . . so isolated."

"It's okay, Page. Cry it out."

She did. A dam burst, and all of her pent-up anguish gushed forth at once, emptying her.

Lucien said, "There's no reason for you to stay here any longer. The baby's not going anywhere with guards watching. The Dunbar woman is nursing him . . . and it pisses me off every time I think about that, but we'll stop it as soon as the test comes back."

Page straightened and cleared her throat. "It breaks my heart not to be able to nurse him, Luce. That's what I remember most about having Cindy. I try to think of Caroline Dunbar as nothing more than a wet nurse. She's just taking care of our son temporarily."

Moments later Lucien paced the floor, his anger flashing again. "A smartass Yankee doctor, an incompetent nurse, a cheating white-trash slut, and her henpecked husband . . . we had to run into all of 'em at once. I could fart porcupine quills just thinking about those idiots. All of them."

Page opened a drawer and began collecting her things. "I would love to go home if you're sure it's all right. I need to hold Cindy. I want to see Doris. And there's a thousand things I should be doing for Pilgrimage. E-mail is great, but it's important that I visit the open homes myself. It's my responsibility. And I won't be that far away . . . I can drive over here as often as I want."

Lucien opened the door. "I'll check you out while you pack." He started to leave, but turned back. "Did they bring that other baby in here this morning?"

Page stiffened. "Why would you ask that?"

"One of the guards said he thought the nurse came out of this room with that black baby. Early this morning."

Page half laughed, turned away, and began tossing clothes into her suitcase. "Early this morning? You know how I hate to wake up early in the morning, especially with all those tranquilizers and that capsule they give me every night to make me sleep."

Lucien nodded and left.

As she packed, Page tried to justify her answer. Lucien would never understand about her holding the black baby and giving him his bottle.

The phone rang. "Yes, sweetie," Page said into the receiver. It had to be Lucien calling from downstairs—nobody else could get through.

A raspy woman's voice responded, "Nobody's called me sweetie since Arthur died in 1973, and he only said it a time or two that I recall."

Page was thrilled to hear the voice of her only aunt, Belle Braswell. She loved this special woman almost more than her own mother. To tell the truth, she hardly remembered her mother, so Belle and Doris had filled that role.

"Auntie Bellum," Page exclaimed. "How in the world did you get through?"

"Threatened the switchboard operator, of course."

"No, really . . . nobody's gotten through all week."

"The operator used to come out here when she was a little girl and play with my old dolls." Belle paused. "Just wanted to hear your voice, Page, make sure you're all right."

Page cleared her throat, then said, "I'm fine."

"But not very convincing. Do I need to come down there and find out for myself?"

"Really, Auntie Bellum. I was just packing my things to go home, so I'm sorta hurrying."

"Who does baby boy Yarbrough look like?"

Page's stomach knotted up again. "It's hard to say."

"Well, I'll let you get on with your packing. But you bring that baby out to see me real soon."

"I will."

"I miss you, Page. You're so much like your mother. I miss her every day that I live."

"So do I, Auntie. So do I."

* * *

Buford Tallant came into Lucien's office alongside one of the guards they'd posted at the hospital.

"There's trouble in paradise," Buford said. He instructed the guard to tell Lucien what he'd heard.

"I'd gone to the bathroom and was moseying back past Mrs. Dunbar's room last night. I always kind of slow down and listen whenever I walk past, like you told me, to see what's going on in there. Well, I heard plenty. They was shoutin' and cussin' and cryin' something fierce."

"Slow down," Lucien said. "Who was?"

"Mostly that Mr. Dunbar. John, she called him."

"Jonathan."

"Yeah. Anyway, he was doing most of the shoutin', calling her all sorts of names . . . I mean, names my mama has probably never heard."

"Be specific," Lucien said. "Exactly what did he say?"

"He called her a whore, a bitch, a slut . . . let me see . . . he said she'd lied about being a virgin when he married her. Part of the time he must've been facing away from the door, because it was hard to understand what he was sayin' even though he was yellin', and part of the time he came in loud and clear."

Buford grinned at Lucien. Lucien sat with his mouth partly open, listening. But his breathing was faster now.

"Anyhow," the guard said, "the woman . . . Caroline . . . was cryin' like a wounded banshee most of the time. Naturally she denied everything. She just kept sayin' she didn't do it to whatever he said. He called her a Jew lover and a nigger lover. He even said she was a damned communist. And he was tellin' her how much the hospital bill was gonna be and said she'd damn well have to work it out herself because he refused to pay it. That's about it."

"Did they say anything about the baby?"

"Not that I heard. A nurse come down the hall 'long about then and I had to move on. Few minutes later I seen that Jonathan come out and he was really steamin' when he left. Man, he was truckin' on down the road."

After the guard left, Lucien asked Buford what he thought it meant.

"I don't know, but I like it. I have a couple of people checking them out."

Lucien shook his head. "Maybe Mr. Casper Milquetoast Dunbar isn't as henpecked as we thought."

After a brief pause, Lucien asked Buford to close the door. "I've been working on a statement to give the press. With all these lawsuits flying back and forth, we can't hold the reporters off any longer. I'm basically saying there's a misunderstanding about our baby's name, and I can't comment further until the matter is settled. That's true enough, don't you think?"

The following Tuesday, Wylie Marsh and Buford Tallant appeared before Judge Winston. A clerk had mysteriously listed only the attorneys' names on the docket, so the session took place without fanfare. J.L. accompanied Buford. The two of them had advised Lucien to maintain a low profile and stay out of court. The opposing attorneys argued for three hours. When it came to citing cases, Wylie was better prepared than J.L. had expected.

"Don't ever doubt Wylie," Buford told J.L. "He's sharp and he's thorough."

J.L. said, "Between you, Wylie, and Mack Malone, the three best lawyers in Natchez are involved in this case. Excluding Lucien and myself, of course, and don't ever quote me on that around the firm. Wonder what the rest of the city's doing for representation along about now?"

After careful consideration, Judge Winston gave his ruling. "In these unfortunate circumstances, I'll allow DNA test results to be introduced."

J.L. winked at Buford. "Yarbrough and Tallant . . . one. Wylie Marsh . . . zero."

Buford whispered, "Now he'll have to let us introduce the results in all the cases. Against the hospital, the doctor. Everybody.''

The next court session was scheduled for the following week. The first ruling only meant the judge would consider the results if a DNA test was done, not that it had to be done. If the court should agree with Buford Tallant in the next session and order DNA testing of the baby, the results would determine once and for all its natural parents.

Back among family, Page was in her own element, though her thoughts remained with her child at the hospital.

To ease Page's pain, Miss Emma organized a "welcome home" luncheon and invited thirty-five of Page's closest friends and ten of her own. In recent years, Lucien's mother had been lovingly known in Natchez as Miss Emma, a title of respect, though she was most definitely married. As of last June 12, she and J.L. had been married forty-two years. She'd been a blushing bride at twenty.

Page pumped her breasts and checked on her baby before breakfast, then did "house things" with Doris and her daughter. She left Cindy in Doris's capable hands and, after locating her car keys, drove her 1993 red-and-silver Suburban to Miss Emma's. Lucien seemed embarrassed that Page drove the older vehicle, but she preferred it to his new Cadillac. She could haul more in the back, and it was great for chauffeuring Cindy and her friends around, or moving furniture and supplies to and from Pilgrimage houses. Besides, she knew where all the buttons were, and what they did. Lucien had offered to buy her a new one, but she refused. Her Suburban was part of her family. Familiar. She had consented to let Lucien have it overhauled for Christmas, however, then repainted for her birthday next May.

She parked at the rear of the grand estate. A legendary Greek Revival house known as River Oaks Plantation, the thousand-acre property sat just outside the city limits of Natchez, on a hill meandering down to the river. River Oaks was considered one of the more *important* properties by socially conscious residents.

Because the October day was overcast and a bit chilly, the luncheon was held indoors. While it was no longer morning, the morning room provided a magnificent view of the rear of the estate, so an elegant buffet with linen-covered tables had been set up in there. The room was large and circular, with high perimeter windows, and filled with fresh flowers from Miss Emma's greenhouse. The glass in the windows was original to the house, built around 1837, so a few imperfections were visible. These somehow enhanced, rather than detracted from, the view across formal gardens and pebbled paths, down the expanse of manicured lawn to the mighty Mississippi.

Guests arrived dressed to the nines. While most were Page's age, several of the old guard attended as well, wearing regularly used hats and kid gloves. Nobody wore white shoes. In Natchez, as in other proper Southern towns, to wear white shoes after Labor Day and before Easter would be considered tacky—akin to a woman's chewing gum in public or drinking straight from a soda can.

Page had searched for nearly an hour before finding a dress she could get into. While her tummy had gone down dramatically, it had definitely not returned to its normal size. She strained to hold her stomach in, knowing she'd have to diet and exercise for at least three months, as she'd done with Cindy. *Arghh. Torture.*

A uniformed black maid quietly served Miss Emma's renowned lime punch. The recipe was guarded like the formula for "Co-Cola," as Miss Emma pronounced the name of the commercial soft drink.

After hugging and kissing the hostess and marveling over how good Page looked, clutches of women explored the first floor of the house sipping punch, admiring the elegant furnishings, and catching up on the latest local happenings. Guests loved to discuss the history of the plantation—how Lucien's great-grandfather, John Jackson Yarbrough, bought the house and property in the 1800s. Upon his death, title passed to his only son, Jackson Adams Yarbrough, who became a legendary governor of Mississippi. The property then passed to the governor's only son, J.L. Senior, the senator. But it was The Governor, as family and friends reverently referred to Jackson Adams Yarbrough, whose presence filled the home. His books and writings filled an enormous oak-paneled library. Newspaper clippings of his accomplishments covered the walls of two ground-floor parlors. His life-size portraits kept watch over priceless antiques and silver, welcoming guests in the grand entry and front atrium.

"He was something special," one woman said to Page, looking up at a somewhat smaller portrait of The Governor hanging in the living room. "But I just know Lucien will be equally outstanding. I loved what he said about improving the schools and getting tough on crime. Everybody in town voted for him, my relatives in Tupelo, too." The woman hesitated, then asked, "Why was it again they had to keep your baby in the hospital? I heard Mary Lou ask, but I couldn't hear your reply."

"The doctor wanted to do some tests," Page said, aware of a tightening in her insides.

"Well, I hope it's nothing serious. I know you two've been trying forever to have a son. It's about time you got one."

Page reflected on the woman's statement. While excited to have a son, she adored her daughter beyond description. She would love either equally. Actually, because of the honor and importance given to the queen of the Confederate Pageant each year, girls were prized more highly than boys in Natchez. Mothers worked, planned, and schemed for years toward that end. It was one reason Page worked so hard as president of the Confederate Garden Club. She was accumulating "points," actually kept on a scorecard in the club office, to ensure that Cindy might someday be queen.

"I mean, Cindy is a delightful girl, and I know you worship her," the woman continued, "but a man needs a son. So do you . . . you both deserve it." She paused to look at a child's dress framed for display in the hallway. "Who wore this gorgeous little dress?"

"Miss Emma, in the 1943 Confederate Pageant. She was about five years old, but J.L. says that's when she first stole his heart. He was the pageant's Confederate general that year. And a dirty old man, if he was telling the truth." They laughed.

The luncheon was a delightful and welcome change for Page, easing some of the strain she was under. It was reassuring to know she had so many wonderful friends. Being among people she'd grown up with, who genuinely cared about her, provided an enormous sense of security. A needed feeling of belonging.

"Thank you, Mama Yarbrough," Page said later. "I needed that." They stood near eight massive white Corinthian columns lining the front porch, watching the last guest drive out of sight down the oak-lined drive. Miss Emma was a head taller than Page, wore her graying brown hair swept back in a bun, and had an aristocratic look. A handsome woman.

"We all do occasionally, dear. Now . . . I can't stomach the thought of another cup of that seasick green punch. Let's have a glass of sherry and talk. When do you go to court?"

"Wednesday."

"Will John Winston still be judge?"

"Nobody's said anything different."

"Good. I've known John since he was nose-high to a bloodhound. He had a terrible crush on me when we were in high school. That won't influence how he hears the case, mind you . . . he's honest. No-nonsense, but smart, and he's fair."

"That's all we're asking."

They took in the view down the quarter-mile alley

of ancient live oaks. A storm was brewing. After a pause, Miss Emma asked, "How's your father, Page?"

"Fine."

"Have you told him the . . . situation?"

"He calls every few days to check on me. I haven't, because there's nothing he can do. It would just worry him."

"Poor Dr. Briggs. What happened was such a shame, both for your mother and for him. Your mother was a fine woman. I think it was harder on the doctor than on her, in some ways."

"I give him a lot of credit. It wasn't till Laura and I left home that he fell apart. He's basically a strong man. I guess doctors have to be."

"By the way, Dr. Goodson was by yesterday. He asked about you."

"Mark? Was one of the dogs sick?"

"J.L. had him vaccinate the horses. They do it every year."

"I've always liked Mark."

Miss Emma studied Page's face as she said, "Well, he has certainly always liked you . . . that's obvious." She walked inside, down the wide hallway. "Let's go where we can be comfortable."

They sat on a red velvet love seat in a mahogany-paneled parlor, surrounded by memorabilia of The Governor. Page poured Miss Emma a glass of sherry.

"You're not having any?" asked Miss Emma.

"Not while I'm nurs— Well, I'm not actually nursing but I still pump my breasts. And I need to pick Cindy up from her dance lesson at four." Page chose not to add that she'd become afraid to drink anything containing alcohol anymore. Watching her father deteriorate was pure torture.

"Lucien said you go to the hospital twice a day. Couldn't you pump your breasts at home?"

"Maybe, but I . . . the nurse helps me do it. Besides, I like to look in on the baby, even if it is through a glass window."

"Are they still using your milk to feed the little Negro child?"

"Yes."

"Somehow that doesn't seem proper, Page."

"He has to eat, Mama Yarbrough, and there isn't any other way to give him the antibodies he needs. I hate to just pour my milk out, and I need to keep my breasts producing for when I can nurse our baby." Page hadn't meant to raise her voice, but desperately wanted Miss Emma to understand. To approve. Though she might not always agree with Lucien's mother, she had enormous respect for the woman. To Page, that was part of being in the family. Page's not having a mother of her own made Mama Yarbrough especially important to Page. She had come to love her dearly.

Miss Emma narrowed her eyes. After a moment she said, "I suppose. I just don't know as I could do it . . . a Negro." She sipped her sherry, considering. "They're not like us, you know."

"How do you mean?"

"Well, for instance, in nature, there are redbirds and there are bluebirds. . . . God intended it that way. They don't intermingle, they don't mate, and they don't drink each other's milk. I realize they don't drink milk . . . what I mean is, they don't feed each other's young." The older woman pondered the situation, studying her crystal sherry glass. "Still, you'd just throw the milk away, wouldn't you?"

Page didn't respond. She wanted to point out the vast differences in the baby's situation from this gross oversimplification, but she didn't. She couldn't help wondering if Miss Emma might be repeating an explanation she'd heard from her own mother some fifty-odd years ago. It was amazing how childhood values resurfaced decades later. Page waited respectfully.

After a long silence, Miss Emma nodded abruptly and looked up, having arrived at a decision. "I guess what you're doing is all right. Sort of like giving them your leftovers . . . or clothes you can't wear anymore."

CHAPTER EIGHT

Early Monday morning, Doris Kern knocked softly at Page's bedroom door, then entered and opened the drapes, admitting the morning light.

"Good morning, pretty Miss Sleepyhead," Doris said cheerfully. She had awakened Page with that greeting most every morning since Page was six years old and Doris twenty-six. When Page and Lucien married, there was no question that Doris would accompany Page to Yarbrough Hall, as this house was named. It was a given.

Doris said, "Your husband's already gone to work. Mary Lou and Patty are waiting downstairs, and they seem real anxious."

Page quickly pulled on a robe and slippers and brushed her hair. While not as large as River Oaks Plantation, Page's home was one of the finest examples of Greek Revival architecture in town, completed two years before the Civil War. Technically, the home and most of the prewar furnishings belonged to J.L., but Page and Lucien planned to live there until Miss Emma and J.L. were gone. Then they'd move over to River Oaks Plantation and save Yarbrough Hall for Cindy or their son, whoever married first.

While she would've preferred going straight to the hospital, Page felt obligated to join her friends downstairs. For just such an occasion, she purposely stayed one feeding ahead of the baby with milk she pumped from her breasts. Her friends had no idea about the terrible mix-up, but wouldn't think it unusual if she excused herself shortly.

They were Page's age, neatly dressed in skirts and sweaters, and both attractive. Mary Lou Snodgrass was blond, Patty Fulton, a brunette. When Page entered the drawing room, they ran up and embraced her.

"Oh, you poor thing," Mary Lou said. "We had no idea."

"Why didn't you tell us?" asked Patty.

"Tell you what?" asked Page.

"About the hospital trying to say your son is Negro."

Shocked, Page asked, "Where did you hear that?"

"Right here . . . in the paper." Patty presented the daily newspaper.

On the front page, column one, she read:

IS IT GOVERNOR YARBROUGH'S BABY?

The article detailed the dispute fairly accurately, quoting "a reliable source." To Page's dismay, it also gave the time and location of next week's court date.

"Is it true?" asked Patty. "Did they really try to switch a colored baby for yours?"

"How awful," Mary Lou said, answering for Page. "You must've just wanted to die."

Patty said, "I want you to know that everybody in town's behind you. I must've talked to twenty women this morning. They've all said if there's anything . . . anything at all they can do . . . please let them know."

Just then the doorbell rang, buying Page time to think. She was totally unprepared for this onslaught. Three women from the garden club were at the door. Two more cars were pulling up at the curb, and more friends hurried toward the house. The phone was ringing off the wall.

In between dressing herself and her daughter and answering phone calls and the front door, Page helped Doris fix coffee and cheese grits, slice a ham, and bake two pans of buttermilk biscuits. Later everybody searched frantically for the keys to the Suburban, until

Cindy located them in the car's ignition, where Page had left them the night before.

Page raced to the hospital to pump her breasts and check on the baby while her friends ate. Even with people waiting at home, she had to drag herself away when it was time to go.

When she returned home, Page told her friends the only thing she could—exactly what had happened. About the new doctor, the inexperienced nurse, three women delivering at the same time. She even told how she'd had her DNA tested and how Caroline Dunbar had refused to let them test the baby. The women were impressed that Gloria Webb agreed to have her baby tested. Especially since Gloria wasn't even married.

"Well, I'll tell you one thing," Patty said. "Those Dunbars might just as well close that dinky little restaurant of theirs up on Main Street. Nobody'll be eating soup and salad in this town for a long time . . . unless we fix it at home."

"What'll you do about Pilgrimage, Page? And the pageant?"

"My daughter's in that pageant," Page said. "I haven't missed a performance since they let me out of the hospital, and I don't intend to start now. As for Pilgrimage, with Rona's help, I'll still make rounds of the houses every day, as long as I'm not needed in court."

Rona Green spoke up. Rona was nearly six feet tall, and had an aristocratic face and bearing. She was normally quieter than most of their friends, but terribly efficient. And loads of fun when she and Page were in high school. "You shouldn't worry about the homes at a time like this, Page. Several of the girls have been helping, so it's working out just fine. We have a big crowd this year and wonderful docents. You concentrate on getting your baby back. You did plenty just setting up schedules." Rona looked at the others and said, "Can you believe she did that from her hospital room? By e-mail."

"That's just like Page," Patty said, touching Page's hand. "One more reason we love you."

Dr. Briggs called a few minutes before noon—Thomas Briggs, M.D. People still called him Doctor, though he hadn't practiced in years. He supported himself by researching articles in medical literature, as a bibliography service. Busy practicing physicians sometimes subscribed to his services. That was what he did before noon. After noon, Dr. Briggs could be found in one of the seedier bars in a riverfront section of town called Natchez under the Hill. Dapper and eloquent, he would entertain fellow tipplers with humorous stories until he passed out and somebody took him home.

Over the phone, Page explained to her father what was going on. "It's a simple mix-up," she said. "We'll have it straightened out as soon as the test is done. You know how newspapers blow things out of proportion."

"You're sure there's nothing I can do?"

"Not a thing, Daddy. Lucien has everything under control."

As soon as she hung up, the phone rang again. It was Auntie Bellum. Page repeated her story.

"I ought to go down to that newspaper and jerk a knot in somebody's tail," Belle said. "I may do just that."

Page hung up the phone, looked at the wonderful friends surrounding her, and said a silent prayer. She thanked God for her husband, loyal friends, and family, the things she held most dear in life. Without them, she'd never survive a time such as this. Nobody would.

In court the following week, Buford Tallant made notes beside Lucien, Page, and J.L., while Mack Malone presented pretrial motions to the judge. Wylie Marsh sat with Jonathan Dunbar at the defense table, next to the hospital administrator, Steve Griffith. Caroline Dunbar was not present. Judge John P. Winston presided. This was not a jury trial. The judge had changed courtrooms first thing that morning to accommodate the crowd. Reporters present were mostly from the South, but even *The Washington Post* was represented.

Aside from the news media, at least a third of the spectators were Page's friends. Pilgrimage or not, the women of Natchez were fully dressed, coifed, made up, and ready for battle. They had come out in force to support one of their own, and there wasn't a white shoe among them. Miss Emma and six old-guard friends occupied the front row directly behind Lucien and Page.

Page tried not to fidget with the gloves in her lap. She had stopped asking herself why this terrible thing had happened. She only wanted it straightened out as quickly as possible so she could bring her baby home. Lucien glanced over and winked, as if to say, *Everything's going to be just fine, Page. We're an undefeatable team.* She returned his smile and felt herself relax. A little.

When Malone finished his motions, Wylie Marsh stood to speak. Billy Larson tapped Lucien on the shoulder from behind the railing that separated participants from spectators. A sketch artist for the local NBC-affiliate TV station seemed annoyed that Billy was blocking her view. TV cameras were barred from the courtroom. Billy motioned for Lucien to accompany him outside.

After making certain nobody else was in the men's room, Billy stood with his back to the door and said at the speed of flowing honey, "A state trooper friend of mine just pulled me outside to tell me something really interesting about Mr. Jonathan Dunbar. Said he tried to get to us sooner, but his sister's been sick and he had to go pick her up in Greenville."

"What's interesting?"

"Well, the sergeant was patrolling Saturday night, out past the paper mill—"

"Get on with it, Gator. What'd he say?"

"You know that all the highway patrolmen have Dunbar's license number and vehicle description, in order to keep an eye on him."

"I didn't know. Who arranged that?"

"The senator."

"Go on. What happened?"

"Sarge was kind of following at a safe distance, you know, and he saw Dunbar park his car off the side of the road out at the edge of the county and meet another guy in a red Ford pickup. So he followed them."

"Get to the point, Gator. I gotta go back inside."

"He went to a Klan meeting out in the woods with this guy."

"Who did?"

"Dunbar. Had on a white sheet and everything. They swore him in that night, but said he'd been a member for a long time over in Macon, then up in Jackson. Sarge parked up the road, then crept out into the woods and hid. He saw and heard everything."

"Son of a bitch!" Lucien exhaled sharply. "Now it all makes sense. Dunbar would kill his wife for having a black baby. Even if he suspects, he damned well doesn't want proof. The brotherhood would arrange for him and his wife both to disappear some dark night." Lucien shook his head. "To tell the truth, I'm kinda relieved."

"Whadda you mean?"

"I haven't mentioned it to Page, but this nagging worry's been whirling around in my skull that this whole thing might be political. That somebody switched my baby for a Negro just to make me look bad." He opened the door. "Good work, Gator. I can't wait to tell Buford and J.L."

CHAPTER NINE

The case went on for days. Everybody testified who might've seen or heard anything in the hospital—Dr. Benning, the temporary delivery-room nurse, nurse's aides, housekeepers, Page, Lucien.

Under oath, Jonathan Dunbar denied any connection with the Ku Klux Klan. His secrecy oath to the brotherhood was obviously more sacred than his oath before God to tell the truth.

Caroline Dunbar was conspicuously absent throughout the proceedings until the final day. Already thin, she appeared pale and weak that day, as if she hadn't slept for days. She wore a simple blue-and-white cotton print dress and white pumps. Her hair was a mousy brown and her eyes puffy, as though she'd been crying. Her makeup seemed excessively heavy on her left cheek, suggesting it might be hiding a bruise.

After Caroline gave the correct spelling of her name to the court reporter, her attorney questioned her. From Wylie Marsh's prepared questions and Caroline's rehearsed answers, she and Jonathan were the aggrieved parties. They were simple, God-fearing little people being bullied by the powerful Yarbrough machine. This had been Caroline's first pregnancy, thus their first child.

Lucien whispered to his father, "She makes a pretty convincing witness."

J.L. whispered back, loudly enough that several people on the front row could hear, "I think I may puke."

Judge Winston quickly glanced at J.L. and frowned. With no readable expression on his face, J.L. nodded innocently at the judge and tipped his chair back, hands interlaced across his chest.

Finally it was Buford's turn. He courteously introduced himself to Caroline Dunbar and thanked her for leaving the hospital and coming down to help all of them sort out this unfortunate situation. Buford sounded totally sincere, with no hint of sarcasm in his voice.

"I hope I can help," Caroline said.

"We all do, Mrs. Dunbar."

Buford asked several routine questions, allowing Caroline to become comfortable with the process and to discover that Buford wasn't a bad fellow at all. She said she'd never testified before, so he explained the procedure, then took it slow and easy.

After proceeding though her recollection of events surrounding her delivery, Buford asked, "Mrs. Dunbar, what do you normally do on nights when your husband isn't home?"

She said she didn't understand.

"Well, do you maybe wash your hair? Watch TV? I'm just curious how you fill your time. I know my wife likes to crochet. What do you do?"

Wylie objected. Buford said he would show relevance shortly. The judge instructed Caroline to answer.

She glanced at Wylie. "Well, it depends. I might watch TV, if there's anything on that I like. I sew. I make things like blouses, or pillow covers, things like that."

Buford pursued this line of questioning for a while, then switched back to the night in question, at the hospital. He then jumped to when she and her husband had met, in Jackson, then to what she did and where she went to school in her hometown, and how she happened to move from Tupelo to Jackson.

"Isn't it true, Mrs. Dunbar, that you had to leave Tupelo under less than ideal circumstances?"

"Not at all," she said. "I had a job lined up at a bank in Jackson."

"Are you saying you weren't pregnant when you left Tupelo?"

"I wasn't married then."

"I didn't ask if you were married . . . I asked if you were pregnant."

"Certainly not."

"When you're sewing things at home at night, do you cut eyeholes in the pillowcases or does your husband do that himself?"

Caroline said she didn't know what Buford meant.

"Pillowcases, Mrs. Dunbar. Sheets. The ones your husbands wears at his Klan meetings."

She fidgeted with her pocketbook, obviously uncomfortable. "I don't know what you're talking about."

"Are you telling this court you're not aware that your husband is a member of the Ku Klux Klan?"

She didn't answer until the judge ordered her to, despite Wylie Marsh's objections. Finally she said, "I wouldn't know anything about that. I don't ask where Jonathan goes at night."

"Where did you work in Tupelo? After you graduated from high school?"

"At my father's business. The dry cleaners."

"Did you know a Terence James at your father's dry-cleaning establishment?"

"Yes, sir."

"He worked there, too, did he?"

"He picked up the cleaning, then delivered it back to people's houses."

"How well did you know him, Caroline?"

She hesitated. "He just worked there."

Wylie objected from time to time. Judge Winston mostly allowed Caroline to answer, but warned Buford to get on with it. Said it was getting late in the day.

Buford asked, "Do you know where the Planned Parenthood center is located in Jackson, Mrs. Dunbar?"

"Objection."

"Overruled. Answer the question, please."

"I may have driven by it."

"Lots of people drive by it every day. Did you ever stop there, as you were driving by?"

"I don't know what you mean."

"Oh, I think you do. Try to remember . . . I know it's been a long time. It was before you and Jonathan were married that I'm speaking of." Buford opened a file folder and read from it. "Have you ever heard of Dr. Ronald Strahan?"

After hesitating, Caroline said, "I don't think so."

Lucien tried to see Jonathan Dunbar's face, but Jonathan kept his head down, staring at a pencil he tapped against a yellow legal pad. Lucien thought he saw a red flush creeping up from inside the man's collar onto his neck.

"Did this Terence James ever drive you over to the Planned Parenthood center and wait for you?"

"No, sir, he did not."

"And on the day that Mr. Terence James did not drive you over to the Planned Parenthood center, did you also not have an elective termination of pregnancy preformed on that very same day? An abortion, Mrs. Dunbar? Isn't it true that you were carrying Mr. Terence James's baby?"

"Absolutely not. I would never . . ." She broke down, unable to answer while Buford fired more questions amidst Wylie's shouted objections.

Jonathan Dunbar seemed to almost have a stroke. He sat glaring at his wife. Caroline nervously avoided his hate-filled gaze.

Finally she composed herself enough to continue, but her hands were trembling.

"Just one more question," Buford said, smiling— Mr. Nice Guy again. Caroline had not answered his previous questions. "To what race does Mr. Terence James belong?"

She shook her head. "What does that have to do with anything?"

"Please, Caroline, let me ask the questions."

She fidgeted with a handkerchief in her lap, chewing at her lip. "You're trying to destroy my marriage, sir, twisting things around."

"Please just answer the question, ma'am."

"Terence James had nothing to do with anything. He merely worked for my father." Caroline looked at her husband and yelled, "It isn't what he's making it out to be, Jonathan. It isn't."

Page swallowed hard. As badly as she needed the truth about her baby, she felt miserable for this woman. Poor thing. What had Caroline gotten herself into?

Once things were under control, Buford said, "I don't believe I heard your answer earlier, Mrs. Dunbar."

"Which one?"

"To which race does Mr. Terence James belong?"

She looked from her husband to the judge, then back at Buford. Her eyes filled with tears, pleading for help. Suddenly she screamed out, "All right, test the baby! I give my permission!"

"No!" Jonathan shouted. "Nobody's testing that baby!"

Caroline countered, "It isn't true, Jonathan. I didn't do anything. None of what he's saying is true . . . he's twisting everything all around."

"No testing," Jonathan yelled again, blue veins bulging in his reddened neck. His fists were balled at his sides.

"I agree to test baby boy Dunbar," the judge said when things quieted, "but I also order Caroline Dunbar, Jonathan Dunbar, Page Yarbrough, Lucien Yarbrough, and the child identified by the hospital as baby boy Yarbrough to be tested."

Blinking back a tear, Page looked at Lucien. Though thrilled they had achieved what they wanted, she felt a soul-deep sadness for Caroline Dunbar.

Lucien grinned, giving Page a vigorous thumbs-up.

All but Jonathan Dunbar agreed to suspend the proceedings till everyone could be tested. Caroline's consent for their child was adequate—Jonathan's wasn't necessary. Judge Winston laid down the procedure to be followed.

Each side would have their blood drawn by a physician of their choice, while attorneys representing both sides observed. The samples would be placed in a locked container and taken to the state laboratory in Jackson by two armed deputies. The deputies would also accompany the written reports back to the court. Lucien requested a Highway Patrol escort for the deputies, which the judge allowed.

It seemed that every woman in Natchez called to congratulate Page that evening. "I couldn't do it without you," she told them, and meant exactly what she said.

After dinner Page and Lucien watched a Disney movie with Cindy, between phone calls. Page was greatly relieved. Their baby would soon be home. At one point she nuzzled her husband's arm and said, "We did it, Luce."

"We sure as hell did. It's all over but the shouting, Page."

The news media loved it. They reported several versions of the Highway Patrol escort and sheriff's cars delivering the blood samples to Jackson. The Mississippi governor's baby. An article in the *Memphis Press* said it was reminiscent of watching O.J. in the white Bronco. Much of the country looked on.

The specimen arrived at the lab on Thursday. Technicians agreed to work over the weekend, to have the results in Judge Winston's hands by Monday morning.

Page had to force herself to go on with life, mainly for her daughter—and to retain her sanity. She pulled her well-used Suburban into Suellen's driveway two mornings later, her daughter belted in at her side.

Suellen's house was not nearly as large or elegant as the one Page and Lucien lived in, but was lovely nonetheless. A white clapboard with square columns rising up to a second-story balcony, the home was built in 1825 on a Spanish land grant. It was presently furnished in early American. A group was being led into the front entrance by a woman wearing a red-and-white 1860s crinoline walking gown.

"Who else is gonna be here?" asked Cindy.

"Betsy and Emma Sue," Page said.

"Who are all those people?"

"A tour group."

"Can I do the part through the kitchen?"

"We'll see."

"I like to tell them about the secret compartment in the fireplace where they kept the bread warm."

Page joined Suellen on a side veranda while Cindy, Emma Sue, and Betsy played in the yard. Page agreed to call Cindy when the tour group reached the kitchen.

"Sorry I couldn't be in the courtroom," Suellen said. "I had tours here in the mornings and at Patty's every afternoon. There's more people this year than last, and I thought we were busy then." She set a vase of freshly cut flowers on a table next to the swing. "Did they get everybody tested?"

Page had suppressed the memory of having her blood drawn again, but unconsciously touched the bruise on her left arm. "They almost had to handcuff Jonathan Dunbar, but he finally gave in."

"What's his problem?"

"Who knows? He's a strange one. Lucien says he's in the Klan."

"Maybe he has Negro blood in his background and doesn't want anybody to find out."

"Would that show up on a DNA test?"

"Probably . . . it's amazing what they can find out nowadays. If the Negro baby's DNA matches Jonathan's, can you imagine what the Klan will do when they find out?"

"That must be it, Suellen. It makes perfect sense."

A man's voice said from behind them, "Your mare's okay."

They turned to see Dr. Mark Goodson coming a boxwood at the corner of the house.

"Page, hello," Mark said. "What a nice surprise." Goodson wore khaki work pants and a long-sleeved plaid shirt. Built like a swimmer, he had jet black hair, brown eyes, broad shoulders, and good angles to his cheek-bones and chin. He was three years older than Page.

When he was near, Page looked up at him and said, "It's nice to see you, Mark." She asked Suellen, "Do you have a sick horse?"

"Classy Lady came up lame this morning."

"Just a stone bruise," Goodson added. "I wouldn't ride her this week, but she'll be fine by Monday." To Page he said, "I was over at the senator's the other day. He and Miss Emma seem to be handling his retirement well."

"Mama Yarbrough told me you said hello . . . thanks. You seem to be just everywhere. I'm glad you're busy."

"I'm not getting rich, but I sure seem to stay on the run, between the practice and trying to fix up my uncle's place. He'd let it run down pretty bad." Mark referred to the 1811 plantation home he'd inherited. When his uncle died, Mark had been in his final year at Cornell University College of Veterinary Medicine, in New York. Mark's uncle had been a successful Natchez veterinarian.

Mark said, "Give Lucien my congratulations. I haven't seen him since the election."

"I will."

"Sorry to hear about the confusion with your baby . . . that must be awful. Have you straightened it out yet?"

"Not completely."

"Well, I'm sorry you have to go through it."

Suellen excused herself to answer a question for the tour leader.

Goodson said, "You look good, Page."

"Thanks, Mark."

"I'm sure the governor's wife doesn't need any help from a country vet, but if there's ever anything I can do, I'll be there for you."

"I know you would. Thank you."

"Are you certain that new couple has your baby? What's their name?"

"Dunbar. We're waiting for the DNA tests to come back. They should confirm it."

"What's happening to the other baby?"

"Which one?"

"The one nobody's claiming."

"The nurses are taking care of him. I go over twice a day and . . ." Page hesitated. There was no point telling Mark about holding the little black baby . . . nobody needed to know. "I look in the nursery whenever I happen to be there. He seems very healthy."

"Poor little tyke," Mark said. "I feel for all of you." He nodded. "Well, I'd better get on down the road." He turned toward the children playing in the yard. "Which one is Cindy? They're all growing up so fast."

"In the tutu and tights. She has a dance lesson this afternoon."

"She's beautiful . . . and gets it naturally. Looks a lot like you did in high school." He turned to Page, studying her face. "Or like you do now. You haven't changed."

Page didn't reply. She knew that Mark had always had a thing for her since high school. Some even said she was the reason he'd never married. Lord knows, enough women had tried to snag him. He was good-looking, intelligent, and as charming as a man could be. But Page had the man she loved, and had adored from the moment they met. Lucien. She wasn't interested in any other, and Mark knew it. Everybody knew.

Mark turned to leave. "Tell Suellen I left some Banamine on the shelf in the tackroom, in case the mare is in pain. She knows how to give it." He stepped off the veranda. "Remember what I said . . . if there's ever anything I can do . . ."

"I'll remember."

The Yarbroughs collectively relaxed, confident their family dilemma would soon be resolved. On Saturday, as they did once or twice a month, J.L. and Miss Emma had friends over for cocktails and dinner—the movers and shakers of the city. Many were descended from families of enormous wealth, and enjoyed reminding each other that before the War between the States, Natchez had more millionaires per capita than any city in the United States. It had been the fourth-richest city in the country after New York, Philadelphia, and Boston. Architects from those northern cities had designed plantation homes that, like River Oaks and Yarbrough Hall, were decorated with linens from Ireland, marble from Italy, silks, mirrors, and armoires from France, and tea tables from England. Because Union troops occupied their homes during the war, the structures were preserved rather than burned to the ground. Though they didn't talk much about it, the guests were painfully aware that money to maintain the homes had vanished after the war.

When Pilgrimage started in 1931, descendants of antebellum ancestors discovered the means to hang on to their magnificent estates by opening their doors to tourists. Money collected paid for repainting and refurbishing, and allowed a slightly tarnished return of the polished society of a hundred and fifty years earlier. Natchez *was* opulence and hospitality in the mid-1800s. A few of the women's dresses tonight had been mended or made over, and more than one man's suit sported frayed collars and sleeves. On the surface, however, Natchez had reclaimed much of its former elegance, as evidenced by guests at the senator and Miss Emma's party. They were living life as their antebellum ancestors knew it, or as close as tourist dollars would allow.

Page and Lucien dropped by after the Confederate Pageant, bringing Cindy along. Lucien apologized to his father, saying they would have been there sooner, but Page had insisted on going by the hospital to say good night to their baby.

Still wearing her ruffled pink costume, Cindy was the hit of Grampa and Granda's party, as she had been on numerous occasions. Granda insisted on taking yet another photo of her granddaughter.

"Reach me my Kodak," Miss Emma said. J.L. fetched the Minolta 110 from a nearby shelf. Cindy posed with the senator while Page sipped sparkling water with lime.

Cindy teased, "You have your finger over the lens again, Granda."

J.L. added, "I don't know why you won't use that new thirty-five-millimeter job with the zoom. It takes better pictures."

"My pictures are just fine," Miss Emma said. "Aren't they, Cindy?"

"Yes, Granda. Don't forget to wind the film before you count to three."

When the photo session was over, Page had Cindy demonstrate a dance she was already rehearsing for next year's pageant. Miss Emma played piano and J.L. danced as Cindy's partner.

Page appreciated everyone's confidence and congratulations, but couldn't suppress a nagging sense of concern. Her baby wasn't safe in her arms yet.

Lucien guided Buford into the gentlemen's parlor while Cindy entertained. With so much going on, they'd had little chance to speak privately since the last day in court. Buford lit a cigar.

"How'd you find out about that abortion?" Lucien asked.

"What abortion?"

"Caroline Dunbar's abortion."

"I never said she had an abortion, did I?"

"You said . . . No, you didn't, did you? You only asked if she did."

"Hey . . . you can ask anything."

"Then she didn't?"

"Not that I know of. As I recollect, she said she did not."

"What about that Terence James fella? Was he black?"

"That much is correct."

"Was she fooling around with him?"

"Beats me. She said she wasn't, so I guess not. They worked together for about three years."

"Who was the doctor you asked about? When you were reading from some chart?"

"Ron Strahan? A buddy of mine from Atlanta. I just asked if she knew him. She said she didn't."

Lucien shook his head, smiling. "What was the deal with the Planned Parenthood center?"

"A lucky break. I had an investigator check every clinic and counseling center in Jackson to see if she'd ever been anywhere for anything . . . abortion, venereal disease, anything at all. She went there once for contraception counseling. They gave her a prescription for birth-control pills." Buford exhaled a cloud of noxious smoke. "That was before she hooked up with Jonathan. I thought she might be a little nervous about him knowing that."

Lucien started to ask how Buford gained access to privileged information, but decided he preferred not to know. "You're amazing, Buford. You made it appear . . . Hell, even I believed she'd had an abortion of a black man's baby two years ago. And he drove her there."

Buford shook a finger at Lucien, grinning. "You have a dirty mind, Governor."

"Yeah, and so does her husband. No wonder she cracked . . . he'll never believe her. I wouldn't be surprised if she's about two states away from the SOB by now."

Bright and early Monday morning, TV cameras recorded the sheriff's entourage, escorted by the Mississippi Highway Patrol, from Jackson to Natchez. They were bringing the DNA-test results to Judge Winston.

The courtroom was jammed, with people standing in the back and along the sides. Page waved confidently to several of her friends. The women were out in force again, as were J.L.'s and Lucien's cronies. All had happy faces and words of support and assurance.

Page had mixed emotions about her sixty-four-year-old father standing to one side of the room. Dapper as always, if outdated, he wore a brown tweed suit and vest and held a brown hat under his chin to prevent its being crushed. When Page waved, his lips parted in a smile below a thin silver mustache. Talk about standing room only—if Dr. Briggs passed out, which he'd been known to do in other public places, he couldn't possibly fall to the floor because of being packed in so tightly. People jammed in like Vienna sausages would support him where he stood.

Lucien expressed surprise when Caroline Dunbar took a seat beside Wylie Marsh. Her husband came in minutes later, but sat stiffly on the opposite side of their attorney, refusing to look at his wife.

"Heavy makeup on both cheeks this morning," Lucien whispered to Buford. "Jonathan probably beat the crap out of her."

Buford said, "Perhaps I overdid it. Do you think I should tell him I made a mistake when this is over?"

"After what that little tramp put us through? Don't forget, that's still her pickaninny over at the hospital. Little Black Sambo didn't come from no damned stork."

The court was called to order and Judge Winston entered. Moments later three deputies approached the bench. You could've heard a canary feather float to the floor. Somebody coughed nervously.

Though she was confident of what the results would show, Page's heart drummed against her ribs. She forced a nervous smile at Lucien.

Judge Winston said, "I've asked Dr. George Crisp, the director of the lab in Jackson, to read the test results. Dr. Crisp is an M.D., a board-certified pathologist, and an expert in laboratory procedures."

About fifty-five, Crisp was a large man with broad shoulders and a clean-cut face. He was sworn in.

Dr. Crisp cleared his throat. "First let me say that we checked for any two samples in which DNA characteristics were identical to an accuracy level of at least one in ten million. This means once DNA characteristics of a sample are identified, we'd have to test approximately ten million unrelated people before finding another sample with a significant number of matching characteristics. As a double check, we sent portions of each sample to the laboratory at the University of Tennessee, in Memphis, where they assigned their two most experienced technicians. Our test results agree completely with theirs."

Page was reassured that the doctor took his responsibility so seriously. However, the suspense was driving her up the wall. Thank God this bizarre nightmare would soon be over.

The deputies unlocked a metal container and presented a sealed envelope to Judge Winston. The judge, in turn, handed the envelope to Dr. Crisp.

"First," Dr. Crisp said, "we compared the sample labeled 'Baby Boy Dunbar' to samples from each of the four adults. I'll read the results in random order. Caroline Dunbar . . . positive. A definite match."

"Damn!" Lucien slammed his open palm against the table in front of him.

Page clenched her fists so tightly, her nails dug into her skin. Her only thought was, *If not this baby, who? Where is my child?* A vision flashed of ignorant rednecks in white sheets racing off with her son. She heard herself groan. She felt physically ill. She didn't know how much more she could take.

"Lucien Yarbrough . . . negative. No match."

In an attempt to lighten the mood, Buford whispered to Lucien, "Well, we know *you* weren't screwing Caroline Dunbar."

Dr. Crisp continued. "Page Yarbrough . . . negative. No match."

Lucien had heard all he needed. He leaned close to Buford and whispered, "We'll have to retest every baby that went home, and fast. If it isn't one of them, some son of a bitch has kidnapped my son."

"Jonathan Dunbar . . . positive. A definite match."

Caroline jumped up and threw her arms in the air. "I told you so, Jonathan! I told you so!"

Jonathan looked shocked. For the first time since their baby's parentage had been questioned, he actually smiled, appearing dumbfounded. Caroline ran over and threw her arms around his neck, but Jonathan seemed embarrassed. He forced her to sit quietly beside him.

Page didn't know why she still listened to the DNA expert. Probably because her mind was totally empty. She was so completely unnerved and disappointed that her mental processes seemed to shut down. She stared blankly ahead and listened, fighting a surge of nausea.

"Next," Dr. Crisp said, "we compared the sample labeled 'Baby Boy Yarbrough' to the same samples from each of the four adults. The results are as follows: Caroline Dunbar, negative. No match."

Lucien and J.L. huddled close to Buford Tallant, planning their next move. Once the Dunbar baby proved not to be Lucien and Page's, the suspense was over. It was time to regroup.

"Jonathan Dunbar . . . negative. No match," Dr. Crisp said.

Buford whispered, "The hospital's still on the hook, and Dr. Benning. They let somebody take your baby out of there."

"Lucien Yarbrough . . . negative. No match."

Glancing up when he heard his name, Lucien winked at his father. "Big wow, Dad, the little pickaninny's not mine."

Dr. Crisp went on. "Page Yarbrough . . . positive. A match."

"What!"

Page jumped to her feet, struggling against a tidal wave of panic. She shrieked, "What did you say?"

The courtroom went deathly silent. A siren wailed somewhere in the distance.

Dr. Crisp cleared his throat before answering. "I said, Page Yarbrough . . . positive. We have a definite match with the sample labeled 'Baby Boy Yarbrough.' "

Page slumped to the floor in a heap. Unconscious.

CHAPTER TEN

Judge Winston broke the handle of his gavel trying to restore order. Finally he called a one-hour recess.

Four deputies shielded Page and Lucien from reporters. Lucien carried Page's limp form into a small room behind the courtroom. He placed her on a worn vinyl couch and propped her feet on a cushion.

A deputy broke a vial of ammonia beneath Page's nostrils.

Page made a terrible face and pulled away from the offensive aroma. She opened her eyes. "Wha' happened?"

"You fainted," Lucien said anxiously.

Page shook her head, trying to clear the mist. She struggled to sit up. The deputy held a paper cup filled with water to Page's lips. She sipped it, then whispered, "I'm so sorry. . . ." She tugged her skirt down over her knees.

Buford glanced at Lucien. Lucien focused his full attention on his wife.

J.L. said, "Sorry for what?"

"I'm embarrassed."

"Why are you embarrassed?"

"I've never fainted before." Page's eyes were beginning to focus. She shook her head again and strained, trying to think. She heard herself ask, "Did he straighten it out?"

"Who?"

"That doctor. He read it wrong."

"Well, he . . ." Lucien bit something inside his

cheek. "He will, Page, when we go back in. The judge called a recess when you fainted."

Judge Winston came into the room and asked about Page.

"She's okay," Lucien said.

"I'm fine, Your Honor," Page said weakly. "Please forgive me."

"Perfectly all right," Judge Winston said. To Buford, he added, "I'm sure you'll have questions for Dr. Crisp, so I asked him to remain until we're back in session. I've ordered the courtroom closed to spectators."

Buford said, "Thank you, Your Honor."

Page managed to sit up. "I'm ready to go back in, Judge."

"You're sure? I don't want to rush you."

She stood unsteadily, holding on to her husband's arm. "I'm sure. We have to straighten this out now."

Letting out a long breath, the judge looked from Lucien to Buford. "I'm as shocked as you are, gentlemen."

Back in the courtroom, Page sat silent, confused but alert, while Buford Tallant questioned Dr. Crisp. Reporters and sketch artists were still present, along with Lucien's mother and Page's father. All were uncomfortably quiet. Page gripped the arms of her chair for support.

Crisp confirmed that the specimens had been guarded from the time the blood was drawn until the results were recorded on the report he'd just read. He even had a duplicate report in his pocket, in case the first was lost or damaged. After exhaustive questioning, Buford asked if either Lucien or J.L. could think of anything more to ask.

Lucien sat motionless too, as stunned as Page. He couldn't offer a single question. Page had suggested several to Buford earlier, and all had been answered.

After a few moments of visibly cogitating, Lucien's father stood, asking Buford to take his seat. There was a sadness in his voice when he said, "Doctor, I am not a medical person, so please bear with me if I ask you to repeat what you may have already explained. Permit me to go over one or two points, to clarify things in my own mind."

"Certainly, Senator."

"Without using the terms positive or negative, or matches or mismatches, you tested the blood of that little Negro baby, labeled 'Baby Boy Yarbrough' . . . right?"

"That's correct."

"According to your tests, who is that Negro baby's mother? His mama?"

"Page Briggs Yarbrough."

"You're certain of that?"

"Absolutely."

Pause. "There's no chance of a mistake with the blood samples or testing procedures?"

"I can't imagine how, sir."

"With what degree of certainty can you make that statement, Doctor?"

"Ten million to one. Maybe more."

"All right," J.L. said. His face flushed as if he'd suddenly developed a high fever. An uncharacteristic tremor appeared when he absently touched his cheek. "Now, Dr. Crisp, who do these tests show is that Negro baby's father? His daddy?"

"They don't."

"Excuse me?"

"They don't identify the baby's father. We have no match from either of the adult males tested."

"What about the sample from J. Lucien Yarbrough Junior? Did you test that sample?" J.L. was beginning to pace now as he spoke, raising his voice.

"We did."

"Just in your laboratory, Doctor?"

"No, sir. That sample was tested at the University of Tennessee as well."

"All right," J.L. said. "In these tests, performed both in your laboratory and in a totally separate laboratory at the University of Tennessee, completely in another state from Mississippi, what did the test of

J. Lucien Yarbrough Junior's blood show?" The senator turned to face the reporters, fixing their gazes.

"No match."

"Let me phrase the question this way, Doctor." The senator was almost shouting. "Is J. Lucien Yarbrough Junior the father of that Negro baby?"

"No, sir. He is not."

"Would you repeat your answer, please?"

"J. Lucien Yarbrough Junior is not the father of the Negro baby."

"Thank you, Doctor."

Dr. Crisp tilted his head to one side. "There were some similarities in the samples, but—"

"Dr. Crisp," J.L. said harshly, "please! Let me ask you once more . . . answer only the question I ask. Can you say with absolute certainly whether J. Lucien Yarbrough Junior is or is not the father of that Negro baby?"

"Yes, sir, I can. No, sir, he is not. He absolutely is not the father."

"Thank you, Doctor." J.L. sat heavily, his chin dropping to his chest. He squeezed his eyes shut and grimaced as if in pain.

Though Page's eyes had followed J.L. as he returned to their counsel table, her mind hadn't. She had no idea what final questions the senator had asked, or what the doctor had replied. Echoing in her mind were the senator's words: *who is that Negro baby's mother? His mama?* And the doctor's reply—the last name in the world she'd expected to hear—*Page Briggs Yarbrough.*

Page wanted to stand and scream out that the doctor was mistaken. The test was wrong.

But the doctor had calmly answered every question she was capable of formulating. He had countered her every objection. As limp as cooked spinach, Page knew she'd wake up any second now to realize that this entire miserable, ungodly experience had been a ghastly dream.

If not, she wanted to die.

* * *

In an effort to avoid clamoring reporters, three deputies hustled Page, Lucien, J.L., and Buford out a side door. Still in a daze, Page spotted Mama Yarbrough on the sidewalk next to her Lincoln Town Car, with some of her friends. Miss Emma stared at Page for a long moment, expressionless, then turned away. Moments later, Sam Walker, the senator's black driver, helped Miss Emma into the car and they drove off.

Rona Green was waiting outside, scanning the exit doors. The instant she saw Page, she raced over. A deputy refused to let her near.

"It's all right," Page said. "She's my friend."

Wet mascara streamed down Rona's face. It was the only time Page had ever seen her cry. "Oh, Page, my heart pours out to you. What can I do to help?" They embraced in silence.

J.L. said something to Lucien. A group of reporters lurking near the parking lot headed their way.

Lucien said, "Rona, would you please drive Page home? I have to go to the office with Dad and Buford."

"Of course." Rona and Page hurried toward Rona's car.

"Don't say anything to anybody," Lucien cautioned Page. "Don't answer any questions." The three men went off in the opposite direction, reporters at their heels.

When Page arrived at home, the front door flew open and Doris Kern ran onto the porch, an apron over her full cotton dress. Doris grabbed Page and hugged her till she could hardly catch her breath.

"What have they tried to do to you, baby? I ask my Lord above, what is going on in this world today?"

Page was too overcome to answer.

Rona Green asked, "What did you hear, Doris?"

"Everything . . . on the radio. Somebody trying to say that little black baby is yours? Why would they say that? Who'd want to lie about you? You've never

hurt anybody in your life." Doris walked arm in arm
with Page to the door. "You'd best be calling your
aunt Belle, too. She's telephoned three times already."

Inside, Doris fixed a ham sandwich and a Coke for
Rona. Page wasn't hungry, but Doris insisted she
drink a cup of sassafras tea. Page phoned Belle Braswell, assuring her the tests were somehow wrong.

Later Page pulled a chair up to the mahogany dining table while Rona ate. Rona asked, "What
happened?"

"I don't know. Those crazy tests . . . Dr. Crisp . . .
it's all a terrible nightmare, Rona."

"Is it . . . I mean . . . is there any way it could
be . . . ?"

"Rona, you know better than that. Of course not.
My God, I'd never dream of cheating on Lucien. It
makes me feel dirty even to think of it."

"I didn't mean you; I meant the test. Is there any
way a test can say it's you when it isn't? Can tests
be wrong?"

"They are wrong. I just don't understand why."

"Why what?"

"Why all this is happening. It's like . . . at first we
thought it was an honest mistake, that the nurse put
the wrong ID on our baby because she was new. Then
we started thinking about other possibilities. Suellen
said something one day that really upset me. She said
it might be more than a mistake . . . that somebody
switched babies on purpose to make Lucien look bad,
or to get even because he campaigned for the black
vote. Now this." Page shook her head. "Why would
somebody give them the wrong blood to test instead
of mine? Or was Dr. Crisp lying? Politics is a dirty
business, but if somebody's trying to make Lucien
look bad, is Dr. Crisp in on it? None of this makes
any sense, Rona, and my innocent little baby's the one
who's suffering. I am so totally confused."

Doris answered the door when the bell rang. When
they turned to look, Page's father entered, navigating
a reasonably straight line. He wore his habitual tweed

suit and carried his hat. His shirt was crisp and white, his tie neatly knotted. A walking cane assisted his precarious balance.

Page met him halfway across the room and they hugged.

Dr. Briggs nodded politely to Rona. "You're looking pink and healthy, Rona. Must be eating your vegetables." He eyed the ham sandwich she was working on with a raised eyebrow.

"So are you, Dr. Briggs." She raised an eyebrow right back at him. He was pale and drawn.

Briggs tried to shrug, swaying to one side for an instant. Page guided him to a nearby chair.

"I'd like to speak privately, daughter." He wasn't too drunk to talk—just to stand unassisted.

Rona joined Doris in the kitchen.

"I was in the courtroom this morning."

"I saw you . . . remember?"

"You've always been able to come to me, Page, if you had something you needed to discuss. Ever since we lost your mother."

"I know, Daddy. You were a wonderful listener."

"Is there anything you'd like to tell me now?"

"You were in the courtroom, so you know as much as I do."

"Hmmm."

"I didn't do anything wrong, Daddy. I wouldn't."

"I tried to raise you with proper values. You and Laura."

"And I respect those values."

He belched. The sour smell of cheap whiskey was overpowering. "Sorry. Perhaps I shouldn't have come just now, but I had to see you." His words were beginning to slur. He tried to stand, but slipped back into the chair. "Oops."

Page helped him to his feet. "Did you walk all the way over here?"

He wiped at something on his chin, trying to focus on whatever he thought he'd removed. "My friend Harry drove me."

Page shuddered at the thought. A part-time house painter, Harry drank as heavily as her father. Though he professed that he didn't drive by choice, Dr. Briggs simply couldn't spend what he did on booze each month and afford an automobile. So he'd made his choice—he walked. Knowing this sometimes depressed Page, but more often gave her a strange sense of relief. At least her father wasn't on the roads in his chronically impaired condition. A beat-up old Studebaker sat in her driveway, a ladder tied to its top. She helped her father to the door and down the front stairs.

"I can manage," he said proudly, aiming his cane toward the sidewalk.

"That wasn't exactly an in-depth talk, Daddy."

"You said you didn't do anything wrong. That's all I need to know."

Beginning to regain her wits, Page said, "Before you go, I think I may know what happened. Oh, God, I hope so. If I . . . Let me start over. In the hospital, they gave my milk to that baby from the day he was born. Wouldn't that shape his DNA? I know it molds his immune system."

Her father slowly shook his head. When he replied, he made an obvious effort to speak distinctly. "Colostrum in mother's milk carries antibodies against infection, so a mother transfers passive resistance to a nursing child until his own immune system matures sufficiently to provide active immunity. It affects primarily immune globulins A and G. That is a different situation altogether."

"Is that a no?"

"It is. DNA is permanent. It can't be changed from the time a child is conceived." He raised his eyebrows proudly and smiled.

"I see." Page was deflated. "Is there anything you'd like to ask me?"

"I have the answer I came for."

"But you heard Dr. Crisp . . . all those tests . . ."

"Tests can be wrong and doctors can be wrong . . .

who knows that better than I? I merely wanted to be certain that, if a mistake had been made, it wasn't yours." He put on his hat, tipped it courteously, and weaved his way toward Harry's Studebaker as if it were a waiting Rolls-Royce limousine. "Good day, daughter."

Rona stayed all afternoon, even drove Page to pick Cindy up after school. To prevent Cindy's noticing that she'd been crying, Page washed her face in cold water and applied new makeup before they went. It didn't work.

When they returned, Rona said she needed to call the antebellum houses to see how the afternoon tours were going. She asked Doris if the phone was working.

Doris picked up a nearby receiver and listened. "It's working. Why did you ask?"

"It just dawned on me," Rona said, "whenever I've come over before, the phone has rung constantly. We must've been here five hours now. It hasn't rung a single time."

CHAPTER ELEVEN

Over her daughter's very vocal protests, Page notified the pageant coordinator that Cindy wouldn't attend tonight. Forcing herself to put everything else out of her mind when Rona left, Page had dinner with her daughter. Then, when all homework was finished, they read stories and practiced dance steps until nine.

After Cindy went to bed, Page took a shower and sat alone in the downstairs parlor, munching potato chips and waiting for her husband to come home. She had called his office several times during the day, but neither he, J.L., nor Buford were to be found. At this hour the offices had long since been closed. The maid at River Oaks Plantation informed Page that J.L. and Miss Emma were out. She promised, however, to leave the message that Page had called. Six times.

Doris checked on Page again, asking if there was anything she could do.

"No, thanks," Page said. Feeling guilty about spoiling her diet, she hid the empty bag of potato chips behind her. "I'll just wait up for Lucien . . . we have to figure out what to do next. You go on to bed now. I'll see you in the morning."

Doris smiled her sweet smile. "I'll say a prayer for you both. I always do."

"Thank you, Doris. We can sure use that. Good night and God bless you."

After Doris left, Page heard something brushing against a screen outside the front window. Nothing was there when she peered out. She went through the house turning lights on. Where was Lucien? She hated being alone at night.

At ten-thirty the phone finally rang. Page jumped, startled, but answered on the first ring.

"Sorry I couldn't call before now," Suellen Whitford said. "Emma Sue filled in for Cindy in the second act, so by the time she finished and we took them out for a bite to eat . . . Bryan hadn't even had dinner yet . . . we just got home. How're you doing? Are you okay?"

Disappointed it wasn't her husband, Page said, "As well as can be expected, I guess. Did you see your brother anywhere?"

"I figured he'd be . . . Mama called before the pageant and said Daddy had a meeting with Buford. Lucien's probably with them."

"I especially need him at home tonight. I'm here all by myself."

"Oh, he'll be home before long."

"Have you spoken with Miss Emma? I've tried to reach her all night."

"She went to bed with a migraine. Won't talk to anybody when she gets one of those."

Suellen finally got around to what she'd obviously called to ask. "Is there anything you'd like to tell me, Page? You know it won't go beyond the two of us."

"Like what?"

"Oh . . . anything. We've never kept secrets from each other."

"What are you suggesting, Suellen?"

"I haven't suggested anything. I just want you to know I'm still your friend, no matter what anybody says."

"What has anybody said?"

"Well, you know . . . I'm sure you can guess. After the tests turned out the way they did, and all."

"Surely nobody believes those tests."

There was a silence on the other end of the line. Finally Suellen said, "I didn't say I believed them, but with all the security around the blood samples and everything, you can understand how some people might."

"Well, they're wrong." Page hesitated, trying to hide her irritation. "What are they saying?"

"Sure you want to know?"

"Yes."

"You won't get mad at me if I tell you?"

"Why would I get mad at you?"

"Well . . . some people think you may have had an affair."

"I would never do such a thing. My God, I'd never be able to hold my head up in this town if I did anything like that."

Suellen continued, "With a . . . shall we say . . . dark and handsome man. Dark, anyway."

"Suellen, how dare you! I'm insulted you'd even repeat such a ridiculous rumor. That is the most preposterous thing I've ever heard."

"You promised not to get mad, remember? I only told you what I heard at the pageant."

"Does anybody actually believe I'd do something like that? Don't these people know me? Certainly not my friends. None of my friends believe that . . . do they?"

"A couple of them were your friends. Or I thought they were."

"Who was it? I want to know."

"They were just saying it seemed that way, Page, based on all the blood-test evidence. They didn't say they actually knew that it happened or anything, just that they couldn't think of another explanation."

"What'd you tell them?"

"I said it wasn't possible. That you're married to my brother, and you'd be the last person in the world to have an affair. With anybody, let alone a damned . . ."

"Go ahead, say it."

" 'With a damned Negro', is what I said. I was angry at the time."

"Well, you're right . . . I wouldn't and I didn't. I want to know who's saying that about me. I'll call them right now and give them a piece of my mind. Better yet, I'll drive to their houses tonight. I won't have people spreading vicious rumors about me, trying to take my dignity away." Page's voice was trembling by the time she finished.

"Calm down, now; you're not in any frame of mind to be calling anybody or driving anywhere. Take one of those sleeping pills they gave you in the hospital. Things'll look brighter in the morning."

Page forced herself not to respond. She counted to ten, willing her anger to subside. This was her friend. Finally she said, "Oh, God, I hope you're right, Suellen. I can't imagine how this is happening to me. I don't even know what's happening. All I know is, whatever is going on, I want it over with. I want Lucien to come home. I want things the way they've always been."

Page felt a huge surge of relief when Lucien arrived home at one-thirty. Though she tried to hug him as he entered, he evaded her, going into the powder room beneath the curved staircase. Lucien wore a suit and tie, but his shirt collar was open and his tie was loose at the neck. From the stench of bourbon following him, she could tell he'd been drinking. And he'd had more than a little. He flushed the toilet and came back outside, zipping his trousers. There was no sound to suggest that he'd put the lid down. She'd do that later. He didn't even say anything about her having every light in the house on, which confirmed that he was more than two sheets to the wind. He hated it when she did that.

As nonchalantly as possible, Page asked, "Where have you been?"

"What do you care?"

"I always care where you are, Luce. I missed you. I've been by myself all night, honey, and thought I heard something outside. I was getting worried when you didn't call."

He started up the staircase. "Had a meeting," he mumbled.

Page followed him up to the master bedroom. "What meeting?" She picked up his jacket when he tossed it on the bed, hanging it in his closet.

"Just a meeting." He kicked off his loafers and tried to remove his trousers, but lost his balance. He had to sit on the bench at the foot of the canopied bed. Page hung the trousers on his night caddy.

When she tried to sit beside him, he immediately got up. He yanked down the white cotton bedspread, quilts, and sheets on his side of the bed, then climbed in, thumping the pillow into the shape he liked.

"Lucien . . . honey . . . we need to talk. I know you're upset about what that doctor said, but we should decide what to do next."

"Not now."

Page took in a long breath, then let it out. "I'd like to hear what you and Buford think we—"

"Dammit, Page, leave it alone!" Lucien flicked off the rose-colored *Gone with the Wind* bedside lamp, almost tipping it over. "Go sleep in the front bedroom. We'll talk tomorrow. I need time to think, unerupted . . . un-inrupted." He licked his lips and smacked his mouth, then said, very carefully, "Un-in-ter-rupted."

Page started to protest his ordering her to sleep in another room, but something in his tone stopped her. Such a command was unlike Lucien, but he clearly meant what he'd said. And he was drunk. Instead of arguing, she switched off the overhead light and left the room, knowing she'd never be able to sleep. She carried her pillow and a book with her.

Other than the times Lucien had been out of town, this would be the first night she'd slept alone since the day they were married, ten years ago last May 18. A Saturday. She remembered Lucien smiling so confidently that day at the church, waiting beside J.L. as

Page walked nervously down the aisle. She had clung tightly to the man who filled in for her father. What she needed tonight was to have Lucien hold her the way only he could, and assure her that together they would get to the bottom of this. As Lucien often said during the election campaign, they were an unstoppable team. Unfortunately, her half of the team would have to wait for the other half to sober up.

At eight a.m., Doris entered the guest bedroom where Page had slept—in a high tester bed with its carved cherrywood headboard. The drapes were already open, since Page hadn't remembered to close them when she finally dozed off at four-thirty.

"Time you're gettin' outta that bed, Miss Sleepyhead. You get any more beauty sleep, you gonna be too beautiful to look at." Doris laughed. "Come on, now; they've already started coming by."

"Who?"

"Your friends. Wash that pretty face and put on some makeup. You'll want to look especially good today. Which skirt you want to wear?"

"The tan wool, if I can get into it, with the yellow cashmere sweater." Hopefully, her morning sit-ups were beginning to flatten her stomach. With all the confusion, she hadn't been able to diet like she should've, even before the potato-chip binge last night. Page didn't feel like visiting with friends. She and Lucien needed to formulate a plan. "Why especially good today, Doris?"

Doris turned to look at Page and put both hands on her hips. "Because these women have come to look you over . . . to see if you are who they thought you were. We're gonna show 'em that you're still Page Briggs Yarbrough, the governor's wife, Cindy's mother, and the finest woman in Natchez. Now scoot. I got coffee all fixed, a ham sliced, and biscuits baking. Your orange juice is on the mantel there."

"Is Lucien up?"

"Up and gone. The senator had him out by six-thirty this morning."

Downstairs, Page was hugged by three members of her garden club. Doris welcomed two more at the front door. While not Page's closest friends, these were women she'd worked and socialized with most of her life. Since the senator had tied Lucien up for the morning, Page was pleased to see them. She knew Lucien and J.L. would be working feverishly with Buford on solving their DNA dilemma. She'd much prefer to be with Lucien, actively participating, but he'd never allow that. It was a man thing.

Page desperately needed somebody to talk to. As it happened, she mostly listened.

"Oh, Page, it's just awful," one woman said. "Because one silly test is wrong, they're trying to make it look like you did something terrible."

Another added, "I never trusted that DNA thing anyway."

"Me, neither, Joanne. Just look at what happened with the O.J. fiasco. It obviously didn't work then, either."

"What are you gonna do about your baby, Page? Your real baby. Do you have any idea where he could be?"

Before Page could answer, another said, "I'd demand a different kind of test. I mean, we know you'd never do what they're saying you did."

"That's right, sweetie. No matter what anybody says, we know you wouldn't do anything like that."

Somebody added, "I know a couple of women in this town who would . . . I mean, I wouldn't put it past them, and you know who I'm talking about. There's one who'd sleep with a rototiller . . . but not you. And with that handsome, rich husband of yours? I mean, why would you?"

"It doesn't make any sense."

Page thanked them for their support. "I can't tell you how much this means to me," she said. "It's like

I've been thrust into some cheap horror movie ever since the night I delivered. You are so sweet . . . I love you all for being here."

More than twenty young women came by that morning. Several wore bright-colored crinoline walking gowns or silk ball gowns, and a few even had bonnets on. Most were helping with afternoon house tours, but assured Page that women from the morning tours would be by after lunch. They ate, talked, consoled Page, and offered their unanimous and undying support. Just before noon, they left.

With tears of gratitude in her eyes, Page closed the front door. "Aren't they wonderful?"

Doris hugged her. "You did fine, Page . . . you're a lady through and through. Now we better hurry and fix some sandwiches and cookies for the afternoon shift."

Neither Page nor Doris heard one of the exiting women say to the others, "Can you believe she'd sit there all innocent-looking and teary-eyed like that when she has to realize that we know exactly what she did? I mean, what does she think we are . . . stupid?"

"Penny Lee was at the courtroom door when that expert explained the test to the senator. She said it was better than ten million to one that Page had sex with a black man. Not one million, mind you. Ten million to one."

"Wouldn't you love to know who?"

"What do you mean?"

"Who he was . . . the Negro she slept with."

"I'll bet Patty and Mary Lou know."

"They'd never tell us. Would they?"

"Don't be too sure. Mary Lou couldn't keep a secret in a pail. And Patty knows everything."

"Well, whoever he was, I hope it was worth it. Lucien was out with his buddies last night and got real drunk. A waitress over at the hotel lounge said they were in there after midnight and he was real upset."

"He'll leave her in a hot second."

"Would you blame him?"

"Not really. Especially with him being the next governor and all. I mean, what else can he do? He can't run the affairs of an entire state and meanwhile be worried that his wife's out sleeping with every good-looking black man who comes along."

"Was he good-looking? Who told you that?"

"You wouldn't expect her to pick an ugly one, would you?"

"Say what you want; nobody's ever accused Page of having bad taste."

They all laughed.

"I wonder if it's true what they say about black men. About, you know . . . their things."

"Why don't you ask her?"

The woman giggled. "Now, that would be just too tacky."

CHAPTER TWELVE

Page collected Cindy from her piano lesson at four-thirty that afternoon. The last of the Pilgrimage ladies had departed shortly before. When she arrived back home with her daughter, she was delighted to see Lucien's Cadillac in the circular drive. She hurried inside and told Cindy to rehearse dance steps for a while, then get ready for tonight's pageant.

Lucien was in the master bedroom, packing two suitcases. Page hurried to his side, but he didn't look up.

"Are we going somewhere?" she asked.

"I have to go to Jackson for a few days."

"Why?"

"Everything's all screwed up for the inauguration, and Jake needs my help. That, plus I need to finalize staff appointments."

"How long will you be gone?"

"I'll let you know once I'm there."

She could tell he was in no mood to talk. Lucien's response to stress was to clam up and try to solve the problem himself. Page preferred to talk things out, to explore their options. She needed to hear there was hope.

"Luce, do you think this is such a good time to be away? Shouldn't we be figuring out what we need to do? What about our baby? We don't even know where he is."

His back was to her when he said, "He's over at the hospital, Page."

"He is? Oh, Lucien . . ." The surge she'd felt

crashed down like a breaking wave when she realized what he had meant.

"In fact," Lucien said, "I told Mack Malone you'd come over and pick him up first thing in the morning. They're charging me damn near a thousand dollars a day for his keep."

"Lucien, what are you saying? Surely, you don't believe . . ."

He turned to face her, his face florid. "What the hell do you expect me to believe?"

The horror of what he was saying hit like a SCUD missile. "I expect you to believe me. Those tests are wrong. Believe *me,* Lucien . . . your wife."

"Don't give me that innocent-victim act, Page. Not anymore."

"Dammit, Lucien, I'm telling you the way it is. Why won't you listen?" She was totally unprepared for this reaction. Hurt, defenseless. About to be sick, she held to the bedpost for support.

"Listen to what? More lies? I spent ten hours and God knows how much money on the telephone yesterday. Between Buford and Dad and me, we talked to every DNA expert in the country and half of Europe. Hell, I had Dr. Crisp fax them the full technical reports from both labs. Every expert said the same thing."

"And what was that?"

"That it's your baby. It sure as hell isn't mine, but that little Negro is yours. The one you've been sneaking over every day to feed your milk. Oh, yeah, I talked to the nurses, too. How do you do it, Page? Do you let him suck on your tits the same as his daddy did the night he got you pregnant? Or was it during the day when I was working my ass off to support all this?" He waved an arm angrily about the room. "While you were supposedly out soliciting homes for the garden club all those times."

Page had never seen Lucien in such a blind rage—foul, abusive, profane. She was too shocked to respond.

He hardly paused for breath. "Where'd it happen, right here in this bedroom? In our bed? Or in the backseat of a beat-up old car on some lonely road out in the woods?"

Subtlety had just flown out the window. Page screamed at him, "Stop it! Stop it right now! What is the matter with you?" She doubled over with the agony she felt in her very core. Who was this stranger shouting at the top of his lungs, so full of venom?

Lucien slammed and snapped the suitcase lids shut. He started for the door.

"Please," Page heard herself say, "don't go."

"Oh, no," he said, mimicking the tremor in her voice. "Don't go and leave poor, sweet, innocent Page all by herself. I should give you time to dream up more lies." He paused, breathing hard. "You expect me to stay here so everybody in Natchez can laugh and point and make signs behind my back?" He demonstrated the Italian "cuckolded" sign, clenching his teeth together. His eyes brimmed with tears. "Do you know what you've done, Page? You knew how bad I needed that money. My one chance to come up with it and what do you do? You go screw some damned nigger and get yourself pregnant. If you had to whore around, why couldn't you pick a white guy? At least we'd have gotten the money." He left.

Page had slid down the bedpost as Lucien shouted and railed at her. Too weak to rise, she clung to the post and gasped for breath, crying hysterically. She moaned, then called out softly. Finally she shrieked until Doris found her some time later.

That evening Page forced herself to dress, covering her puffy eyes with makeup. With the help of a medieval girdle, she squeezed into her nicest outfit. She refused to take a tranquilizer, knowing she would need all her wits about her if she ran into Lucien or his family. None of them had been available all day. The ice packs Doris made helped her eyelids a little, but she still needed dark glasses. Cindy was upset about arriving at the pageant ten minutes late, but Page assured her it would be all right. She wasn't scheduled to go on until the second act.

Backstage, mothers quickly busied themselves when Page came close, adjusting or repairing costumes or otherwise readying their children for the performance.

Page fought back tears when she thought of the night Lucien had made his announcement about their son. It seemed like a thousand years ago.

As the evening's performance began, Page hugged and kissed Cindy and wished her good luck, then slipped into one of six permanently reserved Yarbrough seats in the front row of the auditorium. The other five seats remained conspicuously empty throughout the performance.

On the way home that night, Cindy asked, "Mommy, what's a nigger?"

Page dimmed her lights for an approaching car, and crossed Devereaux Drive. "That isn't a nice word, sweetie. Where did you hear it?"

"Bobby Treadway said it."

"Well, he shouldn't have. It's a terrible thing to call somebody."

"What is it? Am I a nigger?"

"No, you're not."

"Is Daddy?"

"No, Cindy."

"But you love me, don't you? And you love Daddy."

"Of course I do." Page suddenly realized what the Treadway youngster must have said. Fuming inside, she said, "Let's not talk about that anymore. You did an excellent job tonight, and your green dress worked out just fine. In fact, I liked it better than the pink one." She forcefully relaxed her grip on the steering wheel when her knuckles began to ache.

"I like the pink one."

"You can't wear the same dress every night."

"Daddy likes the pink one best. He told me."

"When did he say that?"

"Tonight, before he left."

"Did he come to your room?"

"Uh-huh. I gave him an extra-big kiss because he said he might not be back for a long time. Why, Mommy? Where's he going? Is he going to tell more people to vote for him?"

Page's depression deepened even further, but she'd never let Cindy know. Although she was an emotionally overcharged roller coaster, she had to appear on track for Cindy. "Daddy went to get things ready for when we all move up to Jackson. When Daddy starts being governor."

"Like Great-granddaddy was?"

"Exactly."

"I don't want to move. I like my pretty house."

"Mommy'll make that house just as pretty. Especially your room."

"Will Daddy put his picture and letters and things all over Granda's house when he's the governor?"

"Maybe. We'll see."

"I think they're ugly."

"Cindy . . . that isn't very nice."

"They're just a lot of writing. I like pictures of dogs and horses and flowers and girls in pretty dresses . . . pretty things."

"So do I, baby. But your great-grandfather was a very important man, so things he wrote or signed are important, too. That's why Granda had them framed and keeps them on her walls." Page tried to focus on her driving, but her mind was on Lucien. Where was he? When would he be home? This would never do. They had to talk.

Cindy sat silent for a while, staring straight at the dashboard. As they pulled into their driveway, she said, "Bobby Treadway isn't very nice, anyway. He said *damn* one time, right out loud. When we were onstage at the pageant." She looked up at her mother and grinned. "I sorta stepped on his toes."

*   *   *

The first thing Page noticed from her friends was how they seemed to become so occupied when she went by the tour houses each day. To keep from going crazy until Lucien might come home, she continued to check on her staff, making sure all docents showed up before each house was officially open, and knew significant details about the home and its furnishings. She made sure the girls knew all about the families who'd lived in each home before the war. Some of the docents were still fairly new, so Page emphasized special items, like a tea set that had belonged to Napoléon and Josephine, and some of the silver that George and Martha Washington had used. She reminded them to tell how each family wrapped their silver in burlap bags and hid it in muddy pond bottoms before the Yankees came. She checked to be certain none of the docents chewed gum or wore nylon gloves. Focusing on trivial concerns was far superior to the alternative—facing reality. Aware that she was not as lenient as usual with small infractions of rules, she even tried to be more patient.

Rona Green worked as hard as Page, and by sharing the load, they managed to visit each house on the tour every day. Doris Kern watched Cindy on Saturdays and Sundays, but Page insisted on taking Cindy to, and picking her up from, school, piano, dance, and charm-school classes.

Page visited Belle Braswell one morning after dropping Cindy off at school, but they only chatted briefly. Belle had been giving a tour of her plantation, which she insisted on doing personally. She wound up all tours with a dollop of sherry for each guest and one for herself, served in antique crystal glasses. She never charged for tours of her home, but demurely mentioned that she did accept gratuities. Belle refused to consider selling any of the priceless antiques or museum-quality silver pieces that filled her residence. With no income beyond a widow's Social Security, she hadn't paid insurance premiums for years. Gratuities from tours paid the taxes and limited maintenance on her gracious home. A twelve-gauge shotgun insured her against theft.

Page also managed to swing by the hospital twice a day to deliver milk evacuated from her breasts. She could no longer bring herself to hold the black baby, however, while he took his bottle. A nurse was certainly capable of doing that. Page told Suellen that the only reason she went at all was to keep her swollen breasts from hurting. She'd never admit how much she looked forward to each visit. The other children were gone from the hospital now, except for new ones who couldn't possibly be hers. But she still went. Hoping.

A week went by without accomplishing her primary objective—speaking with Lucien. He had his new secretary, Fayrene, call twice to ask about Cindy, then tell Page the governor was terribly busy, but would try to phone her the next day. He never did. Page sent lengthy e-mail letters that went unanswered. She had never felt so alone. With the exception of Suellen— and to a lesser extent Rona Green—she had nobody she could talk to. Nobody who would understand. Doris was wonderful, of course, and did understand. She was always available to listen, and to do whatever she could to help, but nobody could give Page the thing she needed so desperately. Nobody but Lucien, and he wasn't ready to be found. Aunt Belle, as kind and loving as she was, lived in her own world in another time. Page prayed every morning and every night that Lucien would come home. Or call. As capable as she was, she depended on him. They belonged together.

Buford Tallant and J.L. never seemed to be at the law offices. Buford was constantly in court, and nobody admitted to seeing the senator. One secretary thought he might be in Jackson.

Page's father called once a week to see how she was doing. He never pressed for details, merely offered his assistance. Page knew there was nothing he could do. Also, he might promise more than he was capable of delivering, then get drunk and not show up, as he'd done for her wedding. But she appreciated his calls and emotional support.

"I've never doubted your capability, daughter. You inherited my penchant for detail and your mother's drive. If anybody can sort it out, you will. Give my love to Cindy."

Wednesday morning, Page received a call from Steve Griffith, the administrator of Doctors' Memorial Hospital.

"Governor Yarbrough said you'd be picking him up, Mrs. Yarbrough."

"Why should I? He's not my child."

"I understand how you feel, ma'am, but we can't continue to keep him here. The baby is legally yours. Naturally, that means you're responsible for the bill."

Page argued to no avail. She couldn't believe this man's nerve. She asked, "How much is the bill?"

"Fifteen thousand, seven hundred thirty-three dollars, if you pick him up today. We reduced the charge for the first two weeks, when all the confusion was going on."

"Let me get in touch with my husband, Mr. Griffith. I'll call you back shortly."

Still unable to reach Lucien, Page left another message with his secretary in Jackson. She also spoke with the newest partner in the law firm, Troy Carter. Troy said he couldn't advise her on what to do. He was courteous, however, and promised to locate Lucien, Buford Tallant, or the senator. Nobody called back.

That afternoon Page received a return call from Lucien's secretary, Fayrene. The woman had a sickeningly sweet manner of speaking.

"He says for you to pick the baby up from the hospital, Mrs. Yarbrough, honey, and take him home."

"I can't do that. It's like admitting he's ours, and he isn't."

"I don't know anything about that, honey. I'm only delivering the governor's message. He says you should pick the baby up . . . that he'll not be responsible for the baby's expenses.''

Page wanted to scream, but forced her voice to remain calm. "Tell him the bill is nearly sixteen thousand dollars. I don't have that kind of money. I don't have any money except what's left in the house account for groceries and incidentals.''

"I know how you feel, honey, but all I can do is give him the message. He's so busy, you know.''

Page had had it with Lucien's adolescent behavior, and she'd certainly had it with this cloying excuse for a secretary.

"Busy, is he? Well, tell him something for me. I'm busy, too, taking care of our home and our daughter. You tell the governor that if I don't hear from him personally before midnight tonight, I'll be in Jackson first thing tomorrow. If he won't talk to me today, tell him the next call he makes had better be for reinforcements, 'cause I'm coming to talk and he's damn well gonna listen and it'll take the whole damned state militia to stop me. You got that, Fayrene?'' After a beat, Page added, as sugary as possible, "Honey?''

Page slammed down the phone, shaking all over. A soft slapping sound came from behind her. Doris Kern stood there with a huge smile on her face, applauding at what she'd overheard.

"Good for you, baby,'' Doris said lovingly. "Now, that's the Page I raised.''

CHAPTER THIRTEEN

At nine o'clock the next morning, Page entered the office building where Lucien's campaign manager, Jake Meadows, worked. She'd been there several times during the campaign. Lucien hadn't said anything about renting a new office, so she assumed he was sharing Jake's.

Minutes later she walked out of the ladies' bathroom on the fourth floor and headed straight for Jake's door—dressed to the teeth and looking good.

Fayrene-honey wore a skirt too short for Cindy, and had one of those peroxide jobs stacked in a bird's-nest 'do that made her look six inches taller than she was. She needed the extra height, with those boobs. Sexual-harassment bait in spiked heels.

Fayrene closed a file drawer and said, "I'm sorry, ma'am, but you can't—"

"Step aside, sister. A lady's coming through."

Page took a giant breath, sucked in her stomach, and opened the door to the inner office. Instead of entering right away, she stood in the doorway, just looking at her husband—and giving him a good look at her.

Fayrene squawked something frantic through the intercom.

Lucien stood behind a shiny mahogany desk. His aide, Billy Larson, sat alligatorlike in one of two chairs at the side of the desk. Jake Meadows was halfway out of the other, his mouth open as if to speak.

Jake and Billy instantly forced their saccharine campaign smiles.

"Good morning, Page. Don't you look lovely today."

"How nice to see you, Mrs. Yarbrough. Here, take my seat. Can I get you some coffee? A glass of water?"

Page remained standing, her gaze frozen on Lucien. The others quietly excused themselves, closing the door as they left. She finally exhaled.

Lucien's face had flushed when she entered, but the red was receding back under his starched collar. He pressed his lips together. "You look nice," he finally said.

"Didn't want you to forget."

"Page, I'm not ready to talk. I need to focus on the inauguration and getting my staff organized. It's a big job. I have a million things to get done."

"Make it a million and one."

He exhaled sharply. "What do you want?"

"My husband back."

"You should've thought of that sooner."

"Are you saying you're not coming back?"

"I'm saying I'm too busy to think about it right now."

"Do you not consider it important?"

"Of course it's important . . . just not right now. I promised the voters new roads; now I have to get them built. I promised better schools, and I'm meeting with educators from all over the state for their suggestions. I promised law and order, and I'm trying to find the money to hire a thousand new deputies. I don't have time to talk to you now."

Page started to ask if he had time to drive Fayrene home a couple of nights a week, or maybe buy her dinner at some discreet, out-of-the-way restaurant that just happened to be on the way to her apartment. That was certainly the impression Fayrene had given. Page didn't ask. Bad timing.

"We're your family, Lucien. Don't we deserve a little of your time?"

"Who is we?"

"Cindy and I. Wouldn't you like to talk to your

daughter in person sometime, or would you rather have Fayrene-honey out there just keep relaying messages?"

"You forgot somebody."

"Who?"

"Little Black Sambo. Don't you include him in the family now? He is your kid." Hatred suffused Lucien's face again. "Next time why don't you fuck a Chinaman or a Jap? Hell, if we can get a couple of Arabs and an Israeli to knock you up, we can start our own U.N. right here in Mississippi." Breathing hard, he added, "Whadda you think you've done to my mother and father? You know how their friends feel about blacks. They're ashamed to go out in public."

Page fought to hold back her tears. She'd done enough groveling in recent weeks. She forced her shoulders back and her head a little higher, determined to ignore his insults. "Lucien, you're being very juvenile about this. I know you're hurt . . . but it's because of what you think, not something I've done. I did not do anything wrong."

Just then Lucien's father came into the room. He nodded his stately head toward her. "Page," he said, always the politician. "You're looking lovely."

"Hello, Senator," she replied. "I've been trying to reach you."

"Well, dear, we've been terribly busy, as you can imagine."

"A family characteristic of late." Page shifted her weight to the other foot. Her new shoes were killing her. "Cindy asks about you and Granda every day. She doesn't understand why she can't come see you, or why you don't call."

J.L. said, "And that's a terrible thing. I'll see that it's corrected immediately. Is Cindy at home? I'll call her right now."

"She's in school. She'll be home by one." Page spoke to J.L. but continued to look directly at Lucien. Damned if she'd be the first to look away.

"Fine," J.L. said. "Now, if you'll forgive us, Page, we have some extremely urgent business to attend to."

Without moving, Page said, "Is he in Jackson?"

"Who?"

"Your urgent business. I seem to remember you two saying you'd search to the ends of the earth for him. Our son. Finding him. What could be more urgent than that?"

Lucien spoke up. "Your son. We know where he is . . . the hospital administrator calls twice a day. I thought you were going to pick him up."

"Not that baby," Page said. "*Our* son, Lucien. Yours and mine."

"You must have me confused with somebody else," Lucien said sarcastically. "I finally figured out that you must be color-blind, but look at my lips . . . check out my nose. Feel my hair, Page; it isn't kinky. Listen to the way I say 'ask,' and 'poor.' " He was in her face now, almost snarling.

"That's enough," J.L. said. He moved in between them.

At that moment Page wanted to strangle her husband; anything to throttle those vitriolic insults. She was too angry to speak. Her perfect world was falling apart before her very eyes, and she was doing a lousy job of trying to piece it back together. She grasped one gloved hand tightly in the other, struggling to keep them from trembling so furiously. Or at least to not let Lucien see.

J.L. gently took her by the arm. He spoke very softly, in a voice filled with compassion. "Why don't you and I step outside for a minute, Page? Maybe go get us a Co-Cola or something. Give Junior time to collect his thoughts."

In the coffee shop across the street, Page strangled and drowned a tea bag in a cup of hot water while J.L. talked. All she could think of was the anger in Lucien's eyes and the horrible accusations he'd made. Why wouldn't he stop and think and listen to what she was telling him? She loved him so much. She needed him now more than ever before in her entire life, and she knew he needed her. Didn't he realize that?

J.L. was saying, "We haven't given up, Page. I've had men checking new white babies all over this state and into Louisiana. You know that's hard. You can't just walk in and take their blood. We're making sure their neighbors saw the mama pregnant, or we've tried to talk to their doctors to make sure they actually delivered those babies."

"What about the first three that went home? The ones where nobody watched their blood being drawn."

"We had 'em all retested. They're with their own mamas."

"Why didn't I hear anything about that?"

"We kept it as quiet as we could. I apologize. I should have told you."

"Those mothers went along without a fight?"

"Two of 'em. They wanted to be sure themselves. One father held out for a while."

"How'd you change his mind?"

J.L. rubbed his fingers together in the universal money sign.

"You paid him?"

"It only works about a hundred percent of the time. I didn't want any long, drawn-out court battles. We're still trying to get things settled between us and the hospital and Dr. Benning."

"What's happening with all that?"

"Oh, it'll cost some money, but we're a lot closer than we were." J.L. pulled out a pocket watch and checked the time. "I need to get back upstairs. Why don't you drive on home now so you'll be there when Cindy gets out of school."

"I need to speak with Lucien. There's so many things we need to discuss. Important things."

"Give him a couple of days, Page . . . let me talk to him. I guarantee you'll hear from him by then." He smiled. "Two days. Okay?"

"They call me every day from the hospital. I keep telling them I'm not responsible for the bill, that it isn't my baby, but they won't listen. They're threatening to turn us over to a collection agency. I don't have any money anyway . . . we've used up what we had in our checking account. I need to pay Doris and I need money for groceries. I'm desperate, Senator. I can't wait a couple of days."

J.L. took five hundred-dollar bills from his wallet, handing them to her. "Everybody needs a little walking-around money. Go pick out whatever groceries you and Cindy need, but don't go to that supermarket you like. Go to the Jitney Jungle where Emma shops . . . I'll call the manager. Whatever you pick out, they'll deliver to your house this afternoon. Charge it to my account."

"Thank you. What should I tell Cindy? Is Mama Yarbrough ever going to be home to us?"

"Why don't you take Cindy on over there this afternoon and leave her for a while? Emma's been feeling kinda poorly, so she won't be much in a mood to visit, but I know she'd enjoy seeing Cindy. Maybe they can crochet something or play the piano." He rested his hand on hers. "And do me a favor, Page . . . go pick up the little Negro baby. Take him home from the hospital."

Page started to object, but he silenced her with a finger to her lips. "Hear me out. . . . Doris'll take better care of that baby than they can at the hospital. It'll save a lot of money, and it won't be any hardship on you. Just till we get things straightened out. The last thing Lucien needs is somebody turning his wife over for collection, or getting a judgment against him. Especially with that savings-and-loan situation still up in the air. None of us need that."

"It's a mistake, Senator." She hesitated. "But I'll think about it." Page formed a mental picture of the baby still in the nursery. Alone. Her heart ached for him, but he wasn't hers. It would be a major strategic mistake for her to take him to her home.

"It might be better to wait till after dark. Take Doris along . . . maybe you should just walk on ahead and let Doris carry him out of the hospital, in case anybody's around that we might know."

Page reluctantly agreed to wait two more days to speak with Lucien. However, she insisted on going back to his office before driving home. She wanted to study his eyes once more, to see if there was any love left for her. Any love at all.

In the office, Fayrene-honey informed Page that the governor had split in a big hurry with Billy and Jake. They hadn't said where they were going or when they might return.

Page seethed with anger, but wanted to cry. J.L. had quietly and cleverly ushered her right out of Lucien's office. Or his life. She reminded herself that it was only for two days. She could stand on her head that long. Besides, two days would give her time to plan exactly what she'd say to Lucien. Even to rehearse it.

She didn't bother to thank Fayrene as she left.

Page and Doris went to the hospital when the pageant was over that evening. Rona Green stayed with Cindy. Even though Page had called to say she was coming over, the night supervisor refused to let her take the baby without a release slip from the business office. Doris watched TV in the reception area while Page went to straighten out the confusion.

Since the business office closed at five, Page was directed to the admissions desk in the front lobby. There, a young night clerk with acne pulled the Yarbrough file up on his computer. Open textbooks lay nearby. The clerk looked old enough to be in high school, too young for college.

"That'll be $17,511.23." He stared at the total. "Wow. Don't you have medical insurance?"

"They already paid their portion. Can you bill my husband?"

"I'm sorry, ma'am, but we're instructed to get payment in full before a patient leaves. If you want to come back tomorrow, my supervisor will be here during the day and you can discuss it with her."

"That won't be necessary. May I borrow a pen, please?" Page wrote a check for the full amount from her household account—which showed a zero balance. So? It was a joint account. Lucien wanted her to take the baby home; let Lucien make the check good. Taking this child to her house was not Page's idea in the first place.

The clerk looked at the check, then at Page. She could tell he was embarrassed to ask, so she volunteered her driver's license. Both Page's and Lucien's names appeared on the face of the check. The clerk finally spoke. "Is that the Yarbrough who's our new governor?"

"Yes."

"He brought his wife in here to have a baby one night a few weeks ago. We're supposed to verify the funds on any check over five hundred dollars, but with the banks closed at this hour, I can't do that. Besides . . . are you the governor's wife?"

"I am."

"Oh. I mean, yes, ma'am, this will be fine." The young man's demeanor changed the instant he realized who Page was. "I actually shook his hand." He gave her a nerdy smile and stamped the bill *paid*.

A nurse had a shopping bag full of paraphernalia to accompany the baby—bottles, a blue blanket, disposable diapers, samples of formula, and brochures advertising various products and services.

"It's a little something we do," the nurse said, "along with some of the local merchants and diaper services. Don't try the formula, though. We gave him some one day when you were late bringing your milk in, and it made him sick. Colicky, you know. The paperwork is tucked inside right over here."

On top of the pile was an official-looking document: a birth certificate, dated the night she had delivered, signed by Dr. Robert Benning. The name on the certificate read *Jackson Adams Yarbrough, II.* Page was listed as the mother, and Lucien the father.

Page said, "That isn't this baby's name."

The nurse read the certificate. "Well, it certainly seems to be, ma'am." She read it again.

"The information on this certificate is not correct. Who can change it for me?"

"We're not allowed to make changes once it's been signed by the doctor. You might check with the clerk in the front office. He can tell you who to talk to tomorrow."

Back downstairs, the same clerk placed a page marker in his textbook, read the certificate, and explained how it came to be.

"I did the admission myself," he said proudly. "That's how I met the governor. I remember two or three of his friends came in while we were filling out the paperwork, and he told them that his wife—that would be you—had already gone upstairs in a wheelchair, then—"

"Please," Page said, "I'm in a hurry. Can you just change the name on this certificate? It isn't even a change; just take the name off."

"Oh, no, ma'am. The original has already been sent in to the state. This is only a copy."

"But it isn't correct."

The clerk's tone became defensive. "Yes, ma'am, it is . . . I remember. The governor was so pleased it was gonna be a boy . . . he said he already knew because they'd done that amniocentesis thing and the doctor told them. Excuse me, I guess you'd know all about that, wouldn't you?"

"How do I get this name off this certificate?"

"I can give you the address, the Mississippi State Bureau of Vital Statistics." He foraged through a drawer and produced something with an address on it. "But I know that's the name the governor wanted . . . I typed it myself."

"When?"

"That night. He was bragging to his friends about having a son. They were passing a flask around right here while I typed out the birth certificate, which they're not supposed to do, but being as he's the next governor, I didn't say anything. Anyway, I left the 's' off of Adams the first time, and he made me retype it. Then he told me to take it upstairs so the doctor could sign it the minute the baby was born. I did."

The clerk shrugged. "If you've changed your mind about the name, just write to the bureau there. I don't think you need a lawyer, but you might. To tell the truth, I've never known anybody to actually change the name once they've got a birth certificate and everything."

Page collected Doris and went back to the nursery. Baby boy Yarbrough was bundled up and ready for his first major journey.

Doris's face lit up when she took the baby in her arms. "Oh, my, this child is beautiful," she exclaimed. "Look at those eyes, Page. These little hands. He reminds me of my William when he was a baby." Doris hugged the infant to her and rocked gently back and forth, marveling at his beauty. "This sweet little thing has been over here all by hisself all this time. Well, I'm gonna take care of you, pretty little baby boy. Oh, yes. You're gonna get you some lovin' now."

Page couldn't help smiling. Maybe she'd made the right decision after all. She opened the side door for Doris and the baby, and carried the bag of supplies toward her car.

Senator Yarbrough always bragged that his word was his bond. And once again, he was true to his word. As he had personally guaranteed, Page heard from Lucien two days after her trip to Jackson. Not by the personal visit she'd hoped for. Nor a phone call. It wasn't exactly a letter—not even a short, scribbled note on one of those little yellow sticky pads. Hand-delivered to her door, Page received Lucien's petition for divorce. Included was his demand for custody of their daughter, Cindy.

After Page's eleventh frantic phone call to Lucien's office in Jackson, Fayrene-honey switched on the answering machine. An impersonal and unemotional recorded message said the office would be closed until further notice. It then instructed the caller to please leave a message.

Page did. Her message to Lucien was not rehearsed or well thought out, as she had planned. It wasn't ladylike, and it certainly wasn't impersonal. On the best of days, there was absolutely no way it could ever be classified as unemotional. If Page hadn't been teetering right on the brink of hysteria, she would've personally considered the message she left tacky. Real tacky.

CHAPTER FOURTEEN

During the next several days, Page ran the gamut of emotional responses. She cried, she cursed, she threw things, she shrieked, she sat silent, morose. She wrote a hundred letters or e-mails, but tore them all up or deleted them. She didn't sleep and couldn't eat, if you didn't count potato chips, pretzels, diet colas, or chocolate. She smoked half a pack of cigarettes, though she hadn't smoked since her Chi Omega days at Ole Miss, and she drank a full bottle of chardonnay in a single evening. The wine not only gave her absolutely no solace, but the hangover was excruciating till well into the next afternoon. She realized then she could never be an alcoholic, genetic predisposition or not.

Page spent hours on the telephone with Rona Green and Suellen Whitford. She swore them both to secrecy, of course. She didn't dare tell Patty or Mary Lou that Lucien had filed for divorce, though she considered them close. Once she and Lucien reconciled their differences, she didn't want the whole world to know. Deep down, she knew they would reconcile.

"You know how he is," Suellen said. "Lets himself get all pushed out of shape at first, ranting and raving. He's done that since he was about . . . well, I'm thirty-three, and I remember his temper tantrums since I was around five or six, so he must've been about eight or nine. Mama and Daddy both let him get away with it because he was a boy. You know how boys are prized in this family, 'cause there's so few of them. I tell you, I didn't get away with much. Anyway, Page, give him a few days. Then call him. He'll settle down.

Incidentally, have you figured out how all this came about?"

"The divorce papers?"

"The baby. Being black."

"Of course I figured it out. He isn't mine."

"Have you had any more tests done? That DNA stuff?"

"Not yet, but I'm going to, in a lab where they don't know Lucien. Probably a different state. I'm so upset thinking about a divorce, I can't worry about having tests done. I should, but I haven't. I was waiting to discuss it with Lucien. And him threatening to take Cindy away from me? Suellen, that isn't like him. He knows I'm a good mother. He'd never try to do something like that."

"Like I said, give him a little time. As guys always say, he needs his space right now. Maybe you should go somewhere. When you come back he'll be waiting with arms open and tail between his legs, begging you to forgive him."

"I'd never go away at a time like this. Besides, there's so much to do with Cindy in school, plus her being in the pageant every night. Even the open houses."

"That's almost over."

"But there's a huge volume of paperwork after the tourists leave, plus getting organized for next year. We've already started working on Christmas Pilgrimage. I lined up the Mass choir and we're doing Christmas lights all over the grounds of Longwood." She paused. "I can't leave, anyway . . . my baby's in somebody else's arms right now, and I want him back. I won't stop searching till I have him at home. I've even hired a private investigator."

"Are you serious?"

"You don't see Lucien making any effort to find him, do you? I'll have to do it on my own."

The next morning Page hurried alongside Cindy out the front door. It was a raw, blustery morning.

"Wrap your scarf around your neck, baby," Page said, fishing through her purse for car keys.

"It itches."

"It's Burberry wool. They don't scratch."

Cindy ran on ahead. "What's that?"

"Where?"

"Somebody wrote words on our car, Mommy."

Page looked up from her purse and joined her daughter. Spray-painted in iridescent green across the passenger side of her Suburban was one word: *SLUT!* Furious, Page raced around the vehicle. Diagonally across the rear was the single word *WHORE*.

"What does it say, Mommy?"

"Nothing, baby . . . it's just a prank, like at Halloween. Let's go inside now. Mommy can't find her keys again. We'll take a cab this morning."

Page and Doris spent most of the day removing graffiti from her truck, along with flakes and chips of the original paint. Lucien had insisted on having it repainted for her birthday next May. She'd gladly accept his offer now, but wouldn't dare tell him about this occurrence.

A few evenings later Page walked from the rear of her home down a pebble path to the garden house. Originally the kitchen for the main house, the small brick building now served as the "servants' quarters," where Doris lived.

Inside, Doris had a living room complete with rocking chair, sofa, TV, a large brick fireplace once used to prepare meals for the main house, and a newer addition containing a bedroom and bath. It was immaculate and neat, like Doris herself. Cozy. A wood fire crackled in the fireplace to ward off the fall evening's chill. Doris carried the baby in her arms when she came to the door.

Stepping inside, Page handed Doris the bottle of breast milk.

"He sure is ready to eat," Doris said. "I been dippin' the pacifier in molasses to keep him quiet, but it

don't work . . . this baby knows that isn't his dinner."
She automatically tested the milk's temperature, then
gave the bottle to the child.

Page warmed herself by the fire and watched.
"What did your friends say?"

"Nobody has seen or heard a thing."

"Who'd you talk to?"

"Bessie Mae and Wilma. Those two know everybody in town, and they said nobody has a white baby.
What they actually said was, nobody's crazy enough
to do something like that in this town. Wilma even
talked to one daughter in Greenville and one in Hattiesburg. They're all looking, and so are their friends.
If he's with a black family anywhere, we'll find him."

"I pray every day that we do, Doris."

"What does that private detective say?"

"He's searching everywhere we can think of. Mostly
talking to people at the hospital. He hasn't come up
with anything promising yet."

"Have you talked to Lucien?"

"He told his secretary I should have my lawyer
communicate with his lawyer from now on. He won't
speak to me. None of the family will, except Suellen.
You'd think I'd suddenly developed leprosy or something."

Doris didn't comment. Her eyes were focused on
the black child's face. Hers were ancient eyes, filled
with an understanding not learned from schools or
books or pleasant experiences.

After a while, Doris chuckled. "This baby's about
to suck this nipple right off of this bottle."

Page decided to try one more law office after taking
Cindy to school on Wednesday, a full week since receiving Lucien's petition. She'd first tried asking someone in the Yarbrough firm what she should do, but
soon realized she was being naive. The attorneys there
smiled courteously, but wouldn't give her the time of
day.

In desperation, Page had driven to Jackson the day

before, only to discover Jake Meadows's office closed. The building manager had no forwarding address.

Where it involved Page, Lucien had disappeared. J.L. and Miss Emma were never home. Page became increasingly concerned with each passing day. She spoke with Wylie Marsh, then Mack Malone, only to be told neither could represent or advise her because of the continuing suits and cross-complaints between the Yarbroughs, including her, and the Dunbars, Dr. Benning, and the hospital. Conflict of interest. Page tried every firm she'd ever heard of, then ones she hadn't. Nobody was willing to take her on as a client or make any suggestions about how she might get in touch with Lucien.

She was particularly disappointed that the few women attorneys in town limited their practices to criminal law, business and corporate law, or personal injury cases. None of them handled divorces. One woman came right out and told Page she should hire a big gun from out of town. Said she'd need one.

Page located a last-ditch address from the phone book. The entrance on the right side of the small building was for a chiropractor. The other was for the law firm of Jones and Wilson. Mr. Wilson's secretary had at least given her an appointment.

Page was running out of time. She'd heard lawyers grumble about how long it took to get a case heard nowadays. Obviously Lucien had pushed this one to the top of the heap, railroading it through. And Page couldn't find an attorney to represent her. She wasn't about to risk having Cindy taken away. This attorney would help her. He had to. He was her final chance.

After explaining her situation to Mr. Wilson, Page heard, "Regardless of how we might vote, nobody in his right mind's gonna go up against Lucien and the senator in Natchez, Mrs. Yarbrough. We all make our living here." The attorney must have weighed three hundred pounds and was losing his hair. He hung over his chair on all sides.

"What are you so frightened of? I'm Cindy's

mother. Everybody in town knows I take outstanding care of her."

"I'm sure you do, ma'am, but I have my own children to feed. If I represented you against the governor after what those DNA tests showed, people wouldn't hire me to notarize a signature, let alone for legal work."

Coward, she thought. *Try sharing your own food with your children. That'd feed a sizable orphanage for years.* She asked, "Do you actually believe those tests?"

"I wasn't in the courtroom, but it sounded like they were pretty foolproof, with all the security and them using two different labs."

Page stood, tightly clasping her pocketbook with both hands. "I can see I've wasted your time and mine." She walked to the door, but looked back. "Isn't there anybody in this town who might help me, Mr. Wilson? My husband is trying to take my daughter away, and I haven't done anything to deserve that." She tried to stop the trembling of her chin, brushing away a tear before it could run down her cheek.

"I don't know of anybody, Mrs. Yarbrough. I'm sorry." He didn't bother to rise. Or couldn't.

Page walked out, certain she didn't want to be represented by this incompetent. But where was she to go? A big gun from out of town would require a huge retainer. Lawyers went where the money was, and she was broke. A sense of impending doom settled on her. As she hurried toward her car, a woman's voice called out behind her.

An attractive African-American woman of about thirty ran toward Page. The woman wore a simple black cotton dress and conservative makeup, and her hair was pulled back neatly in a bun.

"I don't mean to interfere," the woman said.

"With what?"

"I couldn't help overhearing when you were talking to Mr. Wilson. I'm a secretary for Jones and Wilson."

She glanced over her shoulder toward the building Page had just left.

"Yes?"

She handed Page a piece of yellow paper with a name and phone number handwritten on it. "You might try calling this man. He's supposed to be exceptionally smart."

Page read the name—David Fields. "An attorney in Natchez?"

"Yes, ma'am. He's in that building on the river, down in Natchez under the Hill. The one they started to paint but never finished."

"I never heard of him."

"Not many people have. He's . . ." The woman hesitated, looking uncomfortable. "Well, he's only been in town for a year or so."

"You started to say something else. What was it?" Page guessed what the woman probably meant. "Is he black?"

"No, ma'am . . ." It was obvious the woman had wanted to say more. She didn't.

"What then?"

"Well, he's . . . Jewish. Some folks don't like him because of that. I know he could use the work."

"How do you know?"

"Nights and weekends, I do typing for some of the legal secretaries in town." She looked around to be certain nobody could overhear, lowering her voice. "Please don't ever say anything about that, or I could lose this job."

"I won't."

"Mr. Fields doesn't have a secretary of his own, so he calls me sometimes, when he has work." The woman shook her head. "That isn't very often. But he's smart, and he'll probably take cases that nobody else wants."

"Why are you telling me this?"

"It has nothing to do with your baby being black, Mrs. Yarbrough. I don't know what you did or didn't do, and it's none of my business. But I have a little girl, too. I know how I'd feel if somebody tried to take her from me." She glanced behind her again. "I'd better get on back inside." She smiled. "Good luck."

"Wait," Page said. "What's your name?"

"Presious. It's spelled with an 's' but sounds like it's a 'c,' like 'precious.' My mama couldn't read nor write."

"Thank you, Presious. I appreciate your help."

Presious had been right about somebody beginning to paint the building and not completing the job. The side facing the river was bright pink, its front a dirty gray. After hobbling in heels across a gravel parking lot, Page walked up two flights of stairs to office number 210.

She was pleasantly surprised. Though small and spartan, the reception area was clean, unlike the hallway leading to the office door. These walls were freshly painted. With no receptionist to greet her, Page took a seat and picked up a magazine, a current issue of *Family Circle*. Seconds later, a man appeared wearing khaki slacks, brown loafers, and an open-collared white dress shirt. He appeared to be about Page's age. Only slightly taller than she, he had a trim build and bushy brown hair. His eyes were set perhaps a little too close together, but were fiercely alive. Blue. And he had a kindly smile.

"Mrs. Yarbrough?"

"Yes."

"Pleased to meet you. I'm David Fields."

His entire suite was smaller than Lucien's private consultation room. A hand-lettered poster board announced that he handled divorces, personal injury cases, medical insurance disputes, wills, taxes, and notary public services. Following him into his inner office, Page noticed a silver dollar–size spot of scalp showing through in the crown of the lawyer's head.

Page took a seat in one of two green wooden chairs in front of a terribly cluttered desk. What she could see of the desk was black metal with a Formica top and chrome legs. Half the drawers of two mismatched file cabinets were open and jammed full of disorganization. It came as no great surprise, then, when Fields sat next to her rather than behind his desk. That chair was occupied by open law books and manila folders with papers hanging out on all sides. She could only hope such disorganization reflected his brilliance and preoccupation with obscure legal technicalities.

"Please," Fields said. "Tell me how I might be of help."

He was the first attorney who hadn't offered coffee, tea, soda pop, or even a glass of water. Perhaps there wasn't a bathroom on this floor, so he couldn't risk filling his rare client with fluids. If she had to go find a bathroom, she might not return.

Fields slipped on a pair of round wire-rim glasses. He held a yellow legal pad and a ballpoint pen that advertised the Jefferson Davis Ice Cream Parlor. They both ignored a folder that slid off the backside of the desk and scattered its contents across the floor.

Page began, "I spend every waking minute trying to find my son. Meanwhile my husband is attempting to take my daughter away from me." Silence. "Actually, it's probably his family more than him. His father. I don't believe he'd do that on his own." More silence. Was this man an attorney or a psychologist? "Look, maybe we should discuss your fee first. I have very little money, and until I get some kind of settlement or maybe alimony from our divorce—if we actually get a divorce—I don't have any means of paying you."

Fields wrote something on the yellow pad. "What's your daughter's name?"

"Cindy. Cindy Lou. We named her after my mother, who is deceased. Did you hear what I said about the money?"

"Yes, ma'am. How old is Cindy, Mrs. Yarbrough?"

"Six. She'll be seven in January. She's absolutely beautiful."

"Why is your husband suing for divorce? And custody?"

Page studied Mr. Fields's face to see if he was putting her on. None of the other attorneys she'd consulted had asked that question. They already knew. Everybody knew. She finally said, "Have you been living under a rock, Mr. Fields?"

"No, ma'am."

"My husband won't talk to me, either in person or on the phone. He hasn't answered my letters or telegrams, and he's closed his office in Jackson. He's the incoming governor, Mr. Fields. If I had an emergency, I wouldn't even know where to find him. You ask why he wants a divorce? Our situation has been in every newspaper in the country and on TV every night. You probably know as much about his reasons as I do. Maybe more."

Fields lifted his gaze from the yellow legal pad and pushed his glasses up on his nose. "I generally don't believe what I read in the papers, Mrs. Yarbrough. That goes double for televised news. What actually happened? From the beginning."

Page hesitated, then said, "Mr. Fields, before I answer that . . . and this is embarrassing for me, but do you mind if I ask you a personal question?"

"Sure . . . go ahead."

"Are you a good attorney?"

He smiled. "Yes, ma'am, I am."

She watched his eyes as he answered. Oh, God, how could you tell? After lengthy consideration, she said, "Well, it all started when Lucien and I . . ."

Three nights later, Page was awakened by something outside her window—muffled sounds at first; then they grew louder. Men's voices. She jumped out of bed and parted the curtains. On the lawn below were six men wearing white sheets and hoods.

Page groaned. One of the men lit a torch, laughing at something another said. Page's heart jumped into her throat. She grabbed up a robe and ran for the door. Her first concerns were to get Cindy out of the house and make sure Doris and Adam were all right.

Unable to find a flashlight, she raced to the front door and threw it open. "What are you doing?" she shrieked.

Somebody touched the torch to a cloth-wrapped cross on her lawn, setting it ablaze. Black smoke rose into the air, and a heavy stench of kerosene filled Page's nostrils. A strange sense of relief swept over her because it was a makeshift cross burning. Not her home. She was incensed, however, that hoodlums would violate her property at all. Her only sanctuary.

Page ran onto the porch and yelled, "You no-good bastards. I dare you to take those hoods off and let me see your faces. Cowards."

The men laughed and ran toward a red pickup waiting at the street. As they climbed inside, one of them yelled back, "Where's your nigger boyfriend now, Page?" They screeched off and left.

"Mommy, there's a fire."

Page turned to see Cindy standing in the doorway, rubbing her eyes. Doris raced around a corner of the house with Adam in her arms.

Page grabbed her daughter up and hugged her close. "It's all right, baby. It's over." Page's heart was pounding so loudly in her ears, she could hardly hear herself speak. The cross was fully ablaze just yards away, its dancing flames heating her cheeks. She kissed Cindy and watched Doris hurry up the front stairs, her eyes wide with fright. How would she ever explain this to Cindy? How could she prevent its happening again?

CHAPTER FIFTEEN

On the morning of the divorce and custody hearing, Troy Carter stood with Lucien and the senator in the hallway outside the courtroom. The newest partner in Yarbrough, Yarbrough, Tallant, and McCann, Carter had worked as an associate for five years before being made a partner the year before. In addition to being an excellent family-law attorney, he was one of Lucien's drinking buddies. While they waited to be called inside, Lucien smiled and shook hands with nearly every person who walked by.

From down the hall, Page had attempted, unsuccessfully, to catch Lucien's gaze. She continued to try, still hopeful they might work something out. Divorce sounded so final.

Meanwhile, J.L. was loudly telling Troy the way things used to be, when he'd started the firm years before. "Hell, I didn't have any money of my own," J.L. said loudly, "and the only cases I could drum up were nigger divorces. The going rate for a nigger divorce was fifty dollars, so I did them for thirty-five . . . they paid cash money up front, don't you know."

Page cringed.

Lucien interrupted his father and whispered something in his ear. J.L. appeared to object at first, then shrugged. His tone was more subdued when he continued.

"Well, that's what we called them," the senator explained to Troy and anybody else who cared to listen. "Anyhow, I was too proud to ask my father for anything, plus he wanted me to prove myself. He was governor of the state, but he didn't give me a dime after I finished law school. Anyhow, Glover McCann worked with me back then, and he was in worse shape financially than I was. So everything we needed to buy, we equated to how many . . ." The senator hesitated. "Well, you know . . . divorces we'd have to represent to get it. I remember a typewriter we wanted. Glover said, 'Hell, Jackson,'—that's what he called me—'we can't afford that typewriter. It's two whole blankety-blank divorces.' When we moved to a new office down on Commerce Street, our rent was three blankety-blank divorces a month. And our first car . . . we bought one car between us and shared it for the first two years . . . that was ten blankety-blank divorces down and three blankety-blank divorces a month." The senator shook his elegant white head. "The story loses something when you can't even say the right words anymore. They're not politically correct, you know."

Page and David Fields sat quietly on a wooden bench down the hall. Page tried again to catch Lucien's attention as he turned her way, but he was laughing at something J.L. said, and his glance skipped past her like a pebble skimming water. David Fields appeared almost as uncomfortable as Page felt. Page let out a long sigh. Lucien looked good—dammit.

Page's thoughts drifted back to the first time she'd noticed Lucien. Oh, she'd seen him around town when she was a child, been in pageants and social functions where he was, but it wasn't the same as that day she really noticed him at Gayle and Dennis Lynds's wedding. Page was about to graduate from Ole Miss, and had come home specifically for the wedding. Dennis's best man Lucien was the most devastatingly handsome hunk of human flesh Page had ever seen. He'd stood in that gazebo like some Greek god, wearing a gray tuxedo with tails, in that garden on that sunny afternoon in May. At that specific moment, Page had known beyond any doubt that God had created Lucien Yarbrough to be her husband. Her partner in life.

For the first time Page had suddenly understood what it meant to be smitten.

She and Lucien were married in that same gazebo a year later, on May 18. Suzie Mayo had called them Ken and Barbie in her society-page column. God, Lucien had looked good that day. He still did.

Now here they were, perched nervously on uncomfortable benches in a dingy hall in a musty old courthouse. Page blinked back her tears. She was still in a daze that the man she adored—or his father—could reduce their perfect love to this. What had become of their bliss-filled ten years together? Didn't they matter at all? Page didn't want a divorce from Lucien. She wanted to cling tightly to him and tell him how deeply she loved him.

When Page's stomach growled she quickly covered it with her pocketbook and gloves, embarrassed. Though she hadn't been hungry that morning, Doris had insisted she eat a sausage biscuit and have a cup of tea. Despite half a roll of antacid tablets since, she could still taste the sausage. When a bailiff called her name, she swallowed several times, trying desperately to keep from throwing up.

As she approached the courtroom, Page's hopes soared. Lucien unexpectedly came back into the hall, toward her.

"Lucien, why are you doing this? We need to talk."

Lucien glared at her. "Stop pretending, Page. How dumb do you think I am?"

"I am telling you the truth . . . I always have. Why in God's name would you try to take Cindy? You know I'm a good mother, Lucien. That's a terrible thing to do to her."

Lucien pushed past and hurried toward the men's room.

Just then J.L. came into the hall, his face hard. "Anything you have to say, Page, tell it to your attorney. Have him speak with Troy."

"But, Senator, I—"

David Fields stepped up to Page's side. The senator

ignored him, saying, "It's too late for talk, young woman . . . actions speak louder than words. Your actions came through loud and clear—and black." J.L. whirled around and went back inside the courtroom.

Rona Green arrived at that moment, her eyes wide, questioning the scene she had partially witnessed. They all went inside.

An hour later, David Fields and Rona Green had to support Page as they guided her from the courtroom.

Overwrought with grief, Page sobbed. "Oh, God, no . . . not my Cindy. My baby girl."

Fields said, "Try to walk, Page. We'll go outside into the fresh air."

Rona was too upset to say anything except, "It isn't fair, Page. It just isn't fair."

Aside from the participants and their attorneys, nobody had come to the proceeding except Rona Green. Once again the Yarbrough name had mysteriously not made the court docket. Page was convinced that none of her so-called friends would've come anyway. Almost none of the town women had had anything to do with her since hearing about the upcoming divorce. They'd felt obligated to pick a side. Nobody liked to stand with a loser.

Page had even received a letter the week before from the Junior League. While it didn't come right out and say her membership had been terminated— not in so many words—it said the members were aware of her "personal problems," and she was being relieved of her duties as secretary of the organization. It also said they would understand if she was unable to attend future meetings. While the Junior League was somewhat less direct than the Klan, their message was the same: they didn't want her kind there.

"They smile so sweetly," Page had told Rona, "sugar wouldn't melt in their mouths. Then they stab me in the back. And to think I was their president last year. I edited that entire cookbook they're selling today."

Two days after the Junior League's letter arrived, a similar letter came from her Wednesday Morning Club. Next came the Confederate Garden Club, saying they wouldn't need her to help with Christmas Pilgrimage, but thanking her for her assistance in the past.

Page had thought that a devastating blow until today. No agony in her thirty-two years had prepared her for the paralyzing despair she felt when the judge decreed that Cindy had to be taken away. She would've preferred being bludgeoned to death with a dull ax.

That afternoon Rona Green and Suellen Whitford sat with Page while Cindy and Suellen's daughters played outside. The adults watched through a bay window. Doris Kern cried so hard, Suellen had to assist her to her quarters. Though Doris pleaded to stay with Page, Suellen finally convinced her to give Page some time alone.

"I'll be glad to call my doctor," Suellen told Page, "get a prescription for Valium. They help me when I'm upset. I hate to say it about my own brother, but he's a shit for not giving you something . . . if not alimony, at least a settlement of some kind. You'll need money to live on till you find a job. Take my suggestion, Page . . . let me get you a Valium."

Page shook her head, dabbing her eyes with a soggy tissue.

"The best thing is to just go ahead and cry it out," Rona said. After a moment Rona asked, "Do you think having David Fields as your lawyer hurt your case?"

"It couldn't help," Suellen answered, "unless the judge was Jewish, which he obviously wasn't." She glanced at Page and added, "You know what Daddy says about how they stick together."

"I like my attorney," Page said. "He's smart and he's kind." She took in a deep breath and let it out. "He's also the only one who wasn't afraid to go up against Lucien and your dad." She sniffed, then cleared her throat. "He said he could tell after we were in there about five minutes that they had it wired. We never stood a chance." She dropped her head into her hands again.

Neither Rona nor Suellen said anything. Friends of Page's for years, they knew her to not only be beautiful but smart and capable. She'd cope.

As afternoon merged into dusk, Doris fixed sandwiches and sodas for Suellen and Rona, then sat in a corner of the kitchen, sobbing, while they ate. Later Doris held a cool cloth to Page's forehead while she threw up in the downstairs bathroom.

When Suellen started to call the children inside, Page said, "I don't want Cindy to see me like this, but I can't look at her without breaking down. I have to stop crying."

"Really, Page, a couple of Valiums would help a whole bunch. Or at least a glass of wine."

"I can't let anything cloud my mind. The private investigator's coming by later, so I have to talk with him. Plus, in whatever time I have left with Cindy, I need all my senses about me. I want to enjoy what little—" Her voice cut off and her body shook with sobs.

The next day was warm and sunny, but Page froze with fear when Lucien and Miss Emma came to pick Cindy up in the afternoon. She had to stop them, but had no earthly idea how. Two Adams County sheriff's cruisers lurked outside the driveway, the deputies watching from their cars. It was Lucien's way of letting Page know he meant business. She could either comply with the judge's order or go to jail. Her initial decision had been easy—she'd take jail any day rather than give up her daughter. But Suellen had convinced her it would be better for Cindy if nobody made a scene.

Page knew she had little or no chance to overturn the judge's decision, but David Fields had agreed to try, and was already drawing up the papers. Unless and until Page prevailed, Lucien and Miss Emma had full custody until Cindy turned eighteen. Page could phone three times a week, and would be allowed to visit for four hours at a time, once every two weeks. With supervision.

As best she could, Page had explained that Cindy would be staying with Granda for a little while. That Mother had some terribly urgent things to do that required her to go away. She promised to call often and to visit every chance she got, so they would be together as much as possible. With Lucien standing in the driveway, Page told Cindy again how much she loved her. Doris was crying so hard she had to hide behind the front door.

Cindy didn't buy it. None of the explanation. When it came time to turn her mother loose, Cindy cried, she screamed, she kicked, she threw herself to the ground, she hollered, she held her breath till she was almost blue. Before it was over, Page didn't behave any better. With four sizable deputies struggling to restrain Page and Doris, Page watched her ex-husband and her ex-mother-in-law kidnap her daughter and bodily drag her away—an act Page would never forget—or forgive.

Life as Page knew it came to an end that day. Somebody had pulled her world right out from under her feet.

Incapacitated for the remainder of the day, Page went to bed and locked her door, incapable of thought or action. Finally she came downstairs and collapsed on the sofa, incessantly crying. She couldn't accept that Lucien would do this to her. Not even J.L. She wanted to die. She alternated between shrieking out at God for being so cruel, then begging on her knees for his help.

Rona Green found someone to take over her own responsibilities, and stayed with Page and Doris all day. Doris was almost as bad off as Page, but managed to look after the baby between sessions with Page.

They cried, talked, and fumed. None of it eased Page's pain.

In the late afternoon, Doris came into the room where Page and Rona sat. Though the light was going, they hadn't bothered to turn on a lamp.

Doris took Page into her arms and rocked her as she had when Page was a little girl. "I'll take care of you, baby. Nobody's gonna do anything else bad to you as long as there's breath left in me. Nobody."

Page clung to Doris. "We'll take care of each other. We always have." Page's heart felt as if somebody had stomped on it.

"People need somebody to blame, baby. They're wrong . . . but they're blaming you." A few minutes later, Doris whispered, "I need to ask you something private." She helped Page into the kitchen.

"What is it?"

Doris took the plastic breast pump from a dress pocket and handed it to Page. "The baby's hungry. I was wondering if you could pump out some milk now."

That particular request launched Page's emotional roller coaster right off its tracks. She shouted, "You interrupt me at a time like this for that?"

"He's crying something terrible, Page. He's almost sucked a hole in his pacifier."

"Well, he can starve, for all I care. Who do you think caused this disaster in the first place?" Page threw the breast pump against the kitchen wall, smashing it to bits. "Him and his damnable black skin." She turned and ran to her bedroom, sobbing hysterically.

A half hour later, Page came downstairs in robe and slippers, consumed with guilt about what she'd done. She had to know if the child was all right. He was only a baby, and hungry. Rona was nowhere to be found, so Page went through the house in search of Doris and the child. Her face felt like an abandoned jack-o'-lantern the week after Halloween.

Inside the garden house, Page could hardly understand Doris above the baby's screams.

"He took that formula from the can," Doris said, "and it came right back up. He has the stomach colic, but he's still hungry. What can I do?"

"Check the bag the nurses gave us. Maybe there's another breast pump in with all those things." She had to yell to be heard.

"Already looked. There isn't another one."

"Well, I don't know what to do. Are there any other sample cans of formula? Some other kind?"

"They're all the same. They'll just make him sicker."

Page watched the baby's little contorted face. He was screaming at a level to shatter crystal, hungry, miserable, and unable to comprehend. Her guilt deepened, depressing her even further, if that was possible. She couldn't seem to do anything right anymore. "I'm sorry about what I said, Doris. I'm just so miserable about Cindy."

"Of course you are . . . so am I." Doris spoke, but didn't look at Page.

"I do care what happens. I wouldn't let him starve . . . I wouldn't let any baby starve, and the color of his skin has nothing to do with it."

Doris didn't speak. She rocked the screaming infant back and forth, humming some tune Page didn't recognize.

Page asked, "Do you have anything we can pump my breasts with? A rubber bulb of some sort?"

"That turkey baster's got a rubber bulb over in the kitchen drawer, but it won't pump milk." There was something strange about Doris's tone. The warmth was missing.

"Then I'll drive to the hospital and pick up another one." Page hesitated. "But what if Cindy calls and I'm not here? They might let her call me. I wish we'd done this sooner, during the day."

"There is another way."

"What?" Page saw Doris's expression change, and her intention hit Page like a cold towel in the face.

"No . . . oh, no, Doris, I wouldn't. I couldn't. He's not even my baby."

Doris fixed Page's gaze. In no uncertain terms she said, "This baby needs to eat. Now."

"Well, there's nothing I can do about it. When we find his mother, she'll nurse him, okay? Meanwhile he'll just have to wait till I can go find another breast pump."

Doris glared at her. Page had never seen so scornful a look on Doris's face. It was almost scary.

"It isn't my fault," Page shouted above the baby's screams. "I can't even nurse my own baby. What do you want from me?"

Equally as loud, Doris yelled back, "Quit thinking of yourself for two minutes, Page. Stop being so damned selfish!"

Page almost fell backward, shocked at Doris's intensity. "What did you say, Doris Kern? How dare you challenge me."

Doris refused to back down, a terrible scowl on her face. "Look at this child, sick from hunger. Just because you're miserable, does the whole world have to suffer? Stop feeling sorry for yourself. Are you too good to nurse him because you're white and he's not?"

"That has nothing to do with it."

"The hell it don't. He's starving, Page. Look at him . . . he's a hungry little baby and your titties are busting out with milk. He don't know he's the wrong color." Fuming, Doris spun around and opened a kitchen cabinet, breathing hard. She held the screaming infant on one hip.

Doris's statement jolted Page. She voiced every objection she could think of. She couldn't transfer milk directly from her breasts to this child for a very simple reason—he wasn't her baby. Nobody in their right mind would expect her to.

Page's anger slowly subsided as she watched Doris improvise.

Doris filled a square of cheesecloth with honey, then let the child feed voraciously on it between cries.

Seconds later the cheesecloth was sucked through. And though Page objected, less vehemently now, Doris placed the wailing infant in Page's arms and began to open the robe, staring directly into Page's eyes the entire time. Seconds later the child's eager lips frantically searched for, then found, Page's distended nipple. He sucked furiously for several pulls, then nestled close against her, drinking more slowly. The contortions in his little face relaxed, and his expression became one of divine contentment. At last he was receiving his fill.

What Page experienced, watching and feeling this child nurse, was beyond her comprehension. She no longer had the strength or the will to resist. She closed her eyes and imagined that this was her baby. Her very own son. She pulled him even tighter against her. And began to sob aloud.

"There, there," Doris said softly. Her callused fingers gently stroked the back of the baby's head. "That's what he's been needin' all along."

Between sobs, Page said, "Don't you dare tell anybody I did this, Doris Kern, and don't expect me to do it again. The only reason I'm nursing him now is because he's so hungry and I smashed that breast pump. I just . . . well, I feel guilty about what I said, and he is a little baby no matter what color he is, and I am the one who broke that pump. Oh, Doris, I don't know . . . I don't think I said no because he's black. I've never been prejudiced in my life. It isn't that I think I'm too good because I'm white. I've never believed I'm better than anybody else. I'm not prejudiced about people's color. Oh, God, I hope I'm not. I don't want to be. I've tried to be a better person than that. Am I, Doris? Am I a hypocrite?"

"You were raised in Mississippi, Page. You're a good woman, but you can't help knowing he's different from you. So am I. Black people feel the same about white people. We're all different. He's not your baby, but you can still love him. You and Laura were different from me, but I loved you. I still do."

"I do want to help him, Doris. I care for him. I don't want him to be hungry. I don't want his little stomach to ache. But something deep inside tells me what I'm doing is wrong . . . nursing him is like abandoning my own baby in my heart. Something even deeper tells me it's perfectly all right. Oh, God, it feels so good. So absolutely right. Surely this can't be wrong."

"I hear you." A slow smile crept across Doris's face. Moments later she visibly relaxed and chuckled softly. "He understands, too. Look at that little face, Page. Adam knows. He knows exactly what you mean. Don't you, Adam?"

CHAPTER SIXTEEN

In the third week of November, Page received a letter from Yarbrough, Yarbrough, Tallant, and McCann. She rushed into the kitchen as she tore it open, excitedly telling Doris, "Maybe Lucien's changed his mind and he'll let Cindy come home."

"That's wonderful," Doris said.

Page's elation vanished when she read the first line. It was not a letter from Lucien at all. It was an eviction notice.

When J.L. and Miss Emma had married, J.L. had received Yarbrough Hall as a gift from his father, The Governor. Then, when the senator and Miss Emma moved into River Oaks after The Governor's death, they kept Yarbrough Hall vacant until Lucien and Page married. Page had expected to remain in Yarbrough Hall until she and Lucien and their children someday inherited River Oaks, where she presumed they'd all eventually grow old, die, and be buried. Until today. The senator had just given Page thirty days to vacate the premises. She wouldn't even be able to stay through Christmas.

Page crumpled the notice and threw it into the trash. "Dammit," she said.

"Cindy's not coming home after all?"

"There'll be no home to come to. The senator's throwing us out, and Lucien is letting him do it." She stormed out of the room.

"Where you going in such a fury?"

"To my lawyer's office." Page continued as she

marched down the hall, "If I knew where Lucien was, I'd tell him and his father both what jerks they are. Lucien's letting his father tell him what to do, and that makes him no better than the old man. I thought I was a better judge of character, but I'm obviously not. I can't believe I married that son of a bitch. Well, good riddance. Who needs him anyway? Who needs any of them?" To herself, she said, "Page Briggs Yarbrough, you get hold of yourself . . . you are out of control. You are a Southern lady, not some uncouth, foulmouthed piece of street trash."

Page forced herself to remain silent as she ascended the stairs, but her brow knotted into a terrible scowl. When she reached the top, she said, "You asshole! I'll show you!"

Early the next morning Page was awakened by the telephone.

"Mrs. Yarbrough?" asked a male voice.

Page's heart raced. "Yes?" It sounded like her private investigator. He'd found her son.

"My name is Victor Brandt, with the trust department of First Mississippi Bank and Trust Company. Is your husband in, please?"

"No, he isn't." Disappointed, Page sat up and flicked on the bedside lamp.

"I'm calling about the trust we're holding for your son, Mrs. Yarbrough. Jackson Adams Yarbrough the second."

Page didn't respond.

"Mr. Yarbrough had everything set up to be transferred into his name as trustee, but he never called back and I was wondering what happened."

"Excuse me?"

"I should've called sooner, but I've been away for a while. I was visiting my sister up in Baltimore, and I had a gallbladder attack. It turned out I had to have my whole gallbladder removed."

Page apologized for not being fully awake, and asked Mr. Brandt for the details. Not about his gallbladder, but about what Lucien had done. This time she made notes as he spoke.

"Our institution has held this trust since . . . oh, lordy now, I guess it's over sixty years. Here it is . . . 1931 is when Governor Jackson Yarbrough set it up. I need to have somebody sign these forms as trustee. It can be a parent . . . or a legal guardian, for that matter, but that wouldn't apply to you, since you are his parents. I should've sent them out as soon as Mr. Yarbrough called, but, being away, then with my gall-bladder and all, I didn't. Mainly I wanted to confirm your home address. Do you still live at Yarbrough Hall, 615 Serticoy Street?"

"Yes."

"Then I'll mail these out right away. You have a nice day now, you hear?"

Page said, "Mr. Brandt, it might speed things up if you address the envelope to my attention, Mrs. Page Yarbrough. I'll make sure they're taken care of."

Later that morning, Page faced her attorney in front of his cluttered desk. For anybody as un-busy as David Fields, his office was a disaster. There were even more stacks of paper and more open books than on her previous visits.

Page wore a green-plaid wool suit to ward off the morning's chill, and loafers. She'd already ruined two pairs of heels walking across the gravel parking lot.

Fields was saying, "Our chances of regaining custody of Cindy are better than of your staying at Yarbrough Hall. Considering who we're up against, neither looks very good. Real estate law is pretty cut and dried: Senator Yarbrough owns the property and you don't have a written lease, so your tenancy is month-to-month. You can refuse to leave, of course, and he'll be forced to physically evict you and your possessions. That would buy a little time, but he'll eventually get you out."

"I'm more concerned about Cindy, David. I don't care where I live as long as she's with me."

Fields removed his glasses and pinched the bridge of his nose. "You may not like what I'm about to say, Mrs. Yarbrough. . . ."

"Please call me Page. I'm not terribly fond of being a Yarbrough right now."

"I understand. The documents your husband had prepared indicate that he wanted control of the assets of the trust."

"Of course he did. He's talked about it since before we started trying to get pregnant."

"But he had the documents drawn up after he knew the baby was black. Is that correct?"

"No. Lucien called Mr. Brandt before the baby was born . . . he wanted to make sure they'd be ready. Mr. Brandt didn't draw them up until later."

"Why would Lucien do that?"

"He's desperate for money. I told you, he and his father are worried about an arrangement they had with Confederate and Southern Savings and Loan. Something went wrong with the deal."

"Do you know exactly what's held in trust?"

"Nobody's ever said. Jackson Adams Yarbrough— that's Lucien's grandfather—set up two trusts when he was the governor of Mississippi. Around 1930. He'd already given Yarbrough Hall and some other property to his son, Jackson Lucien Yarbrough, the senator. The first trust was to be held for his first grandson, who he said must be named Jackson Yarbrough. That's Lucien. He only tolerated the name Lucien because Lucien was Esmeralda's father's name. Esmeralda was The Governor's wife. The grandson had to be by blood."

"By blood?"

"That's what I was told. He insisted that his estate go only to direct descendants. Miss Emma said he was afraid his wife might outlive him and remarry, possibly have other children or marry somebody with children who could inherit his things. So Lucien, who is Jackson Lucien Yarbrough Junior, was the . . . what do you call it?"

"Beneficiary."

"Yes. There was mostly land in that first trust. Lucien got the property out next to the paper mill—it had cotton on it at one time—and about a thousand acres along Natchez Trace Parkway, plus some smaller parcels around town that have apartment buildings on them now. He sold some of those about five years ago, and put the rest up for collateral on a loan. That was when he went into that supermall shopping center they did in Jackson."

"The one that fell through."

"It eventually got done, but by somebody else. The men Lucien went in with stole most of the money and skipped out. He was left holding the bag. That's where the savings-and-loan people came into it. J.L. was a good friend of the chairman of the board."

Fields took notes as Page spoke. "What about the second trust?"

"Lucien never told me much about it. Just that it was set up for The Governor's first great-grandson, who had to be named Jackson Adams Yarbrough the second."

"By blood?"

"I guess so."

"It could be important. Do you know if the second trust specified that the great-grandson be by blood, not by marriage?"

"What are you getting at?"

"Your husband was awfully eager to be named trustee of that trust. When he filled out the birth certificate on the little black child, naming him Jackson Adams Yarbrough the second, that inadvertently fulfilled the second requirement of the trust. The first requirement, from what you tell me, is that the child be a boy, which he is."

"But he's not—"

"Hear me out. I'm not saying you'd want to pursue this, but as an attorney, I'm obliged to explain the possibility. Lucien may've created a very uncomfortable situation for himself . . . a loophole we might use as leverage to get Cindy back."

Page leaned back in the hard green chair and listened.

"Legally, you and Lucien were married at the time of the black baby's birth, as evidenced by your marriage certificate and your recent divorce verifying that the marriage had been valid. Since the birth certificate identifies you and Lucien as the parents, this baby is technically the great-grandson of Jackson Adams Yarbrough the first, The Governor."

"But he isn't."

"Not by blood. But we need to know what the trust documents specify."

Page crossed her legs. "I'd be uncomfortable trying to claim the trust, David. It isn't mine, and it certainly doesn't belong to the child."

Fields acted as if he hadn't heard. "Are there any other siblings?"

"Just Cindy."

"I mean does Lucien have brothers or sisters?"

"One sister. Suellen."

"Is she married?"

"Yes, to Bryan Whitford. He has the Cadillac dealership up on Broadway."

"Children?"

"Two daughters, Emma Sue and Betsy. They're five and nine. Girls seem to run in the Yarbrough family." She thought of Cindy someday being queen of the Confederate Pageant—if her chances weren't completely ruined.

Fields scribbled something on the yellow pad, then nodded. "A son of Suellen's would qualify, too, if she named him Jackson Adams Yarbrough the second."

"Could she do that after Lucien already used that name on a birth certificate?"

"You can name your own baby anything you want."

Page was getting restless. She needed to find a ladies' room, wherever it was. "Well, it's a moot point, David. The baby isn't my child and I won't say he is, trust or not. In fact, I wrote for that form to remove the Yarbrough name from his birth certificate, but now I don't care if it stays on or not. Quite frankly, it'd serve Lucien right. Just concentrate on trying to get Cindy back. I have to go. I need to find a job and a place to live." She stood and extended her hand to him. "I'll pay you as soon as I have a job. I promise."

"I know you will."

"You're awfully kind to help me, David, even though you're not making very much from it."

He shrugged and smiled. "Having something to do keeps me on my toes. Besides, it isn't like I'm turning clients away. How many times have you had to wait to get an appointment with me?"

What he said was true. She'd never seen anybody else in his office. "You're an unusual lawyer. Tell your wife I think she's a very lucky woman to have you. You're a gentleman."

"She may not always agree, but I'll tell her." He paused. "Anything encouraging from your investigator?"

"No. And he's not able to put in the time I want him to. I . . . don't have the money to pay him."

"I could loan you some."

His offer warmed her heart, but it wouldn't be right. "I can't let you do that," she said, "but thank you. I'll sell some things to keep him searching as long as I can. Maybe hire somebody else. He's about ready to give up anyway . . . he hasn't found a single lead."

Fields accompanied Page to the office door. As she walked away he said, "Don't do anything about that birth certificate just yet, and don't tell anybody. It still might help us negotiate with Lucien."

"I don't know who I'd tell, David. Nobody in this town talks to me anymore."

"Well, in case anybody does." He smiled warmly. "Let it be our little secret. Okay?"

CHAPTER SEVENTEEN

Page's father called while she and Doris were in the midst of packing dishes into moving boxes. Page had just wrapped the first of two deviled-egg plates in heavy paper. When her father asked what she was doing, she told him. He'd find out soon enough anyway. She had less than a week to get out, and confided this to her father.

"Where will you go?"

"I don't know yet, Daddy. Every place I look at seems to suddenly get rented . . . the ones I think I can afford. I've even called friends with guesthouses. Two have already been rented and the others never even called back."

"Why is that?"

"Well, I'm not looking just for me. I won't go anywhere without Doris. And you know she has the baby now, so there's three of us." It was left unsaid that, even in the twenty-first century, racial prejudice existed in Natchez, just as it did nearly everywhere in the world. With all the publicity Page and the baby had received, people were not exactly clamoring to have her live with them.

"Have you considered taking two separate places? One for you, another for Doris and the child?"

"Can't afford it. Frankly, I don't know how long I can pay for one place. I haven't found a job yet, either."

"You can stay here until you find something, but I only have an efficiency. I'll stay with Harry for a while. Of course, there's no way three people can sleep on a sofa bed, even if one is a baby. What are you going to do about him?"

"Doris has checked with everybody she knows, and nobody claims him. So we'll keep him until I find my baby. Doris sure loves him, and I can't blame her—he's adorable. If we don't find his real mother, Doris might just raise him as her own."

"I received two hundred dollars from a new subscriber this week. I'll be glad to bring it—"

"Thanks, Daddy, but you keep it. I sold my jewelry and some of my clothes to a resale shop. I didn't need them anyway. And don't worry about the apartment. We'll be okay as soon as I find a job."

"What type work will you do?"

Page laughed. "Well, let's see . . . what are my qualifications? I'm great at giving dinner parties and I can organize a buffet luncheon for a bridge club in a matter of minutes. I write creative invitations and thank-you notes, and I was terrific at arranging flowers and rushing girls for Chi-O in college. I can solicit homes to put on the tour for Pilgrimage, hang drapes and curtains, I know how to edit a cookbook, I wallpapered my own room once in high school, which I'm sure you'd rather forget, and I'm a great mother for the daughter I don't have." She broke down for an instant but caught herself. "Oh, and I almost forgot . . . I can also clean house, plant a flower or vegetable garden, and polish silver." She paused. "Sorry, Daddy, you taught me better than that."

"You're an intelligent, capable young woman, daughter. With your talents, you could run Delta Air Lines. And, as you did as a child, you'll come through this time unscathed and very likely improved. Remember, every adversity carries its own seed of equivalent or greater benefit . . . but you must look for it. Napoleon Hill said that in 1936, and he learned it from billionaire Andrew Carnegie. It's equally true today." Dr. Briggs coughed. "Excuse me. Try and find something soon. It'd be nice if you were settled in before

Christmas. Shall I reschedule the blood tests for January?"

"That'll be great, Daddy. Thank you."

When she hung up, Page heard additional words of reassurance, this time from Doris.

"We're gonna be just fine, Page. You'll see. We just have to cope, that's all. You and me and Adam . . . we'll just have to cope."

Page spent a wonderful four hours with Cindy at River Oaks Plantation after lunch, even though Lucien's mother remained closer than was comfortable. Miss Emma hovered like a hummingbird working a trumpet vine.

Page certainly didn't appreciate not being believed. However, she could understand Miss Emma's conviction that Page had gone to bed with a black man. The presence of the black baby and supporting DNA tests were proof enough. Her baby boy—her Lucien—had been wronged by a woman, and Emma was angry. Nothing Page could say or do would change that. Despite her memory of Miss Emma hauling Cindy away, Page knew the two of them would have to be civil in the future, for Cindy's sake.

On her way out, Page tried once again to convey her feelings to her mother-in-law. "I understand how you feel, Mama Yarbrough, but no matter how it appears, I never once cheated on Lucien."

Miss Emma angled her head back to study Page, one hand on the door. "The next thing you'll ask me to believe is that you're actually a virgin, Page. And that Negro child of yours is the new Messiah. Really, my dear . . . you insult my intelligence." She closed and locked the door behind Page.

After leaving River Oaks, Page went on interviews for two more jobs she'd found listed in the classified section of the morning newspaper. The first was for a receptionist in a law firm on Commerce Street. She'd purposely not given her last name when she scheduled the appointment, for fear an attorney might be reluctant to hire Lucien's ex-wife. She was right. The attorney didn't come right out and laugh, but might as well have. His expression said it all. And they had somehow miraculously filled the position in the short time since Page had called.

The other job was for a receptionist in a doctor's office. Though it hadn't been specified in the paper, the physician was an obstetrician and gynecologist. At least the doctor was more honest than the attorney, which, Page concluded, was no big task. The doctor was quite young, but attempted to conduct himself like a wise old man. He reminded Page of overly dramatic little boys in the pageant.

The doctor said, "I'm just building my practice, Mrs. Yarbrough, and I deliver babies. Quite frankly, with all the notoriety you and your Negro baby received, I'd be afraid to have patients know you work here. If you try to sue me for discrimination of some sort, I'll deny I ever said that . . . but that's the way it is. Frankly, I'll be amazed if there's a doctor in town who'll hire you."

In the kitchen that evening, Page nursed Jackson Adams Yarbrough II while Doris fixed dinner.

"Ooooee!" Doris said as chicken sizzled in an iron skillet nearby. "That's a sight I never thought I would see."

"What is?"

"A black baby sucking at a white titty."

"Don't you ever tell anybody. You haven't, have you?"

"Haven't said a word. Used to be it was t'other way around."

"What do you mean?"

"White babies have nursed black titties lotsa times. I've known one or two myself. Mostly it was when my mama was growing up and even before, when blacks were slaves. If a mammy had milk from her own baby, she'd give some to the white child too, whenever it got hungry. Children don't care. All milk is white . . . it all tastes the same when a baby's hungry."

Page thought back to the first night she'd nursed Adam. In all her years with Doris, that was the only time they'd fought. She also thought of when Doris used to carry Laura on one hip and William on the other. They were the same age, and Page remembered watching Doris nurse William. She asked, "Did you ever nurse Laura?"

Doris smiled and sort of shrugged. "I don't rightly remember."

Page knew full well that whenever Doris used that "don't rightly remember" phrase, she was capitalizing on people's stereotyped impressions of poor, ignorant blacks to avoid giving an answer. "Aunt Jemima-ing," Doris called it. Page didn't press the issue. Doris's expression was answer enough.

Stepping back when the sizzling grease popped out at her, Doris nodded toward Adam. "You think that baby cares if your titty is white?"

"I'm sure he doesn't know the difference."

Doris checked the biscuits in the oven. "World would be better off if nobody did. People sure do make it out to be some big difference." She turned off the gas burner underneath the skillet. "How many pieces you want, Page?"

Page watched the baby nurse, a little brown hand wrapped around her finger, his face against her snowy white breast. "Just one . . . I'm not very hungry. Save the rest for lunch tomorrow."

Page awoke with a start the following Thursday morning. Somebody was ringing her doorbell. She stumbled out of bed and parted the drapes enough to see out the window. A sheriff's cruiser was in her driveway. She grabbed a robe and slippers and went downstairs. It was six a.m. and freezing cold inside the house.

When she opened the door, a deputy handed her a sheaf of papers.

"Sorry to wake you, ma'am, but it's the twenty-third of December. According to these documents, you were to vacate this house yesterday." His breath steamed when he spoke, quickly carried away by a gusty wind.

"I've tried to leave, Officer, but can't find a place to go. There's either nothing available or whatever there is, I can't afford. With Christmas around the corner, I'm gonna need a few extra days." Page pulled her robe tighter around her, then folded her arms across her chest. Her teeth began to chatter. David Fields had told Page she had no grounds for staying beyond the twenty-second. She knew she had exhausted her legal delays. But, considering the time of year, maybe the deputy would understand.

"Sorry, ma'am, you're already past the deadline. You'll have to be out today."

"I don't have anyplace to go. And there's my housekeeper and a baby. You can't just throw us out in the street." Maybe the deputy had a family. A child. It was almost Christmas.

"We don't have any choice, ma'am. It's the law, and the property owner wants you out. If you're not gone by noon, we'll be forced to evict you and your belongings." He repeated, "It's the law." Exhibiting no readable expression, he added, "We can keep your personal possessions in county storage, but that'll be at your expense. I'd suggest you pack up and leave of your own free will." He tipped his hat. "Merry Christmas, ma'am. I'll be back at noon."

When the deputy left, Page raced to the telephone and dialed River Oaks Plantation. Lucien's father answered the phone. She told him about the deputy, and said she hadn't found a place to move. She'd need a couple of weeks more.

"Sorry you're having a difficult time, Page," the senator replied, "but it's out of my hands. Emma already contracted a decorator, and they'll be in there first thing tomorrow to remove everything from the house and put it in storage. They'll be repainting, changing the carpets, putting in a new heating system. Nobody can live there while they're doing all that."

"Can't it wait till after the holidays?"

"She's using the Speriagowski brothers, and you know how tough it is to get on their schedule. This was the only time they had." After a short pause, he said, "You were given plenty of notice."

Page gripped the receiver so tightly one of her fingers popped. "Give me a little consideration, Senator. This is not some stranger you're talking to. This is Page Yarbrough . . . part of the family."

"Oh, no," J.L. adamantly replied. "No, Page, you got that wrong. I thought you were part of our family, but you proved me wrong. Anybody who'd do what you did never has been and never will be part of my family."

"Senator, I didn't do anything. Won't you at least—"

He cut her off. "You are not a Yarbrough. Yarbroughs don't sleep with niggers." He slammed the receiver down.

Sputtering expletives under her breath, Page hurried into the garden house to nurse the baby. If she showered and dressed quickly, perhaps she could finalize a lease before noon on the last place she'd seen. It was in a terrible neighborhood, but at least the landlord hadn't objected to taking the three of them. It beat sleeping in the car. A cold front had moved in two nights earlier—nothing could chill bones faster than a wintry wind off the Mississippi. She asked Doris to pack up the essentials and put them in the Suburban.

Back upstairs, a car horn sounded outside before Page finished getting dressed. Then the doorbell rang and rang and rang. She yanked back a curtain to look out, certain the sheriff had returned.

Page froze in position when she looked. A blue pickup was parked near the front steps. Somebody in the truck blew the horn again. She raced for the stairs, adrenaline surging. What a terrible time for another visit from the Klan.

When Page opened the door, Mark Goodson stood grinning at her, snug and toasty in a fleece-lined denim jacket, jeans, and boots.

"You'd wake the dead," Page said, relieved, "with all that racket."

"We thought you'd be up early. Especially today."

"Why today?"

"It's moving day." He winked. "We're here to help."

Page heard a truck door slam. Belle Braswell came around the front of the pickup, a cane lending support to her bad leg. Belle wore a black wool overcoat, fur hat, and leather gloves.

"Auntie Bellum. What're you doing here?"

"You're too proud to come to me, so I came to you. Go inside and finish your makeup and fix your hair. There's a gentleman present."

Goodson said, "I talked to your father yesterday. Actually I drove him home. He told me you needed a place to live. I offered my place, but Auntie Bellum said that wouldn't be proper."

"It not only isn't proper, it's downright sinful." The seventy-five-year-old woman winked. "Or it would be if it was me staying with such a good-looking young fella." With Goodson's help, Belle made it up the last step onto the porch, short of breath.

Page said, "You're awfully kind, but I couldn't impose like that. Besides, I think I found a place."

"Where?"

"Over on Martin Luther King Boulevard. One side of a duplex."

"Have you paid the rent yet?"

"I was just going over to make sure it's still available."

"I won't hear of it," Belle said. "For years people have been saying I must be crazy to live in that huge house by myself, and they're right. I was. But I've come to my senses, so don't argue with a sane old woman. Go fix yourself while we pack the truck. Where's Doris?"

"Out back. She'll be along shortly. I'm sure she heard you."

"I fixed up the cookhouse for her and the baby. You'll stay in the big house with me."

"Only if you let me pay something. I can give you what I was going to pay for the duplex. Is that all right?"

"Don't be tacky, Page. We'll not discuss money in public. Now, scoot. Go get ready."

Page didn't know whether to laugh or cry, so she did a little of both while hugging and thanking these two incredible people.

Mark Goodson picked up a carton marked Dishes. "Okay if I put this on the truck?"

"Yes, Mark, it certainly is. And God bless you both. I don't know what I would've done without you."

Page turned to see Doris racing around the side of the house, the baby in her arms.

"Look, Doris, it's Dr. Goodson and Auntie Bellum. We have a place to live."

By the time they loaded the Suburban, Page barely had room for Doris and the baby. Things were stacked well above the roof level of Goodson's pickup's cab. He pulled out of the driveway and disappeared down the street with Auntie Bellum at his side—no doubt giving unnecessary directions.

Page chewed at a remnant of the last fingernail she'd saved during the packing, then sighed. That particular problem would have to wait. "Almost everything in the house belonged to the senator," she said, "and we still look like *The Beverly Hillbillies*."

"Sure do," Doris said, laughing. "Especially Auntie Bellum . . . she looks like that grandma woman on TV."

As they started out the driveway, a constable's car pulled in, blocking their exit.

Page rolled down her window. "We're leaving, Officer."

A man wearing a leather jacket, khaki pants, and

Western boots swaggered up to Page's window. He leaned an arm against the car and peered inside, flashing a toothy smile. "Are you Page Briggs Yarbrough?"

"Yes."

"I have some papers for you, ma'am." He handed her a stack of documents and walked away.

Reading what she'd received, Page said, "Damn!" She scanned several pages, then said, "Merry Christmas to you, too."

"What now?" asked Doris.

"Those creeps are suing me because those other people are suing them."

"Say what?"

"Lucien and his father. They've sued me because the hospital and Dr. Benning and the Dunbars are suing them. According to this, I caused the whole problem, so I'm solely responsible for any monetary damages. Those no-good sons of . . . excuse me, Doris; I'm trying to remember that I'm a lady."

Page tossed the papers on top of a cardboard box and drove off, the Suburban lurching and bellowing blue smoke from its exhaust. In her current financial situation, a tune-up was out of the question.

CHAPTER EIGHTEEN

David and Sarah Fields drove to Belle Braswell's Willowdale Plantation for lunch on Christmas Eve. David told Page his office was closed for the holidays, though he doubted if anybody would notice. Said that while they didn't celebrate Christmas from a religious point of view, he and Sarah very much enjoyed the festive season.

Of the original thousand acres, Belle still owned twenty-five acres surrounding her 1823 Southern planter's residence. The beautiful Federal mansion, heirloom furnishings, and manicured gardens kept tourists returning time and again. That and Belle's stories. Page's favorite part of the property was the family cemetery that dated back to 1840, when Belle's great-grandfather purchased Willowdale as a wedding present for his daughter and her husband. Unlike the homes that were open only during Pilgrimage months, Belle kept Willowdale open year-round.

While Belle took Sarah Fields on an extended tour, Page and David talked in the parlor. They sat on a blue velvet sofa with antique lace on the back and arms hiding most of the places that had worn through. Page had helped Belle string lights and ornaments on an aromatic cedar tree the night before. An ornately carved breakfront in one corner contained museum-quality pieces of silver, and fine china hand-painted by John J. Audubon. The walls were Dresden blue, hung with portraits of long-gone ancestors. A fire crackling in the fireplace gave off scents of oak and pine. Red flannel stockings hung from the mantel, one each for Belle, Page, Doris, and Adam. There was even one for Mark Goodson, who considered Belle's place his second home.

Page asked David about his personal life. He confessed that he was writing a book on tax law for the layman. Between the government and attorneys making things so complicated, he said, almost nobody understood how to take their rightful deductions. Trained as a CPA and tax attorney, David hoped to explain the law in simple, understandable terms. Having such a small practice had turned out to be a blessing in disguise, giving him time to research and write his book. His wife's interests included gardening, antiques, and American history, particularly the Civil War period, which was the primary reason they'd settled in Natchez.

When Belle and Sarah rejoined them, Belle inquired about David's upbringing. He said he was born in Baton Rouge, Louisiana, but when he was two months old, his parents moved to Philadelphia, then to Long Island. To Belle, where you were from meant where you were born. You might've lived in Natchez for fifty years, but if you were born in Meridien, then Meridien was where you were from. To her, Fields would forever be from Baton Rouge.

David's father had been a successful pharmacist with the Rexall chain, steadily ascending the corporate ladder. He had eventually taken an interest in politics, but only as a supporter of men with vision whose actions he approved. David's mother was a Southern girl who never got over leaving her home. She'd spent hours telling David and his sister, Rose, about life in the South, and about the magnificent homes along the Mississippi River. Her dream was to return to Louisiana or Mississippi, buy an antebellum river home, and restore it to its former grandeur. Breast cancer prevented his mother's realizing her dream, but not the dream itself. David's father had long since retired and sold enough stock to travel the world quite comfortably, but enough remained for the family to live in whatever style they desired for about a thousand years. David and Sarah had purchased a grand home on a hundred acres overlooking the Mississippi, and restored it with great care.

When Page asked why David chose the office he did, he said a former professor had explained that clients resent a show of wealth when you're young, while they expect it as you grow older. So David spent his money on his home, where he and his wife could enjoy it together.

David and Sarah Fields had never opened their home to tours or as part of the Pilgrimage for two reasons. First, they treasured their privacy and preferred small, intimate gatherings of friends. Second, nobody from the community had ever asked.

When Page finally brought up business, David reviewed the summons and complaint she'd received. "This is a tactical maneuver, Page. Probably because we asked to have Cindy's custody reviewed."

"They know I don't have any money. I could never pay those people anything."

Fields idly tugged at his lower lip, thinking. "Do you have any significant assets?"

"My Suburban. I'm surprised Lucien hadn't borrowed against that, too, but he hadn't. It's on its last legs, but it's the only thing in my name."

"No bank accounts, stocks, bonds, insurance policies with cash value?"

"I'm destitute, David. Lucien kept everything in his name. Whenever I needed money to run the house, I wrote checks. He canceled our credit cards and charge accounts right after he moved out."

"Jewelry? Diamond ring, expensive watch, earrings?"

"Gone. I needed money for Cindy's dance lessons and charm school."

"Then we should file chapter seven, but let's wait till they start to pressure you. Maybe let them get a judgment or two."

"What's chapter seven?"

"Bankruptcy. You have no assets and no possible means of paying a large judgment. Bankruptcy wipes out existing debts and claims against you, including these lawsuits, so you start fresh. Whatever you earn from this point forward is yours. Nobody can come back later and make a claim on anything you make after you file. So when you get a job, you keep whatever you earn."

"How humiliating," Page said. "I've never known anybody who declared bankruptcy."

"You probably know several people—some pretty prominent. They just don't talk about it. I'll bet Lucien considered the possibility when that shopping center failed. Are you likely to inherit any substantial sums in the near future, or does anybody owe you money?"

"My father's the only family I have, besides Cindy and my sister. He probably has less than I do."

"Isn't he a doctor?"

"He was. Now he researches articles for other doctors . . . he barely earns a living. Plus he drinks. A lot."

"Why?"

Page let out a long breath. "He was a very good doctor once. A surgeon, trained at Harvard and Johns Hopkins. He loved history and he loved stories about the old South, so he finished his residency down here, fell madly in love with my mom, and they got married. She was Aunt Belle's younger sister."

Fields didn't speak, but his expression asked for more.

"Anyway, they had me. Then almost five years later they had my sister, Laura. A couple of years after that, my mother died."

"She must've been very young."

"Twenty-nine. Daddy was several years older than she."

"What happened?"

"They'd wanted another child and she got pregnant,

but it settled in one of her tubes. . . . Daddy called it an ectopic pregnancy."

"I've heard of that."

"As the pregnancy grew, it caused the tube to rupture, and Mother went into shock. I guess she lost a tremendous amount of blood."

"I know of a case where they went in and stopped the bleeding."

"There was a big surgery convention in New Orleans at the time, and my father was the only surgeon left in town."

"You're not serious. Did he operate on her?"

"There wasn't time to get anybody else . . . she was hemorrhaging badly." Page shook her head. "She died on the operating table."

"I'm so sorry."

A long silence was punctuated by the ticking of a wall clock. Finally Page said, "That's why Daddy drinks. He's a brilliant man, but he never practiced after that night."

"So you grew up without a mother."

"Daddy was mother and father to Laura and me. He was wonderful, and he didn't drink then. He used up his inheritance doing it, but he saw to it that we learned everything Mother had wanted us to—dancing, singing, piano. He sent me to charm school, and made sure I knew how to set a table, serve tea, arrange flowers. I became the lady of the house for him. Looking back, he probably hated doing it, but he entertained fairly often just to be certain Laura and I learned our social graces. I'll never forget the time I did my first pink tea."

"Your what?"

Page laughed. "It's a tea where everything is pink. An old Southern tradition. Well, the tea itself doesn't have to be pink, but everything else is. The flowers are pink, the tablecloths, napkins, the plates and cups and saucers, the hostess's dress, her shoes, sometimes her hair. Even the butter mints and petit fours are pink."

"Why?"

"David, anybody can have a plain old tea. It's fun to do something different . . . have a theme."

"If you say so."

"Anyway, Daddy did the things our mother would have done. Before he sent us off to college, he rehearsed us for marriage. That's really what it was all about. If I hadn't known how to do those things, Lucien wouldn't have looked at me twice." She reconsidered. "Well, that isn't quite true. He would've asked me out because he always thought I was pretty, but he wouldn't have married me. His mother would never have allowed it."

"You never considered a career?"

"Being a wife and mother was my career. The only one I ever considered."

Later David asked how those huge round front-porch columns were made.

"That's why plantations had ponds," Belle said. "They took mud from the pond bottom and packed it into pie-shaped molds along with horsehair, straw, or grass to bind it together, then baked them in a big oven. The pie-shaped bricks were arranged in a circle, one layer on top of the other, till they had a column. Then they painted them white."

"Wow," David said. "I want to see that done."

"Why are you so interested in columns?" asked Page.

"Why not?" David responded.

Sarah laughed. "He has a voracious appetite for knowledge. Wants to know everything, whether it's useful or not. Don't you, dear?"

Late that afternoon, Page bundled up in a jacket, jeans, and a sweater and walked outside for some air. Passing beneath a row of giant live oaks, she walked around the pond where Belle's mother had buried silver and china in burlap bags during the War of Northern Aggression, as Belle called it.

The crisp air was absolutely marvelous. It was one

of those days that made her glad to be alive. That thought surprised Page. She was no longer married to an extremely successful man. No longer part of the most prominent family in town, perhaps in the state. No longer able to call one of the finest Greek Revival houses in the entire South her home. She was devastated that she hadn't found her son and couldn't be with her beloved Cindy. But somehow, in spite of her heavy heart, she was glad to be alive. She couldn't explain why, but she was. Survival instinct, she guessed.

She walked, and she thought. Despite all evidence to the contrary, something deep inside gave Page hope that she'd find her son somehow, someday. And she would get Cindy back. Strangely, she credited Lucien with giving her the will to go on. Precisely because he'd turned out to be such a jerk, Page had learned to use her anger to force herself out of bed each morning. Thinking of Lucien made her angry right now, but also made her heart sad. She hated to admit it, but despite everything he'd done—and she did not want him back—she missed him.

"Belle said I'd find you at the cemetery."

Startled, Page turned to see Mark Goodson approaching. "I was hardly aware of where I was," she said.

They meandered through the old cemetery, making small talk while reading names and dates from headstones of Belle's ancestors.

After a while Page said, "You've never asked me about the baby, Mark. Why?"

"Your father told me you're still looking for your son. That the black baby isn't yours."

"You're satisfied with that?"

"He said that's what you told him. I've never known him to lie." Mark chuckled. "Drink a little too much, yes . . . but not lie."

"So you believe me?"

"Remember that time I got thrown out of high school?"

"When you were trying to be James Dean and the Fonz rolled into one?"

"I suppose." He nodded, remembering. "Actually, my folks had divorced. My dad got drunk and beat me up a lot because I reminded him of my mother. My mom stayed half-zonked on sleeping pills and tranquilizers till she finally just up and left one day. I didn't handle it very well."

"Such as when you drove your father's car through the side of the gymnasium?"

"I was drunk."

"I heard. Everybody in school heard."

"My dad almost killed me."

"Is that why you ran away?"

"Mostly I was embarrassed at the way he carried on."

"But you came back."

"Thanks to you."

Page stopped walking. "You never told me that. What did I do?"

"You don't remember?"

"Are you talking about when I ran into you down at the river?"

"Yes. Remember what you said?"

Page ran her fingers lightly across a moss-covered headstone. A weeping willow frond tickled her cheek. "I said I thought you were capable of so much more."

Goodson stood looking at Page, studying her face. "Before that. Don't you remember the coach accusing me of stealing money? From Jimmy Green's locker?"

"I'd forgotten that."

"Nobody believed me when I said I hadn't done it. Especially my father. That's why I got drunk in the first place."

"That had completely slipped my mind."

"That day by the river I asked why you never brought it up about me stealing the money. You just looked at me and replied, 'Because you said you didn't do it.' That's all. You didn't bug me about it. No third degree. You just believed me." He shook his head. "You were the only one who did."

"Did they ever find out who took it?"

"Yeah, nobody. Brian Garfield found it stuffed inside his track shoes about a week later. Jimmy had used Brian's locker that day, then forgot it."

"I also said I thought you were smart. You were. You were great at figuring things out in math and in science class."

"Nobody had believed in me in a long time, Page. I needed that. I never actually thanked you before, but if it hadn't been for you, and then my uncle's taking me in hand, I'd probably be dead by now."

"I doubt that."

"I was headed full-speed down a real steep road that wasn't going anywhere good."

They walked through the crooked gate of an iron fence surrounding the cemetery, then started back toward the main house.

"For what it's worth," Page said, "I've never been with another man since I fell in love with Lucien, so that child cannot be mine . . . no matter what those DNA tests said. I don't know how, but I intend to prove that if it takes the rest of my life."

"Can I do anything to help?"

"Daddy arranged for us to be retested at a lab in Baton Rouge. I've had to cancel three times because of court dates and then moving, but we're going over the first week in January. I'd rather nobody knows about it, but I'm sure we'll get an honest report this time."

"You think somebody got the lab to falsify the first results?"

Page didn't answer. She looked at Mark knowingly. "Who?"

"At first I thought it might be some white-supremacist group, or even the Ku Klux Klan. But now I don't think so. I think maybe somebody wanted to split Lucien and me up. I don't know why, but his father sure jumped into the middle of things and took

over mighty fast. That's the senator's personality, but
he's been superintense about this. Downright rigid. I
haven't understood Lucien's reactions since the results
came back. I mean, he never even listened to me after
that day in court, no matter what I tried to say, and
that isn't the Lucien I knew. He flat made his mind
up then and there, and that was that. Or somebody
made it up for him."

"The male ego can be pretty fragile sometimes."

"Maybe. Or maybe the senator felt Lucien couldn't
risk the scandal politically, so he distanced the whole
family from me as quickly as possible. Including my
daughter. There has to be more to it than I'm seeing.
I keep wondering why anybody would want to split
us up. I don't know who would do it, and I can't
imagine why . . . but if that was the reason, it worked
like a charm. One day I'm happily married with the
ideal husband and perfect family, then poof . . . it all
disappears and I'm helpless to stop it."

After saying her prayers that evening, Page lay in
the dark, staring up toward her bedroom ceiling. Her
thoughts drifted to Mark Goodson, what they'd discussed about growing up, and how helpful he had been
recently. Mark was a good man. Tall and rangy, he
was handsome too, considered dashing and gallant by
the women in town. A fine catch. And she thought
of Lucien—stubborn, pigheaded, refusing to hear her
account of what she had not done. A tear trickled
down her cheek and into one ear.

"Damn you, Lucien."

CHAPTER NINETEEN

Page drove to Baton Rouge the Wednesday after New Year's with Doris and the baby beside her.

Doris said, "Why wouldn't they let you bring Cindy home for a little while? On Christmas Day? Page, that's not right."

"At least I got to see her. The first time I asked, Miss Emma wanted me just to talk to her on the phone. Told me to drop her presents off at the law office."

"I know how bad it pains you, but it isn't good for Cindy either. That girl needs her mama around . . . I don't care what anybody says."

Once they found the lab, the samples were drawn in a matter of minutes, amidst the baby's shrill protests. Page was a little quieter about it. Very little.

"How soon can I have the results?" Page asked as they were leaving.

"Monday," the technician replied. "Call us around noon."

Aware that the tests could be done within three days, she started to object, but didn't. A sign in the window indicated they were closed on Saturdays. She didn't have the clout of Lucien or the senator to make them stay open just for her. Not anymore. She didn't even use the Yarbrough name. She had signed in as Page Ann Briggs—her maiden name. The only Yarbrough being tested that day was Jackson Adams Yarbrough II. Page had grinned as she signed him in. She'd taken her attorney's advice and never filled out the forms to change Adam's name. She enjoyed knowing that Lucien had probably forgotten all about putting that name on the baby's birth certificate. She chuckled every time she thought about it. J.L. and Miss Emma would just die if they knew. When the time was right, she'd make certain they found out—in a very public place.

At noon the next day, Page went on an interview for the first job she felt confident she could do. The Natchez Oaks Hotel needed someone to handle public relations, plus help with advertising and marketing.

During the interview, Page excitedly told the hotel manager, "This is exactly what I've done for the past ten years. First for the Junior League, then for the Confederate Garden Club and the Pilgrimage tours. Our organizations brought close to seventy million dollars into Natchez last year."

The manager wore a dark suit, a narrow tie, and an almost undetectable hairpiece. Mr. Webber. Page had dealt with him on numerous occasions, organizing luncheons, bridal showers, and awards banquets for the garden club. He was well aware of her ability to organize and work with others, and her attention to detail.

"You'll be perfect," he told her. "You're exactly what we've needed. When can you start?"

"How soon do you need me?"

"Tomorrow, if possible. Nine a.m.?"

"I'll be here."

Page was so thrilled, she could hardly keep from jumping in the air and twirling about the room. She started for the door to leave.

Webber said, "Don't you want to know what you'll be making?"

"Oh, that's right . . . I didn't want to mention it, since you appear to be a very fair person. I'm confident the salary is commensurate with the responsibility of the position." She smiled broadly. "But since you brought it up, what does it pay?"

There was no way Page could go straight back to Willowdale. She wanted to share her wonderful news with a friend, do something fun, go shopping or to lunch. She glanced at a clock in the grand lobby of the hotel. Twelve forty-five. She'd been too nervous to eat before her job interview, but now that it was over and she'd been hired, she was starving. She'd prefer to have a companion for lunch, but Rona Green and Suellen were both tied up today, and Auntie Bellum hated going out for lunch.

Page knew that the hotel dining room was lovely, and she'd be comfortable dining alone there. Plus they made chicken salad almost as good as her own. They'd even slice the crusts off the bread for you. What the heck—it had been way too long since she'd had anything to celebrate, and she felt absolutely marvelous. She freshened up in the ladies' room, then walked past the more casual Mimosa restaurant and into Café La Sere. This elegant restaurant was known for its fine continental cuisine—which, of course, included chicken salad with homemade mayonnaise.

The maitre d' bowed slightly and smiled. "How nice to see you, Mrs. Yarbrough. Are you having lunch with us?"

"Yes, Armand. Something by a window, please."

They made their way across the crowded dining room beneath crystal chandeliers, past tables set with pink tablecloths and fine china. The room was filled with fresh flowers and Chippendale chairs. Page saw many familiar faces. Women from rival garden clubs filled two tables of eight, at opposite ends of the room. They stopped their conversations to watch her walk by. Most of the women in those clubs were near Miss Emma's age. Page smiled at several friends along the way, mostly in groups of three or four. One girl smiled back. The others averted their eyes the instant they recognized her, suddenly becoming engrossed in all-consuming conversations.

Directly in the path between Page and the window, Mary Lou Snodgrass looked up and waved—a sort of halfhearted, *almost*-wave. Mary Lou sat with two women from the Confederate Garden Club, of which

Page was still the official president, despite the letter she had received—the one suggesting so graciously that she not show up at future meetings. Page stopped, eager to share the good news about her job.

"Why, Page," Mary Lou said, "how nice to see you. I love your hair that way . . . you look marvelous. Doesn't she look marvelous, girls?"

The other two women agreed that Page looked absolutely radiant. "We heard about your divorce. What are you doing now?"

Page could hardly wait to reply. "I just took a position here at the hotel, starting tomorrow as the new public-relations director, so I came in to celebrate and have lunch." She glanced at the empty chair beside Mary Lou.

One of the women touched the chair and said, "Why, that's wonderful. We'd invite you to join us, except we're expecting somebody any minute."

Another woman checked a wristwatch that hadn't kept time in months, then said, "Patty Fulton. She should've been here before now."

"I don't know where she can be," Mary Lou said. "You probably have somebody joining you anyway, right? I mean, who goes to lunch alone? But it's good to see you, Page. Keep your hair that way. It's really flattering."

What Page felt from their rejection was somewhere between anger and agony. Disappointment, perhaps, and a sense of being truly alone. Turning away, she spotted two other women she'd known for years, at a nearby table for four. Though they didn't acknowledge her, one woman pointedly picked her pocketbook off the floor and placed it on one empty chair while the second woman followed suit with the other. Their conversation became more animated as they pretended not to watch Page make her way to the empty table by the window, overlooking a small garden outside.

Page took her seat, thanked Armand, and removed a paperback novel from her own pocketbook. Rather than allow the hurt she experienced to ruin her glorious day, she'd simply read while she ate, a chicken-salad sandwich on white bread—crusts cut off, of course, and no sprouts. She'd sit there as dignified as any woman in the room, pretending not to notice her former friends, who were pretending not to notice her.

After lunch, Page stopped at the Toddler Shop on Main. She paused outside the display window, admiring assorted baby clothes as she had so many times in recent weeks. Inside she found the perfect outfit for Adam: adorable yellow overalls with matching shoes and cap, and a white long-sleeved cotton shirt. It cost more than she should've spent, but what the heck—she was employed now.

On an impulse, she bought a second outfit, for *her* son: a blue jumpsuit with leather athletic shoes about the size of her thumb. Uncertain of his current height or weight, she bought one size larger for him.

At eight-thirty the next morning, Page wheeled her wheezing Suburban into the employee parking lot of the Natchez Oaks Hotel, jumped out, and raced inside. Too excited to sleep, she had stayed up till two a.m. jotting down promotional ideas and PR campaigns she knew would work for the hotel. Her pocketbook contained a list of contacts she could count on in other states to assist her efforts. She'd get their e-mail addresses first thing. She hurried into and through the lobby, an irrepressible smile on her face, cheerfully greeting everybody she saw. As soon as work was over today, she intended to treat herself to a manicure—her first in weeks.

As she floated down the hall toward her new office, the manager came around the corner unexpectedly.

"Good morning, Mr. Webber," Page sang. "Isn't it a glorious day?"

"Uh, yes, it is. Ms. Briggs . . . or Mrs. Yarbrough. I'm afraid I need to speak with you immediately. I have some bad news."

"Sure." Her office was probably being repainted or carpeted, or maybe her secretary would be a few minutes late. So? She could handle that. It was still a beautiful day.

"To put it bluntly, we're going to have to let you go."

"Excuse me?"

"From your job. We won't be needing your services after all."

"But . . . why?"

"Actually, we're not letting you go. We never hired you. Not really."

Page's heart sank right down to her navy pumps. "I don't understand. What did I do?"

"You didn't do anything. I mean, not here."

"Then why would you let me go? I'll be great for the hotel."

"I am sorry."

Page fumbled to retrieve the contact list from her pocketbook. "Look . . . you just hired me yesterday. You said you needed me to start as soon as possible. I'm ready to begin, and I have some very creative ideas—"

The hotel manager interrupted. "Mrs. Yarbrough, I don't have time to discuss this. I'm sorry for any inconvenience, but there's no job for you here. All right?"

"No, it isn't all right, Mr. Webber. You have no idea how badly I need this job. I'm struggling to support myself, plus my housekeeper and a child. I'm divorced, so I have no husband to help me. You said you needed somebody to do public relations, and I can do it better than anybody in town. Won't you please reconsider?"

Webber was becoming impatient. "Look, I'm not being arbitrary. Personally, I . . . what I mean is . . ." He exhaled sharply. "If you must know, several women came into my office yesterday . . . good customers, you understand. Most of them didn't exactly come right out and say it, but one or two did. The bottom line was, if you were going to be working at the hotel, they'd take their business elsewhere."

Page was dumbfounded. She stared at the hotel manager, trying to imagine what he'd just described.

"I'm sorry, but I've already discussed it with our corporate headquarters. We can't afford to lose that business."

"But I haven't done anything to those women. They're friends of mine."

"They didn't act like friends . . . they were extremely upset. And it wasn't just one or two. There was a parade of them in here starting right after lunch."

Page seethed inside at being judged again, and so unfairly. Though she knew it was hopeless, she said, "Mr. Webber, I've always supported this hotel. I brought you thousands of dollars every year. Are you seriously going to allow a few women who may be jealous of me for totally different reasons to tell you how to run your business?"

"I have no choice, ma'am." He glanced at his watch. "I gave you my decision."

"And your decision stinks. You need more than public-relations help, sir. You need lessons in human psychology and sound business practices. Good day."

The funk that descended during the long walk back to her car was far lower than the high Page had experienced only minutes earlier, skipping in for the first day on her new job. She couldn't help recalling an incident the year before, when a Midwestern publisher compiled a magnificent book on antebellum mansions in Natchez. Though the book's arrival generated much excitement, it vanished from local booksellers' shelves overnight. The reason? Two *important* homes had been left out of the book during the editing process. One of the two belonged to a current officer of a rival garden club.

When Page reached her car and finally located her keys, it wouldn't start. The battery had given up the ghost.

CHAPTER TWENTY

·

Late that afternoon Page went to the converted cook-house behind the main house at Willowdale Plantation. She and Doris agreed not to discuss either Page's experience at the hotel or having to buy a new battery. Those things were behind them, and they needed to go forward. Doris loved the outfits Page had bought for the babies, especially Adam's.

Belle had done a superb job of making the wooden building cozy for Doris and the baby. A huge open brick fireplace still worked, and Doris had a small fire going with an iron pot hanging over the coals. Whatever was cooking inside the pot smelled wonderful. Page asked.

"Beef stew," Doris said. "Your favorite thing for a winter day. I'll make some corn bread when the stew's almost ready."

Doris had converted a wicker basket into a bassinet for the baby. It rested on a bench opposite an old pine kitchen table. Page walked over and spoke to the baby, gently stroking his tiny hands. He grasped her finger tightly and cooed.

"You're just precious, little Adam," Page said. "You know you are, don't you? Yes, you do. You are. Wait'll you see what I bought you."

Doris said, "Isn't he pretty?"

"Adorable. He does remind me of William." Page referred to Doris's son, now twenty-eight, in the navy. Doris had commented several times that this child was as pretty as William was at that age. Page said, "He even has one of those dark spots on one finger, like a little ring. Is that common in black babies?"

Preoccupied, Doris didn't respond. She was busy adding something to the pot of stew. Besides, talking about William as a baby usually brought up some discussion of William's father, Antwann Kern, whom Doris preferred to forget. Antwann was a charming but uneducated man who'd swept Doris off her feet when they had met thirty years earlier. He worked as a laborer on farms in the area. Though they'd never formally divorced, Doris had thrown her husband out over twenty years ago, for his chronic drinking and for having a girlfriend on the side. She still saw Antwann around town occasionally, but ignored him as if he'd never been born.

Page continued. "He has those great big eyes, like William did, and look . . . he already has long eyelashes. Why is it always the boys who get the long eyelashes?"

The baby began to fuss.

"Could he be wet, Doris?"

"I just changed him a little bit ago, but that doesn't mean he's not wet again. He may be hungry. What time is it?"

Page glanced at her watch, checked the baby's diaper, and picked him up. She sat in a wooden rocking chair near the fire and opened her blouse. The baby found her nipple with the eagerness of a newborn calf.

"You're right, Doris, he was hungry. He sure has an appetite."

"You did too, and so did little Cindy. But this baby eats like you did. You always were hungry till you got to be about ten years old. Then you wouldn't eat for nothing. I thought you were gonna starve to death . . . I swear I did. Your daddy used to say, 'Doris, you got to get that child to eat better. I don't know what's wrong with her, but she's gettin' too skinny.' So I did. I'd make you up that cornmeal mush with milk and sugar on it, and bananas. You always did like bananas."

"Did you love me, Doris? When I was a baby?"

"Course I did. I still do. You and Laura. I love you like you're my own flesh and blood."

"Maybe we should keep him."

Doris cocked her head to one side.

Page continued, talking mostly to herself. "I know I shouldn't think that way. Just as I'm suffering not knowing who has my baby, this child's mother must be hysterical without him. But he is so precious. I sure would miss him."

"It's been too long since we had a little baby around. They sure do make days go by fast, just doing for 'em. I like it, too."

"We may never find his mother, Doris. It's possible that whoever took my baby stole Adam from his mother as well, and exchanged them. We'll certainly try to find her, but if we don't, would it be terrible if we kept them both?"

"Nothing wrong with that."

"They could grow up together. They'd have each other, like when William and Laura and I used to play together. Even though they were younger than me, it was great." She watched the little black baby nurse for a while. "I sure would hate to give him up."

Somebody knocked on the door, and Belle Braswell called, "Page, are you in there?"

"Just a minute." Page scurried to pass Adam to Doris before Belle could come in. She didn't dare let anybody else know she nursed the baby. As she buttoned her blouse, Adam began to cry. Handing Doris a pacifier, Page opened the door and smiled.

"Telephone," Belle said. "It's that nice young lawyer fella who was out here with his wife."

Page hurried to the only phone Belle had—in the front parlor.

"Sorry to disappoint you," David Fields said, "but we won't be able to use that technicality to negotiate after all. The trust specifies three requirements: one, that the child be a boy, The Governor's first great-grandson; second, he must be named Jackson Adams

Yarbrough the second, like you said; third, he must be The Governor's own descendant, not the result of marriage or adoption."

"I figured as much."

"Also, the judge denied our request for reconsideration of custody. The earliest we can go back is ninety days from the original hearing."

Page felt her hopes slip even farther away. It was hard to stay up when everything she tried slammed her back down. She said, "Nearly all the judges are friends of Lucien's or the senator's. The deck's stacked against us." She exhaled noisily. "When I get the blood tests back, we'll have a fighting chance, David. Once I prove this baby isn't mine, things will change. Lucien and the senator might even help look for my baby again."

"Probably. Lucien's gonna want whatever's in the trust. Speaking of which, did he ever say what's in it?"

"A long time ago he told me how The Governor divvied up his estate. His widow, of course, got the house and money to support her during her lifetime. His son, Senator J.L., got Yarbrough Hall until his mother died. Then he and Miss Emma also received River Oaks, plus most of The Governor's cotton plantations here and across the river in Louisiana. Those represented the most valuable part of the estate. Next, his grandson, Lucien, got the land I told you about along Natchez Trace Parkway and in town. That was the second most valuable part of the estate, although the oil leases weren't worth much by then. The final part, to go to the great-grandson, was mostly stocks and bonds, I think. There may've been a little land in it, but Lucien couldn't figure out where it would've been. The Governor wanted each trust kept private until it went to each heir. I remember the senator talking about the trust one time. He said The Governor should've stuck to politics and cotton farming. He knew a couple of railroad stocks his father had liked that went under for sure."

"Then Lucien's concern was probably for naught.

I've researched old trusts and wills through the years, studying the tax consequences. Old stocks generally aren't worth the paper they're printed on.''

Fields was silent for a moment, then tried to lighten the mood. ''Well, that's enough bad news for one day. Let's talk about something on a happier note. How was your first day at work?''

On Saturday Mark Goodson dropped by Willowdale. Auntie Bellum poured sherry for the veterinarian and herself, and asked Page to join them on the veranda. The temperature had warmed up to the sixties, and the sun was at the perfect angle to enjoy its warmth. Page sat in a porch swing with Aunt Belle, while Mark perched on the wooden railing. Belle told Mark about Page's losing her job.

''You know,'' he said, ''I could use some help in my office.''

''I don't know anything about animals,'' Page said.

''That's *my* job. I need somebody to help answer phones, make appointments, and clean up the paperwork. I'm awfully bad with that.''

''Do you really need somebody, Mark, or are you just saying that to help me out? I don't want charity.''

''Ask Belle . . . she's been there.''

Belle Braswell nodded in agreement, pushing the swing back and forth with her good leg. ''Believe me, he needs you. I'll guarantee he's got bills he hasn't sent for animals he treated three or four months ago. Some longer. That little girl who answers the phone is more interested in chewing gum and talking to her boyfriend than in making appointments.''

''If you're serious, Mark, I'd love to help. I can start whenever you say.''

''Monday, then. I can't pay much, but it'll give you something to do till you find what you want. Plus, I'll enjoy having you there. It's kinda fitting.''

Belle asked what he meant.

''Page is partially responsible for me becoming a veterinarian. I got myself all messed up in high school, and nobody much wanted anything to do with me. Page always took the time to talk when I came around. She wouldn't go out with me, but she talked to me."

"You never asked," Page said.

"I did, too. For the hayride, our senior year. You turned me down."

"I already had a date."

"Yeah, with a college boy." Goodson sipped his sherry. "Anyway, Page knew how much I liked animals, and how I didn't get on so great with people. She kept telling me I should do what my uncle did."

"You had a special way with them, Mark. Dogs, cats, horses . . . they just took to you."

"Well," he said, "so did you. You were great with dogs and children. I'll bet you still are."

Page's eyes misted over at the thought of her missing children. She swallowed hard. "If you'll excuse me for a minute, I'd better check on Doris. I need her to do some ironing for me."

After dinner that evening, Auntie Bellum took a phone call in the foyer, then slammed the phone down. "Some idiot says the Kluckers are gonna burn my house down tonight."

"The who?"

"Kluckers. Ku Klux Klanners."

"I'll call the sheriff," Page said.

"Lot of good that'll do."

"They'll protect your property."

"We've been having sheriffs in Adams County since I was a girl. Far as I can tell, they've never slowed the Kluckers down one bit."

At midnight, Page, Mark, and Doris sat nervously in a darkened front room, listening and watching. Belle Braswell was nowhere to be found. Wearing his Tweetie Bird shirt, Adam was asleep on Doris's lap.

"It's all my fault," Page said quietly. "I never should've come here." She chewed at what was left of one fingernail, worried sick. "Where could she have gone?" The wall clock ticked louder than their voices.

Mark answered. "She must've gone with the deputy when he left."

"I hope so. It isn't like her to leave and not tell us."

Doris said, "Aunt Bellum's nobody's fool. She probably went down to the police station to jerk a knot in somebody's tail, like she always says. She'll be coming home soon, and bringing the police with her. You'll see."

Moments later they watched from the window as a pickup coasted into the front driveway, its headlights off. Two hooded figures jumped from the bed of the truck, and two more slipped out of the cab.

Mark Goodson started for the door.

"No, Mark," Page said, grasping his arm. "It's too dangerous. I'll call the sheriff back out."

"No time for that," Mark said, raising his voice. "Somebody has to stop these cretins."

Before he could open the door, two thunderous explosions shattered the night. Mark ran outside, with Page right behind him.

A familiar voice shouted from somewhere in the dark. "Try burnin' another cross on my property and I'll blow your hairy little testicles up around your ears, you no-'count, worthless, inbred bastards. . . ."

The men clamored into the pickup and started the engine, one of them tossing an empty beer can out the window. Auntie Bellum stepped out from behind a live oak and reloaded her shotgun. She fired two more shots, blowing out a brake light before the truck disappeared into the night.

"By God," Belle said, "if the Yankees didn't burn Willowdale, I'll damn sure not let some no-good ignorant rednecks do it." She limped toward the porch, where Mark and Page stood grinning at her. "I need a glass of sherry," the old woman stated. She ejected the spent shells. "They'll not be back tonight. Humph. If they know what's good for 'em, they won't be back at all."

* * *

After nursing Jackson Adams Yarbrough II Monday morning, Page went to Goodson's office. Mark practiced in a one-story brick building near the county road, just inside the property he'd inherited from his uncle. Uncle Matthew had practiced there for nearly fifty years. Mark kept several of the outdated surgical instruments on display in a glass cabinet in the waiting room. Things like mortars and pestles for mixing medications, stainless-steel syringes and saws, and horse-hair sutures for sewing up wounds.

Mark introduced Page to his staff of one receptionist and one veterinary assistant. The receptionist was about twenty, Caucasian, slightly overweight, but with a pretty face and innocent eyes. Her name was Betty. Mark's assistant was an African-American man of about fifty, thin and wiry, who had a gold tooth on one side of his mouth. His name was Rudolph.

While Goodson went on farm calls, mostly to treat sick animals too large to bring easily to the clinic, Page went to work cataloging and filing. She found charts, invoices, and scraps of paper with notations about patients with names like Prissy-cat, Muffin, and Scruffy.

A little after ten that morning, Page phoned David Fields's office. After they laughed about what Auntie Bellum had done, she told him about her employment.

"I was about to ask you to help me," Fields said. "I have all these great cases and notes I use as reference material, but can't seem to find the ones I need when I need them. Guess I sorta let things get cluttered."

"I noticed, and I'd love to help you once I get things organized here. Mark won't need me full-time."

"I'll pay you."

"Figure out what I'm worth, David; then take it off what I owe you. I'm embarrassed that I haven't paid you before now . . . I just haven't had the money."

"Did you get your DNA results yet?"

"They said not to call before noon. I've been checking my watch every five minutes. Mark probably thinks I'm a clock-watcher, and I am . . . but not for the usual reasons. I'm so excited about getting an honest test that I hardly slept all weekend."

"Call me the minute you hear. . . . I'll wait here over lunch. When this test shows what we know it must, you're home free, Page. We'll win all the suits against you . . . the hospital, the doctor, the Dunbars, plus the one your husband and father-in-law filed. Hands down, we'll win."

"And get Cindy back. Right, David? The judge can't say I'm an unfit mother after we prove that Adam isn't mine."

Minutes after Page hung up, Suellen Whitford called.

"Page, you're not gonna believe what I just heard."

"What?"

"I can't believe it myself. My own brother."

"Tell me." Page glanced at the pile of manila folders and unfiled papers. She didn't have time for gossip.

"Lucien's married."

Page fell back in her chair, unbelieving. "You're kidding me. The ink isn't dry on our divorce papers."

"It's the Lord's truth, Page, I swear."

"To who?"

"Kay Rae Talwell."

"I'm insulted. I thought he had better taste."

As Suellen provided details, Page listened to the words, but had trouble believing the facts. She heard herself say, "Mary Lou saw Kay Rae drink beer straight from a can once at an Ole Miss tailgate picnic." And, "I heard that her boobs are pure silicone." She'd never made such statements before.

"There's more."

"I'm not up to hearing more. What is it?"

"She's pregnant."

"Tell me the truth, Suellen."

"Patty Fulton says she knows for sure. Mary Lou's sister works for Kay Rae's gynecologist."

"How far along?"

"Patty thinks three months, but she'll find out for sure as soon as Mary Lou's sister breaks for lunch."

Page said, "I can't believe what I'm hearing. Why, that girl's just trash."

"Her daddy's got money."

"But she has no breeding . . . they're from Arkansas. She wouldn't know a salad fork from a dessert spoon." Page paused. Surely this was a joke. "When did they get married?"

"This past weekend."

"Where?"

"They flew to Las Vegas."

"That's about what I'd expect from Kay Rae."

"You know what I think?"

"What?"

Suellen lowered her voice to a whisper. "I haven't said this to anybody, but I think Lucien got her pregnant on purpose."

"Why would he do that?"

"To get the money from the trust."

"Well, first off, I'm surprised he could get her pregnant. And with her reputation, she probably doesn't know whose it is. Lucien's sperm count is so low we had to try for five years and take all sorts of medicines. . . ." Page realized what she'd been saying, and stopped. "Besides, there's nothing in the trust but a bunch of worthless old stock certificates."

"I'm not so sure." Suellen said this as though she were privy to some big secret.

"Why do you say that?"

"Because I know my brother and, even more so, my father. I don't care what Granddaddy's will said; Daddy and Lucien sure were anxious for him to have the first grandson. There's probably a whole pisspot full of money in there, and I'll bet they know exactly how much. More'n likely, he was working on gettin' Kay Rae pregnant while he was still married to you, just in case. When you didn't give him what he wanted, he dropped you like a hot horseshoe and moved on to somebody who would. Daddy probably engineered the whole thing. Or at least encouraged it."

"Nobody could be that coldhearted." A cold, damp sadness seeped into Page like London fog. Surely Lucien would never have done what his sister was saying.

"Page, I've known them both a lot longer than you, and Lucien's always done whatever Daddy told him to. Believe me, sweetie, he would. Hell, they're both lawyers. And politicians. Why would you expect anything different?"

CHAPTER TWENTY-ONE

Unable to wait any longer, Page phoned the lab in Baton Rouge at eleven-thirty. A receptionist said a technician would give her the report, if it was ready. Seconds later, somebody else came on the line.

A young-sounding male voice said, "Mrs. Briggs? Mrs. Page Briggs?"

"Yes." Page's pulse was pounding with anticipation.

"That was a DNA profile on you and on Jackson Adams Yarbrough the second, right?"

"Correct."

"Okay, here it is." There was a moment's pause. "Yes, ma'am, it's a match."

"Excuse me?"

"It is a match, ma'am. Jackson Adams Yarbrough the second is definitely the child of Mrs. Page Briggs. Did you need anything else?"

"No. No, I don't."

"Shall I mail the reports to your Natchez address, ma'am? I have Willowdale Plantation . . ." He read off the address and Page confirmed it without actually hearing what he said.

Too stunned to ask anything more, when she thought to look, she had somehow hung up the receiver. Her mind circled like a toy train on a track, finding no conclusion on which it could stop. Nothing made sense today—it hadn't in a very long time. What Suellen said earlier about Lucien couldn't be true. And nobody could've tampered with the DNA test she'd just learned about, because nobody knew she was having it done. She had told only Doris, her father, and David Fields, all of whom she trusted implicitly. And Mark Goodson. She had even used her maiden name.

Page sat staring at the telephone, unable to speak or move. Her last particle of hope, of reason—of any explanation she might comprehend—had just vanished.

Was she losing her mind? It was the only conclusion that made any sense.

Page locked the door, then told David Fields about the results. Her hands shook as she held the phone.

There was a long silence on the other end of the line before Fields said, "When you and Lucien were trying to have a child, did you always go to the same doctor?"

"Yes. Dr. Archer."

"Why did he say you had trouble conceiving?"

Page forced herself to answer slowly and distinctly. "I went through a battery of tests in the beginning, because we assumed the problem was with me. It turned out I was fine, but Lucien had a low sperm count. He isn't sterile, but he produces a smaller than average number of sperm. The doctor put him on some medicines."

"What medications?"

"Testosterone. And something else."

"Did it help?"

"I assumed so. What are you getting at?"

"Just a wild idea. How close were Lucien and the doctor?"

"Not particularly close."

"Did Dr. Archer ever mention the possibility of concentrating Lucien's sperm and inseminating you with them?"

"Lucien said we'd get pregnant the old-fashioned way, or die trying. It was an ego thing with him, I think. Questioning his masculinity. Why, David?"

"It's pretty far-fetched, but do you remember that doctor from Virginia who used his own sperm to impregnate patients? Somebody found out and sued him for child support or something. My thought was, if your doctor did anything like that, even without your knowledge, he might've got hold of some African-American sperm by mistake."

"Dr. Archer would never do anything without my permission. Besides, I kept an ovulation chart for months."

"What does that do?"

"I recorded my temperature and Ovumeter readings twice a day."

"A what meter?"

Being forced to focus on her attorney's questions was helping Page think better. "Ovumeter," she said. "You put this little probe thing on your tongue, and it measures some kind of electrical impulses in your saliva . . . that's what the doctor said . . . and a digital readout gives you a number." Page had also used the probe to measure the electrical conductivity of her vaginal mucus each morning and evening, but declined to share this information. "You write the number on a chart. When the numbers dip and your temperature rises, it means your ovary has produced an egg that's ready to drop. In other words, you ovulate. That's the only time a woman can get pregnant."

"How long did you keep that chart?"

"Almost a year."

"So you know exactly when you ovulated?"

"Sure. It was the night before we left on our Caribbean cruise. I looked it up when I got out of the hospital."

"Did the doctor examine you the day you ovulated?"

"No, it'd been at least a week. Maybe more."

Fields let out an audible sigh. "Well, so much for that theory. The only other possibility is, there must be Negro blood in either your or your husband's background. Are you absolutely certain about your own?"

"Belle Braswell knows everybody on my mother's side back to Adam and Eve. My father is familiar with his family for almost as many generations. Both are lily white."

After a long pause, Fields said, "Lucien and his father had somebody watching everybody who was tested, right? The second time."

"Yes."

"Who watched Lucien?"

"I don't know."

"If the Yarbroughs know there's Negro blood in their family, no matter how far back, then they've suspected all along where that baby came from. If nobody was watching Lucien, he or his father could've easily substituted somebody else's blood for his. Then when the baby didn't match with him, but did match with you, Lucien played the role of the injured party. He immediately cried foul and sued for divorce. Am I making sense?"

"I don't know, David. I am so confused. I just . . . from that first night when Lucien told me they'd put our baby in the wrong bassinet, I've been living a bad dream, like some synthetic, parallel universe. And in a state of panic, frantically searching for my child. It never occurred to me this little black baby could be mine. I just . . . well, it threw me for a loop when I found out." She took in several deep breaths, trying to absorb this new information. "I need time to adjust," she said. "I'm so exhausted I can't even think anymore."

"Shall I call you at home later?"

"I don't know, David. I . . . I just don't know." Page hung up the receiver and sat staring into space, tingling all over. She had no feeling in the bottoms of her feet. She couldn't even force herself out of the chair.

Page didn't tell anybody else for several days. In fact, she hardly spoke at all. After work at the clinic each day, she went home to Auntie Bellum's to eat, sleep, and nurse the baby. She wasn't aware when Monday became Tuesday, or Friday became Saturday. She did take the private investigator's suggestion and discontinued his services. He hadn't found a thing, but still took her money. Meanwhile she remained buried in thought. Finally she confided in Belle Braswell.

"Damn sure isn't from the Braswells," Belle said.
"My father's people go back to the *Mayflower*. Mother
was a Byrd, you know, related to Admiral Byrd, the
explorer. They're pure white all the way back to England, before they set foot in America. Your lawyer's
right . . . it's one of Lucien's ancestors. Has to be.
Wonder which one it was?"

"If it is, we'll never prove it. Lucien won't agree to
another blood test with us being divorced and him re-
married. I still can't believe he married that . . . hussy."

"Is Kay Rae that flashy blond girl that kept pushing
to get into your garden club?"

"Herself."

"Drives around town in that little foreign car with
the top down?"

"A yellow Jaguar convertible." Page tried not to
picture Lucien and Kay Rae together in the car. Or
anywhere.

"Well, I've heard a few things about that one. Mind
you, I wouldn't know her from a jackrabbit, but there
has been talk. And you know what they say . . . 'If
everybody's carrying an umbrella, it must be rain-
ing.' " The old woman sipped her sherry. "It has to
be Lucien for sure . . . but how're we ever gonna
prove a thing like that?"

After a long silence, Page said, "I'm amazed that
Mama Yarbrough let Lucien marry Kay Rae. I bet he
didn't tell her beforehand."

"Why'd you say that?"

"Well, Miss Emma is . . . shall we say, wise in the
ways of the world. She's bound to be familiar with
Kay Rae's reputation."

Since learning the baby was hers, Page began to
look at him quite differently. Even before talking to
the lab, she had dreaded the thought of having to give
him up someday. She had definitely bonded with him.
She had tried to think of ways for Doris to keep him,
or so she told herself. She realized now she'd wanted

the baby for herself long before she knew. Or had she known on some primitive level all along?

Before she'd learned the truth, there had always been a feeling that held her back—some restraint or barrier. A nagging sense of guilt had gnawed at her soul for accepting the baby's love, and for loving him back. Some innate prejudice had whispered that the very thing her heart urged her to do was wrong. Unacceptable.

Now the barriers were removed. She could snuggle Adam tightly against her and allow their love to flow as it had during the nine months when he lived inside her—their blood and their love intermingling with each beat of their hearts. She could see herself in him now. His nose was thin like hers, and his lips not as full as those of many African-American children. Adam.

For the first several weeks Page had thought of him as "that other baby." But he wasn't. Over the weeks he had become his own person. He was Adam. The name fit. Created by God, since no one claimed parentage. Whether he was black, white, or chartreuse, Page loved him more than life itself. He was, after all, her very own. Her Adam. Her son.

Now it was time to get on with their lives.

Page was delighted when her sister came to visit one sunny Sunday in late January. Watching Lucien's inauguration on TV the week before had upset Page even more than she already was. She needed company.

Her relationship with her sister remained strained, at best, despite Page's efforts to become closer through the years. Page was prettier, did better in school, had been more popular growing up, and had married better. Tough things for Laura to forgive.

After catching up with Aunt Belle, Laura asked Page to walk with her down to the river. Page agreed, saying she'd have to take the baby along, since Doris had gone to church. She wasn't ready to share her newfound knowledge about her son just yet. How could she explain it?

They walked along a stone path for a way, then through tall grass past the family cemetery and down to the river's edge. Heavy oak branches laden with Spanish moss overhung the slow-moving water.

"I've always loved the river," Laura said.

"I remember having to pull you out by the hair a couple of times to keep you from drowning."

They walked and talked, then sat beneath a massive old tree, filtered sunlight warm on their bodies. Jackson Adams Yarbrough II was bundled securely in the blue corduroy jumpsuit that he'd already grown into, and a blue wool blanket. His big eyes searched everywhere, taking in new sights and sounds. Laura asked what Page planned to do with him.

"Keep him."

"What about his real parents?"

Page hesitated. "What about them?"

"They must be looking for him. And they probably live somewhere in Natchez, don't you imagine?"

"Most likely. Meanwhile Doris takes great care of him. Nobody's better than she is, and she loves him to pieces. He reminds her of her own son."

"William? I haven't heard anything about him in ages. Where is he now?"

"San Diego. In the navy. He's been in school there."

"Good for William. He always was smart."

"And good-looking. Doris has a picture of him in his uniform on the deck of a big ship."

"When's the last time he came to visit?"

"About a year ago."

"Wish I'd known. I would've come by to say hello."

"He was only here for a short time. He caused some sort of trouble and got arrested. Lucien had to get him out of jail."

"What'd he do?"

"Got into an argument with some woman, Lucien said. Disturbing the peace. Nothing really bad."

"He was always a good boy, growing up."

"Doris didn't get to see him because the navy shipped him back to San Diego. She was terribly upset."

The baby fussed for a few moments, then began to cry in earnest. Page checked his diaper, but it was okay. His crying crescendoed steadily in intensity and pitch. Page offered the pacifier but he spat it out. Twice. "He's hungry."

"We just got here. Do we have to go back?"

Page looked upriver toward the graveyard from whence they'd come. The house was a good fifteen-minute walk away. The baby shrieked at the top of his lungs. Page checked quickly to make certain they were alone, then opened her blouse, exposing one breast.

Laura was aghast. "What are you doing?"

Without replying, Page cradled the infant in her arms so that his lips found her nipple. The sudden silence was instant relief.

Laura repeated her question.

"What does it look like?" Page said, not quite hiding the edge in her voice. "Adam's hungry, and there's no time to walk to the house for a bottle."

"Adam? I didn't know . . . Page, he's a Negro." Laura's face displayed her horror.

"He's a hungry child who needs to eat."

Laura was circling like an agitated moth around a lightbulb. "I can't believe what I'm seeing. My God, Page, how long have you been doing this?"

"The nurses pumped my breasts to feed him in the hospital. Otherwise he wouldn't have developed any immunity to disease, which is extremely important for newborns. And it kept my breasts from hurting. I have even more milk this time than I did with Cindy, and you know how engorged I got with her." Page knew she was overexplaining, but couldn't think what else to do. She wanted to be left alone to feed her child.

"That is not the same as letting him actually put his mouth on . . . I mean, right on you."

"I broke the breast pump," Page said, "and I don't have another one. Besides, how is this any different from what Negro women have done for white children for generations?"

"There's a huge difference . . . you're white. And I don't believe that, anyway. A white baby couldn't nurse at a Negro woman's breast . . . the milk would sour in its stomach."

"Did it sour in yours?"

"What are you talking about?"

"When you were a baby and your tummy ached with hunger, do you think you cared who nursed you? Before you answer, let me ask you something else. Did you love Doris when you were little?"

"Of course."

"Remember . . . you and William are about the same age, so Doris had milk for him. I can almost guarantee that Doris nursed you to keep you from crying. You seemed to grow up pretty healthy."

"Page Briggs, that is a lie. I never did such a thing. I wouldn't."

"Doris all but told me."

"Then she's lying. I'd remember something like that."

"If you don't believe me, ask her yourself."

"I wouldn't lower myself to ask such a question. I know better." Laura turned toward Willowdale. "I have to go. Bobby'll be home soon." She left.

Page gradually relaxed, mildly guilty about what she'd done, but relieved that her sister was gone. And she knew Laura would never tell a soul. She'd be too embarrassed.

Watching her son nurse, Page softly said, "Forgive Mommy, little Adam. I didn't deny you because I don't love you. I did it because I do."

Walking from a front pew toward the entrance of the church, Doris Kern adjusted her hat. Perspiration trickled from her armpits onto her chest. It had been a powerful service, certain to renew her strength for another week. Somebody touched Doris's arm from behind.

Bessie Smith said, "We been praying for you, Doris, and that little baby."

"Why, thank you, Bessie. I appreciate that."

"We been praying you find a black family for that boy."

"Why would I want to do that?"

"You know a white woman ain't got no right raisin' a black baby."

"Say what?"

Bessie nodded solemnly, her wide-brimmed hat nearly hitting Doris in the face. She closed both eyes and shook her head. "A black baby needs a black family . . . to learn his roots. White people got different values. They's cold, Doris . . . standoffish. They food's strange . . . they music, too. They even smells funny. And they don't feels things same as we do."

"What about me? I'm there, and I love that baby."

"Ain't the same as having a whole family. How you 'spect him to relate? He gonna need brothers and sisters growin' up. His own kind."

Doris had heard enough. "Bessie, you're wasting your time praying to my God about taking Adam away from me. My Lord is not gonna do that. I love that child, and Page loves that child, and she's a good mama . . . better'n most I know, black or white. Pray about your own self or your own children, and leave us be. We're just fine." Doris spun around and bustled out of the church, fuming.

Outside the church, a woman named Lila told Doris about a white woman and her baby who had moved into a predominantly black neighborhood. Lila was equally critical about mixing the races, especially with children.

"She's part of that same mess," Lila said.

Doris asked what she meant.

"That trial about the governor's baby. She was that other woman where her husband said it wasn't his baby. She's in bad shape. The baby, too."

CHAPTER TWENTY-TWO

The following Monday, Page and Doris got out of Page's Suburban and went to the door of a ramshackle house in the poorest section of Natchez. Black faces, adults and children, watched wearily from nearby doorways and windows. Seconds later Caroline Dunbar answered their knock. Extremely reluctant at first, she finally asked them inside.

Doris sat on an orange crate. Page's heart nearly broke when she saw the conditions this poor woman and her child lived in. She tried to hide her reaction as she joined Caroline and the baby on a rust-colored sofa with a brick where one of its legs had been and one coil of a spring sticking through the back. Wrapped in a fairly new wool blanket, Caroline's baby fell asleep beside them. John Henry Dunbar. He appeared fat and healthy. Page and Doris kept their coats on in the cool room as they tried to learn what had brought Caroline to this pathetic state of affairs.

Almost an hour later, Caroline finally accepted that they were there to help, rather than trying to take her baby away. She said she'd lost nearly everything, not the least of which was her pride.

"I haven't seen Jonathan since the day they padlocked the restaurant," Caroline said without feeling. Whatever emotions this woman harbored in the past had been used up. She was clearly drained.

Page said, "You haven't heard from him at all?"

Caroline shook her head. Later, she told them, "Mr. Wylie Marsh levied our house and Jonathan's car when we couldn't pay the balance of his legal fees.

The hospital attached our furniture." She shrugged helplessly. "I didn't have anyplace else I could go." Her dry eyes scanned the room. "It's all I can afford by the time I buy food for the baby, but it keeps us out of the weather."

Page wanted to cry for this poor soul. The shack she called home was clean, but falling apart. Where there had once been a carpet on the floor, large splotches of wood showed through the occasional patch of faded green threads. On this January day, Caroline's clothes were summer-weight and scant, except for a tattered sweater around her shoulders, and its elbows were badly worn. Her hands were cracked and peeling. Raw.

Caroline explained that she'd finally been accepted for food stamps, but they didn't go very far. The rent ate up the welfare check. John Henry ate up the rest.

Page asked, "Doesn't your mother live in Hattiesburg?"

"Tupelo," Caroline said.

Doris spoke up. "Why didn't you go live with her?"

Caroline studied something in her lap. She finally answered Doris. "Pride, I suppose." She hesitated, then sighed. "And I guess I keep hoping Jonathan will come back. Mama never liked him after she found out . . ." She didn't finish the sentence.

"What? That he beat you?" Even when she'd been angry with Caroline, Page was incensed that she overheard Buford and Lucien discussing that probability in court. She had tried not to imagine what that man had done to this frail creature, but those visions had kept her awake late into several nights.

Caroline nodded, her eyes down. After a moment she raised her head and offered a sad, apologetic smile. "I know Jonathan wasn't perfect, but he's all I had . . . and I caused him to hit me most of the time. He wasn't a bad man. He didn't mean to hurt me."

That's it, Page thought, steaming inside. *We're outta here. All of us.*

*   *   *

That same evening Page phoned Caroline's mother. Two days later, Page, Doris, and Adam drove to Tupelo with Caroline and John Henry Dunbar snug in the seat behind them. They would've left sooner, but Page needed a full day to have her Suburban tuned up before it could make the trip. All of Caroline's worldly belongings were in the rear compartment, with room to spare—even with the extra clothes and food-stuffs Page and Doris had put together.

When Page prayed for God to help Caroline and her baby in the future, she also asked his forgiveness for any role she might've played, however unintentional, in bringing Caroline to her present circumstances.

During the drive home, Page silently considered what she might do in Caroline's situation, if the man involved were Lucien.

Love is not necessarily a constructive emotion, she decided. Not always.

At two-forty-five the next afternoon, Page took a call from David Fields.

"I have a couple of ideas," Fields said. "Would you be willing to undergo a polygraph examination?"

"A lie-detector test?"

"Yes."

"For what purpose?"

"To say you didn't have sex with anyone except your husband during the time period in question."

"It isn't in question, as far as I'm concerned."

"I understand that, but we need to convince a judge."

"What purpose would it serve?"

"Polygraph exams are not universally accepted in courts, but neither is DNA sampling because neither test is a hundred percent conclusive in the eyes of the law. One might argue that results of one test are just as reliable as the other."

"When would it be done? And where?"

"If I arrange the test, Page, it'd have less impact

than if a judge orders you to be tested. Plus, Lucien's attorney could claim we rehearsed you. I'd rather present my argument and let a judge arrive at that decision."

"What makes you think I would pass the polygraph?"

"You told me you had relations only with your husband."

"You believed me?"

"Yes."

"Thank you, David. I'll never be able to express how grateful I am for that."

"Is that a yes?"

"If you think it'll help get Cindy back, yes."

"Great. I'll explain the details in a minute, but I think we also have a decent shot at having Lucien's blood retested. Or perhaps, tested for the first time. If we succeed, I'll be standing there watching this time as the needle goes into his vein."

Leaving Dr. Goodson's office early, Page checked the gift-wrapped packages in the back of her Suburban, then drove to Miss Margaret's Dance Academy and Charm School. It was Cindy's birthday, and Rona Green said they were having a birthday party at the school. This was the day Cindy turned seven. Page could hardly wait to see her. She was growing up so fast. Page felt horribly cheated that she was missing out on so much of Cindy's youth, but felt even worse for Cindy. A girl needed her mother. How well she knew that.

Page parked in the rear lot and entered through the side door, as always. Hurrying up the hallway, she encountered Margaret Murray, the owner of the academy, whom she hadn't seen in months. A birdlike woman in her fifties, Margaret wore a rose-colored leotard and ballet shoes. She probably weighed no more than ninety pounds fully dressed. Page smiled and said hello.

"Page? Is that you?"

"You are so sweet to have a party for Cindy, Margaret. I appreciate it more than I can ever tell you."

Margaret tried to smile, but it came out more of a contortion of her beak. "You're just dropping off some presents?"

"I came for the party. Where is she?" Page headed toward the lunchroom.

"I can't let you go in there."

"Why not?"

"Please . . . think of your daughter. Don't make a scene."

"What scene? I want to give Cindy her birthday presents."

"Miss Emma will have me shut down if I let you near her. Please, Page, give me the gifts. I'll see that Cindy gets them."

Page's anger flared. "Margaret Murray, how many years have I been bringing Cindy to your school?"

"I know, Page, a long time."

"Who do you think selected your school in the first place? I took ballet and tap here long before you ever bought Miss Tuttle out, and that was over twenty years ago. Now you're telling me I can't attend my own daughter's birthday party?" Page was beyond caring that she was raising her voice.

"It isn't anything personal, Page."

"How much more personal can it get? She's my daughter."

Margaret put a finger to her lips. "Shhh," she said.

"Don't you shush me. Where's my daughter?"

"I have strict orders not to let you in. Why are you being so difficult?"

"Orders from whom?"

"Miss Emma and Senator Yarbrough. They are Cindy's legal guardians, you know. They're paying her tuition."

"I'm her mother."

Birdwoman was getting haughty now. Righteous. "If you wanted to be her mother, you should have acted like a mother."

"What does that mean?"

"You had everybody in town fooled, including me. But going out with a black man? That floored me. I'm surprised you have the nerve to stay in Natchez."

Page wanted to scream. "You don't know what you're talking about."

"Oh, don't I? Does number thirty-four for the Saints ring any bells? You think everybody in town doesn't know about those weekend trysts you had in Biloxi, then bringing him into your own home?"

"You're insane."

"Am I, now? Well, no decent woman wants to be in the same room with you after what you did. The only reason I agreed to keep Cindy in the academy was that Miss Emma assured me you'd never come here. If you don't leave immediately, I'll send Cindy home and not let her return."

"You'd penalize my child for something you think I did? Even though I didn't do it?"

"If any of the other mothers see you here, they'll take their daughters out in a wink. You'll ruin me overnight."

Just then the door to the lunchroom opened and Cindy poked her head out. She saw Page and came running, arms extended above her tutu. "Mama! Mama! I heard your voice."

Everything but Cindy ceased to exist in that instant. Page picked her daughter up and hugged her tight, smelling, touching, feeling her wonderful child.

Clinging like a barnacle, Cindy began telling her mother about the party and all the children who were inside. "Come on, Mommy, you have to see. I have a cake and ice cream and everything. I already blew all my candles out." She wriggled to the floor and tugged Page's hand to lead her up the hall.

Page hesitated, watching Margaret Murray, who was glaring like an agitated crow. The woman was serious—she would ask Cindy to leave. Page considered what the academy meant to her daughter, and how embarrassed a child could feel. Cindy wouldn't understand how adults could be so cruel. Page's heart dried right up and crumbled.

"Come on, Mommy."

Page had to clear her throat before answering. "I can't, baby. I need to be somewhere and I'm almost late. I brought your presents so you'd be sure to have them today. Okay?"

"But I want to show you my cake. You have to eat some ice cream, Mommy."

"Save me some, sweetie. Here. Take your presents inside for when you open your other gifts." She took the little girl's face in her hands and kneeled, looking deep into innocent blue eyes. "Happy birthday, Cindy. I love you very much."

"I love you too, Mommy."

"Don't you ever forget that. Mommy loves you very, very much."

The innocent blue eyes looked back into hers, questioning. "Is that two verys or three?"

"Three. I love you very, very, very much. I'll come to see you next Thursday, okay? At Grandma's house."

"Okay, Mommy, I guess." The child's disappointment was shattering.

Page hugged her daughter again, then left. She managed to hide her anger and tears until she was out of earshot of her daughter. When she exploded, it was not a pretty sight, or fit for a child's ears to hear.

David Fields filed Page's bankruptcy petition the last week in January. Page had borrowed against her Suburban as David suggested, and insisted on settling all debts she had personally incurred before allowing Fields to file.

With so little money involved, Page's no-asset bankruptcy was approved without fanfare. Embarrassment, yes. Humiliation, most definitely. Shame, overwhelming. Legal complications, no.

After legal notice of her bankruptcy appeared in the local newspaper, Page dreamed that she saw headlines all over Mississippi announcing, PAGE BRIGGS YARBROUGH: FIRST CHI-O WOMAN TO DECLARE BANK-RUPTCY. Waking in the dead of night in a cold sweat, she flooded the house with light and sat up till day-break, shivering.

Next, Fields filed documents with First Mississippi Bank and Trust Company requesting that Page be named sole trustee of the trust held for the great-grandson of Governor Jackson Adams Yarbrough. He also requested a full accounting of the trust's assets. Then he waited.

Three days later, his phone began to ring.

Victor Brandt called first, the trust officer who'd phoned Page shortly before she was evicted from Yar-brough Hall. The one with the gallbladder. Or with-out it.

"Certain conditions must be met," Brandt said quite formally.

Just as formally, Fields replied, "My client and I are aware of the conditions. This child qualifies as the legal heir."

"That isn't possible."

"We believe it is. Shall I bring Mrs. Yarbrough by to sign the necessary documents and pick up the ac-counting, or would you prefer to messenger everything to me?"

"Perhaps I should have you speak with our counsel. You seem to have a misconception about the trust requirements."

"Who would your counsel be?"

"Mr. Wylie Marsh, of Marsh and Brandon."

"Please ask Mr. Marsh to phone me. I should be available most of the morning."

Minutes later, Fields received a call from Buford E. Tallant, of Yarbrough, Yarbrough, Tallant, and McCann.

"David? Buford Tallant here. Senator Yarbrough asked me to give you a ring." Buford's voice was warm and cordial. "What is this about Lucien's ex-wife trying to get into some trust The Governor set up?"

As politely as he could, Fields said it did not appear to be any of the senator's business.

"David, what she is attempting is rather preposterous, don't you think?"

"No, Buford, I don't."

"As I understand it, that trust was established to benefit the first great-grandson of The Governor. I can't imagine anybody believing that either Lucien's ex-wife or her Negro child is in any way related to The Governor."

"Mr. Tallant, perhaps I missed it, but exactly what is your role in all this?"

"I told you, the senator asked me to call."

"Do you represent someone with an actual interest in the matter?"

"Consider it a friendly call, David. I don't represent anybody just yet."

"Then I appreciate both your concern as a friend, and the senator's as an uninvolved party. Naturally I won't be able to divulge information pertinent to any of my clients' interests, but I'm always happy to hear from a friend."

After a long pause, Buford said, "Let me give you some advice, Fields. And, though I don't normally operate this way, I won't even charge my usual hourly fee, which is considerable. For you it's free, and might just be the bargain of a lifetime. You're biting off more than you could ever hope to chew. Friend to friend, I suggest you drop this little charade like a white-hot rivet and go on back to remodeling your lovely house out there on the river, or whatever it is you do with your time. You really don't want to go up against a Yarbrough in this town. You or Page."

After an equally long pause, Fields replied, "I certainly appreciate your concern, Buford. If I feel the need of any additional advice in the future, would it be all right if I give you a call?"

Buford laughed. "Anytime, David. Anytime at all,

but this is the last freebie. From now on you will have to pay . . . I flat guarantee that. You have a nice day now, you hear?''

Buford Tallant hung up the phone and turned to look out his office window, considering. This might be exactly the opportunity he'd been waiting for. No point allowing the exposure he'd received to go to waste. If he played his cards right, there could be a great deal more publicity just around the corner. The best kind—when you win.

At one time Buford had considered a circuit-court judgeship to be the ultimate. But now, joined at the hip with Lucien, what was wrong with raising his sights a bit? Lucien had already hinted at taking Buford along if he went to Washington.

Buford smiled to himself. Hell, Bill Clinton had made it from over in Arkansas, and took lots of friends with him.

Fingers interlocked behind his head, and feet crossed on his mahogany desk, Buford fantasized for several moments. Would he rather be secretary of state, a U.S. Supreme Court judge, or attorney general? While he'd already given this a great deal of thought, he was perfectly willing to give it considerably more. It was becoming his favorite pastime. What better way to advance his name and reputation than to have Page and her incompetent lawyer claim that her black bastard son was the progeny of his white friend, law partner, and possibly future president of the United States of America?

David Fields had a conversation with Wylie Marsh later that same morning. Marsh informed him that the trust department would, of course, refuse his request.

"I'd like that in writing," Fields said.

"Naturally," Wylie said.

When he hung up, Fields reviewed the documents he'd already prepared. As soon as he received the written refusal from Wylie Marsh on behalf of First

Mississippi Bank and Trust Company, he'd carry his document to the courthouse personally, and initiate Page's lawsuit.

Buford Tallant and Wylie Marsh spoke on a conference call with Governor Lucien Yarbrough, who was in Jackson.

"The whole thing is preposterous," Buford was saying, "but we have to defend it."

Wylie agreed, adding, "No point in your even comin' down, Lucien. As attorney for the trust department, I can block her request."

Lucien asked, "What do you suppose she's up to? Page is anything but stupid." He paused, then added, "Of course, she doesn't understand the law, either."

Buford said. "Apparently neither does her attorney. Where'd she find this clown?"

Wylie answered. "I heard she tried every lawyer in Mississippi. Nobody'd represent her."

"Maybe I *should* come down for the trial," Lucien said.

Wylie Marsh responded, "Why bother, Luce? They don't have a Popsicle's chance in a sauna of winning. Being governor, you can invoke all kinds of privilege and immunity if you want . . . keep this thing postponed forever."

Buford quickly said, "No, I think you may be right, Lucien. Defending yourself could be good for your national image." He thought, but didn't say, *And mine.*

Lucien said, "I agree with Buford. My public needs to see how this terrible, cheating woman and her greedy lawyer are trying to steal my son's inheritance even before he's born." He was silent for a moment. "The senator's always taught me that, and he's right. I'll be there no matter what they try . . . in the interest of justice. In fact, even if they don't have a case, let's blow it up to make it look as though it's a life-or-death struggle. National-caliber stuff. Might as well give my supporters something to cheer about when we win. And we will win."

*   *   *

David Fields dialed Dr. Mark Goodson's office the next morning. When Page came on the line, he said, "The game's at hand. Or is it afoot? Whatever." His voice projected his excitement.

Page flashed back on Wylie Marsh in the courtroom, representing the Dunbars so eloquently at some ungodly hourly fee, then attaching their home and car. And Buford Tallant: cunning, confident, capable. This time she'd be going up against them both, with Lucien and the senator advising them every step of the way. Was it realistic to think she had any chance of prevailing? She and David Fields, who was long on compassion, but short on experience.

Page swallowed hard and said, "I guess I should've asked before, David, and don't take this the wrong way. I know you're smart, and I like you very much." She hesitated. "That first day in your office, I asked if you were a good lawyer, and you said you were. I do believe you, but how many actual court cases have you had in Natchez?"

"Including your divorce and custody hearing?"

"Yes."

"Three."

"How many have you won?"

"Including yours?"

"Yes."

"Uh . . . actually, none, now that you mention it."

"Oh, my God."

"But don't worry, Page. That can be good. Sarah says it means I'm due."

CHAPTER TWENTY-THREE

Despite Buford's calling in all sorts of favors, it was still late in May before the trust case could be put on the court calendar. Buford Tallant and Wylie Marsh privately considered the entire case a laughing matter, deserving zero respect and a minimum of time. Wylie did remember to bill his highest hourly rate for each time the case crossed his mind, however, which apparently happened often. Such as when he was on the golf course, or singing in the shower, or driving to and from work.

"I get paid for showing up," Wylie told David Fields one day at the courthouse. "How about you?"

Fields didn't respond to the dig. So what if the opposing attorneys were being paid by the hour? He had agreed—no, he had suggested it—to represent Page on contingency. If they won, and if there was anything of value in the trust, he'd receive either one-third of that value or whatever his hourly fee calculated out to be at a hundred dollars an hour. Realistically, he didn't expect a quarter. His reward would be when Page got her daughter back—if his guess was correct about Negro blood in the Yarbrough background.

Surely Lucien and J.L. would relinquish custody of Cindy rather than let that skeleton out of the family closet.

The Honorable James L. Scott was assigned to the case. Scott was a man of about fifty, who had thinning blond hair and wore horn-rimmed glasses. Page was

ready to pack up and go home when she heard who
would preside. Fields asked why.

"He and Lucien play poker together. They've known
each other forever."

"How long since they've played?"

"Two years, maybe three, as far as I know."

Fields chewed at something inside his lip before re-
sponding. "Well, it's a small town. Whoever we get's
gonna know somebody." He shrugged. "We could get
lucky."

"How?"

"Maybe Lucien won."

Judge Scott listened patiently while Fields presented
his case. Page was impressed. Lucien was neither impressed nor unimpressed, but his level of concern was
evident to everybody there. Neither he nor J.L. had
bothered to show up.

Fields was succinct, to the point, mild-mannered but
confident. He wound up by saying, "It is quite simple,
Your Honor. The trust spells out three requirements
for the beneficiary. My client's son fulfills those requirements. As his mother, Page Ann Yarbrough is
entitled to be named trustee until her child reaches
the age of maturity."

When Fields took his seat, the judge nodded toward
Wylie Marsh.

Marsh stood, reviewing a page of notes he'd taken
while David had the floor. "Ya Honor, what Mr.
Fields has explained to the court is just the way things
are . . . but not quite. Mr. Fields overlooked one or
two significant requirements in the language of the
trust. First, the trust requires that the beneficiary be a
male. We'll yield that point to Mr. Fields. The second
requirement is that the beneficiary be named Jackson
Adams Yarbrough the second. Now, since we know
for a fact that the mother of the child in question did
not take the child home from the hospital until two
days before she was served with divorce papers, and
since she openly denied that the child was hers at that

time, she could hardly have named the baby prior to that time. Therefore, we contend that she chose the name only after learning the language of the trust. If that assumption is correct, and we have witnesses to confirm that it is, she had no right to use the Yarbrough name at all when she finally got around to naming him.

"Third, the trust says the beneficiary must be Governor Jackson Adams Yarbrough's first great-grandson." Wylie turned to David Fields and shook his head. "That same paragraph specifies that the great-grandson must be a direct descendant, not by marriage or adoption. Since we know that Governor Lucien Yarbrough is the grandson of Governor Jackson Adams Yarbrough, and we know that both of those gentlemen are white, it seems fairly obvious that the child in question, a Negro, Ya Honor, cannot possibly fulfill this requirement.

"The decision of First Mississippi Bank and Trust Company to refuse Mr. Fields's request on behalf of his client was based upon the requestors not meeting the requirements of the trust. Oh, yes, except that their child is a boy . . . hardly enough to qualify, Ya Honor."

Wylie started to sit, but glanced at his notes and said, "If I may add one thing more, the trust also specifies that the contents of the trust are not to be revealed to anyone other than the beneficiary or the trustee. Therefore, since Mr. Fields's clients do not qualify as either beneficiary or trustee, his request for an accounting was denied for all the same reasons which I just stated." Wylie took his seat.

Judge Scott nodded to Buford Tallant.

Buford stood, hitched up his trousers, and buttoned his suit coat. His voice was cordial and self-assured. "Your Honor, I agree completely with what Mr. Marsh has just said. As the attorney for the Yarbrough family, I'm here to protect their interests and the intentions of Governor Jackson Adams Yarbrough. Unlike some people, we have no desire to waste the court's time, and we feel no need to defend our position, though we are quite capable of doing so."

Buford turned to look directly at Page before continuing, as if to let his message absorb. Turning slowly back to the judge, he said, "We merely want to see the trust instructions carried out exactly as they were written. If someone believes he or she has a legitimate claim on the trust, I say let him or her prove that claim. Thank you, Your Honor."

Judge Scott turned his leather chair on its swivel to face David Fields. "Mr. Fields, I'm inclined to agree with Mr. Tallant. What proof do you offer to substantiate your claim?"

Fields stood. "I appreciate Mr. Marsh's conceding point number one, Your Honor, that Mrs. Yarbrough's son is a male. Can I assume that Mr. Tallant goes along with the concession?"

Buford said he did. He looked at the judge and shook his head sadly, as if in the presence of a retard.

"Regarding point number two," Fields said, "I submit this document from the Mississippi State Department of Health, Bureau of Vital Statistics, for the court's consideration. I ask that you label it exhibit A."

Judge Scott asked, "What is the document, Counselor?"

"A certified copy of the birth certificate of my client's son, Jackson Adams Yarbrough the second."

Marsh and Buford Tallant quickly came to their feet to inspect the document. They wanted to know the exact date the birth certificate was filled out, signed by the attending physician, and filed with the state.

In time, Page testified to what Lucien had done.

When Page finished, and over Marsh's and Tallant's objections, Fields put the night admissions clerk of the hospital on the stand, Chester McDowd. Chester substantiated what Page had said.

On cross-examination, Buford Tallant said to Chester, "You expect us to believe that Governor Lucien Yarbrough filled out the birth certificate on that Negro

baby as his own? Come now, young man, are you
aware that the governor of the great state of Mississippi doesn't even know this child's name, let alone
how the child might've come to have that name?"

The clerk nervously pushed his glasses up on his
nose with one finger, then pulled a piece of paper
from his shirt pocket. "This is the copy he filled out
right here. That's his signature at the bottom."

Tallant studied the signature briefly, then almost
laughed. "Are you in the habit of forging prominent
people's signatures, young man?"

"No, sir."

"I'll bet you have lots of people's signatures at
home, don't you?"

"Yes, sir. I collect autographs."

"Keep them in a special place, do you? Maybe a
photo album?"

"Yes, sir."

"When your friends come over, do you ever take
that album out and show 'em all those famous
signatures?"

"Sometimes."

"Makes you feel good, doesn't it?"

"Yes, sir."

"Important."

"Excuse me?"

"It makes you feel important to show that you got
somebody famous to sign an autograph for you,
doesn't it?"

"I never thought about it."

"Well, think about it now, Chester. What grade are
you in?"

"A senior."

"At Natchez High School?"

"Yes, sir."

"How old are you?"

"Nineteen, sir."

"And you went to Natchez Middle School for your
seventh and eighth grades, correct?"

"Yes, sir."

"Do you recall someone by the name of Mr. Manning at Natchez Middle School, Chester?"

"Yes, sir."

"Who was Mr. Manning?"

"The principal, sir."

Buford stood studying the young man for several seconds. Finally he said, "Chester, did you forge Governor Yarbrough's signature on that phony birth certificate?"

"No, sir."

"Oh, come now, son, nobody's going to prosecute you for stretching the truth just a little bit to make your friends think you got the governor's autograph. I mean, he was in the hospital that night. Everybody knew that, right?"

Chester didn't respond. He shifted uncomfortably in his seat.

Page tried to swallow, but her throat was far too dry. Buford had done his homework, and she and David had committed what Lucien always said was a crucial error when dealing with Buford: they'd underestimated him. Fields perched on the edge of his chair, silent but attentive. Page noticed little dots of perspiration on her attorney's upper lip.

"Well," Buford said, "is that right or not?"

"What?"

"Answer the question, son."

"Which one?"

"Was Governor Lucien Yarbrough in the hospital that night and did everybody know he was?"

"He was there. I don't know who knew it."

"Please answer yes or no."

"Yes, sir."

Buford paced back and forth in front of the witness, stroking his chin. He stopped. "Why were you suspended from school in the eighth grade, Chester?"

The young man shook his head and pushed his glasses up again. He looked to the judge for help. "I don't know how to answer that. It isn't yes, and it isn't no."

Judge Scott asked Buford to rephrase the question.

"Isn't it true that you were suspended from school in the eighth grade?"

"No, sir."

"Oh, come now," Tallant said, "you must know that public-school disciplinary actions are a matter of public record." Buford quickly walked to his table and picked up a piece of paper. He read it silently. "Isn't it true that on April fifteenth, 1994, Mr. Robert Manning had you suspended from school for forging your father's signature on your own report card?"

David Fields lowered his chin to his chest. He let out a long, slow, deflating breath.

Page's eyes narrowed, but she sat perfectly erect in the chair beside Fields.

Chester McDowd picked at something on one of his fingers, but didn't answer. He wiped the tip of his nose with the back of one hand.

Buford Tallant continued, "Isn't it also true that your father had to correct you on several occasions for forging other people's signatures?"

No answer.

Page started to sink lower in her chair, but fought the urge.

Buford was relentless. "Famous people's signatures, Mr. McDowd? I believe Senator Barlow was one of them, wasn't he? Tom Cruise's signature was another when he was filming a movie over in Baton Rouge."

Chester raised his gaze and stared at Buford Tallant, his face screwed up and his glasses well down on his nose. "I don't know what you're talking about, sir."

"Just as you didn't know what Mr. Robert Manning was talking about when he suspended you in April of 1994 for forging your father's signature, just like you forged Governor Yarbrough's signature on that phony birth certificate? How much did the ex-Mrs. Yarbrough pay you, Chester?"

"Objection," Fields said.

"Sustained."

"Did Mrs. Yarbrough pay you to forge the governor's signature, Chester?"

"No, sir."

Tallant stood shaking his head unbelievingly. "I want to get this straight now . . . your testimony is that after Mr. Manning did not suspend you from school in the eighth grade for not forging your own father's signature on your report card, and after you went to work for Doctors' Memorial Hospital and heard that Governor Yarbrough and his wife were in the hospital, you did not fill out this totally contrived birth certificate, nor did you sign the governor's name to it to add to your collection of autographs in your album at home, just as you did not sign your father's name to your report card in the eighth grade. Is that what you expect us to believe here today, Chester McDowd?"

David Fields came to his feet. "Objection, Your Honor, counsel is badgering the witness."

"Then strike the question," Buford said in disgust. "I see no point in asking this witness anything further."

Judge Scott said, "Does that mean you have no objection to entering the birth certificate as exhibit A, Mr. Tallant?"

Buford half shrugged. "No objection, Your Honor, for what it's worth. We might as well ask Mr. Fields to submit the Declaration of Independence while we're at it. I'm sure Mr. McDowd would be glad to sign it for us."

"That'll be enough of that, Mr. Tallant," the judge said.

"Sorry, Your Honor. I apologize."

"Any redirect, Mr. Fields?"

Page leaned over and whispered something to David. What did she have to lose now? They'd already gone down in flames.

David frowned, but listened. Then he nodded and got to his feet. His voice was tentative as he began. "Just one or two questions, Your Honor. Chester, did any of the things that Mr. Tallant just described in such dramatic detail ever actually take place?"

"No, sir."

"Objection. Vague and ambiguous."

"Sustained. Be more specific, Mr. Fields."

"Sorry, Your Honor. Chester, was Mr. Manning the principal of Natchez Middle School when you were in the eighth grade?"

"Yes, sir."

"How long do you suppose he's been the principal there?"

"I'm not sure . . . he's pretty old. A long time."

"And nearly everybody in town knows that he's the principal, right?"

"Yes, sir."

"Which students in Natchez attend Natchez Middle School?"

"All of us, sir."

"So it's no big secret that you would've gone there?"

"No, sir. It's the only school in town that has a seventh and eighth grade."

"Were you ever suspended from school, Chester?"

"No, sir."

"Did you ever forge your father's signature on your report card?"

"No, sir."

"Did you forge Governor Yarbrough's signature on this birth certificate, Chester?"

"No, sir."

"Thank you, Chester. That's all."

From his seat, Buford Tallant said, "One more question of this witness, Your Honor, if you will."

"Go ahead, but be brief."

"Chester, do you have any proof that the signature on that birth certificate right there was actually signed by Governor Lucien Yarbrough?"

Chester shifted in his seat again. "I guess not, sir, except I watched him sign it."

"Just like you watched your father sign your report card that time in the eighth grade, Chester?"

"No, sir."

"So you admit that he didn't sign it?"

"Yes, sir."

"Objection," Fields said. "Who didn't sign what?"

"Let me rephrase the question," Buford said. "All of a sudden you've changed your mind and decided that it wasn't your father's signature on your report card after all, when you were in the eighth grade?"

"Yes, sir."

"That's enough for me," Buford said. "No more questions."

Page nudged David Fields, who stood and said, "Whose signature did appear on the report card in question, Chester?"

"Mr. John Brownlee's."

Fields hesitated, but he was already in this deep. He plunged ahead. "Why didn't your father sign your report card, Chester?"

The young man's face twisted into a grimace as he said, "Because he was dead, sir. My parents were killed in an automobile accident that year. I didn't have anybody to sign the report card, so Mr. Brownlee signed my father's name. They started to suspend me until they realized why, and I guess that got into my record. Mr. Brownlee became my legal guardian later."

CHAPTER TWENTY-FOUR

Walking to Page's Suburban behind the courthouse, David Fields asked, "How did you know?"

Page replied, "I've watched Buford work before. Plus, Lucien used to talk about some of the things he's pulled. Buford has a vivid imagination and tells good stories. Very convincing."

"He had me believing that young Chester lied about the signature, the birth certificate, everything. I'm sure the judge believed him at first."

"Buford's good." Page fished through her pocket-book for the keys. When she found them, she opened the car door and climbed inside. She couldn't wait to go home and take a long, soaking bath. She rolled down the window to finish the conversation. "Same time tomorrow?"

"Be here around eight if you can, and we'll go over your testimony." Fields thought for a moment. "Do you think Lucien will come tomorrow?"

"You're asking the wrong person." Page hadn't accurately predicted anything Lucien would do in months.

"His absence today was planned, to show the judge he doesn't consider us a serious threat. And it worked to his benefit. Buford could say Lucien knew nothing about the birth certificate without Lucien perjuring himself."

"He probably didn't."

"How so?"

"There was so much excitement that night, plus he and his friends were drinking the entire time I was in labor. I'm sure he didn't remember it existed before today."

"Well, he knows now." Fields grinned like a schoolboy, removed his glasses, and put them in his jacket pocket. "The trust has only three requirements, Page. We showed the court that we've already met two of them. Two out of three's not bad."

David's naivete would have been charming in other circumstances. At the moment it was downright disconcerting.

"Right," Page said. "Now all we have to do is convince a white judge from southern Mississippi that the white governor of his state, who just happens to be the judge's poker buddy, fathered my black son. That should be easy enough."

Fields shrugged, slowly losing his grin. "Give my regards to Auntie Bellum."

On the way home, Page stopped at the Natchez Business Center to pick up envelopes and stamps for Dr. Goodson's office. She'd been coming here for fifteen years.

The slender young man behind the counter always managed to be pleasant and efficient at the same time. He bagged Page's order, rang it up, and handed her the receipt and change. "Thanks, Mrs. Yarbrough."

"Briggs," Page said. "My maiden name. I'm recently divorced, Barney."

"Yes, ma'am. Thank you, Ms. Briggs."

As she turned to leave, Page bumped into Mary Lou Snodgrass. "Oh, excuse me," Page said. Recognizing her friend, she exclaimed, "Mary Lou, it's so good to see you. My heavens, it's been . . . months. You look wonderful."

Mary Lou half smiled and stepped to one side as if to get around Page. "Yes, it has. I'm in a real big hurry, Page. I need to get some stamps and Fed-Ex envelopes."

"I'll wait for you. I haven't talked to Patty or Hazel or any of the girls in ages. Are they all okay?"

The woman ignored Page's question and told Barney what she wanted. Minutes later, Mary Lou turned around with supplies in hand. She nervously navigated around Page, now waiting at the door.

"Excuse me," Mary Lou said, staring at the floor as she pushed past.

Page followed her toward their cars. "Mary Lou, what's wrong? Why are you acting this way?"

"As if you didn't know."

"Know what?"

"Why don't you just move away from here, Page? After what you did to all of us, you should be ashamed to show your face in this town."

"What have I ever done except be a good friend?"

"Make us all look bad. You were one of our leaders, Page. Junior League, Pilgrimage, the pageant. Here you're supposed to be a Southern lady setting an example for our daughters, and you turn out to be a tramp. Not just an ordinary tramp, but a . . . well, even worse. It makes the rest of us appear either real stupid or as if we were in on it all along, and we're not either one."

Page was dumbfounded. "Of all people, Mary Lou, I thought you knew me. That morning when you and Patty came to my house, I told you—"

Interrupting, Mary Lou said, "You sat right there and told us a bold-faced lie, Page Yarbrough . . . or Briggs, or whatever you're calling yourself now. I heard all about your boyfriend and it's disgusting."

"I don't have a boyfriend."

"Well, I'm not surprised . . . I guess even a rich Negro is smart enough to dump you. You were probably trying to steal his money, too, and everybody knows he has it. They make millions."

"What're you talking about?" Page's whole body began to shake with anger.

"Oh, we all know what you're up to now. You and that money-grubbing lawyer you got yourself. Trying to steal Lucien's son's rightful inheritance before he's even born."

"Where'd you hear that?"

Mary Lou opened her car door and got in. Before she slammed it in Page's face, she said, "Do you think we're all deaf, dumb, and blind or something? We know what you're up to, Page . . . we watch your every move. Guess you'll be puttin' a move on Dr. Goodson next." With tears in her eyes, Mary Lou almost spit as she added, "Damn you!" She burned rubber as she drove off.

Steaming, Page couldn't believe she'd ever been friends with anybody so pigheaded, prejudiced, and full of . . . misinformation. Page knew that no matter what she might say, Mary Lou's mind was made up—and one hundred percent wrong.

"I've lived here all my life," Page said to the parking lot. "Doesn't anybody in this town know me?"

While Doris ironed clothes that evening, Page cradled Adam to her breast in the rocking chair. Still upset and hurt, she described her encounter with Mary Lou.

Doris's comment was, "Some people sure go out of their way to find somethin' bad to say about people. Always looking to blame somebody."

"It seems that way."

After a brief silence, Doris said, "They're afraid of us."

"Afraid of who?"

"Me. Adam. Black people. Now you, too."

"What makes you think that?"

"Remember what happened up in Lafayette? Was a wealthy town at one time, mostly white. After the schools got integrated, a few white folks moved out. Little while later, African-Americans started running one or two of the stores and buying houses, so more white people moved away. Then black people figured out they were in the majority at voting time, so they elected a black mayor. Next thing was, there wasn't hardly any white folks there. One day even the ones had stayed just up and left. You won't find a white face in Lafayette today. Lot of folks fear that'll happen here."

"What does that have to do with what Mary Lou said?"

"Maybe nothing . . . maybe everything. When folks believe as fine a white woman as you would lay with a black man, they figure black people can take anything they have. They might not talk about it . . . least not out in public . . . but they're scared."

Page didn't comment, but she'd learned long ago to respect this woman's observations. Doris often reduced things to their essentials, seeing people and events for what they actually were. Reflecting on what had happened, she realized that Mary Lou had seemed frightened. Page had been too upset to notice at the time, but Mary Lou could hardly wait to get away. She had been downright terrified.

Page watched Adam drift off to sleep momentarily, wake up just enough to nurse some more, then fall asleep again. One little hand slowly let go of her breast and came to rest against his own cheek. She carried him to his bed, tucked him in, then bent over and kissed him. He was a beautiful baby.

"Good night, sweet Adam," she said. "Sleep well. Mommy loves you." The thought of Cindy going to bed without a mother's kiss came into Page's mind, instantly flooding her eyes with tears.

Doris looked at Adam, then at Page. "He can't walk and he can't talk, but for such an itty-bitty thing, that baby sure has stirred up a heap of trouble."

"He's done that, all right. He has certainly done that."

Doris let out a long sigh. "Somethin' tells me it ain't over yet. Some things have to get worse before they can ever get better."

Page started to leave, but stopped. She looked back at the child. "I'd love to have him sleep beside me tonight."

"Miss Belle will see you if you do. That old woman's still awake in there watching them old movies on TV."

"You could carry him over to my room, then ease out the back door. I'll bring him back before Belle gets up in the morning. I used to love snuggling Cindy at night. Feeling her little warm body close to mine, listening to her breathe."

"What'll you say if you get caught?"

"I'll say you . . . Oh, what difference does it make what I say? He is my baby. The whole world's gonna know soon enough."

"Don't know if Miss Belle's ready for that, Page. She's from the old school. Isn't likely to 'preciate a black child sleeping in the big house. That just wasn't done in her day."

Page opened the door to leave. "Then I'll be right back. I'll stay over here with Adam, and you sleep in my bed tonight. If Auntie Bellum sees you, tell her you brought me something but that when you got there, I was asleep. That'll work, Doris."

"I hear you."

As Page went into the main house, the phone rang. Belle answered it, then called out to Page. "Lucien's sister," she said.

Page eagerly took the call and answered questions about what had happened in court that day.

Suellen said, "You are doing this just to spite Lucien and Kay Rae, aren't you?"

"That isn't the reason at all."

"Do you think you have any chance of winning?"

Suellen was one of Page's very few friends left in the world, but she sounded almost accusatory. Page wanted to keep her abreast of everything, but David Fields had said to tell nobody of their plan.

Page replied. "Of course we do."

"Lucien says the great-grandson has to be a direct descendant. There is no way a Negro baby's going to qualify as that."

Page was taken aback at this reaction, but quickly

surmised the reason. Suellen would consider the implication of Negro blood a slur on her own heritage as well.

Page said, "I thought you and Lucien were on the outs . . . when did you talk to him?"

"He stopped by today to see his nieces . . . he and Kay Rae." Suellen exaggerated her Southern accent on the woman's name.

"So they *were* in town."

"Kay Rae had to get her hair done and do some shopping. Lucien said he talked to Buford this afternoon and that the whole court case is a joke anyway. Says some high school kid forged a birth certificate for the baby. Is that true?"

"No, it isn't." Page paused, then asked, "How are Kay Rae and her fake boobs?"

"She isn't showing yet, but her tits are even bigger than last time I saw them. She's keeping her weight down, though. Lucien got her a personal trainer, so she works out every day. Just lifting that diamond would be a workout for me. Of course, knowing my brother, she probably paid for it herself."

Page chose to ignore that comment. "Is she pregnant for sure?"

"Oh, yeah. They did an amnio test last week and guess what . . . it's a boy."

"Really?" Page felt sick to her stomach.

"She's due in early July. I told you so . . . Lucien got her pregnant to cover his bets. He's determined to get whatever's in that trust for himself."

"I refuse to believe he'd do something like that . . . not while we were still married." Page quickly calculated the elapsed time. "My God, I must still have been in the hospital."

"Get real, Page; he's a man. Give him the right scent and he's a bird dog pointing with his you-know-what. Kay Rae's always been a bitch in heat. Plus, her daddy's loaded and she's an only child. You think Lucien didn't consider that little bonus?" Suellen crunched

something noisily. It sounded like she was eating peanuts. "Speaking of fathers, how's yours?"

"He calls once a week."

"I heard he passed out at Landry's last Friday."

An empty sensation pulled at the pit of Page's stomach. She'd been so preoccupied lately she hadn't
checked on him as she normally did. "Was he sick?"

"Just drunk. It must break your heart to watch him
deteriorate that way. He's self-destructing."

"At least he was in a restaurant. That may be a
good sign if it means he's eating for a change." She
promised herself to call him first thing in the morning.
She'd love to have him over for dinner, but knew he'd
refuse, as always. He was so afraid he might impose.

Page heard something creak and turned to see Doris
tiptoeing up the stairs toward Page's bedroom. She
waved and winked conspiratorially. "Will Lucien be
in court tomorrow?"

"He has some visiting dignitaries this week, but says
he'll be there if it gets juicy. What that means is, if
there's a TV camera around. You know how he loves
to grandstand for his constituency."

"Will he never stop campaigning? He's already
been elected."

"People in Washington are talking about grooming
him to be vice president. Then another four years and
who knows? Daddy says we're destined to have a Yarbrough in the Oval Office yet."

Page thanked Suellen for calling, said good night to
Auntie Bellum in front of the TV, and went back to
Doris's cottage.

Suellen finished her snack, put her daughters to bed,
and took a long bubble bath. When she emerged from
the tub and dried herself, she stepped on the scales,
then studied her figure in the mirror. The hips and
thighs were still good, the breasts full. Amazing what
being pregnant could do for boobs. Her tummy
pooched out a bit, but hardly anybody had noticed,
she told her reflection.

"Granddaughters can have sons too, you know. Besides, medical tests can be wrong. Kay Rae might just have a girl."

Page fell asleep in an old feather bed in Doris's cottage, with Adam's warm little body snuggled close against her. If she had any chance at all of regaining custody of her daughter, tomorrow should be the deciding day.

CHAPTER TWENTY-FIVE

Page wore a beige linen suit and hat in court the next morning. Her sit-ups were working, and she could button most of her skirts again. The opposing attorneys had on their battle uniforms—navy pinstripes to suggest veracity. Suggest, not confirm. Buford Tallant wore his Ole Miss tie.

Page recalled, uncomfortably, that Judge Scott was a dyed-in-the-wool alumnus of Ole Miss. She had never asked where David Fields went to college, but, judging from his accent, she assumed it was somewhere up north. New York, maybe. David wore a brown sports coat and tie with tan trousers and loafers.

Page didn't see her father in the courtroom. When she'd called earlier, he said he'd attend when he finished summarizing the articles he was reviewing. He obviously hadn't.

Fields began by repeating the third requirement of the trust, that the great-grandson be a direct descendant of Governor Jackson Adams Yarbrough.

Buford Tallant and Wylie Marsh pretty much let Fields ramble until he said, "Since my client, Page Briggs Yarbrough, was legally married to Jackson Lucien Yarbrough Junior at the time of conceiving and giving birth to their son, and since she only had sexual relations with her husband during that marriage, the son she bore on October sixth, 2001, is the direct descendant of her husband. The only issue in question, then, is whether Jackson Lucien Yarbrough Junior, or the man presumed to be *his* father, Jackson Lucien

Yarbrough Senior, are, in fact, direct descendants of Governor Jackson Adams Yarbrough."

Buford was instantly on his feet, objecting.

"I object too, Ya Honor," echoed Wylie Marsh.

Marsh, Tallant, and David Fields went back and forth about the aspersions Fields had cast on the Yarbrough lineage.

At one point Wylie Marsh said, "Ya Honor, Mr. Fields is asking us to believe that this blond-haired, blue-eyed white woman, who gave birth to a black baby boy, never had sexual relations with anybody except Governor Lucien Yarbrough, whom we all know to be white. What they are asking us to believe is preposterous. No, Ya Honor, it's worse than preposterous—it is downright insulting."

When Page took the witness stand, Fields asked, "During your marriage, did you have sexual relations with anyone other than your husband, Governor Lucien Yarbrough?"

"No, sir, I did not."

"Mrs. Yarbrough, I remind you that you are under oath before God."

"I realize that, sir."

"Let me ask you again, during your marriage to J. Lucien Yarbrough Junior, did you at any time have sexual relations with any man other than your husband?"

"No, sir, I did not."

"Then let me ask you this. Have you ever had sexual relations with an African-American man?"

"No, sir, I have not."

Wylie interrupted. "How about a Negro? A colored man? A black football player?" He grinned knowingly at the judge.

With only a slight hesitation, Fields said, "All right, Page, have you ever had sexual relations with a Negro, colored man, or a black football player?"

"No, sir, never in my lifetime."

When David finished, Buford Tallant asked Page several innocuous questions. His tone was gentle, almost sympathetic. Even when he asked, "Ms. Briggs, are you familiar with a man by the name of Dejon Washington?" He pronounced the first name *Dee-on*.

"I've heard the name." Page almost said, *Everybody on planet Earth is familiar with him, Buford.* She had to remind herself not to refer to the opposing attorney as Buford, the only name she'd known him by for the past ten years.

"And I believe you know Mr. Washington personally, do you not?"

"No, I don't."

Buford walked to his table and took some papers from his briefcase. "Have you ever been to the Maison de Ville Hotel, Page? In New Orleans?"

"I have."

"Isn't it true that on January twelfth, 2001, you accompanied Mr. Dejon Washington to the Maison de Ville Hotel?"

"No, Counselor." Page kept her composure. It was appropriate to show respect to officers of the court, no matter what she thought of her ex-friend at the moment.

"And I believe you stayed there two nights." Buford consulted his notes again. "Yes, January twelfth and thirteenth. That is correct, isn't it?"

"No, Counselor."

"Do I have one of the dates wrong?"

"Your information is wrong, Counselor. I was never there."

"You just testified that you were there. Which testimony is true?"

"I testified that I had been there. Previously."

Buford waited for her to continue. She didn't. Lucien used to tell Page how he or Buford would agitate witnesses, then let them talk themselves into a trap. She wanted to speak. She wanted to tell Buford exactly what she thought of him and Kay Rae and Lucien and the whole Yarbrough family. Instead she folded her damp hands in her lap and waited.

"You were there previous to January twelfth and thirteenth or previous to now?"

"Both."

"I see. So you and Mr. Dejon Washington were there prior to January twelfth, 2001."

"No, Counselor."

"Do I have the date wrong?"

"Any date would be wrong, Counselor."

"Please answer yes or no."

"Yes, Counselor."

"Yes, I have the date wrong when you and Mr. Washington were together at the Maison de Ville Hotel?"

"Objection, Your Honor."

"Sustained."

Buford persisted in his efforts to make Page say something she shouldn't. Page listened carefully to each question, paused to consider her response, then answered as briefly as she could. Occasionally she had to answer with more than a simple yes or no.

"Ms. Briggs," Buford said, "what would you say if I told you we have several witnesses prepared to come into this court and swear before God that they saw you with their own eyes, on several occasions, in romantic situations with Mr. Dejon Washington, a black man?"

"I'd say they are lying before God, Counselor. Or you are."

Judge Scott reprimanded Page.

"Sorry, Your Honor. I'm trying to answer as honestly as I know how."

Buford continued. "So it will be your word against several highly respected women in Natchez?"

"If they exist, Counselor."

"Are you saying that highly respected women don't exist in Natchez?"

"No, Counselor."

"Good, because they exist, Page . . . they do exist. And they are prepared to testify to what they saw."

She'd had enough. "Then bring them on, Buford, one at a time or as a group." Mary Lou Snodgrass's accusations flashed across Page's mind, the memory instantly heating up her face and quickening her breathing. She could imagine who the others were. Half the women in rival garden clubs might enjoy seeing her suffer.

David Fields cautioned Page with as severe a look as he could muster. Buford ignored her outburst.

Page tried to keep from fidgeting with the pocketbook on her lap. She attempted to slow her breathing and regain her composure.

Tallant established that Dejon Washington played for the New Orleans Saints football team. That he was African-American.

Page said she had heard of him.

Buford asked her to explain.

"Lucien, my ex-husband, watched the Saints play every Sunday. Sometimes he went to the games and sometimes he watched on TV. I occasionally watched with him, so I heard Mr. Washington's name. I'm sure a great many people have."

"On TV."

"Yes, Counselor."

"And people who saw you coming out of Mr. Washington's apartment at 121 Dauphine Street in New Orleans are lying, right?"

She forced herself to appear as calm as possible. "Or mistaken, Counselor."

"And witnesses who saw you in Mr. Washington's car here in Natchez . . . I suppose they're lying too?"

"Or mistaken."

"Please answer yes or no, Ms. Briggs."

"Then ask yes or no questions, Mr. Tallant."

Her response rolled off Buford's back, but he hesitated, considering something. "Have you ever taken a polygraph examination, Ms. Briggs?"

"No, sir." Page shifted in her seat, crossing her legs.

"You do know what it is."

"Yes."

"How do you know what a polygraph is if you've never taken one?"

"I was married to your partner for the past ten years, Buford. He told me." Page folded her arms across her chest. The judge shot her a stern look. It was all she could to keep from telling Buford exactly what she thought of him.

Tallant asked for a moment to confer with his colleague. He and Wylie Marsh whispered back and forth. Finally he returned to Page. "What did your husband tell you about polygraph testing?"

"He said it wasn't reliable."

"Do you believe that?"

"I have no reason to doubt what he said. Or I didn't have then."

"Why do you suppose he said they're not reliable?"

"I don't know." Page hugged her pocketbook to her chest.

"Are you aware that many courts across the country have admitted polygraph testing?"

"I wouldn't know about that." Page was visibly uncomfortable.

Buford asked, "Why are you suddenly so fidgety, Page?"

"I'd rather not say."

"Is it because we're discussing a device that can tell when you're lying? Does that make you nervous?"

"No."

"Let me ask you this . . . if Judge Scott were to agree, would you be willing to take a lie-detector test, Ms. Briggs?"

David Fields was on his feet. "Objection, Your Honor. Polygraph testing is less than a hundred percent reliable, and many sophisticated courts have refused to consider them. New York, Pennsylvania, Massachusetts—"

Buford interrupted, saying, "Your Honor, there are any number of instances where polygraph examinations have been considered, including, I believe, right here in Mississippi. In a situation like this, only Ms. Briggs, her husband, or some black mystery man could've actually been present to know what happened at the time she conceived that Negro child. For all we know, it could have been sired by the Phantom."

"Objection, Your Honor. Mr. Tallant is . . ."

In the end, Judge Scott instructed the attorneys to present their arguments for or against polygraph testing in a separate hearing, to be held the next day.

Before the hearing, as they had done the day before, Page met David Fields for breakfast across from the courthouse. Page had her usual dry toast, hard-boiled egg, and iced tea. She needed to lose another seven pounds. Fields ate scrambled eggs and a bagel with cream cheese as they discussed strategy.

At the hearing, Buford Tallant and Wylie Marsh produced armloads of computer printouts to cite in support of allowing a polygraph into evidence. David Fields showed his inexperience, citing only a few outdated cases from Northern courts. After hearing all arguments, Judge Scott ruled in favor of allowing the test.

The judge said, "Ms. Briggs, it's obvious that there is a discrepancy in what you're telling us and what other people say they've witnessed. All things considered, the preponderance of evidence seems to be against you."

Fields pointed out that no actual witnesses had testified to what Mr. Tallant claimed.

"In the interest of time," Judge Scott said, "Mrs. Yarbrough—or Ms. Briggs—will you voluntarily undergo a polygraph examination?"

"I'd rather not, sir."

"Why not?"

"My husband said they're not a hundred percent reliable. Excuse me, my ex-husband."

"For the purposes of this court, I have determined the test reliable enough to admit. Any future ruling I make will not be based solely on the result of this examination, but I will consider it along with other evidence presented. If you won't agree to take the test voluntarily, I'll be forced to order you to do so."

"Objection, Your Honor."

"Sit down, Mr. Fields . . . you had your chance to present arguments earlier. Page Briggs Yarbrough, I order that you submit yourself for a polygraph examination, to be conducted by the Natchez City Police Department." He told Page where and when, then asked the attorneys to prepare questions they'd like Page to answer.

Page and David Fields maintained their somber posture until they were safely inside Page's Suburban. Then, grinning like an excited chimpanzee, Fields said, "Gotcha!"

"You watch too many reruns, David. But it worked . . . you were less than convincing today. I loved the way you rubbed their noses in what Massachusetts and New York courts have ruled."

"You were brilliant." He mimicked Page's voice, " 'I'd rather not, sir.' And your body language was perfect . . . crossing your legs, arms folded across your chest. You actually looked uncomfortable when Buford kept inching toward using the polygraph."

"I was."

David looked surprised, then concerned. "It's what we wanted from the start, Page. Why would that make you uncomfortable?"

"Not the questions . . . I needed to go to the bathroom. Really badly."

They both laughed. Fields said, "Perfect timing. I'll have all my clients drink iced tea for breakfast in case I ever need that look again."

As he exited her car, Fields asked, "Are you okay with tomorrow for the test?"

Page nodded in reply.

Fields said, "I'll be there with you, but they'll make me wait outside. You understand?"

"Yes."

"You're okay with that?"

"I guess so." Now that they'd achieved what they wanted, she was having second thoughts. What if she got so nervous she flunked it? Could a machine tell the difference?

"Well, I . . . what I mean is . . . do you . . . our whole case hinges on this test, Page. Are you pretty confident you can do it?"

Page gave a half shrug, raising her eyebrows. "We'll see. I've never had a lie-detector test before, remember?" She put her key in the car's ignition.

Suddenly a horrible thought flashed into Page's mind. "They don't stick me with any needles, do they?"

Over the weekend, Mark Goodson asked Page to accompany him to his place, Trail's End Farm. "I'm redoing the first floor," Mark said. "I sure could use some help with paint colors and wallpaper."

"I might go for a little while, but I'll have to take Adam along. Is that all right?"

"Fetch him. I'll bring my truck around back."

At Goodson's plantation, Page quickly went through wallpaper books and paint chips for each downstairs room. Having helped friends restore grand old homes to their antebellum splendor, she was well versed in what worked and what didn't. As far as she was concerned, if a restoration couldn't be authentic, the house would be better left alone.

Her favorite styles were Greek Revival, like Dunleith and Magnolia Hall, or early plantation homes like Fair Oaks, Elgin, and Mount Repose. The home Mark had inherited was considered an early Southern planter's residence, a two-story white wood structure with brick on the front steps, verandas, fireplaces, and chimneys. The house seemed in good repair, but was sorely in need of redecorating.

Page carried Adam in a handled wicker basket padded with blankets and pillows. She tried to juggle a wallpaper book and Adam at the same time.

"I'll carry him," Mark said. "You've got your hands full."

"Sure you don't mind?"

Mark picked up the makeshift bassinet. "He isn't heavy." He bent forward, touching Adam's chin. "Hey, little buddy, how you doing in there?"

Adam gave him a gummy smile.

"You're a cute one, aren't you? Yeah, smile real big."

Page watched Mark with her son. She said, "It doesn't seem to bother you."

"What?"

"That he's black."

Mark shrugged. "He is what he is." He looked back at the baby. "Aren't you, little buddy? Huh? It wasn't your choosing, was it? Or maybe it was. How're we supposed to know?"

Page flipped pages in books of wallpaper samples. "You've never asked me about Adam. Or the last DNA tests."

"I figure if there's anything to tell, you'll get around to it in your own time."

She hesitated, then said, "He is mine, you know."

Goodson didn't comment. He brushed a strand of hair off the baby's forehead.

"But I wasn't with anybody besides Lucien."

"I sorta figured when you stopped looking all over hill and holler, you must've found out something. Hard to figure, isn't it?"

"People here will never accept Adam, but I'm going to raise him. I love him like I love Cindy. He's my son."

"Makes sense."

"I've been thinking about starting over someplace where he'll be more comfortable growing up. I want to do what's best for him, but I don't want to run, either. I haven't done anything wrong, and I won't let people force me out of my home. I do love Natchez. I always will."

"Be a shame to leave."

"Am I wrong, Mark? To want to raise my son, but want to stay here at the same time? Am I being selfish?"

Goodson didn't answer right away. He ran a hand through his hair and shook his head. "I know a whole lot more about animals than I do people, Page. But when a mare has a foal, or a cow a calf, they don't question what the rest of the herd thinks they ought to do. They raise it the best they can wherever God planted them. And no other mare, stallion, cow, or bull had better interfere, or they'll kick the daylights out of them.

"Nature set it up that mamas love their babies better than life itself. And babies learn from their mamas. I don't know what to tell you, Page, except that you're right to love this little boy. If he's got your blood in him, and with you raising him up and setting an example, he'll be a fine man someday . . . I have no doubt about that. Whether you can do it here in Natchez, I don't know. It won't be easy . . . you're already discovering that. People are gonna talk. I don't even know if I can be objective. What I say may be completely selfish . . . but I sure would like to see you stay."

Adam began to cry. Page glanced at her watch and knew why. He was hungry. She asked Mark if she could have some privacy, then went into an adjacent room, checked her baby's diaper, and changed him.

Minutes later Page sat in an overstuffed chair and looked out a den window as she nursed her child. A meadow outside meandered beneath magnolias and weeping willows toward a pond near the river. She held the baby she loved, admiring the countryside she loved, in the city she loved. And wondered what she would do. Though she knew she wasn't, sometimes she felt so helpless. Confused. Alone.

I feel like that weeping willow out there, she thought. *God planted it here, too.* A few moments later, watching her baby smile up at her, Page straightened and let out a sharp breath.

"I may weep," she told Adam, "but I'll damn well not wilt, and I won't break in this storm. If they want to get rid of us, they'll have to chop me down or dig me up, roots and all. Hear that, Lucien Yarbrough! We're here to stay!"

CHAPTER TWENTY-SIX

In addition to Judge Scott and the attorneys, Victor Brandt from the First Mississippi Bank and Trust Company attended court on Monday.

The courtroom had been virtually empty the week before. Today the wooden benches were filled with curiosity seekers, many of whom Page knew.

Page spotted Miss Emma sitting with Patty Fulton near the rear, in their finest dresses, hats, and gloves. There was one empty space next to Miss Emma. Mary Lou Snodgrass sat just in front of Patty, with three of Page's so-called friends. Smug looks of superiority adorned their faces. All but Mary Lou averted their eyes when Page looked around. Mary Lou glared right back. Suellen Whitford took the seat behind Miss Emma, pointing at Miss Emma's hat. She winked at Page.

David Fields leaned over and touched Page's arm. "Are you okay?" he whispered.

She whispered back, "A little nervous."

"You said you'd be sure to go to the bathroom before we started."

"I did."

"You look as though you need to go again."

"I do."

"You did all right, though, didn't you? On the test?"

"I hope so, David. I can't be sure."

"But you think so?"

"You must've asked me that fifteen times. I didn't sleep a wink the night before. When you get there, they put all this paraphernalia on you, measuring your breathing and your heart rate, how much you perspire, and I don't know what all. Then they tell you to relax while everybody in the room stares at you and some electronic gadget measures your every bodily function and can probably read your mind. I perspired right through my blouse before they even asked my name. There's policemen all around, and they're all so solemn, you can tell nobody believes a word you say. They just watch that machine that's gonna tell the world whether you're a saint or a whore. Forgive me, David. I shouldn't have used that word, but it's exactly what they're all thinking. It was very disconcerting. I think I will go to the bathroom once more before we begin, if you don't mind."

The bailiff called the court to order and the judge came in before Page could stand. She could feel her former friends' eyes burning holes through her back. Though she forced herself to sit a little straighter than usual, perspiration trickled down both sides of her chest.

Judge Scott asked the polygraph expert to take the stand, a round-faced man of about fifty with short gray hair and bushy eyebrows. Sergeant Wilms. He wore his police uniform and carried his uniform cap in one hand and a manila folder in the other. He was sworn in.

Sergeant Wilms answered routine questions confirming that he had performed the examination on Page at the appointed date and time, then went through early questions and Page's responses, which established the baseline calibration for the test.

Just then the rear door banged open and several men came inside. Lucien and Senator J. L. Yarbrough hurried up the aisle and through the center gate in the wooden railing. They took the two empty chairs beside Buford Tallant and Wylie Marsh, apologizing to the court for the interruption. Neither man looked at Page. Billy Larson, Jake Meadows, and three men whom Page did not recognize had come in with Lucien and his father, but remained standing in the rear of the courtroom. The governor's entourage.

Page stiffened when she saw Kay Rae saunter in and sit beside Miss Emma. Suellen had told the truth—Kay Rae's fake boobs were bigger than Page remembered. Since she was about seven months pregnant, they were downright obscene. Kay Rae smiled smugly and whispered something to Miss Emma. Page turned back to face the judge.

The room became silent as Sergeant Wilms read each question, Page's answer, then gave his interpretation.

"Question . . . is your name Page Ann Briggs? Answer . . . yes. Interpretation . . . unable to determine.

"Repeat question . . . is your name Page Ann Briggs? Answer . . . yes. Interpretation . . . unable to determine. Probably untrue.

"Rephrased question . . . is your name Page Ann Briggs Yarbrough? Answer . . . yes. Interpretation . . . true.

"Question . . . were you born May eleventh, 1969? Answer . . . yes. Interpretation . . . true.

"Question . . . are you thirty-two years of age? Answer . . . yes. Interpretation . . . true."

The judge asked the sergeant to dispense with using the words *question, answer,* and *interpretation.*

"Is your weight a hundred and fifteen pounds? Yes. Untrue."

Page tried to smile at her attorney. Several chuckles came from benches behind her, but David Fields was not amused. He sat as stiff as frozen laundry on a February clothesline.

"Do you know Mr. Dejon Washington? No. Unable to determine." The courtroom went totally silent.

Page could hear herself breathe, suddenly filled with doubts. Submitting to a polygraph may have been the worst thing she could have done. What if she had completely flunked the test? She clasped her hands tightly together in her lap, fearful of what she might hear next.

The police sergeant continued. "Have you heard of
Mr. Dejon Washington? Yes. True."

Well, what did that prove? Lots of people had heard
of him. Page swallowed hard.

"Have you personally met Mr. Dejon Washington?
No. Unable to determine. Probably untrue."

Page thought her heart would hammer right through
her ribs. Why had she subjected herself to this torture?

"Repeat, have you personally met Mr. Dejon Washington? No. Unable to determine."

Oh, God, Page thought. *I've ruined everything.* Her
frustration continued to mount as she watched the sergeant turn a page in his notebook.

"Have you ever been to Mr. Dejon Washington's
apartment? No. Unable to determine. Probably untrue."

Page fought back an urge to stand and shout at the
officer. Of course they'd thought she was lying. She'd
been scared half to death at the time, with all that
paraphernalia strapped to her and policemen watching
every move she'd made. Who wouldn't have been
nervous?

"Repeat, have you ever been to Mr. Dejon Washington's apartment? Absolutely not. True."

Page felt her breath catch. Had she heard right?
She'd said she'd never been to that man's apartment
and the machine believed her. She was so thrilled she
wanted to jump up and cheer. She couldn't resist
quickly turning to look at Mary Lou Snodgrass. The
way Mary Lou instantly became occupied studying the
ceiling, you would've thought she was in the Sistine
Chapel.

"Have you ever had sexual relations with a Negro?
No. True."

Flooded with relief, Page turned around again to
see Miss Emma's reaction. Mis Emma appeared genuinely confused. Sitting next to Miss Emma, Kay Rae
nonchalantly popped a stick of gum into her mouth
and began chewing.

"Have you ever had sexual relations with a black

man? Most certainly not. Unable to determine. Subject became agitated, moving about in her seat."

Page held her breath again, willing her pulses to slow. These emotional swings were playing havoc with her palms and underarms.

"At any time during your marriage, did you have sexual relations with any man other than your husband, Lucien Yarbrough? No. True.

"Repeat, have you ever had sexual relations with a black man? Answer, no. Interpretation, true."

By the time Sergeant Wilms finished, Page was limp from hanging on to this emotional roller coaster. David Fields, meanwhile, had to cover his mouth to keep from grinning at the judge. The polygraph examination had confirmed every word Page had said.

During a brief recess, Page raced to the women's rest room down the hall, almost running into Miss Emma, coming out of a stall.

Page couldn't resist saying, "Do you believe me now, Mama Yarbrough?"

Before Miss Emma could answer, a toilet flushed and Kay Rae emerged from an adjacent stall. Looking right past Page she intoned, "Lucien said those polygraphs are totally unreliable, Emma. I guess now everybody knows just how right he was."

Page felt her blood boil. "What would it take to convince you, Mama Yarbrough? What'll it take for you to give my daughter back?"

Lucien's mother seemed to have shrunk just a bit. Her shoulders were not as square as Page remembered; she didn't stand quite as erect. "Your son is a Negro," Emma said. "Do you expect me to believe that my Lucien sired that child?"

Kay Rae stepped in. "Oh, come on, Emma. Anybody can beat that test. Her lawyer rehearsed her for days. They always do."

Page wanted to cram a roll of toilet paper down Kay Rae's throat. Instead she said, "It must be easy to sit in judgment, Kay Rae, when you know absolutely nothing about somebody." She almost added, *You pious slut! Didn't you even care that my husband was married?* But Kay Rae and Miss Emma had already escaped out the door.

Back inside, Page tried to focus on what Buford and Wylie Marsh were saying about striking the polygraph results as unreliable. But her thoughts remained on Miss Emma and Kay Rae. She was still fuming. And hurt.

At one point Buford said, "Your Honor, it has already been proven beyond any scientific doubt that Governor Lucien Yarbrough is not the father of—"

David Fields was on his feet in an instant, interrupting. "Objection, inadmissible. We're concerned with evidence submitted for this case only, Your Honor, not some unsubstantiated claim that might have occurred at an unknown location sometime in the distant past."

"Sustained."

Page was impressed. David improved with experience.

Buford attempted several maneuvers to introduce Lucien's DNA test from the earlier lawsuit, but Judge Scott ruled against him each time.

Fields said, "If Mr. Tallant wishes to introduce any new evidence"—he emphasized the word *new*—"let him offer it." David smiled smugly at Page.

Buford agreed that he would introduce new evidence, though it was not what Page and David had expected. He called Mr. Ralph Reynolds to the stand.

"Who's he?" whispered Fields.

"I have no idea," Page replied, but a terribly uneasy sensation crept through her abdomen. What was Buford about this time?

Mr. Reynolds said he lived and worked in New Orleans, as a desk clerk at the Maison de Ville Hotel. He was in his forties, pale and thin, with a shock of black hair that kept falling down over one eye.

Page immediately became glued to the proceedings again. She knew the Maison de Ville Hotel. But who was this man and why was he here?

After some preliminaries, Buford asked if Mr. Reynolds had ever seen Dejon Washington check into the hotel where he worked.

"Yes, sir, I have."

"Do you remember if Mr. Washington checked in around January twelfth, 2001?"

"Yes, sir, he did." The desk clerk pulled a piece of paper from a shirt pocket and read it. "Checked in on January twelfth, checked out on the thirteenth."

"You know Mr. Dejon Washington by sight, do you?"

"Yes, sir, he's one of my favorite players for the Saints. I never miss a game."

"Was Mr. Washington alone?"

"No, sir."

"Who was with him when he checked in?"

"A young woman."

"I believe Mr. Washington is African-American, is he not?"

"He's black as midnight." A murmur of laughter rippled through the room.

"This young woman who accompanied Mr. Washington, I suppose she was also African-American, right?"

"No, sir, she was white as a magnolia blossom. About that pretty, too."

"If you saw this woman again, Mr. Reynolds, would you recognize her?"

"Oh, yes, sir, I would. I do."

Page was becoming increasingly uncomfortable. She didn't trust Buford. Wrong. She did trust him—to come up with something unexpected and bizarre, but convincing for his team. She feared she could guess exactly where he was headed with this witness.

Buford continued, "Do you mean to tell me you see this woman in this courtroom now?"

David Fields watched Page. His own expression was one of great concern. Fields should never play poker.

Page sat stiffly, watching Buford and his witness. She couldn't believe anybody would stoop so low. Lucien had once told her, "Buford only knows one thing, but it's the most important thing in trial law. How to win."

"Could you point that woman out to us, Mr. Reynolds?"

"Why, yes, I can. She's sitting right over there." Reynolds pointed a bony finger straight at Page.

"That's a lie," Page blurted out.

"Silence," ordered the judge. "Counselor, control your client."

Page glared at Buford, then at Lucien. Neither displayed any emotion—certainly not remorse at what they were doing. It was all a production staged for the court. The truth and people's lives be damned. She wanted to slap Lucien's face.

When Page drove home during the noon recess to nurse Adam, she told Doris the results of the polygraph test and about the hotel desk clerk.

Doris responded, "Give some folks a little money, they'll say anything. Or to get theirselves out of trouble."

"If that man ever saw me in his life, it had to be with Lucien. The ones I'm most disappointed with are Lucien and Buford, no doubt helping the clerk remember what they wanted him to. I know they want to win, but I had no idea they played so dirty."

Sweeping the floor across from where Page sat with Adam, Doris said, "That was a bad January . . . unlucky all around."

"Why do you say that?"

"My William got put in jail. I'm not likely to forget that time."

"That's right . . . the morning we left for Miami."

"Was January the thirteenth. I remember that unlucky number. Instead of coming straight home like he should have, William met some girl somewhere. That's how he got hisself arrested and put in jail. They took him back to California the next day, after you and Lucien left on that boat trip."

Page could hardly believe her good fortune. What Doris had reminded her of could make a huge difference. "You're absolutely wonderful, Doris. I love you." Page began to search desperately through her files. Boxes of papers. She had to find what she needed before Lucien took the stand.

In court that afternoon, David Fields questioned Lucien about events in January of 2001.

"Do you recall what you did shortly before you left on your cruise to the Caribbean, Governor?"

Lucien arrogantly asked, "When are you referring to, Mr. Fields? An hour before, a day, a week?"

"Oh, a day or two before."

"I remember that my associate, Troy Carter, was about to get married, so we gave him a bachelor party. I know for sure it was the night before we left because I remember the headache I had the next morning."

Several people laughed out loud, including Troy Carter and Billy Larson. Lucien enjoyed the moment.

"Was your wife, Page, at the bachelor party with you?"

"Oh, no, there were no wives there."

The men laughed again. Lucien winked at them.

"Where was Page that night, Governor Yarbrough?"

"Well, I suppose . . . yes, she was at my mother's home, River Oaks Plantation. Mama gave a bridal shower for Troy's wife . . . well, his fiancée, then. I picked Page up there later that night."

"Where were you the day before that?"

"In my office, I guess. Yes, that's where I was."

"And your wife?"

Lucien smiled. "Do you mean my wife then, or my wife now?"

"Then, Governor, Page Briggs Yarbrough."

"I believe she goes by Page Briggs now." Lucien actually looked at Page, one of the few times he'd done so since their divorce.

Fields continued, "But she was Page Briggs Yarbrough at the time. Where was she the day before the bridal shower?"

"Helping Mama get things ready for the party, and probably packing our suitcases. I remember she took half the house."

Lucien beamed when several spectators chuckled at his comment.

David Fields walked slowly to the counsel table where his briefcase rested. He opened and fished through the briefcase, took out a piece of paper, studied it, then put it back. He took a long look at Buford Tallant, seemed to hesitate, then went back to Lucien.

Somewhat tentatively, Fields said, "Governor Yarbrough, if I told you that I have a copy of the itinerary for your trip, and plane-ticket stubs that show that you and your wife left Natchez, Mississippi, together on January thirteenth, 2001, the same day the desk clerk from New Orleans swears that Page Briggs Yarbrough was in a hotel in the French Quarter with some African-American man whom she has never met, what would you say to that?"

Lucien glanced at Buford and half laughed. "I'd say you're full of crap."

Judge Scott reprimanded Lucien mildly.

David Fields repeated the question, word for word.

"I'd say you need some acting lessons, Mr. Fields. Do you expect me to believe there's anything in your briefcase over there besides a couple of legal pads and maybe a sandwich? You don't have any itinerary or ticket stubs because they don't exist. If they did exist, they'd prove that I'm correct in saying we left on our cruise the last week in January. As I think about it, I'm certain that's when it was. I don't remember where Page was earlier in the month. I was away quite a bit during that time. She could've easily driven to New Orleans for a day or two without me knowing about it. She obviously did."

Fields looked defeated. He stood looking at Lucien, who stared back defiantly as if David were a schoolboy who'd just been taught a painful lesson.

In the silence that followed, Buford Tallant whispered something to Wylie Marsh and they both smiled. Buford winked at Lucien.

David let out an audible sigh. His shoulders sagged. He slowly walked to his table. Instead of sitting beside Page, however, he opened his briefcase, took out the pieces of paper he'd studied, walked back to the witness chair, and presented them to Lucien. "Would you mind reading these to the court, Governor Yarbrough? Out loud, if you don't mind."

"Well, this is not . . . what it . . . these are . . ." Lucien fumbled with the documents, sputtered, and delayed, but with a face reddened by anger and embarrassment, eventually read the printed travel itinerary for his and Page's trip. And the names and dates on their airline-ticket stubs.

"So," David Fields said triumphantly, "you confirm that you and Page Briggs Yarbrough attended separate parties on the night of January twelfth 2001, in Natchez, Mississippi, not New Orleans, Louisiana. And the two of you left town together on the morning of January thirteenth, for Miami, Florida, where you boarded a ship for islands in the Caribbean. Is that correct, Governor Yarbrough?"

Lucien mumbled, "It would appear so."

"I'm sorry, Governor, I couldn't hear your answer. Could you speak a little louder, please?"

"I said yes, if these scraps of paper are accurate, that's the date we left."

"Do you have any reason to think these records might not be accurate, Governor?"

"I guess not."

"I didn't hear your answer."

"No."

"So are you confirming that these records are accurate?"

"As far as I can tell."

"Is that yes or no, Governor?"

"Yes."

"Thank you, Governor. I submit these documents to the court as exhibits B and C, if Your Honor please."

CHAPTER TWENTY-SEVEN

During breakfast the next morning, Page said, "No calls from Lucien or his attorneys?"

"Not yet," Fields replied.

Their window seat looked onto a street facing the courthouse. The restaurant was filled with pinstripe-suited attorneys and anxious clients. A harried waitress asked if they would like anything else, then left the check. Page slid it over near her plate.

"Maybe you should call Buford," Page said. "Just mention that we'd like to discuss custody of Cindy. It might encourage them to offer a compromise."

"If we're right about the Yarbrough bloodline, they'll call us."

"Don't forget, Lucien's a poker player. He's pretty good at not giving his cards away. So are Buford and J.L."

"Let's see what happens today. I'm going to push the polygraph evidence pretty hard. Did you bring that ovulation chart?"

"In my pocketbook. Why?"

"The itinerary and plane tickets destroyed their New Orleans hotel ploy, but they'll come back with something else. Is Dr. Archer willing to testify?"

"As long as he's not doing surgery or a delivery. He said to give him at least a half hour's notice."

In court, Buford said he had spoken with the desk clerk by phone just that morning and confirmed that it was the week before when Page checked in with Dejon Washington.

Fields asked for a brief recess and phoned Dr. Archer.

Lucien, J.L., Wylie, and Buford huddled around their briefcase-laden table.

Page went to the rest room, this time without incident. Miss Emma and Kay Rae hadn't bothered to show up in court. Suellen and former "friends" Patty and Mary Lou sat quietly among the spectators, watching as Page walked by. Suellen smiled at her and winked. Thank heavens there was one considerate Yarbrough left.

Once the physician arrived and was sworn in, Fields established that Dr. Jefferson Archer was a board-certified obstetrician and gynecologist who specialized in fertility challenges. He asked the doctor to explain how a date of conception was calculated. "When the mother actually got pregnant."

"We take the date of delivery," Archer said, "subtract nine months, then add seven days. That gives the approximate date the woman ovulated and conceived. In this instance, Page delivered on October sixth, 2001. Subtracting nine months from October would put us in January. Adding seven days to the sixth would make it the thirteenth. Using this formula, Page ovulated around January thirteenth."

Buford had a field day with Dr. Archer's use of the words *approximate* and *around*. He forced Archer to admit that the calculation was based on an "average" woman's time of gestation, and could be off by as much as two or three weeks.

When Buford sat down, David Fields got back up. He showed Dr. Archer the chart Page had kept, and asked if he was familiar with it.

"I am," Archer replied. "I have all couples with fertility problems keep one."

"Why do you do that?"

"For exactly the reasons Mr. Tallant just pointed out. The calculation we use is approximate, and it's after the fact. When a couple has difficulty conceiving,

we need to know exactly when a woman is going to
ovulate, not wait to calculate it nine months later."

"Would you explain how this chart helps in that
determination, Doctor?"

"Certainly. A woman's ovulatory cycle is based on a
circadian rhythm of twenty-eight days. During that time
there's a delicate balance of estrogen, progesterone,
follicle-stimulating hormone, luteinizing hormone,
and . . ." Archer went into great detail, explaining how
an ovary contained hundreds of immature eggs, called
ova, with each ovum in its own fluid-filled sac, or follicle. When stimulated by the proper hormone balance,
one follicle with its contained egg enlarged, matured,
and ruptured, releasing the egg into the fallopian tube.
That egg was then available to be fertilized by a male's
sperm, which swam up from the vagina, through the
cervix and uterus, and into the fallopian tube.

Archer diagrammed on a blackboard how the
"numbers" changed when measuring the electrical
conductivity of a woman's saliva or vaginal mucus with
an Ovumeter, reflecting changes in her reproductive
hormones.

"When this line dips by several points, and we see
her body temperature rising right here, this tells us
the exact time she ovulates." He pointed to what he
described on the chart Page had kept—a visual graph
of the conductivity numbers and her temperature.

Fields asked, "In Page Briggs Yarbrough's case, exactly when was that, Doctor?"

Archer read the date. "January twelfth, 2001, at
eleven p.m."

"Would it have been possible for Page Briggs Yarbrough to have gotten pregnant a week before that
date?"

"Absolutely not."

"What about a week or ten days later?"

"Impossible."

"Exactly when did she conceive the baby she delivered on October sixth, 2001, Doctor?"

"Normally, it would be within eight hours before

eleven p.m. on January twelfth, or twenty-four hours after eleven p.m. at the outside. With her husband's poor-quality sperm, probably less than eight and twenty-four hours, respectively. It most likely occurred between five p.m. on January twelfth and five p.m. on January thirteenth."

Over loud objections from Buford Tallant, who was being prodded by Lucien, Fields asked what the doctor meant about poor-quality sperm.

"Governor Yarbrough has an extremely low sperm count, meaning he produces less than one-tenth the number of live sperm compared to what the average adult male produces."

"And the quality?"

"Under the microscope, normal sperm are highly motile, meaning they're active, swimming furiously in every direction. To complete fertilization, millions of sperm swim furiously to enable one sperm to penetrate the egg that has been released way up in a woman's fallopian tube. Governor Yarbrough and his wife had been trying for five years to have a child."

"But Mrs. Yarbrough was fine. I mean, she had no problems conceiving, did she?"

"No, we did a complete fertility workup on her at the beginning. It was her husband who had the problem."

"Thank you, Doctor. No further questions."

Moments later Buford Tallant asked, "Dr. Archer, does this chart that Ms. Briggs kept identify whose sperm swam all the way up that long channel and penetrated her egg?"

"No, sir."

"And you've just testified that Governor Yarbrough doesn't produce very many sperm, is that correct?"

"Yes."

"And I believe you said the governor's sperm don't swim very fast or very far."

"I didn't say exactly that, but I would agree, compared to the average adult male."

"It's sort of a competition then, isn't it, so no matter

how many sperm are in there, the strongest one, which can swim the fastest, is the one that gets the egg, right?"

"Yes."

"I see." Buford paced, absently rubbing the back of his neck. "Let me get this straight. All this explanation of how an egg is produced, and how a sperm swims upstream like a little salmon, and this chart that Ms. Briggs says she kept—"

"Objection."

"Sustained."

Buford continued. "All this scientific data merely indicates that Page Briggs got pregnant somewhere between five p.m. on January twelfth and five p.m. on January thirteenth, 2001 . . . is that right, Doctor?"

"Yes."

"It does not prove who got her pregnant, does it?"

"No, sir."

"Is there anything in this information to show that it was Governor Lucien Yarbrough's sperm that fertilized Page Briggs's egg?"

"No, sir."

"You didn't perform any kind of artificial insemination on Ms. Briggs, did you, Doctor?"

"No, Governor Yarbrough refused to consider that."

"Let me ask you this, Doctor . . . if the egg that you say Ms. Briggs produced at eleven p.m. on January twelfth were exposed to another man's sperm—"

Fields was on his feet, objecting to the implication. In time, Buford was allowed to continue.

"If this egg were exposed," Buford repeated, "to an average man's sperm, millions of them swimming fast and furiously, is it likely that Page would have gotten pregnant?"

"Yes."

"What are the chances, Doctor Archer? Ten percent, fifteen? More?"

"It's hard to say."

"Please try, Doctor. You are an expert in this field."

Archer hesitated, raising his brows for a moment. "I'd say, given the conditions you describe, probably a ninety percent chance. Maybe ninety-five percent."

"And this is somebody else's sperm we're talking about, right? Not Governor Yarbrough's?"

"Yes."

David Fields asked to remind the court this was a hypothetical situation, which did not imply that Page was impregnated by anyone's sperm other than her husband's. Judge Scott agreed. Fields also asked that Buford refer to Page as Mrs. Yarbrough or Page Briggs Yarbrough, since she'd been legally married to Lucien Yarbrough at the time under discussion.

Buford continued. "So, speaking hypothetically, if Page Briggs Yarbrough had sex with another man who produced large numbers of healthy, vigorous sperm, there's a better than ninety percent chance she would have gotten pregnant as long as she had sex with that man between five p.m. on January twelfth and five p.m. on January thirteenth, give or take an hour or so. Is that correct, Dr. Archer?"

David Fields tried to derail the line of questioning, to no avail. Archer was allowed to answer the question, which Buford seemed to delight in repeating.

"Yes."

"She would probably have gotten pregnant by the other man, correct?"

"Probably."

"Is that a yes, Doctor?"

"Yes, sir, it is."

From the pounding in her head, Page knew that her blood pressure must be rising. Buford seemed able to turn anything against her, including her own witness. She seethed inside.

Buford hammered away. "Better than ninety percent chance, Doctor? Maybe ninety-five?"

"Yes, sir."

"How long would that take, Doctor Archer?"

"I don't understand the question."

"How long would it take for another man to deposit

his vigorous little sperm where they could begin that journey?"

"Well, I don't . . . it could take . . . it varies considerably."

"Days?"

"Of course not."

"Hours?"

"No."

"Minutes?"

"Usually."

"How many minutes?"

"On average, anywhere from two or three minutes to perhaps ten or fifteen, though it often seems longer."

Several people chuckled softly behind them.

"So during that twenty-four-hour period during which Page Briggs Yarbrough could have got pregnant, it is possible that she could have accomplished that feat within from two to fifteen minutes. Correct, Doctor?"

"Yes."

"It would only have taken from two to fifteen minutes when nobody was watching for her to meet her lover, black or white—"

Fields interrupted, objecting so strenuously that his briefcase spilled over onto the floor. Judge Scott sustained his objection.

Page wanted to throw everything that had fallen out of David's briefcase at Buford, then the briefcase itself. But she controlled herself. Surely nobody would believe what Buford was implying. Then she thought of Kay Rae and Miss Emma. Mary Lou Snodgrass. And knew she was wrong. They'd believe the worst without question. Page's own expert witness had, unwittingly, done her in.

Buford calmly said, "No further questions." He walked back to his table, where Lucien pulled him close and whispered something. Seconds later, Buford held up his hand and said, "Your Honor, with the court's permission, I do have one or two more questions for the doctor."

Judge Scott agreed. Page cringed.

David Fields was busy collecting the last item that had fallen from his briefcase—a sliced-egg sandwich.

"Doctor," Buford said, "when you say Governor Yarbrough had a low sperm count, you're not saying he's sterile, are you?"

"No, sir."

"Not impotent?"

"No."

"There's nothing wrong with his masculinity, is there?"

"No."

"And as far as the size of his . . . male organ . . . there's nothing inadequate about that, is there?"

"On the contrary, he's quite well endowed, as I remember."

Lucien shielded his mouth with one hand, trying not to grin.

Buford continued. "You are not saying that he has trouble performing sexually, are you, Doctor?"

"No."

"So if I told you that Governor Yarbrough is a normal, healthy, adult male who is totally masculine, and performs quite well in the bedroom . . . sexually, that is . . . you'd have no argument with that, Doctor?"

"I would not."

"In fact, didn't some of the medicines you gave Governor Yarbrough even increase his performance ability beyond what an average man might be able to do?"

"Possibly. He was on testosterone, which often enhances the frequency and quality of a man's erections."

"Frequency?"

"How many erections a man can have in a given period. He would have more erections than average."

"Quality?"

"Rigidity, Counselor. How hard he gets."

Several giggles came from the spectators. Page

didn't dare turn to face them. She couldn't believe what she was hearing, and Lucien had put Buford up to it. Not only had they just made her out to be a whore, now they were flaunting Lucien's sexual prowess. Did he seriously think this would gain him more votes?

Lucien did turn to look at the audience, beaming proudly.

Buford said, "Thank you, Doctor. I merely needed to clarify those few points."

CHAPTER TWENTY-EIGHT

It was pouring rain when Page hurried home to feed Adam. When Doris asked how it was going, Page told about the ovulation chart and Dr. Archer. Lightning flashed; then a clap of thunder rattled windowpanes and jarred the floor. Adam began to cry.

"You left early that morning," Doris said. "I remember because I went over to the jail right after Lucien'd been there. And the police wouldn't let me see William, my own boy. From there I went over to Miss Emma's to help Bessie clean up after that party. I haven't seen William since."

As Page hurried up the courthouse steps following the lunch break, Rona Green called out. Page hadn't seen Rona in the crowds all week, didn't know she was there. They ran under cover and closed their umbrellas.

After a quick greeting, Rona said, "I don't know what it is, but Lucien and the senator are up to no good. I overheard them near the water fountain, talking about the surprise they had in store for you."

"What kind of surprise?"

"They clammed up when Lucien spotted me, but they looked as pleased as punch. Be careful, Page. Lord only knows what they'll do to you."

Inside, Page told David Fields about the conversation. Rona's warning had given her a very uneasy feeling that something terrible was about to happen. As if anything worse could happen. Her case was rapidly going to hell in a handbasket.

Fields considered what Page said, then responded, "I'll go ahead and suggest DNA testing before they can pull any fast ones. It's time to turn the heat up on Lucien and his father."

As soon as they were in session, Fields stood and said, "Your Honor, my client has undergone a polygraph examination that corroborates her sworn testimony that she never had sexual relations with any man other than her husband. My client is also willing to undergo further scientific testing to show that the child in question, Jackson Adams Yarbrough the second, is her son. We contend that this same child is, therefore, the son of my client's former husband, J. Lucien Yarbrough Junior, which makes said child the first great-grandson of Governor Jackson Adams Yarbrough. Unless Governor Lucien Yarbrough can prove to the court that this child is not his own, we must assume that Jackson Adams Yarbrough the second is a direct descendant of the maker of the trust, and is, therefore, entitled to whatever benefits the trust may provide."

When David finished, Wylie Marsh stood. "Ya Honor, I don't know what more proof is needed than is already evident." He looked around the room, as though searching for something or somebody. Then he said, "Mr. Fields, is your other client in the courtroom?"

David asked what he meant.

"You keep talking about this Jackson Adams Yarbrough the second, but I haven't seen him here. For all we know, he may not exist. Or am I mistaken? Is he present in the courtroom?"

"He's just a baby."

"And a party to this proceeding." Wylie spoke directly to Judge Scott. "Ya Honor, I would respectfully ask that Jackson Adams Yarbrough the second be present for at least this particular portion of these proceedings."

After much discussion, the judge ordered Page to bring the baby to court the following day.

On the way out, Page told David, "That must have been their big surprise. They want the judge to see that Adam's not white."

Fields shook his head. "It may work, Page. We can introduce all the polygraphs and blood tests in the world, but when this Mississippi judge looks back and forth from his white governor to that little black baby, it just may work. Old Wylie may've come up with their most effective tactic so far."

Page's hopes sank even more. Each maneuver Buford and Lucien engineered proved just how outmatched she was.

A drenching June rain came down hard, and puddles and downed tree branches slowed her progress as Page drove to the veterinary clinic after court. She needed to finish making out invoices for the week. Being in court every day had put her far behind.

Cars and trucks were parked around the clinic, and people sitting alongside big dogs peered hopefully out of their pickups, unable to walk in the grass while they waited. Inside, the reception room was full, with people impatiently holding dogs, cats, one chicken, a duck, and two nervous rabbits. Page shook her umbrella and said hello to the young receptionist, who stopped twisting her hair around a finger long enough to wave back, but never put the phone down. From the girl's body language, Page knew exactly who was on the other end of the line—the boyfriend.

Mark's assistant, Rudolph, came through the back door and into the hall first, a gold tooth gleaming in a quick smile. The doctor followed. They were both drenched and in a hurry. Page said hello and followed them into the lab. Rudolph dried his face and washed his hands, then went toward the front of the office.

"What's up?" she asked.

"The usual," Mark said. "I was out at Hope Farm this morning, vaccinating their cows, then breeding a couple of horses for Mr. Phipps. It took longer than I expected."

"The waiting room's overflowing," Page said.

Mark put something in the refrigerator. "I'd better get started. People hate to wait."

Page worked on bills and medical records until nearly six p.m. As she was finishing, Mark came in. The sleeves of his plaid shirt were rolled up, and he brushed at something gooey that had splattered on his khaki trousers.

"You want your desk back?" she asked.

"No, sit still. Rudolph's putting the next patients in." Goodson plopped into a chair, picked up a bundle of mail, then tossed it aside. "How'd things go today? You're out early."

"Okay, I guess." She told him about having to take Adam tomorrow, and what her attorney had said.

"Fields is right. Jim Scott's as fair a man as I know, but he's also a born-and-bred Southern boy. Sitting up there staring at a white woman with a black baby's gonna make a definite impression on him."

Just then Rudolph came in carrying a rain-splattered cardboard box. "Where you wants 'em, Doctor?"

"Anywhere over there, Rudy. Put some extra bottles and nipples in my truck with the formula before I leave."

Page heard something whimper and got up to see what was in the box. She saw five darling puppies, all shiny black, their eyes still closed. Somebody had put an old bath towel in the box for their bedding. "Awww," she said. "How cute. What kind are they?"

"Mostly Labrador retriever. They look purebred, but I doubt they are."

"Whose are they?"

"Yours if you want 'em. One of the Wallace kids found them down by the river."

"Where's their mother?"

"Who knows? Somebody dumped them, probably figured they'd fall in and drown. It happens all the time."

Page picked up the smallest of the puppies. She held it to her chest and stroked its velvety head with one finger. "What will you do with them?"

"Try to keep 'em alive. Whichever ones survive, I'll raise or find homes for."

"Do you have a dog now?"

"Eight."

"You have *eight* dogs?"

"Plus five cats and a canary, at last count. They seem to find me. Even the canary, Mr. Tweet."

"Mark, you have a good soul."

He stood and grinned. "More likely they know I'm a sucker. Animals see me coming from miles away." He mimicked a dog talking, overly animating his eyebrows. " 'Hey, guys, over here . . . we found us a live one.' " He walked into the hall. "What's the plan for tomorrow?"

"Take Adam to court. What choice do I have?"

"Does he have to stay all day, or can you just take him and then have Doris bring him home? I'll drive her for you."

"I didn't ask."

"What if he gets hungry while you're in court? He's not one to wait for his dinner, but I doubt you'll want to nurse him with half the town watching."

Page looked at Mark's face and her mind went blank. "I hadn't thought of that."

"You can bet Lucien did. Or Buford. And they'll make him stay there till he does."

When Page called to speak with her daughter that evening, Miss Emma answered, nervously saying she would fetch Cindy.

"Before you go, Mama Yarbrough, please let me say something."

"We're not supposed to be talking, you know." She was obviously uncomfortable having to speak with Page. It was awkward for them both.

Page said, "You'll probably never believe me, and

I can live with that if I have to, but please don't take
it out on Cindy."

"She's Lucien's child, Page. She'll always be loved."

"She's my child, too, and she needs to know her
mother. How would you have felt if somebody had
taken Lucien from you at that age?"

"You should've thought of that."

"I'm not going to argue about what I did or didn't
do. I grew up without a mother, Mama Yarbrough, and
believe me, it wasn't easy. It still isn't. No matter what
the reason, if you love Cindy, don't take her mother
away from her. She'll wind up hating you for it."

There was a long pause, then, "Just a minute, Page,
I'll put Cindy on the line."

The weather had let up a bit by morning, with only
a cold, slow drizzle falling now. Once they were in
court, Page had David Fields explain to the judge that
Jackson Adams Yarbrough II would be along shortly.
Judge Scott agreed to go ahead until the child arrived.

It seemed that nearly everybody Page had ever
known was in the small room. Miss Emma and Suellen, Page's sister, Laura, Mary Lou, Patty, and on and
on. Only her father wasn't present. Probably too hung-
over to attend. Kay Rae sauntered in late, but, unfortunately, Miss Emma had saved her a seat.

Fields surprised everybody, including Page, when he
opened that morning by saying, "We all know that
Page Briggs Yarbrough's baby is black." He paused, exaggerating the stunned silence. "Part Negro." He
paused again.

Feet began to shuffle above whispers of shock. Somebody coughed. Such an overt admission obviously
made people uncomfortable.

Fields continued, "How much Negro blood her baby
has, we don't know, but he certainly has some. If his
skin were not black, we wouldn't be here today . . .
this child would be living with his parents, Governor
Lucien Yarbrough and Page Briggs Yarbrough. And
they are his parents. Before you start objecting, Mr.

Tallant, let me issue a challenge. If your client is a hundred percent convinced there is no Negro blood circulating in the limbs of his family tree, let him demonstrate that confidence by submitting himself for DNA testing and prove once and for all that he is not the father of this black child."

Senator J. L. Yarbrough looked as though he might have a stroke. On his feet in an instant, he shouted as he started across the courtroom, "Damn you, Fields, you retract that statement immediately."

Despite quick reactions from Judge Scott, Buford, and Lucien, the snow-haired senator in a pinstripe suit advanced toward David Fields with his head tilted to one side, his fists clenched, his face fiery red. "You besmirch my family name, you little pissant, and by God you'll wish you'd never heard the name of Yarbrough."

Just as the senator reached a retreating David Fields, two deputies grabbed J.L. by the arms. Surprisingly strong for a man in his seventies, J.L. flung one deputy aside, drawing back to strike Fields. The amazed deputy barely recovered in time to halt a balled fist in midswing, quickly twisting J.L.'s arm behind his back. Amidst much shouting, cursing, gavel banging, and scuffling, the deputies wrestled the pugnacious senator to the floor and handcuffed him in view of a roomful of flabbergasted spectators.

". . . will not tolerate such an outburst in my courtroom," Judge Scott was shouting to anybody who might be able to hear above the din.

"No son of a bitch is gonna say there's nigger blood in my family," J.L. shouted, his suit jacket askew. The energized deputies pulled him up to his feet.

"Dad, it's okay," Lucien tried. "Settle down."

"Please, Senator," Buford was saying. "Give me a chance to explain." To Judge Scott, Buford said, "I respectfully request a twenty-minute recess, Your Honor. And please accept my apology for my colleague's inexcusable behavior. I assure you it will not happen again."

"I don't need any damned recess," J.L. retorted. "That bastard's going to apologize."

Page's heart was in her throat. What a way to start a morning she had been dreading all night. She had the ominous feeling that this was definitely not going to be a good day.

Following the recess, all parties returned to the courtroom. The handcuffs had been removed from Senator Yarbrough's wrists, and though he remained silent as proceedings continued, he sat stiffly, glaring at David Fields.

In response to Fields's request, Buford argued, "Millions of people watching TV saw Governor Lucien Yarbrough's blood be delivered to the state laboratory in Jackson, Your Honor. DNA tests proved that the governor is not the father of Page's black baby. How many times will the governor be forced to prove this?"

"You may say it was Lucien's blood," David retorted, "but how are we to know that? I wasn't there to watch the specimen being drawn. To the best of my knowledge, Judge Scott wasn't there. Are we to take your word for it, just as you asked us to do when that hotel clerk from New Orleans called back to say he was mistaken about the date he had fabricated under oath in this courtroom?"

"Objection, Your Honor."

Heated arguments went back and forth. With each exchange, however, Page became more impressed with avid Fields. He had the more convincing points of law as well as logic. David was trying to convince the other attorneys to agree to DNA testing, to avoid a separate hearing specifically for that issue. Finally it seemed they might be about to give in. Even J.L. seemed to have mellowed ever so slightly.

Buford said, "If Your Honor should decide in favor of DNA testing, may I presume that all parties with a direct interest in this trust will be tested?"

Page felt herself begin to relax for the first time

since Rona's warning. Maybe David could obtain what they'd come for—Lucien's DNA. All else would pale by comparison.

Judge Scott said, "Be more specific, Mr. Tallant."

"Specifically, the alleged parents of the child who is being called Jackson Adams Yarbrough the second."

Fields said, "I've already agreed that my client will undergo repeat DNA testing. Her baby, too. The one requiring a court order is the baby's father, Lucien Yarbrough."

Though she had known it was coming, the thought of another needle made Page's blood run cold, both for herself and for Adam. Her son hated needles as much as she did.

Buford corrected David. "You mean *Governor* Yarbrough, the man whom you *allege* to be the baby's father."

"All right," Fields said, "the alleged father."

"So," Buford said, "are we in agreement that, if the court should rule for the testing, the same court will arrange for not only the black child, but also the alleged parents of the black child to undergo DNA testing?"

"I have no objection to that," Fields said. He looked at Page, who nodded her agreement. Was Buford developing Alzheimer's or something? This was exactly what they had requested in the first place.

Judge Scott ordered Page, Adam, and Lucien to undergo DNA testing, and specified the procedure for collecting and delivering samples to the state lab in Jackson. David Fields would be allowed to watch Lucien's blood being drawn to make sure everything was on the up-and-up.

Page was so proud of David at this moment, she wanted to hug him. Finally Lucien would be tested for real, while they watched. J.L.'s violent outburst had made the victory that much sweeter. Perhaps David could joust with the big boys after all.

When the judge finished outlining the procedure to be followed, Buford stood. "If it please the court," he began, "Governor Yarbrough would like to officially allege that the father of the child in question is not himself, but one William Kern, a Negro man presently residing at the San Diego Naval Base in San Diego, California. We therefore ask the court to order that Mr. Kern submit his blood for DNA fingerprinting, following the procedure that Your Honor has outlined."

Page almost fell out of her seat, but hardly had time to react. As Buford spoke, the rear door of the courtroom opened and all eyes turned to watch Doris Kern amble down the center aisle toward Page. Adam was in Doris's arms, screaming at the top of his lungs. Doris handed the little black baby to Page with much of the social register of Natchez watching.

Between his shrieks Doris loudly announced, "He's real hungry, Page, and there wasn't nothing I could do without your milk."

Adam's screaming continued as he groped at Page's breasts, his lips working furiously in anticipation of what would surely follow.

Dr. Thomas Briggs poured two ounces of Wild Turkey into a water glass as he swung his feet over the side of his small bed. With fingers pressing against his throbbing temples, he washed two aspirin down with the liquor. It was eleven a.m. Moments later he sat at his computer in an undershirt and shorts, surfing the Internet. Typing in a password, he activated the search engine at the University of Heidelberg Medical Library. He selected the category *Obstetrics and Gynecology*.

Adam's fretting stopped as if somebody had flipped a switch when Page directed the nipple into his mouth. The bottle contained milk she'd pumped from her breasts before leaving home. Flustered, she had put the bottle in her handbag instead of leaving it with Doris. Along with everyone in the courtroom, Page watched as he ate. His huge, innocent eyes stared right back, one little hand on the bottle, the other wrapped around her smallest finger.

Though incensed at the accusation, Page wanted to laugh that Lucien and the senator had somehow come up with Doris's son for her supposed lover. William. They were grasping at straws now. No matter how pleased J.L. appeared at the moment, even Miss Emma wouldn't be able to believe this one.

Judge Scott said he'd need more than just Lucien's suspicion that Page had "been intimate," as Buford put it, with William Kern, before ordering the man tested.

Page hung on every word, feeding her son. This should be good. People reluctantly moved over on the front row to make room for Doris, but nobody left. All eyes were alert with anxious anticipation.

Buford put Lucien on the stand, and began by establishing just who William Kern was.

"That's his mother right there," Lucien said, pointing toward the front row. "Doris Kern. She pretty much raised Page and Page's sister, Laura, after their mother died. William's father left Doris when William was about eight or ten, so Doris and William stayed with Page up till the time we got married and after. William grew up with Page and Laura, so he was always around the house. He and Page were real close, even as kids."

"Are you aware of anything unusual that occurred when they were all growing up together, Governor? Those two little white girls and that Negro boy?"

"One instance in particular comes to mind. Page is five years older than her sister and William. When William was about four years old, Page's father caught him and Laura with their clothes off, examining each other's . . . you know . . . private parts."

"How do you know this?"

"Page told me about it once."

"What happened as a result of that incident?"

"Page's father made Doris keep William away from

the girls for a while. And Doris gave her son a good whipping."

Unaware she was doing it, Doris nodded in agreement.

Buford said, "Would you say that Page and this black man, William Kern, were close?"

"Very."

"When was the last time you saw William Kern, Governor?"

"The morning of January thirteenth, 2001."

"Where did you see him?"

"At the Natchez City Jail."

"What was the occasion?"

"William was in custody for disturbing the peace and public drunkenness. I arranged his transfer back to the navy base where he's stationed, in San Diego."

Page heard Doris behind her saying, "So that's why."

"How did you happen to be involved, Governor?"

"Page asked me to help him."

After a lengthy pause, Buford said, "So your wife, Page Briggs Yarbrough, asked you to help her close friend William Kern, who was in jail."

"That's correct."

Page felt her anger rising. How could Buford and Lucien twist things around so? She wanted to tell Doris not to take what they said about William personally. Apparently an acceptable courtroom technique for successful attorneys, this was but one more twisted fabrication.

Buford was saying, "When you arranged to have Mr. Kern released, what did he say to you?"

"He told me to go blank myself."

"Blank?"

"I'd rather not use the word with ladies present." Lucien turned toward his mother and smiled. Miss Emma nodded solemnly in return, approving his upbringing.

"Did William use the *F* word?"

"Yes." Lucien lowered his head as if he might blush.

Page nudged David Fields and whispered, "That's Lucien's favorite word, and the senator's. They make me want to throw up with their holier-than-thou act."

Buford continued, "So this man whom you went to help told you to go F yourself. Did he say anything else?"

"He said he had already F'd my wife and I could go F myself too. Me and all the F'ing Yarbroughs."

The spectators stirred like a school of excited minnows.

After another pause, Buford quietly asked, "Did Mr. Kern say exactly when he had F'd your wife?"

"The night before."

"Which would have been?"

"January twelfth, 2001."

Buford turned to Judge Scott. "The exact time, Your Honor, when Mr. Fields's own witness, Dr. Jefferson Archer, testified that Ms. Briggs had just ovulated and was primed to get pregnant. Dr. Archer also testified that her chances of becoming pregnant by another man's sperm—not her husband's—would have been a ninety to ninety-five percent certainty."

Page jumped straight out of her chair. "Lucien's lying," she shouted, Adam in her arms.

CHAPTER TWENTY-NINE

Shocked spectators watching Page and Adam shook their heads.

David Fields objected to the governor's testimony, but it stood.

When finally forced to take her seat, Page told Fields this was the first she'd heard about William making such a statement. She didn't believe it.

On cross-examination, Fields asked Lucien how Page had reacted to what William supposedly said.

"I never told her."

"Why not?"

"I thought William was being a hothead because he was angry. I didn't believe him. That is, I didn't believe him at that time."

"Why was he angry?"

"He was in jail."

"I see. Later on, Governor, when the hospital told you your baby was black, what did you say to your wife about William?"

"Nothing. I still couldn't believe Page would do something like that. To tell the truth, I'd repressed the whole episode with William. I actually thought the hospital had mixed up the babies."

"When did you suddenly decide to believe William's angry proclamation, Governor?"

"When the DNA tests proved beyond any doubt that Page was the mother of that little—"

Fields interrupted. "Objection, inadmissible and immaterial."

Judge Scott said, "You can't object to your own question, Counselor."

"Sorry, Your Honor." David blushed, chagrined. When he recovered, he asked, "What happened to your earlier conviction that Mr. Dejon Washington is the father of your wife's child?"

Lucien hesitated for only an instant. "The date when Dr. Archer said Page ovulated doesn't coincide with when she was in New Orleans with Dejon Washington. It does match exactly with what William told me about the night of January twelfth."

Just then Adam stopped drinking from his bottle and grunted noisily, his face straining. It was one of those moments when everybody stopped talking at the same time. No matter what was happening on the stand, Adam had more important things to do, like having a bowel movement. So with the entire court silently watching—attorneys, judge, clerks, and spectators—he did just that.

Amid a murmur of soft laughter and hushed conversation, Doris rushed the baby outside for a fresh diaper.

The only way he could, Adam had offered his opinion of these legal proceedings to all who cared to listen.

Page thought her son had expressed himself quite well.

Later, Page testified that she knew William was in town the night of the twelfth and morning of the thirteenth, but she never saw him. She learned he was in jail only when Doris came to ask Lucien to help early on the morning of the thirteenth.

Page said, "I was at River Oaks Plantation most of the afternoon of the twelfth and all that evening, helping Lucien's mother with a wedding shower. Lucien came by around eleven o'clock and we went home."

Buford Tallant asked, "Did you leave River Oaks at any time?"

"Just to pick up my daughter from charm school."

"Were you alone?"

"Until I picked up Cindy."

"What time was that?"

"About five p.m."

"On January twelfth?"

"Yes."

"How long were you gone from River Oaks?"

"About a half hour, maybe a few minutes more. I swung by my house and picked up the dresses Cindy and I were going to wear for the shower."

"Did anybody see you there?"

"Doris. She ironed Cindy's dress."

"Doris Kern? William's mother?"

"Yes."

Buford reminded the court that, according to Dr. Archer's testimony, Page required only from two to fifteen minutes to get pregnant on that particular day at the exact time when she was alone, unobserved by others. Supposedly driving somewhere between River Oaks Plantation, her daughter's charm school, and her own home.

From the looks in their eyes, it was obvious to Page that, with the exception of her own attorney, nobody in the courtroom believed her. Especially not the judge.

As Page returned to her seat, Buford Tallant unexpectedly said, "I call Doris Kern to the witness stand." Page held Adam while Doris was sworn in.

Doris confirmed that William and a navy buddy had arrived in town by bus on the evening of the twelfth. William was arrested and taken back to San Diego just as Lucien had said, without ever coming to see his mother. Doris was still upset about that. She seemed terribly nervous being on the witness stand. Buford had to ask her to speak up several times.

"When did William join the navy, Mrs. Kern?"

"Nineteen hundred and ninety-five."

"Why?"

"Why did he join up?"

"Yes."

"Couldn't get a job. Nothing that would pay."

"Is that the only reason?"

Doris thought for a moment. "He liked the uniform. He sure was proud of that."

"Anything else?"

"Not that I know of."

Buford walked closer to Doris. "Isn't it true that your son joined the navy because he had to leave town, Mrs. Kern?"

"No, sir."

"Isn't it also true that he got into trouble with a woman by the name of Rose Marie Johnson right here in Natchez?"

Page clutched David Fields's forearm and squeezed. Hard. She suddenly knew exactly why Buford had insisted that Doris testify.

Doris's eyes seemed to double in size. She began to perspire. "That girl was trailer trash, and that ain't what happened."

"And didn't Rose Marie Johnson's father threaten to shoot your son, William Kern, if he ever came near his daughter again?"

"I don't rightly recollect that."

Buford stopped for a moment. Taking a long breath, he asked, "What color was Rose Marie Johnson, Mrs. Kern?"

Doris studied something in her lap. She wiped one eye with a handkerchief, then looked off to the side of the courtroom. Not at anything in particular, just away from Buford Tallant.

"I didn't hear your answer, Mrs. Kern. Before she left town because of your son, William, what color was Rose Marie Johnson?"

Doris mumbled something inaudible.

"Louder, please."

"White," Doris finally admitted. "She was a white girl, but it wasn't the way you're making it out to be."

As if on cue, Adam began to cry. Page managed

to fight back her own tears as Buford threw her a haughty look.

Buford was building Lucien's fort one brick at a time. Page wondered if, by the time he finished, she'd be able to see over the top. Or if she'd be forever buried beneath the foundation.

Judge Scott ordered that William Kern be DNA tested along with Lucien, Page, and Adam. He raised the question of William's whereabouts, and the steps necessary to have him brought to Natchez. "Since this is not a criminal matter," Scott said, "he'll have to come of his own accord."

David Fields had wanted to insist that William be brought in to testify as well, but decided to consult Page first. He needed to know more about William, whether he was honest, would lie, or might've been bought off by Lucien or J.L.

Buford said, "We have taken the liberty of speaking with Ensign Kern's commanding officer, Your Honor. The U.S. Navy will make the ensign available for testing whenever you say."

To Fields, Page whispered, "Political influence. And dirty politics."

Mark Goodson drove Doris and Adam home, enabling Page to confer with her attorney.

Page wanted to call William immediately, in San Diego, but David thought they should talk first.

Page said, "I don't believe for one second that William said what Lucien claimed. William would never say anything like that, even in anger. He's my friend."

Rather than go to his office, David suggested they sit on a small dock behind David's office building, overlooking the river. They both needed a breather, and agreed not to discuss the case for at least a half hour. After today's events, Page was nonplussed. From the way the senator had carried on, to the strain of having Adam there, and now this latest crazy claim that Doris's son had sired her child, she was exhausted.

Contrasting her mood, the rain had stopped and the day was a beautiful afternoon with summer flowers in bloom beneath an unexpectedly sunny sky. Downtown was filled with tourists even after spring Pilgrimage. Hotels and plantation bed-and-breakfasts remained booked for miles around. Horse-drawn carriages clip-clopped through the streets. Unlike the previous hectic ten years, Page hadn't been asked to help with anything having to do with Pilgrimage or the pageant this year. In fact, nobody from the Confederate Garden Club had even returned her calls. She'd left four voice messages and three e-mails before giving up.

David brought two enormous paper cups filled with iced tea from a restaurant across the street: one for him, plain; one for Page, sweetened. He loosened his tie and opened his collar. They found a dry wooden bench under an overhang at the end of the dock and sat quietly for a long while, watching a flatbed barge struggle against the muddy current, hauling some kind of huge metal pipes upriver. They were in the area of town called Natchez under the Hill. Sounds of a Dixie-land band came from *The Lady Luck*, a riverboat casino permanently moored a few hundred yards away. A brightly colored passenger paddle-wheeler en route from Ohio to New Orleans was docked just beyond.

Page had trained her docents to inform tourists that Natchez was actually two towns in one. On a high bluff overlooking the Mississippi sat Natchez proper. Down below, on the riverfront, was Natchez "improper," an early domain of riverboat gamblers, runaway slaves, prostitutes, and transient vermin. Known in the distant past as "Sodom of the Mississippi," the area had accommodated as many as three or four hundred vessels at a time during the cotton boom. Now there were mostly small fishing boats or barges, and the occasional paddle-wheeler filled with nostalgic tourists.

"The river air smells nice," Page said, inhaling deeply. "I'm so tired of being cooped up in that stuffy old courtroom all day."

"Me too," Fields agreed. "I even like the humidity outdoors."

"You're supposed to be in courtrooms, David. I'm not."

He sipped his tea through a straw, then stirred the ice. "I'd much rather be writing my book or researching tax law. I can do that in short sleeves and jeans with the windows open, or under some shade tree."

"That's certainly comforting to hear."

"I don't mean I'm not pleased to be helping you . . . I am. In fact, I've enjoyed most of it. It's completely different from tax law." He tossed a piece of ice across the water, watching it skip. Both had stayed away from the case as long as they could. "Do you suppose William said anything even close to what Lucien claims he did?"

"No." Page had been pondering exactly the same thought.

"I can't understand why Lucien would say he did. I'm missing something here."

"The whole idea is ludicrous."

"What actually happened with William and the white girl?"

"I only got bits and pieces of the story, but according to Doris, Rose Marie Johnson wasn't a very nice girl. Her family lived in a mobile home out past the tire plant. I guess she saw William around town and had this thing for him. He is a good-looking young man, clean-cut and all, and she made up her mind to . . . do it . . . with a black man. She made a bet with her girlfriends at school. So she set out for William."

"And he got caught?"

"According to what William told Doris, they never actually did anything . . . at least, they didn't go all the way. Rose Marie's daddy came home one afternoon and caught them kissing. He had a conniption, and threatened to kill William. The Johnsons left town later, but it wasn't over William. He was already in the navy by the time they left."

"How old was William when that happened?"

"About seventeen."

"Can you think of any reason William might say what Lucien claims he did? If he was angry enough?"

"No, I . . . not really."

"What? You started to say something else."

"I don't know. William changed when he was about sixteen or seventeen. Not toward me or Laura . . . he was always friendly toward us. Like a brother." Page laughed softly. "From what my friends told me, he was nicer than most brothers. But he got so he didn't seem to care for Lucien. I don't know why, and he never said anything, but you could tell. Know how a dog will sometimes sit over in a corner just watching somebody it doesn't like? Not growling or anything, but you can tell. By its eyes."

Fields understood the analogy.

"That's the way William became whenever Lucien was around. Just sorta sullen, you know?"

"Had Lucien done anything to him?"

"Not really. He did tell William he needed to stay in his place once."

"His house?"

"No, his place. You know, his social position . . . being black and all. He said William didn't know his place anymore. That he was getting uppity."

"How'd William respond to that?"

"He seemed okay, at least as far as I was concerned. I guess I didn't pay a whole lot of attention. I was a new bride and busy with parties and events. I'd just been asked to join the garden club and I was already in the Junior League. I didn't have time to notice."

Her description of that life suddenly felt superficial to Page. Shallow. And sounded that way. She wished now that she had paid attention to more important things.

Fields stared out across the river. It was nearly dusk, and lights were beginning to flicker on patios of restaurants near the casino. "Is there anything for us to worry about, Page? With the blood test?"

"You mean William's?"

"Yes."

"Don't be silly, David."

"I don't mean to be. It's just . . . they ambushed me, didn't they? Buford baited me to push and argue till I achieved exactly what he wanted."

"It appears that way."

"Do you think the senator was helping set me up? The way he overreacted?"

"I doubt it. His reaction seemed genuine."

Fields considered her answer. After a moment he said, "Of course that's why they made you bring Adam to court. They knew I'd start clamoring for DNA tests, the only logical way to counter Judge Scott's impression from seeing Adam." Fields took a mouthful of ice and crunched it noisily. "But why? What could possibly make them want to test William?"

"It defies all reason, David. I don't have the faintest idea."

David turned slowly to face Page. "I don't either. And that worries me big-time."

CHAPTER THIRTY

Mark Goodson's pickup was in the driveway when Page returned to Willowdale Plantation. The truck's specially designed bed overflowed with veterinary supplies.

Mark was having a cup of coffee in the front parlor with Auntie Bellum, listening to tales of idyllic life before the War of Northern Aggression. After checking on Adam and Doris, Page joined them.

Page's brain was so fatigued, it felt good to sit back and listen to something pleasant for a change.

Belle Braswell was telling Mark about when John James Audubon lived nearby, supporting himself as a tutor for children of wealthy cotton growers while he painted local birds. She talked about important homes, Stanton Hall with its enormous white pillars, and Monmouth, a legendary mansion and former residence of General John A. Quitman, Mexican war hero and later governor of Mississippi. Belle knew the names of every original owner and their descendants still living in Natchez today. She could go on for hours about the elegance and charm of that former era.

When Belle paused for a sip of coffee, Page thanked Mark for his help with Doris and Adam.

"Glad to help," Goodson said. "Doris sure is upset."

"I can imagine."

"Your father, too."

"You talked to him? I didn't see him in court."

"He arrived late in the afternoon. I drove him home when court let out."

"To a bar, you mean."

"No, home. He was in pretty good shape today. He sure is furious over Lucien's insinuations about you and William. Almost as mad as the senator was about Negro blood in his family."

"Daddy always liked William."

"He said he did. Said it'd make him laugh if it weren't such an insult to you." Mark toyed with a doily on the arm of the sofa. "Why would Lucien make such a statement?"

"Beats me, Mark. David and I have been trying to figure it out."

Mark nodded. "I like your dad. He's plenty sharp."

"If you catch him before noon."

"Like I said, he was fine today, and it was afternoon. His hands were a little shaky, but his mind's like a laser. He told me about all kinds of new treatments for human ailments, wanted to know if we use them in animals. Most of them we probably should, but don't."

Belle spoke up. "His mind's more like an egg when he's been drinking."

"How's that?" asked Mark.

"Take your pick . . . either scrambled or fried." Belle enjoyed her own humor so much that she spilled her coffee. She wiped it up and went to fetch more.

"How're the new puppies?" asked Page.

"Gettin' bigger every day. They already chewed a hole in their box."

"Oh, no."

"Lab puppies are bad about chewing. But that's part of the deal."

"How do you stop it?"

"Make sure they have something to chew that you don't value. The good Lord designed 'em that way."

"You really like your animals, don't you, Mark? You give them such understanding . . . and love."

"They give back more than I could ever give them." He stood. "Well, best be moving . . . I have a couple of farm calls to make. With all those dogs looking for something to chew, I hope my front porch'll be standing when I get home."

While they prepared dinner that evening, Page commented to Doris that she had no idea why Lucien had suggested a relationship between William and her. Adam lay sleeping in an antique mahogany crib nearby—a gift from Auntie Bellum—and the windows were open. A gentle breeze lifted curtains from the windowsills and carried a hint of summer jasmine into the room.

Doris said, "Remember, I raised you both, so you don't have to tell me. I know you and I know my William."

"He'd never be part of anything with Lucien or the senator, would he?"

"Part of what?"

"I don't know . . . whatever."

"Not against you, he wouldn't, nor Laura neither. You girls are his family, same as I am. I just hope he's all right."

"Do you think the senator might've threatened to mess up his career in the navy somehow?"

"That's what worries me. William won't take no threats. Never did. He wanted to go to that trailer park the time that lawyer was talkin' about, and tell old man Johnson what really happened with his no-'count daughter . . . after that man threatened to shoot him on sight. Would have, too, if I hadn't got him stopped."

"How'd you stop him?"

"I hate to admit it."

"Tell me. I never knew anything about all that."

"The only time I ever had to ask that no-good Antwann for help since the day I threw him outta the house. But he did it . . . he came over and wouldn't let William go. Besides, William isn't gonna kowtow to no Yarbrough, whether it's Lucien or the senator, either one. That doesn't include you, of course. You're not one of them."

"Why, Doris? Antwann's family worked for the Yarbroughs for years. What'd they ever do to William?"

"Since they were slaves," Doris said softly. "That's a mighty long time."

"Do you know what happened?"

"Yes."

"What was it?"

After much prodding, Doris said, "It wasn't exactly William they did it to, but he took it the same as if it was. I wish Antwann never had told him. Antwann always did have a big mouth. And you know how young men are, Page. They're just looking for somethin' to get all riled up about."

Adam woke up, so Page changed his diaper, then played with him as Doris stirred pots, checked biscuits, and related the story. Adam laughed and cooed at the red teddy bear Page had bought.

"Antwann was born right out there at River Oaks Plantation. Antwann's daddy's name was Jim. They called him Big Jim, 'cause he was so big, you know . . . William's granddaddy. Big Jim's wife, Ophelia, had two other children before Big Jim got killed. They were with The Governor for a long time."

"How'd Big Jim get killed?"

"The Governor shot him."

Page was shocked. "Jackson Adams Yarbrough? Shot William's grandfather?"

"Yes," Doris answered quite unemotionally.

"Why, Doris? What happened?"

"He and The Governor got in some kinda argument."

"And The Governor just shot him?"

"Yes."

"What were they arguing about?"

"I don't rightly know."

"You must've heard something. What did Antwann say?"

"I don't recollect what all he said. Didn't matter anyway . . . Big Jim was dead."

"I remember Suellen saying something about The Governor shooting a man. What I heard was, The

Governor caught somebody stealing a keg of whiskey from his shed one night. Was that Big Jim?''

"Must've been.''

"What did they do, Doris? Was there an investigation?"

"I reckon.''

"Was there a trial?''

"No.''

"Why not?''

Doris looked up as if Page were daft. "He was The Governor, Page.''

"Yes, but . . . what'd the police say after the investigation?''

"Antwann said they told The Governor he should be real careful who he hired next time . . . not get 'em so big, so he could make 'em mind without having to shoot 'em.''

"No wonder William was upset with the Yarbroughs.''

"William and some of his friends had watched that *Roots* program on the VCR—more than once; then Antwann opened his mouth about Big Jim. William got real upset over that. I personally believe that's why he left Natchez. It wasn't because of that Johnson girl." Doris spooned steaming stew from an iron kettle onto two plates. "That and no work for him here. Dinner's ready, Page. I already put sugar in the tea.''

Buford Tallant, David Fields, and two court-appointed sheriff's deputies were present when Page went to Dr. Archer's office to have her own and Adam's blood drawn. Television audiences throughout the Southeast would watch and hear once again about Governor Yarbrough's black baby, and about some mystery man's blood being flown in from San Diego—Page's alleged black lover.

Her story made the cover of two supermarket tabloids that week. She felt certain Judge Scott didn't want to be outdone by Judge Winston, who'd received so much publicity during the first round of testing.

"They're all politicians," Page said, "the scariest thought of all."

Explaining that it would be less costly, yet perfectly reliable, Judge Scott elected to have William Kern's blood drawn at the base hospital in San Diego. It would be DNA tested there with a sample sent to the lab in Jackson for confirmation, rather than transporting William to Jackson.

After being ambushed in court, David Fields was taking no chances this time. He insisted on flying to San Diego to witness the sampling. At his own expense.

Fields was on the phone to the base commander as soon as he arrived in his San Diego hotel room.

"Oh, yes, Mr. Fields, Senator Chavitz said you'd be calling. And Senator Turnbull."

"Did the senators mention what I'm calling about?"

"They said you wanted to meet with one of my men. Ensign Kern. When you come out to the base, we'll discuss it. I look forward to showing you around, if you have time. We're quite proud of what we're doing here."

Fields freshened up and took a taxi to the naval base. Yarbroughs weren't the only people who could play politics. David's father had come to know lots of politicians over the years, and had been delighted to make a few calls on his son's behalf. When it came to political influence, a senator was a senator, be he from Mississippi, Pennsylvania, or New York. David sat back in the taxi and smiled, pleased with himself. The base commander hadn't even heard from the vice president yet.

His name recognized instantly by the uniformed guard at the entry gate, David received directions and a snappy salute as his taxi proceeded on base. They drove past rows of long, low gray buildings and squads of marching sailors—young men and women—and U.S. Navy trucks and equipment. Huge gray ships were secured to the biggest docks Fields had ever seen—ships with enormous guns, menacing but silent. There was no sign of life on board except for revolving radar-and-communications antennae, alert, no doubt watching and listening to the world. He could only imagine the bright young technicians inside, and the array of sophisticated electronics at their fingertips. David knew he'd rest securely tonight, less concerned about wild-eyed foreign dictators after observing these sleeping behemoths. He sure was glad they were on the same team.

After a brief tour by the base commander, a second officer escorted Fields onto one of the docked ships, where he was directed to a small office to wait for Ensign Kern.

The room contained two portholes, a single gray metal desk, and assorted chairs. A young man wearing a white uniform entered and quietly closed the door behind him. The sailor's heels could be faintly heard to click together as he straightened and said, "Ensign William Kern, sir. How may I be of service?"

Fields felt as though he should salute. William could've been on a poster enticing young Americans to enlist in the navy. He was immaculate, trim, and athletic. His hair was cropped in a crew cut, his skin a creamy, unblemished chocolate. His smile was gleaming white, and appeared genuine.

David said, "I'm David Fields, an attorney from Natchez." He presented his business card.

The smile in William's eyes faded. He didn't speak.

Fields quickly added, "I represent Page Briggs."

Kern narrowed his eyes. "I thought that was over with."

"You thought what was over with?"

"Her divorce."

"The divorce has been over for a long time." Fields steadied himself with a hand on the desk when the ship moved under his feet. He nodded toward the chairs. "Do you have any objection if we sit for a few minutes and talk?"

"No, sir."

Once seated, David studied the man's face. "What's your job in the navy, William? May I call you William?"

"Yes, sir. I'm a communications specialist, sir."

"I've never been in the military, William, but I respect it and the people in it. I appreciate the job you fellows do for our country. However, I'm a bit uncomfortable with the formality. I'm not used to it."

"Yes, sir, sorry, sir." His answer was a little less snappy, but William sat erect in his seat, shoulders square, chin level, eyes straight ahead.

"Have you spoken with anybody back home about what's going on there?" Fields caught himself slumping in his seat in response to William's rigidity. He swung one ankle up to rest on the opposite knee and tilted his chair back.

"My commanding officer told me Senator Yarbrough had called. Of course, I know about the baby. There's no need for a blood test, Mr. Fields . . . they should've just asked me. I can tell them exactly what the test is going to show."

CHAPTER THIRTY-ONE

Being so concerned with what might be happening in San Diego, Page found it difficult to concentrate on her driving as she went to and from work at the veterinary clinic. She hadn't heard a word from David Fields, and that was most unsettling. She had expected him to call almost as soon as he arrived in California, to say he'd solved the mystery. Why had Lucien and the senator insisted on testing William? It made no sense. But then, what *had* lately? The most frightening thing was knowing that Buford, Lucien, and the senator would never risk public embarrassment. They were experienced schemers, calculating to the most minute detail, and downright cunning. What misery did they intend to heap upon her this time? And who would they coerce or buy off to achieve it?

Surprised at William's comment about the blood test, David Fields asked, "What are you saying?"

"Somebody obviously mixed up the babies in the hospital."

Fields asked what he'd meant about the test.

"Page was married, Mr. Fields. She'd never go with another man. Especially not an African-American."

"What makes you say that?"

William gave a short laugh. "I'm not saying there's anything wrong with African-Americans, mind you, or with interracial relationships, but that isn't how Page was raised."

Fields felt his chest relax somewhat. He took several deep breaths and slowly let them out. "When you were in Natchez in January of 2001, what'd Page think of your uniform?"

"She never saw it, sir."

"Were you wearing civvies, as I believe you fellas call them?"

"No, sir, I was in uniform. But Page didn't see it."

"Why not?"

"When she came by, they wouldn't let her in."

"Who wouldn't?"

"Either the police or her husband. Probably Lucien."

"Came by where?"

"I was in jail, sir."

"Are you talking about the morning Lucien Yarbrough came to get you out of jail?"

William recoiled, a smirk on his face. "That's a joke."

"What do you mean?"

"He came to make sure I couldn't get out. He even called my base to be certain they'd pick me up."

"Let me get this straight. First, let's back up to the day before. Did you see Page for, oh, say, as little as two minutes, or as much as fifteen?"

"No, sir, I told you, I never got to see her at all." William's unwavering gaze came straight back at David.

"Do you know what DNA testing is, William?"

"The whole world knows about DNA, sir, after O.J."

"Then you probably know that the odds of one person's DNA matching up with another person's who is not closely related are pretty slim. Like one in ten million or so."

"I know it's rare, sir."

"What would you say if Page's DNA matched perfectly with the black baby's?"

"The tests are wrong, sir."

"What if they retested and came out the same?"

"I'd say somebody's playing a shell game with the samples."

Without warning, Fields asked, "Did you have sex with Page Yarbrough?"

William almost laughed. "Are you sure you represent Page, Mr. Fields?"

"Didn't your commanding officer tell you that?"

"Yes, sir, but your asking that question makes me think you don't know her at all." William's look said he did not appreciate Fields's making that insinuation.

"Humor me, William. Did you ever have sex with Page Briggs Yarbrough?"

"Of course not. That's ridiculous."

"You're sure?"

"I think I'd remember something like that . . . sir." William was obviously becoming annoyed.

"Why would somebody claim that you did?"

"Who said that? Lucien? His father?"

"Yes."

"Then they're damned liars, sir, and I'll tell 'em to their lying pasty faces." William stood abruptly and walked around his chair, the muscles of his jaw and temples working furiously. His nostrils dilated and he was breathing hard. After he'd stood perfectly rigid for a while, his breathing gradually slowed.

Fields didn't speak. He merely observed.

Finally William spoke. "How long have you lived in Mississippi, Mr. Fields?"

"Two and a half years."

"Who's the governor of Mississippi now?"

"We both know the answer to that."

"Who lives in the biggest house in Natchez? Drives the biggest car? Who was it could get elected to the United States Senate for as long as he could fog a mirror?"

"That would be Senator J. L. Yarbrough."

William slowly shook his head. "If your name is Yarbrough in Mississippi, Mr. Fields, you can make a test show whatever you want it to show. People will say whatever you tell them to say."

"Even doctors? Medical experts?"

"They're people, aren't they?"

*   *   *

Page stood in the rear of Mark Goodson's clinic, holding a particularly uncooperative goat, while Mark prepared to administer an injection. Rudolph hadn't come back from lunch yet, and the owner of the small herd had driven forty miles to have his animals vaccinated. Good thing she'd worn jeans and a cotton blouse to work.

Mark thumped his hand against the goat's rear to mask a needle that he inserted on the third thump, usually a successful technique. Not today. The goat jumped straight in the air, bucking and kicking, knocking Page to the ground. As she attempted to catch herself, one hand went smack into a pile of fresh goat manure.

"Yechhh," she said, hanging on to the lead rope with the other hand. The goat lurched toward an open field, dragging Page behind. She came up on her feet, running, then led the goat back to Mark.

"He didn't escape," she said proudly.

"Are you all right?"

"A little smelly, but that's why they make hot showers and soap."

Just then the receptionist announced that Page had a call.

Page washed her hands and excitedly answered the phone. It was David Fields. She asked where he was.

"At the airport in San Diego. I've just had William Kern take a polygraph examination, administered by U.S. Naval Intelligence."

"Did he say what Lucien said he said?"

"He'd never say anything bad about you, even in anger. He knows you're too much of a lady. But I'll tell you one thing—he sure doesn't like Lucien."

"Doris explained that to me one night . . . it goes way back." Page thought for an instant before asking, "Did you ask him on the lie detector about when he was in town that January, if he and I even saw each other?"

"I had them ask every question both I and the intelligence officer could think of. William confirmed exactly what you said."

"Oh, David, I'm so relieved. I want a copy of the report, in case Cindy ever hears anything different. No matter what happens I'll always be grateful for your getting that report."

"If the polygraph isn't admissible, there's a chance William can testify, depending on their maneuvers schedule."

"That'd be wonderful."

"When's the last time you saw him?"

"About four years ago."

"Did you know the navy put him through school? He has a college degree now."

"Doris said he was in school."

"He's an intelligent, articulate young man."

"So he'll make a good witness?"

"I think so. Look, I have to run. Would you call Sarah, please? Tell her I'll be home tomorrow morning."

Elated, Page danced back to where Mark waited. "Bring me another goat," she said. After hearing David's news, she was ready for anything.

More reporters were in the courtroom than for the previous round of DNA testing, but not as many locals—most had already made up their minds. Page had slept with a black man and everybody knew it. Did it make sense to dignify the act by questioning which one it was? Besides, it'd be in the evening paper and on the six-o'clock news.

The procedure was less drawn out than before. Dr. George Crisp once again delivered the test results under guard, in a locked container.

A court reporter silently punched keys on her transcriber as the judge asked, "Dr. Crisp, did your laboratory perform a DNA test on a blood sample from the infant Jackson Adams Yarbrough the second?"

"We did."

"Did you also test a blood sample from Page Briggs Yarbrough?"

"Yes."

"How does Page Briggs Yarbrough's sample corre-
late with that of the infant?"

"It is a definite match."

"So according to your tests, Page Briggs Yarbrough
is the mother of that infant?"

"Yes, Your Honor."

A clerk looked up from the docket books, then
yawned. Everybody in town knew that Adam was
Page's baby. David Fields had admitted that straight
off; then they'd all seen her giving the baby his bottle.

Page wished she could be so calm. With Lucien and
Buford opposing her, no such luxury was possible. She
trusted them the way she would trust an angry
rattlesnake.

Judge Scott continued. "Did you also test a blood
sample from Governor Jackson Lucien Yarbrough
Junior?"

"We did."

"How does that sample compare with the one from
the infant?"

Under her breath, Page said, "Listen up, Miss
Emma. Here it comes whether you like it or not."

"No match."

What? Page thought she'd surely heard wrong.

"What do you conclude from the test, Doctor?"

Crisp said, "Governor Yarbrough is not the father
of the infant."

Disappointment swept over Page like an onrushing
tsunami. Testing William had been a devious charade
orchestrated by the senator, but how had they arranged to show, once again, that Adam was not Lucien's son? After an insufferably long moment, Page
accepted that everything in her life had been off-kilter
since that first night in the hospital. She exhaled a
sigh of frustration, leaned toward David Fields, and
whispered, "Isn't there a way to at least tell if there's
Negro blood back there somewhere? There has to
be."

Before David could respond, Judge Scott continued,

saying, "Dr. Crisp, did you also test a blood sample from Ensign Kern?"

"We did." Crisp cleared his throat. "It is a definite match. Ensign William Kern is the father of the child."

Fighting a sudden wave of nausea, Page clung tightly to the arms of her chair, afraid she might pass out. Though Dr. Crisp's words resonated throughout her skull, she felt as though she were no longer a party to these proceedings. Or to any reality she had ever known.

CHAPTER THIRTY-TWO

Buford and J.L. huddled immediately. Lucien focused on his father, avoiding everyone else's gaze.

From across the room, Page had some vague awareness that Lucien was livid with anger. Everything around her seemed to be distorted somehow, and moving in slow motion.

Reporters ran for telephones. Everybody in the room suddenly had something to say. There was no hope of restoring order in the courtroom.

Page and David Fields were too stunned to react. Unmoving, Fields stared openmouthed at Dr. Crisp. A quizzical look blanketed David's face, but no words were formed.

Something heavy compressed Page's chest, almost suffocating her. Her eyes were glued to Lucien. Tears began, then streamed down her flushed cheeks. In the throes of complete mental meltdown, she made no effort to wipe them away. Her shoulders slowly sagged; then she dropped her head into her hands and sobbed aloud. She didn't have the energy reserves to scream.

Feeling totally alone in the courtroom, Page realized it was over. Really over this time. She'd lost her daughter, her husband, her home. Friends. Her reputation. All credibility. Even her dignity. Everything that had ever mattered, before Adam.

But how? Why? Her mind whirled, being sucked down some nightmarish dark vortex—the black hole of reason and sanity. The most up-to-date, incontrovertible, scientific evidence had just proved, at better than ten-million-to-one odds, that she had performed an act that only she knew, with absolutely certainty, she had not.

The events of the past several months left her with one inescapable conclusion, which she resigned herself to accept. Too exhausted to continue, she was doomed to surrender. What other course was there? Clearly defeated, she felt as hopeless as she knew she was helpless.

The conclusion? Simple. Obvious, when you considered all the evidence—Page had lost her mind. She'd read about women doing that after childbirth. It happened often enough that they even had a name for it now—postpartum psychosis.

It would be perfectly natural to have had no insight into her condition. After all, how could she, being crazy?

Back in their law offices, Buford exclaimed to J.L., "You hit a homer this time, Senator. How could you be so certain William was the father?"

"The black bastard flat-out told Lucien he'd screwed Page. That morning at the jailhouse."

"My money was on Dejon Washington. What about those anonymous calls from women who'd seen Page with him?"

"Hell, she probably screwed them both. Maybe half a dozen, for all we know. The lying slut."

Mark Goodson came to check on Page on Saturday morning. Even though her gloom had lightened somewhat, she had a terrible headache, and there wasn't an aspirin in the house.

"I have some Bute in my truck," Mark said.

"What's that?"

"Butazolidin . . . sort of a horse aspirin, but it'll work on you. People are animals, too, same as horses and dogs and cows. We think we're smarter, but the jury's still out on that, as far as I'm concerned."

"Pill or capsule?"

"Paste." He grinned. "It may not taste great, but it'll do the job. I generally hold their heads and squeeze some on the back of their tongues to make 'em swallow, but you can mix yours in orange juice, if you prefer."

"At this point I'll try anything, horse medicine or not. I'm not sure I'm as smart as a horse. I feel drunk, and I haven't even had a drink."

When Mark brought the medicine in, he asked what Page's plans were now. She stirred the paste into orange juice and drank it in one long swallow. It was revolting.

When she could speak, she said, "Any hopes I had for the trust are over for sure. Lucien's son will get whatever's in it, thanks to wonderful Kay Rae. With Adam sitting up by himself now, even standing with a little help, he'll be walking in no time. He needs new shoes and bigger clothes, and I need to keep working. If you'll have me."

"You're gonna be just fine, Page. You may not be ready to hear it, but I am glad you're not married anymore."

"Thank you, Mark." She sipped from a fresh glass of orange juice, then said, "You know, here I am in this terrible predicament, and I cannot understand why. I know as much about reproduction as the next person, but I need to know so much more. Will you teach me how babies are made?"

Mark grinned mischievously, his dark eyes flashing. "Hands-on instruction?"

"I'm serious, Mark. Teach me exactly what happens. Technical details. I feel so helpless. If I don't do something constructive, I'm gonna wind up in a straitjacket. Trying to understand what's possible might keep my mind off the impossible . . . which is exactly what happened to me. Am I making any sense?"

"It's as good a place to start as any."

"I know I'm grasping at straws."

"We all do sometimes." After a pause, Mark raised one eyebrow and asked, "How long does a gentleman need to wait after a lady's been through something like you have before he can ask the lady out?"

"Are you serious? You'd go out with me after all you heard this week? Out in public?"

"Sure would."

"Then you don't have to wait at all. I haven't been anywhere in months. I haven't gone out with a man in years, if you don't count Lucien."

"I don't."

Page laughed for the first time in days. "Me, neither. Not anymore."

That afternoon Mark took Page to Phipps Plantation, with its vast green pastures, white rail fences, and the most elegant horses Page had ever seen.

She'd never realized how enormous racehorses could be. Their heads alone seemed the size of her body, and their backs were two feet higher than her head.

Mark led her through a lab complete with stainless-steel counters, a microscope, a refrigerator, and racks of glass tubes.

Minutes later Page watched a man lead a beautiful bay mare into the breeding shed, next to a cylindrical "breeding dummy." The dummy resembled a boxer's canvas punching bag. About four feet long and two feet in diameter, it was mounted horizontally on a sturdy support at the same level as the mare's back. They positioned the mare alongside the dummy.

Two stocky attendants led a muscular stallion into the room. The stallion immediately began tossing his magnificent head, snorting loudly and sniffing with excitement. He kicked and stamped his hooves and dragged his resisting handlers toward the mare as if they were made of straw. Page pressed her back against the wall, grateful for the handlers' presence. Mark grinned.

The power and energy exuded by this massive beast were terrifying, for he was clearly out of control. He was blindly driven by some primordial instinct.

Though his behavior was frightening, it was somehow simultaneously exciting to Page. The stallion's enormous penis dropped from its sheath and became erect instantly. More than a foot long, as big around as her forearm, and solid black, it appeared as rigid as iron pipe.

The mare squealed noisily, stamping her hooves as well, and swung her haunches under the stallion's nose, tail raised in the air. Her vulva opened and closed in rhythmic spasms, winking. Short spurts of urine squirted onto the floor. She half squatted in front of the stallion, eager to be mounted.

Seconds later the stallion reared, raging, forelegs pawing the air, teeth bared, eyes crazed and unseeing, unstoppable now. Upright on his hind legs, this awesome beast lunged at the mare with incredible force. In the same instant the handlers diverted his hurtling bulk onto the breeding dummy, guiding his throbbing penis into a rubber receptacle. Driven by some unseen force to the point of temporary insanity, the stallion hugged the breeding dummy, and with rapid grunting thrusts, came to climax. He snorted loudly, his tail flagging high in the air.

Mere seconds later the stallion melted before their eyes. On the edge of consciousness, he slowly slid off the dummy, spent. He staggered for an instant, eyes dull, glazed over. His magnificent head sank nearly to the floor.

The stallion then straightened, waking from his stupor, and turned away as if the mare didn't exist. The mare backed closer to him and squatted again, still squealing with anticipation. With penis limp and wrinkled and retracting into its sheath, the satisfied stallion turned toward the exit, as docile as a lamb. A single handler accompanied him out toward his stall.

Page's breathing was rapid, her pulse racing. She moistened her lips with the tip of her tongue and unclenched both fists.

Mark walked past on the way to a microscope, a smug smile on his face. He winked.

Page had to clear her throat before she could speak. When she could, she said, "Wow."

Page phoned her father the next morning. Once again he declined her invitation for dinner. Had a very important bridge game.

During their conversation, Page asked how reproduction in humans compared to animals.

"Basically the same," Dr. Briggs said. "Why?"

"Mark's been teaching me about animals . . . which hormones stimulate the ovarian follicle, how it ruptures and drops a ripe egg into the fallopian tubes. But I still can't imagine what happened to me. I had a baby whose DNA matches mine and it matches William Kern's. How is this possible?"

"I'm afraid I can't answer that, and I've given it a great deal of thought."

"I have a zillion questions and not a single answer. I mean . . . can you pick up sperm from a toilet seat? I used the bathroom that morning at the jail. If you can, how did William's sperm get there in the first place? It was the women's rest room on the first floor. The prisoners are kept upstairs."

"I've never heard of that actually happening. In general, even bacteria or viruses on toilet seats dehydrate quickly and lose their virulence. Sperm wouldn't survive in that environment unless they were freshly deposited."

Page shuddered when she considered the possibility. Surely she would have noticed. No, it couldn't be. She was downright fastidious when it came to toilet seats.

"What about medications, Daddy? Lucien was taking things to increase his sperm count. Could any of them have affected his testicles, somehow, to make me have a black baby?"

"No, and even if they could, that wouldn't explain the match with William's DNA."

Page searched her mind. Sperm were tiny. Could one or two have been on the toilet seat? Even being careful, maybe she wouldn't have noticed something microscopic. Her father thought that highly unlikely.

Finally she said, "I'm at my wits' end, Daddy. My whole life's upside down and I don't know why, and I don't know who to turn to. You know about the human body. Can't you help me? Please?"

Briggs cleared his throat. "It is quite inscrutable. I've tried to think of every possibility, but I may have overlooked something. Give me a few days to see what else I can come up with; then we'll get together. All right?"

"That'd be wonderful, Daddy. Thank you." Page hung up, feeling better already. Even if she didn't expect her father to perform miracles.

On Monday morning David Fields told Page he'd like to put her on the witness stand again, to relate exactly what took place the night of January 12, 2001.

Shortly after they were in session, Lucien, J.L., and Kay Rae came in from the rear of the courtroom. After pointedly glaring at David Fields, J.L. went to the counsel table beside Buford Tallant, whispering something. Lucien held Kay Rae's elbow as they proceeded slowly down the center aisle and through the swinging wooden gate. He pulled her chair out and waited till she was comfortable before he sat.

Page couldn't remember the last time he'd been that attentive to her. Yes, she could—when Page had also been pregnant, on the campaign trail, in front of groups of people. In private he'd let her fend for herself.

For the first time Page noticed that Lucien was gaining weight. He also looked as though he was starting to lose his hair. He'd spent the early morning outside, romancing reporters. Kay Rae was dressed like a hooker and had her usual go-to-hell attitude about everybody and everything. Lucien seemed to eat it up.

Though she hated to admit it, Lucien still caused a slight flutter in Page's heart each time he looked her way. *The jerk.* She was definitely going to have to do something about that.

When Fields recalled her to the stand, he asked Page to relate the events of January 12 and January 13, 2001. She told of helping Mama Yarbrough and her maids prepare for the bridal shower. That was the afternoon of the twelfth. She described leaving to collect Cindy and their clothes, then going back to River Oaks Plantation, where she stayed till Lucien picked her up sometime after eleven.

Between questions, Page watched Kay Rae fish through a large purse, then begin chipping polish off her nails. The courtroom activities were apparently like some uninteresting TV program she kept on for background noise. With Kay Rae nearly nine months pregnant, her dress was way too short and cut so low that her boobs nearly fell out. It rode halfway up her thighs whenever she tried to cross her long legs.

Fields said, "After picking up your daughter and your clothes, what time did you arrive back at River Oaks?"

"Six p.m. I remember Mama Yarbrough commenting that we only had an hour before guests would start arriving at seven."

"Did you leave River Oaks anytime between six p.m. and eleven p.m. on the night of the twelfth of January?"

"No. Mama Yarbrough can swear to that, or any of the girls who were there. Some of them are in the courtroom right now." She looked directly at the few former friends who watched the proceedings. They quickly averted their eyes.

Fields said, "After Governor Yarbrough picked you up around eleven and you went home, what did you do?"

"Everything I did?"

"It would be best, yes."

"Well, I went to the bathroom as soon as I got home. I put Cindy to bed. Then I checked my numbers."

"Explain what you mean by that."

Page explained about the Ovumeter, how she checked her saliva and vaginal mucus and her temperature, and what it meant. "When I wrote the numbers down on my chart, I realized I had ovulated because the numbers had dropped fifteen points and my temperature had gone up a full degree."

"What did you do next?"

"I was so excited that I ran in and woke Lucien."

"He was already asleep?"

"He'd had a few drinks with his buddies at the bachelor party while I was at River Oaks. When he drinks, he gets sleepy."

"So you woke him up. Why?"

"Because we had to make love right then."

"Why right then?"

"We'd been trying to have a baby for five years. Dr. Archer told us anytime those numbers dropped like that and my temperature went up, we had to do it right then if we were to have any chance of having the son Lucien wanted so badly. Because of his low sperm count and all."

"His low sperm count?"

"My husband's." Page tried not to look at Lucien, but couldn't help herself. He was busy talking to J.L.

"So what did Lucien do when you woke him?"

"He wasn't interested." Glancing over this time, Page saw Kay Rae smirk. It wasn't glaring, but the smirk was definitely there.

"Why not?"

"I don't know . . . he just . . . sometimes when he came home late, or he'd been drinking . . . he likes vodka and tonics or mint juleps, mostly. Or sometimes he just wouldn't be interested, and that was okay with me except he kept saying we had to have a son and I didn't want to disappoint him. So I made him."

"Made him what?"

"You know . . . make love to me." When she looked, Kay Rae was holding one hand at a distance, inspecting her nails, oblivious to whatever Page might be saying.

"What time was that?"

"Eleven-thirty."

"P.M.?"

"Yes."

"On January twelfth, 2001?"

"Yes, sir."

"And it was successful?"

"Well, yes, once he was awake. Lucien never had that problem, especially after Dr. Archer started giving him those shots." When she looked this time, Lucien was watching her. A hint of a smile pulled at his lips. She automatically smiled back.

"What happened next?"

"He rolled over and started snoring like he was in a coma."

"Lucien did?"

"He fell fast asleep. We both did. The next thing I knew, Doris was banging on the door about seven-thirty the next morning and woke us up."

"Doris is your housekeeper?"

"She's more than that; she's like my mother. Doris and my father raised me after my mother died."

"Why was she banging on the door, Page?"

"She said William was in jail and she didn't know what to do."

"That would be William Kern? Doris's son?"

"Yes."

"So Lucien went to the jail to get him out."

"We both did."

"Did you see William at the jail?"

"No."

"Why not?"

"Lucien said they had a rule about more than one visitor, so I waited in the car while he went in. Oh, except when I had to use the ladies' room downstairs."

"Did Lucien get William out of jail?"

"He said he did."

"Did you see William that day?"

"No."

"Why not?"

"Lucien and I left straight from there to go to Miami. We started our cruise through the Caribbean the next morning."

"How long were you away?"

"Ten days."

"Do you know what William did after he got out of jail?"

"No. I know he didn't go see his mother, because Doris was quite hurt. She said he went straight back to San Diego, where he's stationed. He's in the navy."

Fields confirmed again that Page never saw William anytime during the period under consideration, then turned the questioning over to Buford Tallant.

CHAPTER THIRTY-THREE

Buford tried his best to make Page out to be a liar. He suggested that she secretly met William on the way from River Oaks to pick up Cindy, or the day before, when William sneaked into town without telling anybody. He even offered the possibility that William was on board ship during their entire cruise. Page never wavered in her testimony. She'd heard about and witnessed Buford's tactics too many times to be intimidated, but could only pray the judge believed her. Nobody else in town did. Without William present to refute what Buford and Lucien claimed, it was becoming evident that the judge wouldn't either.

"Your Honor," Page said, "I am telling the truth."

Kay Rae stopped doing her nails and excused herself. Her expression conveyed her boredom.

If Lucien thought I was bad about using the bathroom when I was pregnant, Page thought, *that cow has to go every ten minutes. He didn't know how good he had it. Her and her fake boobs.*

When Buford exhausted his questions, Page returned to her seat alongside David Fields. "I'm sorry I wasn't a better witness," she said. "How can anybody prove they didn't do something?"

"You did fine, Page."

Judge Scott was saying, ". . . your next witness, Mr. Fields."

Exhaling a long sigh, Page said to David, "We don't have anybody else. Does this mean we're finished?"

She knew it was over. And she had lost. She would never get Cindy back now.

"Not exactly." Fields stood, saying, "Your Honor, I call Ensign William Kern." He turned to grin mischievously at Page.

Page's heart leaped into her throat. David hadn't told her William had arrived. The last she'd heard, he was out of touch, on maneuvers somewhere. She had wondered why David seemed so secretive the past couple of days. He'd obviously wanted to surprise her.

Looking like the poster man Fields had first seen in San Diego, William walked smartly down the aisle in his white uniform. Moments later he stood proud, tall, and confident, taking the oath to tell the truth, whole truth, and nothing but the truth. Perhaps most important, he looked like a man who *would* tell the truth.

Lucien and J.L. watched William curiously from the defense table. A very pregnant Kay Rae returned from the rest room and began filing her nails. She glanced up as William took the witness chair.

Fields allowed William to settle in with routine questions of background and training, then asked about his visit to Natchez in January of 2001.

"How did you travel to Natchez, Ensign Kern?"

"By bus, sir."

"Were you alone?"

"No, sir. My friend, Ensign Cyril Thatcher, came with me."

"Do you recall what time you arrived?"

"Nineteen-hundred hours, sir. The bus was on time."

"That would be seven o'clock in the evening?"

"Yes, sir, on twelve January."

"What did you do then, Ensign?"

"I phoned a friend, sir, and Ensign Thatcher and I went over for a drink."

"You didn't go to Yarbrough Hall to see your mother, or Page Yarbrough?"

"No, sir. I planned to do that later in the evening. My friend had plans for later, so we went there first."

"Your friend who came with you from San Diego?"

"No, sir, the friend we went to have a drink with, had plans at twenty-one-hundred hours . . . nine o'clock, sir."

William hardly looked at Page, but occasionally glanced toward the defense table. Buford, J.L., and Lucien sometimes whispered among themselves, but mostly sat and doodled on lined yellow pads.

Kay Rae appeared to be listening, while smoothing her nails with an emery board.

Fields continued, "And you were arrested that evening and put in jail, where you stayed until being transferred back to San Diego by the U.S. Navy the next day. Is that correct?"

"Yes, sir."

"On what charges were you arrested, William?"

"Public drunkenness, sir, and disturbing the peace."

"Were you doing those things?"

"I'd had a few drinks, sir. I wasn't drunk."

"Why do you think you were arrested?"

"For being at the wrong place at the wrong time, sir."

"Explain that, if you will."

Lucien and Buford quickly conferred; then Buford objected to this entire line of questioning. Judge Scott allowed Fields to continue only when he assured the judge he could and would show relevance.

Fields repeated, "Explain what you mean about being at the wrong place at the wrong time, Ensign Kern."

"Well, sir, Ensign Thatcher and I were leaving my friend's apartment when somebody arrived and demanded to know what I was doing there."

"Where were you at that time?"

"On the sidewalk out near the street. We were discussing whether we should walk to my house or call a cab when this other man came up."

"What time was that?"

"Twenty-one-hundred hours."

"That's nine p.m., civilian time?"

"Yes, sir."

"Go ahead."

"He was real nasty, telling me I was shiftless and calling me names. He kept asking what I was doing in town and wanted to know what was I doing out there on that sidewalk. I told him it was none of his business."

"In those words?"

"Not exactly, sir. I told him it was none of his damned business."

"This is to the person who had arrived in front of your friend's apartment."

"Yes, sir."

"Go on. What did this person say next?"

"He told me I was a smartass nigger, and he was gonna teach me a lesson. He shoved me off the curb into the street. I could tell he'd been drinking."

"What did you do?"

"Called him some names right back, and said some things I shouldn't have."

"What did you say?"

"I told him to go fuck himself, sir." William turned to the judge. "Mr. Fields told me I should repeat the exact words I used. I apologize for using them in front of ladies."

David asked, "What happened then?"

"He went inside and locked the door. I tried to follow, but he wouldn't let me in. A few minutes later the police arrived and arrested Ensign Thatcher and me and took us to jail."

"What time would that have been?"

"Twenty-one-fifteen hours . . . excuse me, nine-fifteen p.m., sir."

"What happened the next morning?"

"They allowed me one phone call, so I called Mama and asked her to get me out of jail. I told her not to say anything to Lucien or Page, but to come get me herself."

"By Lucien or Page, you mean Governor Lucien Yarbrough and his then wife, Page Briggs Yarbrough?

Your mother lived on their property and worked for them, didn't she? Your mother is Doris Kern?"

"Yes, sir."

"Why would you ask your mother not to say anything specifically to those two people, William?"

"Lucien had me arrested in the first place. That's who I had the fight with the night before."

Page nearly came out of her seat.

Everybody at Lucien's table huddled together. Everybody except Kay Rae. She waved the testimony off, but glared at William.

"Let me get this straight," Fields said. "The man whom you argued with the night before, the man who pushed you off the sidewalk into the street, and who then went inside and called the police was Governor Lucien Yarbrough?"

"He wasn't governor then," replied William. His voice went stone cold and he glowered at Lucien as he spoke. "He was just an ordinary citizen, like you or me."

Page was in shock. How in God's name could her husband have been out on some street brawling with William? Lucien had been at a bachelor party that entire evening.

Buford tried several angles to block this line of questioning.

When David was ultimately allowed to continue, he said, "The next morning, while you and your buddy sat in jail, did your mother do as you'd asked her?"

"No, sir."

"Who came to the jail that morning, William?"

"Lucien Yarbrough."

"To get you out of jail?"

"No, sir, to make sure I didn't get out. He called my commanding officer in San Diego, who sent two shore-patrol officers to take me back to base. I was thrown in the brig for the rest of my leave. Ensign Thatcher, too, and he hadn't said a word to Lucien." William tried to fix Lucien's gaze, but Lucien was deep in conversation with Buford and the senator.

"How do you know he made that call?"

"He told me so. He said I'd be damned sorry I came back to Natchez, and he was gonna have my uppity black butt—excuse me, ladies—hauled out of town once and for all, and I'd better never let the sun set on my trifling nigger ass in Mississippi again."

"I see."

The room went totally silent. Fields walked to his counsel table and flipped through his notes. From the table he asked, "William, did you have sex with Lucien's wife, Page Briggs Yarbrough, while you were in Natchez that January?"

"No, sir."

"You've known Page for many years, have you not?"

"Yes, sir, we grew up together."

"Have you ever had sex with her?"

"No, sir."

"Have you ever had any sort of romantic or physical relationship with Page?"

William shook his head. "Page isn't that kind of girl, Mr. Fields. She'd never do something like that."

"Why not? You're a handsome young man."

"She's a lady."

"It's my understanding that some ladies enjoy sex nowadays. Even interracial sex."

"Not Page. Not on your life."

Page turned to see if Lucien's mother was in the courtroom. She wasn't. *Damn.* Page would've loved for Miss Emma to hear this.

"Are you saying that you have never in your lifetime had any sort of sexual relationship with Page Briggs Yarbrough? Is that correct?"

"Yes, sir, that is correct."

"Then why would you say to her husband, Lucien Yarbrough, that you had fucked his wife?" A shock wave jolted the roomful of spectators at David's use of the King's English.

"I didn't, sir."

Overly polite, clean-cut, boyish-looking, naive-sounding David Fields pushed his glasses higher on his nose and raised his voice. "Please remember that you are under oath, Ensign Kern. An oath before God."

"Yes, sir, I remember. I never made that statement."

"Governor Yarbrough said you did, right in this courtroom."

Buford objected.

Sustained.

Fields rephrased. "If Governor Yarbrough should say that you told him you fucked his wife—excuse us, ladies and gentlemen, but it is extremely important that I make His Honor aware of the exact words used—how would you respond, William?"

"Lucien is lying. I never made that statement." William turned to look at Page. "I'd never say anything like that about Page because it would never be true."

"What *did* you say to Governor Yarbrough that morning, William? While you were in jail?"

"When Lucien told me he'd called my commanding officer, and then said what he did about hauling my black ass out of town, I went berserk. I felt bad about it later, but I completely lost it. Went ballistic."

"You mean you got angry."

"Very. I told him to go fuck himself. I told him I had fucked his woman better than he ever could, and I'd kick his scrawny ass halfway to New Orleans if he had the balls to come inside the cell and—"

Fields cut him off. "Wait a minute. You testified earlier that you never said you fucked Page . . . Lucien's wife."

"I didn't."

"But you just said—"

"I said, I told him I had fucked his *woman*, Mr. Fields. Not his wife. I wasn't talking about Page."

"Who were you talking about?"

"His woman. His girlfriend. Kay Rae Talwell. That's who I went to see the night before."

Kay Rae dropped her emery board on the floor.

CHAPTER THIRTY-FOUR

Objections and counterobjections flew until Judge Scott called a recess. When court was back in session, the spectator seats overflowed as if people had materialized from molecules in the air—made-up, coifed, fully attired in hats and gloves and white shoes. They appeared to've been waiting at home for just such an occasion, all dressed up and ready to go.

Buford, J.L., and Lucien conferred with Kay Rae, who shook her head in denial while Lucien's face passed through increasingly vibrant shades of Tabasco red.

Spectators gasped in disbelief when, without warning, Kay Rae slapped Lucien across the face. The sharp report still resounded in the stunned silence when she shouted, "Fuck you, you pompous asshole!"

Lucien's rage was obvious to all; but J.L. and Buford managed to restrain him. Their ravings were punctuated by stern orders and threats from the judge. With much prodding, Lucien finally sat, clenching and unclenching his fists and jaw.

Kay Rae spun around in a huff, scowling at a wall away from her husband. Several minutes elapsed before she reluctantly agreed to take her seat.

Page was aghast. She had never seen Lucien so angry. Well, once—that day in their bedroom as he packed to leave. In all the years she had known him, he had never shown his temper in public before.

What William said had jolted Page, too. Hurt her to the core. In retrospect, she realized she'd ignored the occasional rumor of Lucien's affairs because she didn't believe them. Hadn't wanted to. Her hero simply wouldn't do that to her. Page had chosen to believe that Lucien was a loyal, loving husband and father, despite women constantly throwing themselves at him. Recurring hints and sidelong glances from her friends had been nothing more than jealousy. Now she remembered, some of the rumors had mentioned Kay Rae. She reflected on those rumors as her adrenaline rush gradually subsided, and watched Lucien struggle to reassemble his public facade.

Something began to nibble at the fringes of Page's mind. Something fuzzy that she couldn't yet identify, as though it were out of focus.

As Fields had feared, Judge Scott refused to allow William's polygraph examination. His reason: the opposing side had not been afforded the opportunity to submit questions. A valuable piece of documentation lost, to substantiate William's credibility.

On cross-examination, Buford focused on William's blood test, which showed that William's DNA matched Adam's. If Buford said it once, he said it a hundred times—William's DNA matched that of Page's black baby; therefore, William and Page obviously had sex. Period, the end. Elementary. That was how reproduction worked.

Buford speculated that William's fabrication regarding Kay Rae was cleverly designed to shift attention away from what William and Page were actually doing that day. The sexual encounter both were clearly lying about now.

Kay Rae and Lucien disputed everything William had said. Fields asked if they would submit to a polygraph examination. Though they had calmed down considerably, both defiantly felt such an examination not only beneath their dignity, but worthless.

"They are notoriously unreliable," Lucien said.

Lucien admitted that William had been on the street that night, though Kay Rae denied ever seeing William in her life. She'd had no idea who was banging on her door until Lucien told her.

Fields asked Lucien, "Were you, in fact, visiting your mistress that night?"

"She's my wife."

"She wasn't at that time, Governor. You were married to Page."

"Kay Rae was a friend. I merely stopped by to say hello."

"Weren't you supposed to be at a bachelor party for your new partner, Troy Carter, that evening?"

"I had been, and I went right back there."

"After you told your girlfriend . . . *hello.*"

"Yes."

"I see."

Page swallowed hard. Her heart couldn't hurt any worse if it'd been run through by a wooden stake.

Fields continued. "What time did you arrive at Kay Rae's?"

"About nine o'clock, nine-fifteen."

"How long did you stay in Kay Rae's apartment that evening, Governor?"

"Oh, twenty minutes or so. Till the police came and took William away."

"And then you left?"

"Yes."

"What time was that?"

"I don't remember. Sometime before ten o'clock."

"After you had . . . said *hello,* I believe is the way you put it."

"Yes."

"Why did you call the police?"

"William was like a crazy man. He was banging on the apartment door, trying to force his way inside, yelling all kinds of threats and insults at me."

"But he never came inside."

"That's what I said."

Fields asked Kay Rae if William had ever been inside her apartment.

"Never," she said, spitting out the word. She tried to cross her legs but couldn't. She didn't know William, had never met him, and wouldn't know who he was today if she hadn't heard his name here in court. William had come to her door only because he followed Lucien there. Lucien had told her that he and William never liked each other.

Page believed William, but almost wished she could believe Kay Rae. What she wanted to believe was that Lucien hadn't gone to Kay Rae's at all. Ever. She also wished that whatever was tantalizing her brain would either show itself or leave her alone. And she tried to will her gut to stop twisting so miserably.

Fields recalled William and asked him to describe Kay Rae's apartment. William had an exceptional recollection of colors and mirrors and scented candles, particularly in the bedroom. He recalled one particular item in some detail—a crystal statue of a horse rearing on its hind legs, its mane blowing in the wind. It rested beside Kay Rae's king-size waterbed.

Lucien tried unsuccessfully not to glare at Kay Rae during that testimony. Kay Rae stared daggers at William.

When David returned to the counsel table, Page's face felt flushed. She was burning up. She pulled David down and whispered, louder than she intended, "Lucien gave me a horse statue exactly like that a year ago Christmas. It's a Lalique. He must've gotten a volume discount." She pulled back, then leaned close again and added, "Now I wonder how many other women got one." Page was seething inside, at least part of her pain now transformed to anger. Her eyes bored into Lucien, who looked the other way. No heart flutter this time—only a sense of betrayal.

Page had thought they were through for the day, but Fields called his final witness. Another delightful surprise, the woman was the interior decorator who'd done Kay Rae's apartment. The decorator confirmed every detail William had described.

Page asked David, "How'd you find out who did her apartment?"

"People in wallpaper and paint stores talk. Sarah

and I just restored an entire house, remember, so they know me in those places." He shrugged. "See the advantages of not having much of a practice? Gives me lots of time to snoop around."

Judge Scott adjourned court for the day after the decorator. Lucien and J.L. hurried out well ahead of Kay Rae, who waddled along alone, spraddle-legged, toward the ladies' room.

"Look at her," Page said to David Fields. "Boobs so big she has to lean backward to keep from falling on her face. I don't know what Lucien sees in that cow. I never will. But right now I can't help feeling sorry for her."

To settle herself down, Page drove into the countryside before going home. She reflected on William's testimony as she journeyed along white fences and green pastures past the racehorse farm. She recalled the day Mark had taken her into the horse-breeding shed. She thought of that magnificent stallion, of the rubber boot for collecting sperm, and the canvas breeding dummy.

"Horses . . . cows . . . we're all just animals," Page muttered to herself. "Oh, my God."

Page jerked her Suburban to the side of the road and stopped, her mind reeling. She stared at this bucolic scene—sleek horses grazing lush pastures. A cold sweat drenched her forehead, both hands tightly gripping the steering wheel. Could it be? The ethereal vision that had tormented her consciousness all afternoon suddenly came into focus. She knew exactly what had happened. But was it possible?

CHAPTER THIRTY-FIVE

David Fields asked the judge for a one-week continuance after Page shared her sudden illumination. A family emergency, Fields explained—which this most definitely was.

Following a very hectic week for everyone around Page, the case resumed. David called Page's father to the stand.

Dr. Briggs was nattily dressed in a brown suit and bow tie, though the July day was nearing ninety outside and the humidity was becoming unbearable. Even with air-conditioning it was plenty warm inside, and Briggs perspired heavily as he testified, wiping his brow often with his handkerchief. He spoke like a professor, eloquently and precisely. Sitting with matchstick-thin legs crossed and one hand on the cane at his side, he appeared ready to stand and lecture at any moment.

Fields established Dr. Briggs's medical credentials. They were impressive.

"You're not in practice now, Dr. Briggs?"

"I am not."

"What do you do currently?"

"Operate a medical-research business."

"What do you research?"

"The worldwide medical literature. I provide clients a bibliography and summaries of articles published in medical journals from around the globe."

"Who are your clients?"

"People too busy to do research themselves. Other physicians, hospitals, clinics, Ph.D. candidates."

"Do you do this by hand, or by going to a medical library somewhere?"

"Objection . . . relevance."

"I will show relevance shortly, Your Honor."

"I certainly hope so, Mr. Fields."

"Dr. Briggs, which libraries do you utilize?"

"Through computer hookups, I access medical books and journals in the New York Medical Association Library, perhaps the largest medical library in the world; the UCLA Medical Library in California; the Harvard University Medical School Library; the Oxford University—"

Fields cut him off. "We get the point, Doctor. Now, as a physician holding the degree of Doctor of Medicine, are you familiar with artificial insemination?"

"Objection . . . irrelevant and immaterial."

"I'll allow it, Mr. Tallant. Proceed."

Dr. Briggs said he was familiar with AI.

"Have you recently had occasion to search your sources about unusual instances of artificial insemination, Doctor?"

"I have."

"Would you please tell the court about one such instance you discovered."

"Of course. Following a recent discussion with Dr. Mark Goodson, a veterinarian, I performed an extensive search not only of international reference material on human medicine, but literature on veterinary medicine as well. I discovered an experiment performed in Austria after a horse breeder reported a strange occurrence among his horses. He raised Arabian horses and Lippizaners, quite different in size, color, and overall appearance. On two occasions, Arabian mares that had been exposed only to Arabian stallions gave birth to foals by a Lippizaner stallion. They had Lippizaner babies.

"The horse breeder used a sterile Arabian stallion—sterile from birth—as a teaser horse, to excite mares in preparation for breeding to a fertile stallion. Because this teaser horse was sterile, he was allowed to roam freely among both Arabian and Lippizaner mares, and he performed normally, having intercourse with mares whenever they were in heat. He just couldn't produce sperm. The breeder consulted veterinarians from a nearby university. The veterinarians flushed out samples from the penis of the sterile Arabian stallion after he'd serviced a Lippizaner mare. Under the microscope, they found live sperm from a Lippizaner stallion in the Arabian horse's penis. The sperm survived for more than twenty-four hours in that environment."

When some of the spectators began to talk among themselves, Judge Scott had to ask them to be silent.

Consulting his notes, Fields asked, "Dr. Briggs, does artificial insemination work pretty much the same in a human as it does in, say, a horse or cow?"

"Pretty much, yes."

"What might the difference be, from a human to a horse?"

"The function of the male is the same: to provide large numbers of viable sperm. In the female, the only difference would be that the horse's cervix opens widely during her heat cycle, whereas the human female doesn't go into heat."

A few people in the courtroom sniggered, making muffled comments to their neighbors.

Judge Scott demanded silence. "Continue, Doctor."

Briggs wiped his forehead, then leaned forward on his cane. His hands were trembling visibly. "As I was saying, the human female's cervix, which separates the vagina from the uterus, does not dilate widely, the way a horse's does. The passageway between the human vagina and uterus is much smaller."

"How large is the opening?"

"About a millimeter."

"How big is that in inches?"

"A millimeter is one-twenty-fifth of an inch."

"Can a man's sperm swim through that small an opening?"

"Oh, yes, they're tiny. And remarkable little swimmers. A sperm swimming through a millimeter opening is comparable to me riding a bicycle down the center of a four-lane highway."

Page visualized that scene in her mind.

"How do they know in which direction to swim?"

"Well, of course, they don't. They swim in every conceivable direction as long as it's moist and warm and they have the proper degree of acidity."

"How warm, Doctor?"

"Body temperature, thirty-seven degrees Celsius in a human. If it's too cold, they stop swimming. They don't die, but they're not active. If it's dry, or too acid or too alkaline, they die."

"What is the ideal acid or alkaline level for sperm, and how do you measure it?"

"It's called pH. The human body averages an ideal pH of seven point four."

"I see." Fields consulted his notes again. "I have no further questions at this time, Your Honor."

"Cross-examine, Mr. Tallant?"

Buford stood and buttoned his navy suit coat over his vest. "Your Honor, I'm reluctant to dignify this dog-and-pony show, other than to ask what relevance some Austrian horse of a different color could possibly have to do with this case."

"Is that a question, Mr. Tallant?"

"No, Your Honor." Buford let out a long breath, then said, "Dr. Briggs, are you licensed to practice veterinary medicine?"

"I am not."

"So you have not personally performed artificial insemination on any horses, is that correct?"

"Correct."

"Either Lippizaner or Arabians or any other breed?"

"No, sir, I have not."

"Have you, in fact, ever performed artificial insemination on humans, Doctor?"

"No, sir."

"So you are not an expert in the field of reproduction at all. Is that correct, Dr. Briggs?"

"It is."

Buford paused, then asked, "Are you related to Page Briggs Yarbrough?"

"I'm her father."

"So you would say pretty much anything you felt necessary to help her win this case, wouldn't you?"

"I would not, sir, though I certainly believe she deserves to—"

Buford cut him off, asking him to please respond directly to his questions. "Would you lie under oath, Doctor?"

"No, sir."

"Have you lied under oath here today?"

"I have not."

Buford paced in front of the witness. "Tell me, Doctor, when did you stop practicing medicine?"

"April 17, 1972."

"Why did you stop?"

Briggs hesitated. "I felt that I was better suited for research than for practice."

"Why is that?"

"It was a decision I arrived at after considerable thought."

"Did anything occur in your practice that prompted that decision?"

Briggs unfolded his legs, then recrossed them. "My wife had died, sir. I had two small children who needed me at home."

Buford walked closer to the witness stand. "I don't mean to dredge up unpleasant memories, Doctor, but would you please tell this court the circumstances surrounding your wife's death?"

Page came to the edge of her seat. She bit her lip.

"Objection, Your Honor," Fields began.

"No, Mr. Fields," Dr. Briggs said, "it's all right. I'd

like to answer." He fixed Buford's gaze. "I operated
on my wife, Counselor. She died on the operating
table. I killed her." A tear trickled down the old doctor's cheek. His hands shook even harder on the cane
he clung to, but his gaze never wavered from the attorney's face. "Is that what you wanted everybody to
hear, Mr. Tallant? Am I being honest enough for
you now?"

Buford conferred briefly with Lucien and J.L., then
dismissed the witness.

Page leaned close to David Fields. "That lowlife."
She couldn't believe Buford could be so cruel—to any-
body, let alone a broken old man who would never
willingly hurt anybody. Under her breath she said,
"You're a son of a bitch, Buford. You always were.
An arrogant son of a bitch."

Judge Scott looked at his watch and called an end
to the morning's session. The courtroom was abuzz
with speculation about what Dr. Briggs's testimony
might mean.

Lucien and Buford made a beeline to reporters outside, using words like American justice, responsibility
to the people, and defending one's honor. Page expected to hear something about motherhood and
apple pie. Maybe she was just concerned about Adam
and Cindy. Or hungry. She hurried to find her father,
to make sure he was all right.

After lunch Fields called Dr. Thomas Stephenson
to the stand, a man of about sixty with thin white
hair combed straight back, and no legs. A professor
of obstetrics and gynecology at the University of Tennessee College of Medicine in Memphis, Dr. Stephenson testified from his wheelchair.

Page turned to see her father and Mark Goodson
seated together near the front of the spectator seats.
They smiled conspiratorially and waved to her.

Fields was saying, "Have you written articles in recognized medical journals, Doctor?"

"Over two hundred." Stephenson's tone was not arrogant or superior, nor was he the retiring sort. He answered quite matter-of-factly. The confidence he exuded made everyone quickly forget he was in a wheelchair, focusing instead on what he had to say.

"What have you written besides articles?"

"A textbook on artificial insemination."

"Where is your textbook used?"

"In official medical-school curriculums in the United States, Canada, Australia, and England. It has also been translated into four languages for medical practitioners . . . Japanese, Spanish, Russian, and German."

"Thank you. Now, if I may ask some rather basic questions . . . please bear with me, Doctor, knowing that I'm not a medical person. When a man has sex with a woman, he deposits sperm into her vagina, is that correct?"

"If he's fertile, yes."

"Meaning, if his testicles make sperm?"

"Yes, and if the delivery system is functioning properly."

"All right. Now, if you took a little glass tube of some sort and removed some of that live sperm from a woman's vagina, would it be possible to transfer it to another woman?"

"Of course."

"Would the sperm still be alive?"

"If they're transferred quickly enough."

"How quickly?"

"That would depend upon the temperature of the glass tube, its moisture content, and its pH. How the sperm is stored."

"Say it's kept moist, at average body temperature, and normal body pH."

"Sperm would survive under those conditions for several hours."

"How many hours is several?"

"At least eight to twelve, if the specimen isn't allowed to dry out. Probably more."

"If you removed this live sperm from one woman,

Doctor, and transferred it to another, would it be capable of impregnating the second woman?"

"As long as she provides a proper ovum."

"An ovum is an egg?"

"Yes."

"If you had a woman on one examination table with fresh sperm in her vagina, and a second woman on the table next to her with no sperm in her vagina, you could take the sperm from the first woman's vagina and transfer it to the second and it could impregnate the second woman if she had an egg. Right?"

"Yes."

"With what degree of likelihood could you do that, Doctor? What percent success?"

"Practically a hundred percent."

"What if the second woman was in the next room?"

"That wouldn't change anything. The transfer would be equally successful."

"What if she was, say, a hundred yards away?"

"Distance isn't important. What is important is how much time elapses between when the sperm is initially deposited and when it's transferred to the second woman."

"So the second woman could be across town, five or six miles away, as long as the transfer was made within, say, four hours?"

"Yes."

"And she would get pregnant if you exposed her to that particular sperm."

"If she had a proper egg, yes." Dr. Stephenson looked at Fields quizzically. The curious smile on his face said, *But why would anybody want to do a stupid thing like that?*

Fields consulted his notes. "Now, as an expert in the field of human reproduction, let me put a second hypothetical situation to you. If a man who is not sterile but relatively infertile—"

The physician interrupted. "Do you mean he has a low sperm count or low quality?"

"Both."

"All right."

"If this man had sex with a woman who had just had sex with another man—"

Buford Tallant interrupted in his most exasperated tone. "Objection, Your Honor. Mr. Fields is so far out on this fishing expedition, he's trying to make us all lose sight of the issues of this case."

Judge Scott agreed. "This testimony does seem rather remote, Mr. Fields."

"If Your Honor please," Fields responded, "some extremely complex medical issues having a direct bearing on this case need to be understood by the court. I promise to show relevance very soon."

Fields was finally allowed to continue, but was perspiring when he asked, "As I was saying, Doctor, if this man with a low sperm count had sex with a woman who had just had sex with a man with a normal sperm count, say a half hour or so earlier, then this man with the low sperm count traveled a few miles and had sex with another woman who has just ovulated, is it possible that the woman who had just ovulated could become pregnant with the man's sperm that was deposited into the vagina of the first woman the man had sex with?"

Buford tossed his pen down on the table. "Objection, Your Honor. Mr. Fields has moved from absurd to incomprehensible."

Judge Scott said, "Straighten it out, Mr. Fields. I certainly couldn't follow it."

"Yes, Your Honor. All right, Dr. Stephenson, let's say a black man has sex with woman A at eight-thirty p.m."

Buford started to object, but Lucien pulled him back into his seat. Kay Rae searched for something in her oversize purse.

"Let's try again, Doctor." Fields wheeled a green chalkboard to the front of the room. He wrote and drew symbols as he spoke. "Woman A has sex with black man B, of average fertility, at eight forty-five p.m. Less than an hour later, around nine-thirty p.m., a relatively infertile white man, W, has sex with the same woman A. About two hours later, say eleven-thirty p.m., the white man, W, has sex across town with white woman C, who has just ovulated. Got the picture?"

"I have it."

"Is it possible for the infertile white man, W, to pick up some of the fertile black man's—B's—sperm from the first woman, A, then transfer them to the second woman, C, impregnating her with the black man's sperm?"

"Yes, sir. It is."

CHAPTER THIRTY-SIX

Judge Scott had to remove several people from the courtroom to restore order. That almost included Senator J. L. Yarbrough. Buford was finally able to convince J.L. to take his seat. When he did, he was scowling furiously, his jaw set at an odd angle.

Fields was allowed to continue. "You answered rather quickly, Doctor. Wouldn't you like more time to think about the situation I presented?"

"I don't need to think about it."

"May I ask why not?"

"Because I described a virtually identical scenario in the *Newsletter of the New England Gynecological Society* in 1965. In that instance, the man who impregnated a woman with another man's sperm was completely sterile."

Fields asked the physician to explain.

"The man had been rendered totally sterile following mumps in childhood. The mumps virus had settled in his testicles, called orchitis. In my article I referred to him as Mr. Carrier. Mrs. Carrier, a woman with rigid puritanical values, became pregnant. However, she'd never had sex with any other man. Mr. Carrier later admitted that he had been with a prostitute only hours before having sex with his wife, exactly nine months before their baby was born. When questioned later, the prostitute admitted that she had been with another man less than an hour before having sex with Mr. Carrier."

"What proof existed that Mrs. Carrier was telling

the truth about not having sex with anyone besides her husband?"

"Two very strong indications. One: Mr. and Mrs. Carrier were the sole residents on a small island in the South Pacific. Being prone to seasickness, Mrs. Carrier hadn't left the island for several months before or after becoming pregnant, and no other men visited their island during that time. Mr. Carrier had sailed to another island for supplies, had a couple of drinks, and visited a local prostitute. He then returned to his island and had sex with his wife later that day. Mrs. Carrier's mother was visiting while he was away, and she confirmed that no other man came to the island during Mr. Carrier's absence. That was point number one. Point number two was, both Mr. and Mrs. Carrier had dark hair. Everybody in their family for three generations back had dark hair. Their baby was born with red hair. The man who had intercourse with the prostitute an hour before Mr. Carrier was Irish. He had bright red hair."

"Were any of these people DNA tested?"

"No, that wasn't readily available then."

"I see." The courtroom had become deadly silent. "Are you aware of any other instances, Doctor?"

"Though it was never written up, a similar case was verbally presented at a meeting of the British Society of Obstetrics and Gynecology in 1968, in London. The physician involved wrote to me because he was familiar with the case I had reported three years earlier. A Caucasian woman married to a Caucasian man gave birth to an Asian baby. In that instance, the Caucasian husband admitted to his wife's obstetrician that he had had sex with an Asian woman exactly nine months prior to the Asian child's birth. On investigation, the Asian woman confirmed that she'd had intercourse with an Asian man approximately four hours before having intercourse with the Caucasian man. The presumption was that the Caucasian man picked up live sperm that the Asian man had deposited into the

Asian woman's vagina four hours earlier, then transferred them to his Caucasian wife."

An audible and visible stir swept through the courtroom.

Fields continued. "How could those sperm survive so long, Doctor?"

"It's the perfect medium for them to live in, isn't it?"

Fields formulated his next words carefully. "To inseminate a woman, Doctor, what would be the most ideal equipment for delivering sperm?"

"The male penis."

"How so?"

"It maintains the perfect temperature for sperm survival, which is normal body temperature. It maintains the proper pH. Its length and circumference are designed for a perfect fit for transfer of sperm into the female vagina without leakage. It is moist. It emits seminal fluid, the perfect vehicle with ideal pH, moisture content, and viscosity to both deliver the sperm and insure its survival. All that's required is to fill it with live sperm."

"In this hypothetical instance, or in the examples you cite, how would that have been accomplished?"

"By exposing the penis to a closed container holding live, active sperm swimming furiously in all directions. In this instance, a vagina. Sperm would swim into the opening of the penis and up the channel inside, called the urethra. Finding a warm, dark, moist environment, they would survive quite nicely for many hours, like stowaways. The next time the man ejaculated, the stowaway sperm would be washed out into the next vagina, then begin their new journey through the cervix, into the uterus and fallopian tubes of the female. Finding a ripe egg waiting, they could accomplish their sole life's mission, and fertilize it."

In an absolutely silent courtroom, Fields waited for this information to sink in before asking, "Does a sterile man ejaculate? Or a relatively infertile man?"

"Being sterile, or having either low-quality sperm

or a low sperm count, hardly affects the ejaculate. The same amount of seminal fluid comes forth with a climax. It merely contains fewer than normal—or weaker than normal—sperm. That would actually be a more ideal situation for the scenario you describe because there are fewer sperm present to compete with the stowaway sperm picked up from the first man's ejaculate. The stowaways would undoubtedly reach the ripe egg first. You might say if the second man typically fires blanks, the first man provided live ammunition for the second man's gun."

Fields waited until the spectators calmed down. "Could sperm from the first man actually swim up inside a second man's penis?"

"Spirochetes and bacteria do it all the time, which is how venereal diseases are transmitted. Syphilis, gonorrhea. Or the HIV virus. Sperm easily navigate a woman's cervix, which has a much smaller opening."

"How much smaller?"

"The opening in an average man's penis would be at least twice or three times as wide as the opening in a woman's cervix."

"So if the passage through a woman's cervix were a four-lane highway, the opening in an average man's penis would be like an eight-lane superhighway for a sperm?"

"Something like that."

David glanced at Lucien, who was sitting perfectly upright, his face impassive. "What if the man had a larger than average penis?"

"That would make it all the easier for the sperm to gain access."

"How many sperm could get up inside the second man?"

"Millions."

"More than enough to impregnate a woman, if it was the right time of month for her?"

"Impregnation requires only one live sperm."

Fields started to ask something else but didn't. He hesitated again, then walked to his table. "Thank you,

Doctor." He submitted copies of the articles as exhibits, then sat beside Page.

Page sat wide-eyed and dry-mouthed, trying to swallow the lump in her throat. Would anybody believe the explanation just offered? She turned to see her father grinning at her. Mark Goodson winked.

"Cross-examine, Mr. Tallant?"

Buford stood, adjusted his trousers, and shook his head while staring at the physician in the wheelchair. He was thinking, *Attorney general's office, here I come.* He said, "Dr. Stephenson, are you licensed to practice in the state of Mississippi?"

"I am not."

"Did you perform any sort of artificial insemination on the plaintiff, Ms. Page Briggs?"

"I did not."

"You didn't take any sperm from some woman on one examining table, then wheel yourself into the next room and spurt it into Ms. Briggs?"

"Of course not."

"Have you ever even examined the plaintiff, Page Briggs, Doctor?"

"No."

"Have you examined my client, Governor Lucien Yarbrough?"

"No."

"So you don't know, of your own personal knowledge, how many sperm the governor produces, do you?"

"No."

"Or what quality sperm he produces?"

"No, I don't."

"Or whether they swim fast or slow, or north or south, or east or west . . . right, Doctor?"

"That's correct."

"Where were you on the twelfth and thirteenth of January, in 2001?"

"In Barcelona, Spain, at a medical seminar."

"You weren't in Natchez, Mississippi, or Miami, Florida?"

"No, sir."

"You didn't happen to be on a cruise ship sailing through the warm, tropical waters of the Caribbean that week?"

"No."

"So you weren't in the bedroom of Ms. Page Briggs anytime during the days surrounding January twelfth or thirteenth, Doctor?"

"I was not."

"Fine." Buford walked closer to the witness. "Isn't it true, Dr. Stephenson, that since you weren't present when Page Briggs Yarbrough got herself pregnant, you do not and cannot possibly know how or when or by whom she got pregnant?"

"That's true. I can only respond to the hypothetical—"

Buford interrupted. "You do not know how, when, or by whom she got pregnant. Is that correct?"

"Correct."

"Thank you. In fact, Doctor, if I told you that we have a witness who actually saw Page Briggs having sex with a certain Negro man, you couldn't refute that, could you?"

Page was on her feet. "Buford Tallant, that's a cheap, dirty lie."

Judge Scott quickly banged his gavel. "That will be quite enough, Mrs. Yarbrough."

"You're damned right it's enough," responded Page. "I'm sick and tired of his lies and accusations when he knows they're false." Her pulse throbbed painfully in her head.

"Mr. Fields," said Judge Scott, "either control your client or I'll have her held in contempt."

Fields pleaded with Page to take her seat.

"I'm sorry, David, but I've had it." She was still shouting, and now tears streamed down Page's cheeks. She pointed a finger toward Lucien and J.L. "They don't give a damn about the truth; they want to believe Buford's lies. The only thing Yarbroughs care

about is winning, no matter who gets hurt. That's all
they've ever known."

"Ms. Briggs," warned the judge again, "do you want
to spend the night in jail?"

Page couldn't stop. "You threaten me for telling the
truth? Why don't you put Buford in jail for perjury?
Or Lucien or Kay Rae? Nobody saw me do what they
claim because I never did it, even if everybody in town
believes I did. They already took my daughter away.
Do you think jail scares me, compared to that?"

Prompted by David Fields's pleading, Page finally
sat. Judge Scott called a recess. Page, meanwhile,
struggled to regain her composure.

When they returned, Page apologized for her outburst, though she still seethed inside. "What I said
was true, Your Honor; however, I apologize for any
disrespect shown the court, and for using profanity.
I'm genuinely embarrassed about my behavior."

Buford Tallant quickly resumed his questioning of
Dr. Stephenson. Page gritted her teeth to keep from
shouting at Buford again when he asked the doctor,
"If a witness swore that she saw Page Briggs having
sex with a certain Negro man, could you refute that
testimony?"

"No, I could not."

"Thank you, Doctor; that's all I need to know."
Buford started to take his seat, but Lucien pulled him
low and whispered something into his ear. Buford then
said, "Just one more question, Dr. Stephenson. If a
man urinated after these mysterious little stowaway
sperm somehow got up inside him, wouldn't that wash
them away?"

"Some of them. Not all."

"Aren't they just sitting in that channel inside a
man's penis, where a strong stream of urine would
flush them right out?"

"They're not all in the urethra, the channel you
speak of. Many would be in the seminal vesicles, small
storage sacs off to one side of that channel."

"What do these seminal vesicles do? What are they for?"

"They store sperm and seminal fluid until the next time a man ejaculates. Then they 'spurt' out, to use your term, to begin their new journey."

Buford smiled. "That is, if they're as smart as you would have us believe, and could actually get in there in the first place." He quickly turned away from the doctor. "No further questions of this witness, Your Honor. I move to strike his entire testimony on the grounds that it's irrelevant and immaterial."

Mark Goodson picked Page up in his red Corvette at six p.m. on Friday. She desperately needed a break from the stress of the trial. Tonight would make the fourth time they'd been out together since he took her to dinner for her birthday. Page especially looked forward to the evening. They had reservations at Monmouth Plantation, called "one of the ten most romantic places in the USA" by *Glamour* magazine and *USA Today*. She had toured the twenty-six landscaped acres years before, but had somehow never found time to return. She knew the history of Monmouth from when it was built for, and presented to, a bride—an incredibly romantic gesture.

They purposely arrived early to walk the grounds before dark. Mark wore a blue blazer with gray slacks and a white turtleneck rather than his usual work shirt and jeans. Working alongside him daily, Page sometimes failed to notice what a good-looking man he was. He exuded a quiet confidence and charm.

Azaleas and camellias filled old-fashioned gardens on either side of the pebble paths they followed. They meandered hand in hand beneath sweet-olive trees and past manicured boxwood hedges to cross an arched bridge over a pond complete with swans. They sat quietly in a gazebo surrounded by Audubon's Mississippi songbirds and moss-draped oak trees. A scent of honeysuckle filled the warm summer night as dusk settled.

Later they joined other guests in an elegant down-stairs parlor for cocktails. Mark and Page were the only locals, the others hailing from as far away as San Francisco and London. Even though Pilgrimage was over, tourists still abounded.

The evening sparkled with candlelight, crystal, sterling silver, and stimulating conversation throughout the five-course gourmet dinner. Service by a uniformed black staff was quiet, courteous, and efficient, reminiscent of days gone by. Page felt a twinge of guilt when she considered the elegance and grandeur of her surroundings compared to what the wait staff must be receiving for their unsung role. Since her divorce, she'd become painfully aware of the wages offered for entry-level jobs, when they were available.

"People can't afford to live like this anymore," a Northern woman was saying.

"Even paying minimum wage," the woman's husband added, "the cost of help today is prohibitive."

Wafting a bejeweled hand about the room, another woman said, "Maybe slavery wasn't all bad. I'm told most owners took very good care of them." The woman took a second helping of green beans from a silent African-American waitress.

Another man said, "I never realized it, but a good slave sold for about ten thousand dollars in the 1860s. Can you imagine what that's equivalent to in today's money? You wouldn't abuse something you'd paid that much for. They were valued commodities."

Page put down her fork. She couldn't believe the insensitivity of these people. What were they thinking?

A woman with a Midwestern accent turned to Page and said, "Since you live here, you must have some idea what it was like. Was life as grand as it appears to have been?"

Page replied, "That depended upon what color you were." She set her napkin on the elegant table, adding softly, "It still does."

In the awkward hush that followed, Page said to

Mark, "Do you mind if we go outside for some air? I don't care to have dessert."

Page regained her composure as they sat in a gazebo near the pond, taking in the night sounds. Frogs croaked and crickets chirped and something slithered into the far end of the pond.

Mark said, "Their conversation really got to you."

"I guess it was that. I don't know, I . . ." Page didn't finish her thought. Moments later she said, "It wasn't any one comment in particular, but the entire scene made me question what I grew up believing in. Pilgrimage, the Confederate Pageant, our antebellum costumes . . . the old South. I've been forced to see another side of all that, and the view from the dark side isn't very pretty."

"The old South is a romanticized memory. A fantasy. We all know how inaccurate fantasies and memories are."

"I grew up worshiping that fantasy . . . everybody I knew did, too. If you took a poll today, I'll bet most of the women in my garden club would gladly go back to the 1860s if they could."

"And give up dishwashers and TVs?"

"If they had slaves to do everything for them. I see people in a different light now. Take Doris, for instance. What a loyal, sweet, loving human being she is. Barely educated, unskilled in terms of today's employment requirements, but a genuine, dear woman. She doesn't ask for anything, she doesn't expect anything, but she's always ready to give. I took her for granted most of my life. I don't anymore. She's . . . she really is the mother I never had. I love her just as I love Adam and Cindy."

Page shook her head, continuing. "Human beings are not commodities. We're all created and loved equally by God." She squeezed Mark's hand. "I felt ashamed sitting in that magnificent dining room amidst all its splendor, having had a glimpse of the tribulations others endured to make it possible."

"That's a very loving, humane view."

"I hope I didn't spoil your evening, Mark. You look so handsome all dressed up, and you were wonderful to bring me here. The plantation is lovely and I did enjoy it. I love being with you."

Mark turned her face to him. It was a tender kiss at first, but then their breathing changed and the kiss became the expression of what they'd felt for each other for a long time. Page drew back, searching the depths of Mark's eyes, then put her mouth on his again and gave in to her passion.

Moments later Mark said, "I want you."

Page hugged him close, breathing hard. God, how she wanted him, too. It had been so long since she'd been with Lucien. "I'm not ready, Mark."

"I've wanted you since I can remember."

"Give me some time . . . please. I care a great deal for you, but I won't rush into something. I just can't."

Mark pulled back and looked at her. His breathing slowed. "You're worth waiting for. . . . I've already waited fifteen years."

"Hold me, Mark. Please just hold me. I love being in your arms. Talk to me. Tell me my life will get better."

When the mosquitoes got to be more than they could bear, Mark and Page went back to his plantation. There, an owl hooted in a nearby live oak as they drank iced tea in the moonlight. They sat arm in arm on a screened porch surrounded by dogs chewing on rawhide bones, and talked into the wee hours.

CHAPTER THIRTY-SEVEN

The next morning at breakfast, Page told David Fields that as soon as Dr. Stephenson had begun his testimony, she knew her father'd had something to do with finding him.

"He had everything to do with it," Fields said. "When you explained what you thought might have happened, I called Mark Goodson. Mark called your dad to see what was possible in humans. Then he and Mark and I got together to discuss it."

"Before noon."

"At all hours. Your dad hasn't had a drink all week. He's burned up phone lines between his computer and medical libraries all over the world. That's how he came up with Dr. Stephenson and found the article on the stallions in Austria. Even Stephenson wasn't aware of that little jewel till your dad got a translated copy of the study. Mark was absolutely right . . . your dad knows his medical trivia. And he sure loves you. He convinced Stephenson to cancel a lecture in Ontario to be here this week."

On the walk toward the courthouse, Page asked if David thought people believed William. She said, "It's William's word against Lucien's and Kay Rae's that he was ever anywhere near Kay Rae."

"I thought William made a good witness," Fields said, "but to be perfectly honest, with the polygraph exam not being admissible, the odds are against the judge believing him." He started to say something else, but didn't. His lips pressed together into a thin line.

Page realized that Dr. Stephenson's theory was all well and good. However, it could only apply if William were telling the truth about Kay Rae. If the judge didn't believe William, Page had no case at all.

As soon as she saw their next witness walk to the stand, Page knew why David had clammed up earlier. Buford tried one legal maneuver after another to prevent Ensign Cyril Thatcher's testimony. David appeared quite pleased with himself. He loved pleasant surprises, and Page had had too few of them recently.

Page didn't know if she could take much more uncertainty, but her hopes soared as Fields swore the uniformed ensign in. Thatcher could've been on the same poster with William. He was the same age, about the same height, clean-cut, equally good-looking, and appeared to be in very good physical condition. There was one major difference, however: Ensign Thatcher was white. His only downside, if there was one, was his accent. He was from New Jersey. There was no way to hide that.

Thatcher confirmed everything William had said. He, too, described the interior of Kay Rae's apartment, except for the bedroom.

Fields asked, "Why can't you describe the bedroom, Ensign Thatcher?"

"Well, see, I waited out in the living room and watched TV while she and William went in there."

"She?"

"That one right there." Thatcher pointed to Kay Rae. "But she wasn't pregnant when I saw her."

Page could almost see the steam rising from Kay Rae's head. Lucien sat like a fence post, rigid and unmoving.

"You waited in the living room while William Kern and Kay Rae Yarbrough, whom you just identified, went inside the bedroom of her apartment . . . is that your testimony?"

"That's right. But her name wasn't Yarbrough, either. It was Tall-something. I remember because of her legs, you know. I couldn't help noticing them tall legs in a skirt so short, whenever she sat down or bent over, which she did a lot."

Fields asked Thatcher how long he waited in the living room while William and Kay Rae were in the bedroom.

"How long is *Wings*?"

"How long are what kind of wings?"

"The TV show *Wings*. That was starting when they went in there. A rerun. Then it finished and *The Nanny* came on. I always liked that Fran whatever girl. I like the way she talks. We had to leave before it was over and I never did find out how it ended."

"So William and Kay Rae were in the bedroom for, oh, more than thirty minutes and less than an hour, right?"

"That's right. I had to turn the volume up on the TV because she"—he pointed to Kay Rae again—"was yelling so loud every time she orgasmed, you know."

Fields waited for scattered sniggers among the spectators to die down, then asked, "What happened next?"

"Then they came out buttoning up their clothes and this Kay Rae chick says we gotta leave, pronto, because her boyfriend is coming over at nine and he's major important. So we split. We're almost outta there, carrying our duffel bags out to the street, trying to decide whether to walk to William's mom's place or go back inside and call a taxi, when this guy over here shows up and starts beratin' us, you know, and I never even saw the bum before. Next thing I know, him and William are pushing and shoving each other and the guy runs inside and calls the cops. Man, he must be important . . . they were there in record time."

"Were you drinking at the time, Ensign Thatcher?"

"Not with what she had to offer."

"Why not?"

"I'm a scotch man. All this girl has is vodka and

tonic or those . . . what do you call them . . . mint tulip things. Her and William were soaking up Smirnoff like it's going out of style. She said that's what her boy-friend drinks, too, which is why she had so much on hand—he kept a stash there." Thatcher pointed to Lucien Yarbrough. "Him. She fixed me one of them mint tulips but I almost tossed my cookies. Man, them things are sweet."

Fields had to promise once again to show the rele-vance of his questions.

Thatcher also confirmed William's testimony about what was said at the jail the next morning. Word for word.

When Fields finished, Buford asked several ques-tions. In the end, he implied that Thatcher would lie for his friend William.

Thatcher laughed. "Maybe I would . . . I don't know. But it isn't his case, right? It's that Page-some-body's case over there, and nobody's even intro-duced us."

"So why are you here?"

"Hey . . . I'm in the navy, you know? My command-ing officer says I'm going to Mississippi, I go to Mississippi."

"Did he also tell you what to say?"

"As a matter of fact, he did."

"Very interesting," Buford said. He smiled know-ingly at Judge Scott.

Lucien was suddenly on the edge of his chair.

J.L. angled his head to one side and opened his mouth, his intense gaze never leaving the sailor's face.

Page pressed her lower lip between her teeth, her heart suddenly darkening. She couldn't breathe. Bu-ford seemed to know exactly how to despoil every witness they'd had.

Buford let the sailor's answer register fully, then continued. "What exactly did your commanding offi-cer tell you to say, Ensign Thatcher?"

"He said that, as an American sworn to serve and protect my country, I should tell the truth."

Page almost jumped out of her chair with delight. She wanted to kiss Thatcher's cheek. He was a godsend, and totally believable. At least to her.

At the exact moment Ensign Thatcher stood to leave the stand, Kay Rae's water broke—the last thing Page ever wanted to witness. An emergency recess was called, and Lucien rushed his wife to the hospital. The spectator section twittered with excitement.

Though she wasn't sure why she did it, Page broke down and cried. All she could think of was how excited she'd been just last October, when Lucien had rushed her to the hospital to have their long-awaited son. These wild emotional ups and downs had drained her to the point of total exhaustion.

Moments later Page heard somebody call her name. She turned to see Suellen Whitford at the railing, her pregnancy really beginning to show.

Dabbing at her eyes, Page managed to tell Suellen she looked good.

"Not bad for seven and a half months," Suellen said. "I'm gonna be so upset if Kay Rae has a boy."

"Have you had the amniocentesis yet?"

"I told you, I'm afraid to. If something went wrong and I lost it, I'd just die. But I'm sure it's a boy . . . they run in Bryan's family. I've already painted his room blue. I don't care about the money, Page, if there is any in the trust. But one time in my life, I'd like to get something from my family before my brother does. Just once."

"You *don't* care about money, do you? Are you sure you're related to Lucien and J.L.?"

Suellen laughed. "Sometimes I wish I weren't."

Page could understand Suellen's feeling of competition with Lucien, growing up knowing absolutely that Lucien was both her mother's and her father's favorite. She'd handled it as well as anybody could. Page asked how long Suellen had been present in the courtroom.

"Long enough to know what happened."

"Did you believe William and his friend?"

"Honey, everybody in town'll believe them. Kay Rae would bed a camel and not give a tinker's damn who knew it. She probably has."

Kay Rae delivered a seven-pound, five-ounce baby boy. Lucien had the birth certificate filled out and signed before the baby was dry. Jackson Adams Yarbrough II had arrived. Again.

"The real Jackson Adams Yarbrough the second," Lucien told J.L. and Billy Larson outside the nursery.

"I kinda liked the first one, Loosh," Billy teased. "There was somethin' about him reminded me a' you."

"Still jealous, Gator?" Lucien grinned, motioning for the nurse to bring the baby closer to the observation window.

"Yes!" Lucien said when he saw his son for the first time. He threw a fist into the air and shouted, "The little son of a bitch is white! Now lower his diaper."

David and Sarah Fields joined Page, William, and Auntie Bellum for dinner at Willowdale Plantation the next evening. Mark Goodson was on an emergency call. Ensign Thatcher had already returned to San Diego, and Page's father had a bridge game with friends who desperately needed him to make a foursome.

Page and Doris had done the cooking, and they put on a feast. The table was loaded with fried chicken and baked ham, sweet potatoes, green beans, collard greens, mashed potatoes, fried okra, yellow squash, and tasty, homegrown tomatoes. They had biscuits and corn bread and milk gravy and redeye gravy. They were celebrating, Southern style, and toasted their victory with iced tea garnished with mint picked fresh from Belle's creek bank.

The trial itself wouldn't be over until Kay Rae and Lucien returned, when Judge Scott would make a determination regarding the rightful heir to The Governor's trust. But as far as this group was concerned,

Page had won. At least, she'd won a personal victory.
She not only had her son; she now knew exactly how
he came to be. As word spread about Lucien firing
someone else's bullets from his very own gun, her dignity might even be restored in the community. And
Page felt hopeful that she'd eventually regain custody
of Cindy. She had reason to celebrate.

William was too energized to eat, preferring to hold,
cuddle, look at, and talk to Adam—his son. He was
as excited as any proud papa, regardless of how indi-
rectly Adam had been sired. He said God must've
wanted that child born in the worst way to have gone
to all that trouble. William promised Adam a football,
baseball, catcher's mitt, and college education, in
that order.

Though Page insisted more than once, Doris refused
to join them at the table, professing to have things to
do in the kitchen.

After dinner Page finally convinced William that
Adam needed his sleep, and put him to bed. They sat
in the front parlor of the big house and chatted. A
freshening honeysuckle breeze drifted in through an
open window, stirring the lace curtains. When Mark
Goodson returned from his call, he asked William how
he happened to meet Kay Rae. Doris was out of the
room.

"I went after her on purpose."

"Why?"

The others listened without interrupting. The wall
clock chimed nine o'clock. A chorus of crickets went
silent as a car drove by outside. When the car disappeared down the road, the crickets started up again.
Page sat erect on the sofa next to Mark, eager to hear
why William had zeroed in on Kay Rae.

William said, "I wanted to get even with Lucien."

"For what?"

"What his family did to mine."

Page said, "You're talking about The Governor
shooting your grandfather?"

"It was more than that, Page."

She asked William to explain.

"My granddaddy was Big Jim Kern . . . a hardworking, honest man. Uneducated, of course, like all African-Americans back then. My grandmother was Ophelia, a pretty woman. That story they told about Big Jim stealing a keg of whiskey was a pack of lies. Granddaddy wasn't a thief and he didn't even drink. The argument he had with The Governor was over Ophelia, Granddaddy's wife. The Governor had moved Ophelia up to the big house, where he worked. Years later she told my daddy how The Governor was always putting his hands on her anytime they were alone in a room, trying to feel under her dress. It got so bad she finally complained to Big Jim. I guess Big Jim hit The Governor and The Governor went after a gun. He shot Big Jim and killed him."

"That's terrible," Page said.

Mark agreed. "I'm surprised somebody didn't report *him.*"

Belle Braswell chimed in. "Nobody would dare challenge a man as powerful as The Governor. That's not such an unusual story, either, back then."

Goodson asked, "How long were you aware that Kay Rae was Lucien's girlfriend?"

"A long time," William replied. "Lucien didn't make any big secret about it, except around Page. I used to hear him talking on the phone to Kay Rae whenever Page wasn't there and I'd be trimming hedges or waxing floors or something, helping Mama. Lucien acted like I either couldn't see or hear or didn't have the sense to know what was going on. I saw Kay Rae and him a couple of times, driving out by the river. I'd heard she was pretty fast, so I just started watching and paying attention to where she went. My experience with the Johnson girl gave me the idea. Kay Rae smiled at me a coupla times and I'd smile back. One day when nobody was around I went up and talked to her, told her I thought she was real pretty. She said she'd noticed me, too, and what did I think I could do for a white girl that her boyfriend couldn't do. One thing led to another and she asked me up to her apartment one day, to help her move some heavy boxes. So I did."

Mark said, "And you two . . . went to bed?"

"Not then. About the third time I was there. After that, I went by at least once a week. I'm not saying I didn't enjoy it, mind you. I was just a kid . . . eighteen or so when it started. But every time I was with her, I'd think about Lucien. How he'd react if he knew. A Yarbrough. I wanted him to know."

William turned to Page. "I never would've done anything to hurt you or Laura, Page, but I couldn't bear the sight of Lucien after I knew. And then, him stepping out on you like that, he wasn't any better than his grandfather. The only difference was, he didn't have to force anybody. Best I could see, Kay Rae would give it to any man that asked."

Page said, "I'm surprised you didn't use protection with her, William. Weren't you afraid of catching something? Like AIDS?"

"Kay Rae hated condoms. She always insisted on feeling flesh against flesh. And she swore she was clean."

Fields asked for more details, but William declined. "I've said enough. It's an old wound, but it'll heal now. I got even the only way I knew how." He paused. "I'm sorry I caused all this trouble for you, Page."

Page responded, "Lucien caused my troubles, William, not you. We were married . . . he had no business at Kay Rae's. Besides, Adam is a wonderful child and I love him to pieces."

William flashed a broad smile. "He is a handsome little dude, if I say so myself. Sorta reminds me . . . of me." They all laughed.

Page asked, "Do you ever hear from Antwann?"

"Not since that trouble I was in. Is he still around town?"

Doris answered from the doorway. "He's around, but he's no good. You got no business askin' about him."

"He's my daddy, Mama. I wouldn't mind seeing him before I go back."

David Fields said, "I'd like to meet him, too. I'll go with you."

Everybody looked questioningly at Fields at the same time. "Why?" they asked.

Fields shrugged, his expression one of wide-eyed innocence. "Why not?"

CHAPTER THIRTY-EIGHT

Lucien paced the floor of the hospital room while Kay Rae nursed their son. When the aide took the baby back to the nursery, Lucien said to his wife, "You slept with William Kern. You know it, I know it, now the whole state of Mississippi knows it. What I really want to know is how long it'd been going on."

"Don't be ridiculous, Lucien. You're not gonna take William's word over mine, are you?"

"That guy from New Jersey sure as hell knew what was in your apartment."

"I told you, their lawyer bought the decorator off. Or my maid . . . I never did trust her. Those creeps wouldn't know my apartment from a submarine."

"Not even the Lalique horse? Do you have any idea what that cost? William sure seemed to appreciate it, and my Smirnoff. What else did he enjoy while he was there?"

"Screw you."

"You already have. I need to get elected every four years . . . how much can my reputation take? Two wives in a row are out humping black guys. What's the matter, don't I satisfy you?"

"You're okay, I guess."

He stopped pacing and looked visibly pained. "What does that mean?"

"It means, don't be so damned insecure. Men! All you care about is how you measure up in bed."

"You never made any bones about what you want in bed."

"So I like a big one . . . is that a crime?"

"No matter what color it is?"

"You're shouting again, Governor. Do you want the entire hospital to hear?"

Lucien lowered his voice. "I should leave you. Maybe I will."

"Yeah, right . . . do that. And I'll take your son and the trust."

"You couldn't do that."

"Try me, big man. My daddy's got five times the money you Yarbroughs have. He'll sue your red ass blue, and we'll hire lawyers that'll make you tremble in your boots, not some little Yankee still wet behind the ears. As the rightful mama, I'll get full custody of Jackson Adams Two out there and I'll be the sole administrator of the whole friggin' trust. Chew on that for a while, numb nuts."

Lucien fumed. Though his insides burned, there wasn't a thing he could do about it. She was absolutely right. Blind with rage, he stormed out of the room and slammed the door. Seconds later he roared back inside, breathing hard. "Did you?"

Kay Rae was dialing the phone. She slammed the receiver down, exasperated. "Did I what? I thought I was rid of you for today."

"Did you screw him?"

"Give me a break . . . go piss on a tree or something and leave me alone."

Lucien forced his voice to remain steady. He walked to the side of her bed. Kay Rae already had her makeup on, including too much eye shadow. She wore a see-through negligee and was hanging out of a bed jacket. He could actually see her nipples. Anybody could. He let out a long breath.

"Look," Lucien said. He stripped off his jacket and showed the back of his shirt. "I'm not wearing a wire. There's nobody in the room but you and me. And you're right. I can't afford to divorce you and risk losing the money in the trust."

Kay Rae watched him sweat.

"But I have to know. It won't change a thing, but I can't go through the rest of my life not knowing."

"Knowing what?"

"Did you have sex with William that night like he said?"

"What is this, a scene from *The Godfather*? Suddenly you're Diane Keaton and I'm Al Pacino?" She smirked. "Remember, Lucien . . . Pacino lied."

"You have no reason to lie. It won't change a thing."

Kay Rae laughed. "Just this once, right? The only time you'll ask and the last time you'll ever bring it up, right? Agreed?"

"Agreed. Just tell me."

After a lengthy silence, she said, "All right. Yes, I screwed him. William Kern. That night before I screwed you, just like he said. I screamed every time I came, which was about five times, and he came twice, and his is bigger than yours. Now get out of here so I can make my phone calls. If I don't get a decent hairdresser over here immediately, I'm gonna rip my hair out by the roots. And if you ever tell anybody, I'll sue you for slander and deny it till your dying day."

She stopped, then smiled spitefully. "Or I'll tell the *National Enquirer* what I just told you. Being a governor's wife isn't all it's cracked up to be anyway, so personally, I don't give a shit." She glared at Lucien, who was staring dumbly at her, slack-jawed. "Go. Get out," she said. "A deal's a deal."

Kay Rae turned and picked up the phone to dial, but stopped, suddenly rigid. "Miss Emma! How long have you . . . ?"

Lucien turned to see his mother in the open doorway, hand in hand with Cindy. "Oh, God, Mama," Lucien cried. "She didn't mean any of that."

Standing there, fully decked out in her best Sunday outfit, Miss Emma had an expression that conveyed shock and consternation. Her mouth worked long before any sound emerged. "Ci . . . Cindy wanted to see

her new brother. I see we've come at a bad time."
She spun around and left, taking Cindy with her.

Lucien hurried after his mother.

Seconds later Kay Rae said into the phone in her sweetest Southern accent, "Avian, this is Kay Rae Yarbrough . . . the governor's wife? I was just wondering if you could come over to the hospital and do my hair. I'll send my limo for you. It's positively dreadful, and I just can't live with it like this for another minute."

The case resumed once Kay Rae and her baby were out of the hospital. The issue now was, which Jackson Adams Yarbrough the second was The Governor's legal heir. Page and David Fields returned to the plaintiff's table. Lucien, J.L., Buford Tallant, Wylie Marsh, and Victor Brandt of the First Mississippi Bank and Trust Company sat at the opposite table across the room, alongside Kay Rae. Six against two. Page had grown accustomed to such odds.

Natchez society came out in full force once again. A few women silently cheered for Page this time, but weren't ready to publicly voice their support. Even if what that artificial-insemination doctor had said was correct, nobody could prove that was how Page had had a black baby. Not for sure.

During the continuance, David Fields had read and reread his trial notes. The third time through, he'd fixed on a statement made in all innocence, not realizing how significant it might become. He had said that the only issue in question was whether Lucien and Lucien's father, J.L. Senior, were direct descendants of Governor Jackson Adams Yarbrough, as the trust specified.

What David hoped to accomplish now would require a DNA sample from Jackson Adams Yarbrough the first—The Governor himself. As greatly as that man was still revered, any judge in Mississippi would be extremely reluctant to order an exhumation. Especially with the present governor, a former senator, and a formidable team of attorneys objecting every step of the way. Unless . . .

Without sharing his entire plan even with Page, Fields cast his bait upon the waters. He alleged that Senator J. L. Yarbrough was not the son of the maker of the trust, The Governor.

J.L. had a fit. Two deputies intercepted the raging snow-haired man halfway to where David Fields stood.

Page suddenly worried that the senator might have a heart attack, the way he struggled to get at David. The things he yelled weren't fit for human ears to hear. Unable to silence him, Judge Scott ordered that the senator be removed from the courtroom and held in contempt. Lucien appeared almost as livid as his father.

Following a recess to allow tempers to ebb, David Fields was allowed to continue. Senator Yarbrough was nowhere in sight.

"If Governor Lucien Yarbrough's baby isn't a direct descendant of The Governor," David told the crowded courtroom, "he doesn't fulfill the requirements of the trust." Fields also pointed out, much to the delight of Suellen Whitford, that other heirs might qualify instead. And who was to say that Lucien was actually J.L.'s son? Fields said a rumor was circulating that J.L. was sterile. Suellen wasn't nearly as thrilled with that supposition.

Even David was relieved that the senator was out of the room when he offered that bit of fabrication.

Judge Scott grew impatient. He asked the warring parties to present their evidence and get this over with. Lucien was particularly eager to do so, because transfer of the trust was being held up. He needed the trust money immediately.

After an intense huddle with his clients, and to settle this argument once and for all, Buford Tallant suggested that Senator J. L. Yarbrough and his father, Governor Jackson Adams Yarbrough, have their DNA tested, along with Lucien's son. He and Lucien assured the court they could convince J.L. to go along.

Secretly delighted they had taken the bait, Fields felt obliged to argue that DNA fingerprinting would be unreliable on anyone dead as long as The Governor. After all, he'd been buried right out there at River Oaks in 1940, and that was over sixty years ago.

Buford and Wylie Marsh decisively squashed David's argument. Scientists had DNA tested dinosaur bones that were millions of years old, confirmed by carbon dating. DNA didn't change with time.

David meekly said he hadn't been aware of that, but still objected—on general principles.

Buford and Wylie shook their heads in concert. Had this turkey actually passed the bar exam?

Buford pointed out that Lucien's DNA was on record at the lab and in court records, and he and Wylie had clearly demonstrated that DNA did not change with time. Accordingly, Judge Scott deemed that all test results on record would be acceptable for these proceedings.

Fields did not contest the ruling.

Judge Scott had J.L. brought into the courtroom to hear his ruling. Free of handcuffs now, but with deputies at the ready nearby, the senator reluctantly agreed to what Buford and Lucien suggested.

Since the immediate family had volunteered, it was a simple legal matter to have The Governor's remains exhumed. State troopers cordoned off River Oaks Plantation to keep newspaper photographers and TV cameras from documenting every ghoulish detail. More resourceful reporters rented barges and dropped anchor in the middle of the Mississippi River. Using telescopic lenses, they photographed first a yellow backhoe, then African-American laborers with shovels, digging The Governor up. One of those laborers was Antwann Kern.

Following several days of waiting, the DNA results arrived to an overflowing courtroom, delivered by armed guards.

Buford, Lucien, and J.L. beamed proudly when all tests confirmed that the sacred Yarbrough lineage was exactly as Lucien and J.L. claimed. Their precious family tree remained unblemished.

The way Buford expressed it, "Governor Jackson Adams Yarbrough the first begat Senator Jackson Lucien Yarbrough Senior, who begat Governor Jackson Lucien Yarbrough Junior, who begat Lucien's and Kay Rae Yarbrough's son, Jackson Adams Yarbrough the second . . . a direct descendant, as the trust specifies."

Buford turned arrogantly to Page and David Fields. "I would hope that Mr. Fields and his client are finally satisfied."

David slowly came to his feet and removed his glasses. "If the court please, there is one other person who needs testing."

Page held her breath.

Judge Scott looked as if he might throw his gavel at David. "Is there anybody in Adams County who hasn't been tested, Mr. Fields?"

"One individual for certain, Your Honor."

Judge Scott displayed a totally incredulous look on his face. "Who is this person?"

"Antwann Kern, your Honor. Mr. Kern is in the courtroom, if you'd hear my reasons for making this request of the court."

Large, uneducated, slow moving, and polite to the point of being deferential, Antwann Kern humbly sat in the witness chair in worn overalls. Dried mud from The Governor's grave clung to the soles of Antwann's heavy work boots. In a basso-profundo voice he solemnly told how his mother, Ophelia, had been repeatedly molested by The Governor. Then, after shooting and killing Antwann's father—Big Jim Kern—The Governor had moved in on Ophelia in a big way.

"Mama told me how The Governor would come down to the little shack she lived in, especially nights when he'd been drinking, and force hisself on her."

"Do you mean, he raped her?" asked Fields.

"Yassuh. Over and over. People that worked there said you could hear Mama crying out in the night, just sobbin' and wailin' whenever The Governor would take her that way, but there wasn't nothin' they could do about it."

Page's heart cramped into a painful knot for poor Ophelia, and for Antwann. As she watched and listened, she could see why Doris had been attracted to this man. He still carried quite a twinkle in his eye. He was a larger and older version of William.

Buford Tallant objected to nearly every question posed and answered, as "hearsay," but Judge Scott allowed Fields to proceed. Said he was only trying to decide whether to have Antwann DNA tested.

David asked, "Do you have anything in writing about Big Jim's death, Antwann?"

Antwann fumbled in the front zipper pocket of his overalls, extracting a yellowed piece of newspaper. He handed it to David.

"Your Honor, Mr. Kern has presented me with a clipping from the *Natchez Gazette,* dated May twelfth, 1932, which lists the death of one Big Jim Kern. According to this account, Mr. Kern was killed by gunfire." Fields turned to Antwann. "Is that correct, sir?"

"Yassuh. 'Twas a shotgun."

Fields entered the newspaper clipping as an exhibit, then continued. "Do you have any record of your birth, Mr. Kern?"

"Yassuh." Antwann held a Bible, tattered and worn from years of use. He opened the cover and presented it to Fields.

"I have here a family Bible, Your Honor, which lists the births and deaths of Mr. Kern's family members from 1925 through 1970. You'll note that Mr. Antwann Kern's date of birth is listed as March fifth, 1933. Mr. William Kern's birth date is July twenty-third, 1973."

Buford rose to inspect the Bible before it was entered as David's exhibit. He said, "Your Honor, I might point out that the entries in this Bible are in different scripts . . . different handwriting."

"Yassuh, you'd be right," Antwann said. "Mama couldn't read nor write. Miss Esmeralda writ them first few birthdays in there for her."

"And who was Miss Esmeralda, Antwann?"

"She be The Governor's wife . . . Miss Esmeralda Yarbrough." Antwann looked over at J.L. "The senator's mama."

J.L.'s mouth tightened, but he offered no objection. He and Lucien huddled in conversation with Wylie Marsh, who appeared perplexed. Buford listened to Fields and Antwann, making an occasional note on his yellow pad. Victor Brandt sat with fingers interlaced across his gallbladderless abdomen, listening and watching curiously. Kay Rae ate a chocolate bar, totally bored.

Fields paced in front of his witness for a moment, then said, "According to my calculations, Mr. Antwann Kern was born ten months after his father of record, Big Jim Kern, was killed by Governor Yarbrough. Because of what he related to us about the governor repeatedly forcing his mother to engage in unprotected sexual intercourse, I contend that Antwann Kern is not the blood son of Big Jim Kern, but was sired by Governor Jackson Adams Yarbrough the first. This means that Antwann's son, William Kern, and his grandson, Jackson Adams Yarbrough the second, are direct descendants—blood relatives, if you will—of the maker of the trust." Fields drew in a huge breath.

"Your Honor," Buford began, "this is preposterous—"

Judge Scott raised a hand, waving Buford off. "Probably," he admitted, "but there's one sure way to find out. Besides, what's one more?"

He ordered that Antwann Kern's blood be DNA tested, exactly as the others had been.

When Fields sat down, Page whispered, "When did you have him tested?"

"I didn't."

"But you said . . ." Realization dawned. "David, why would you take such a huge gamble?"

"It's not really a gamble."

Panic welled up inside Page. Everything hinged on this one piece of evidence. A single blood test. "What if Antwann isn't The Governor's son after all?"

"Big Jim was killed ten months before Antwann was born, Page."

"I heard. But what if his mother went with somebody else? Other than The Governor?"

"She wouldn't."

"You don't know that."

Fields smiled confidently. "Sure I do. I asked my wife . . . Sarah knows about women."

"Oh, my God."

CHAPTER THIRTY-NINE

Silence filled the room as Dr. George Crisp took the stand. Judge Scott had moved the trial to the largest courtroom in Adams County, yet people filled every inch of sitting or standing room, and still they spilled out into the halls, down the steps, and onto the lawn outside.

When the locked container was opened, Judge Scott asked Dr. Crisp to read the results.

Crisp said, "The DNA sample from Antwann Kern matches with the sample from the remains of Governor Jackson Adams Yarbrough. Antwann Kern is the son of Governor Jackson Adams Yarbrough. Antwann Kern is also the father of William Kern, according to the sample we have on file, and the grandfather of Jackson Adams Yarbrough the second. The one whose specimen was drawn on November eighteenth, 2001."

Page and David Fields came out of their seats. Several spectators cheered openly, and reporters dashed madly to public phones downstairs or to their cell phones.

Buford was on his feet objecting, but Lucien and J.L. were clearly stunned. Lucien's face was ashen, totally devoid of healthful color. J.L. sat with his mouth open, shaking his head in disbelief. He appeared to have aged twenty years.

Judge Scott banged his gavel, demanding order. David and Page hugged, and David kept repeating, "We won, we won . . . Adam gets the inheritance. You get the trust."

Page suddenly stopped, drew back, and looked at David. "What do you suppose he'll get?"

Fields shrugged, "Who knows? Whatever it is, it's Adam's."

CHAPTER FORTY

On a windy Saturday in March when Adam was four years old, Doris Kern admired a new silk dress in her bedroom mirror, turning from side to side. Red had always been her favorite color. She smiled at her reflection and voiced the comment a male friend had made just days before. "Lookin' good, Mama, lookin' good."

Adjusting an earring, Doris hurried out her front entrance, past white columns, and down the stairs. She didn't bother to lock up, since she was only going next door, to Yarbrough Hall.

Once there, Doris spoke briefly with Page, then made certain her grandson had a sausage biscuit and glass of milk before he went out to play. As Adam raced from the kitchen, she said, "He truly is a beautiful child, and does look like William. But not Antwann, thank God. Adam doesn't have a bone in his body like Antwann. Now, The Governor? Well, that's another story."

Suellen Whitford dropped by later that day, bringing her children to play. Disappointed that her own child hadn't qualified for the trust, Suellen was nonetheless delighted that Page and Adam received the proceeds rather than Lucien.

Suellen's oldest girls, Betsy and Emma Sue, were now fourteen and ten. Page's daughter, Cindy, was eleven, and hadn't had a nightmare or stomachache since she'd returned home to live with Page. Suellen's youngest child was named Hilary. Suellen and Page sat by a bay window in the front parlor, watching the children race about outside.

Suellen said, "Did you hear the latest about Lucien?"

"Now what?"

"He's moving his practice to Tupelo."

"Why?"

"Losing the election finally convinced him that women are thoroughly pissed off at him. And after that savings-and-loan scandal, nobody in Natchez will use him as an attorney, including his old cronies. He's the harbinger of doom around here."

Cindy ran into the room with Emma Sue and Betsy right behind. "Mama, do I have to wear a sweater if we practice dance steps in the driveway? Emma Sue isn't wearing one."

"Yes, you do. You don't want to catch a cold right before the pageant, do you?"

"See?" Betsy said. "I told you so."

"What about Adam? He took his off."

Adam darted out from behind his sister, grinning. "Don't need a sweater, Mommy. I'm hot." He was developing a bone structure like William's, an angular face with high cheekbones. His nose was going to be narrow and his lips as thin as Page's. His skin was like Grandma Doris's, the color of milk chocolate, and his eyes were dark brown.

Page picked Adam up and hugged him. "Yes, you do, young man. Bring it here."

"He's bothering us, Mama," Cindy said.

"I am not."

"You are too. You were throwing gravel. You're just a dumb boy. Boys don't even know how to dance."

"I do too."

"Do not. Girls are better dancers than boys."

"Are not."

Page put the sweater on Adam and shooed them outside, turning her attention back to Suellen. "How's Miss Emma handling things?"

Page referred to the senator's declaring bankruptcy after the savings and loan went under, along with Lucien. The senator had cosigned Lucien's notes at the bank. Adam's trust had bought River Oaks the day it went into foreclosure, but allowed Miss Emma and the senator to live there for a nominal rent. Month-to-month.

Page and Cindy preferred to live in Yarbrough Hall, Cindy's "pretty house," with paintings of flowers and animals and people on the walls. Cindy did agree to one painting of The Governor, which hung over the mantel in the living room. It depicted The Governor with a hand to his chin, pondering something.

"Probably trying to figure out how to get into Ophelia's pants," Suellen said, "or how much it'll cost to buy somebody's vote."

Mama Yarbrough had given the painting to Cindy at her birthday party the year before. Miss Emma apologized to Page that same day for not having believed her from the beginning.

If you looked closely at The Governor's hand in the painting, you could make out a small birthmark on one finger. It was dark, and in the exact shape of a signet ring—identical to the mark Adam bore.

Discussing Miss Emma, Suellen said, "Oh, you know Mama; she can handle anything as long as she has a tea party every month or so."

"Anything except Kay Rae."

"She was definitely happy to see that one go. Mama don't let nobody treat her baby boy that way."

"Is he seeing anybody?"

"Three or four . . . you know Lucien."

"Nobody special?" Though no longer romantically interested in him, Page couldn't help remembering Lucien in that gazebo on that long-ago Saturday—a Greek god. Her eyes stung momentarily. What a fool he'd been. They'd had it all, and he threw it away.

Suellen was saying, "Are you kidding? Women fall all over him, same as always, but he'll be a bachelor till he dies. After Kay Rae, he says marriage is one institution he can live without. Says if he ever feels a craving for an institution again, he'll just check himself into the nearest psycho ward.''

"The way he respects his vows, he'd be better off." Page sipped her tea, then calmly set it down. "Did I tell you I ran into Judge Scott last week?"

"No."

"I told him how scared I was having our case in his court, knowing he was a poker buddy of Lucien's."

"What was his response?"

"He said he'd known something about Lucien long before I figured it out."

"What?"

"Lucien cheats."

Suellen howled with laughter. While they were enjoying the joke, the doorbell rang. Doris's housekeeper-trainee answered the door and showed Mary Lou Snodgrass and Patty Fulton into the front parlor. They were decked out in spring colors and hats, but their shoes were appropriately dark. Easter was still a month away.

Patty spoke first. "Page Yarbrough, you look absolutely marvelous . . . I love your hair up like that. Doesn't she look marvelous, Mary Lou? Hi, Suellen."

When they got around to the reason for their visit, Mary Lou said, "We really appreciate your contribution to the Junior League, Page, and what you've done for the garden club. The committee met and made its selections for next year's pageant. We wanted to be the first to tell you that Cindy is to be queen, and Adam the lead child around the maypole, if that's all right with you. Rona Green suggested it, and it was unanimously agreed."

Page glanced at Suellen. "I'll have to ask Cindy . . . she's still a bit young to be queen. And Adam isn't interested in the pageant yet, but he might be by next year."

Suellen couldn't resist it. "Why would you want Adam dancing around the maypole? Has anybody noticed that he's black?"

Patty straightened in her chair and quickly retorted, "There were lots of affluent Negroes in the South before the war, Suellen. William Johnson, for one, a businessman-barber. He owned that big plantation up on the Natchez Trace."

"Absolutely," Mary Lou quickly added. "Colored people played an important role in our society. At Page's suggestion, we're having several African-Americans in the pageant next year."

That evening, Suellen kept the children while Page and her husband went to the most romantic restaurant in town for dinner. Though Page continued to work in the office, they rarely got to be alone. Even for special occasions.

Touching his wineglass to hers, Mark said, "I love you, Mrs. Goodson. You were definitely worth waiting for."

"And I love you, Dr. Goodson," Page replied. "Thank you for waiting. Happy anniversary, darling."

Adam's birth not only changed Page's life, it affected others as well. Condom sales were up fifty-four percent in Adams County alone. Rona Green said Page should receive a commission on every sale. She said Adam's birth proved there was such a thing as a second coming.

Page had just gotten it organized when David Fields shut down his law office and became a successful author of books on taxes, investments, and trusts. He retained one client—Adam.

In addition to working in Mark's office, Page played an active role in her church and the garden club, as well as several national charitable organizations. She was especially pleased that Adam would be able to obtain his undergraduate education at home in Natchez. Adam's trust had endowed a college on Jefferson Street that encouraged minorities to enroll. Page had insisted it be named Yarbrough College, and placed two life-size portraits in the entry hall—The Governor, and his great-grandson, Adam.

Page harbored no doubt that her son would go into politics. Every night at bedtime, she reminded him of two things: One—"No matter what happens in life, good or bad, remind yourself that it's a blessing . . . then search until you find the good in it." Two—"You may be governor of the great state of Mississippi someday . . . president of the United States, if you want it."

A Yarbrough had never been president. Yet. She hadn't informed Adam that he was wealthy. He'd find that out in due time.

All things considered, and with more than eight million dollars remaining in the trust she directed for her son, life was good for Page. She and her children were as active as they cared to be, and were invited to every social event worthy of a deviled-egg plate or a cut-glass punchbowl. Page and both children. After the first year they were in full circulation, people hardly noticed that Adam was black.

If they did, they never mentioned it.

But of course they wouldn't. Since before the war, Natchez has been a genteel society. It remains so today.

Always one to have the final word, Patty Fulton told Mary Lou, "Saying anything about *that* would be just too tacky for words."